# the HOURGLASS

# TRACY REES

# Quercus

First published in Great Britain in 2017 by

Quercus Editions Ltd
Carmelite House
50 Victoria Embankment
London EC4Y 0DZ

An Hachette UK company

A CIP catalogue record for this book is available
from the British Library

PB ISBN 978 1 78429 626 1
EBOOK ISBN 978 1 78429 625 4

10 9 8 7 6 5 4 3 2 1

Typeset by CC Book Production

Printed and bound in Great Britain by Clays Ltd, St Ives plc

For my amazing parents – and this one's for the family, too.

# Welsh words and phrases in *The Hourglass*

*bach* – little one

*cariad* – darling

*cwtch* – cuddle

*Duw* – God

*hiraeth* – similar to homesickness, but a sharper longing

*Mae'n ddrwg gen i* – I'm sorry

*mochyn* – pig

*twp* – stupid

# Prologue

*Sometimes, you have to ask for what you want.*

The old woman rose from her bed in the deepest watches of the night. She'd always liked that phrase – *the watches of the night* – suggestive as it was of vigil. It made her feel as though someone, somewhere, was witnessing the passing hours and minutes of her life, and cared. She struggled into her robe. It was yellow and fluffy, making her feel like a newly hatched chick, when actually she was at quite the opposite end of life's arc. Never mind slippers. She couldn't sleep and the time had come.

She flipped her hair out from her collar and pulled it over her left shoulder, a gesture that had been with her many years. She drew a deep breath, pressing her hands to her cheeks. They were soft as tissues, their plump resilience long gone. All the more reason, then, to make her demand. She didn't like the idea of *demanding*, but then a request was too soft, and this was important. Utterly unaccustomed to asking for anything for herself, she wasn't sure how it would feel, how it would be received. But she had decided. She'd lain awake too many nights now. Well then.

She moved through indigo shadows to the window and drew back the curtains on a glittering sky. Despite her trepidation, she smiled. The stars were scattered across the blackness like breadcrumbs; it filled her soul to see them. Fields stretched in every direction, dark and empty. At least, they *looked* empty but she knew that out there foxes moved, owls hunted, mice crept.

She knelt down – that hurt – and rested her forearms on the windowsill, hands clasped together. The silence was indigo too.

'Dear God,' she began, but her voice was soft, tentative, her usual voice.

'Dear God,' she said again in the voice she saved only for very rare occasions. She had used it long ago when the teacher wrongly accused one of the children of mischief. She had used it when the boys reached their troublesome teens and needed to be told 'no', in no uncertain terms. She used it for speaking to the doctor.

'I thank you as always for all my blessings, Lord. You have granted me a long life filled with many good things and I have been grateful, you know that. But Lord, I cannot bear this situation now and I want an end to it.'

Her eyes filled with tears as she looked into the fathomless night, her own reflection a faint imprint upon the window, a familiar-strange overlaying of elderly woman and young girl.

'It hurts too much, Lord, that's the thing. I've never asked you for anything for myself, only for the family. But there's a first time for everything, they say, and this prayer is for me. I'm not pretending otherwise. All for me.

'I'll be honest, I can't see why you wouldn't grant it. We both know I'm not going to be here much longer. But I think you should and I trust you will and I'll . . . I'll accept nothing less, God. Enough, now. In your infinite mercy and might, you can make this happen. Somehow.'

She hesitated. But sometimes, you have to ask for what you want.

'So please, Lord, before I go, bring my girls home to me. That's all I want now. Bring my girls home. Amen.'

The tears trickled free. Her words drifted into the dark corners to settle like dust, and shivered through the glass to float over the inky plains of the night sky. There was no sound or movement. If God had heard, He sent her no sign.

Still, as she leaned heavily on the windowsill to struggle to her feet, she felt she had made her point. She felt she had been very clear.

# Nora

*December 2014*

After Nora had been in therapy for a while, things did start to change. It's just that they didn't change in any of the ways she'd expected. Before her first session, on a dusty evening back in June, she had made a list of all the ways she *hoped* her life would improve. Never having had counselling before, she didn't want to be underprepared.

For a while life had continued as usual, except for these once-weekly trips to Belsize Park to see Jennifer. Then, after about three months, the nightmares became more persistent, her anxiety intensified and her relationship with her mother got much worse. She also split up with her partner, Simon, just months before her fortieth birthday. None of these things had been on her list.

Now, on a frosty evening in December, she stood at the window of Jennifer's cream waiting room, staring into the clear darkness of a quiet North London street. One or two faded leaves ghosted past on a winter wind, drifting through a beam of lamplight. Nora didn't mind the wait. She was too busy wondering how to explain to Jennifer what she'd done now.

'I resigned today!' she blurted out, forty minutes later. Jennifer had commented that she often did that – bit her tongue over something really important until late in the session so there was no time to discuss it properly. Usually Nora didn't recognise how significant these omissions were until Jennifer seized on them like an archaeologist examining an apparently ordinary bit of stone and pronouncing it an arrowhead. But even Nora knew *this* was important.

She would have loved to put off the revelation for another week but if she couldn't say it to Jennifer, who was trained to bear witness to the vagaries of human motivation, how would she tell her staff at the office? How would she tell Simon (who still kept in touch even though she had broken up with him)? And – oh God – how would she tell her mother?

'I see. Would you like to say a bit more about that?' asked Jennifer, betraying none of the alarm Nora was certain she must feel. Jennifer had a shock of auburn hair and lovely creamy skin. She was probably only ten years older than Nora at the most, but she seemed somehow aeons ahead. Wise? Motherly?

'Um, well, I did it after lunch,' said Nora, then grimaced. *That* was not what Jennifer meant, clearly. 'Olivia was really surprised but quite nice about it. I don't know why I did it. Um . . . I saw a beach.'

'A beach?'

Nora sighed. There was no way to explain this without

sounding barking mad. She probably was. People didn't just quit their jobs because they wanted to go to the beach!

'Yes. In my mind's eye. I know it sounds crazy. I . . . I don't know why I did it,' she repeated.

How could she ever explain? Surely it had been nothing more than an idle daydream . . . but she *wanted* to call it a vision. It had felt almost breathtakingly significant. Sudden, diamond-bright and impossible to resist, it made her feel something unfamiliar and buoyant. Hope, perhaps. But now, on top of everything else, she would soon be unemployed. Jennifer had said that when a person started therapy things often got worse before they got better. She wasn't kidding!

'We've only got a few minutes left, Nora . . .' Jennifer began. A therapy hour, for some reason, was fifty minutes long. She hadn't glanced at her watch and the only clock in the room was above her head, but Jennifer seemed to have time running through her veins. 'However, I'm happy for you to stay an extra few minutes if you'd like to explore it a little further.'

'*Really?*' Jennifer never ran over. Perhaps she was more shocked than she appeared. 'Thank you.'

'Then why don't you tell me exactly what happened today, as if it's unfolding now?'

Nora nodded. She closed her eyes as Jennifer had taught her and took herself back to a memory of earlier that day. Just like that she was back at work: lunchtime. The rest of the department had gone out but, as usual, she was eating at her desk. She could see the filing cabinet's grey metallic gleam out of the corner of her eye, the white glow of her computer monitor and the black stapler ranged neatly behind the keyboard.

'It's lunchtime,' she began. 'I'm in the office. I'm telling myself I'm lucky because my office has two windows. Except, when I look out of one of them, I see the corridor. And the other one looks over the indoor courtyard. What's the point of an *indoor* courtyard? But at least there's greenery — some ferns growing over some rocks . . . Remember you said last week that—'

'Concentrate, Nora,' Jennifer's voice murmured. 'You're in the office . . .'

'Oh, yes. So I decide to go down to the courtyard to stretch my legs. I go over to the ferns and I touch them and . . . they're plastic.

'I feel completely betrayed. So I get a Kit-Kat from the vending machine and go back to my office. I think, no wonder I never look up from my desk — I'll just get on with my work. But when I sit down again all I can see is this *beach* . . .'

And she could still see it. It hadn't really left her the rest of the day. A cool, clear sweep of beach, golden sand turning oyster coloured in the pale, clear light, miles of walking, under a silver sky.

'I mean, I can *see* it — as clearly as if it's the actual view from my window! And it's beautiful . . . It's winter, but the sky is bright and the wind is blowing . . . and I'm filled with this yearning . . . It's not *just* that it's beautiful, it's the feeling it gives me. It's a feeling of freedom and of something . . . *real* . . .

7

I want so badly to be there. And it's not *just* that I want to be somewhere beautiful, though I do. It feels . . .' Nora sighed again and shook her head. 'It feels as if I'm *meant* to be there, like it's calling me. *Commanding* me, actually. As if it holds the key to a great secret – though I didn't even know there *was* a secret!

'Then Nick comes back from lunch. He's my assistant,' Nora added, opening one eye, in case Jennifer had forgotten. But she hadn't, of course; she just motioned for Nora to continue.

'He bursts through the door – the office doors are hideous by the way, this really horrible shade of green. I mean, *who* saw that colour paint and thought, *Yes, let's go for this one?* Anyway, so Nick bursts in and I look at him – I mean, really *look* at him. His hair's untidy, so I realise it's windy out, but I wouldn't have known otherwise because I'm in this hermetically sealed building. I'm never outside. I'm either at the office, or the gym, or on the Tube, or in the flat . . . He's holding his battered old satchel. It's always crammed with those black Moleskine notebooks because he's attempting to write the great British novel. And I realise that my bag contains absolutely *nothing* I'm passionate about. Only my purse and phone and make-up – essential stuff. Then Nick gets back to work and I can *still* see the beach. It's *clamouring* at me. So I walk down the corridor and knock on Olivia's vile green door, and tell her I'm leaving. Oh, I gave a month's notice, of course, I wouldn't leave them in the lurch. But after that . . .'

Nora opened her eyes. Jennifer was nodding slowly. 'Your

wish for a life of your own making is calling loudly now,' she said at last. 'It doesn't seem as though you can run from it any more.'

'Nowhere to run, nowhere to hide,' Nora laughed nervously. 'I've left Simon and I've left my job and I don't know what I'm going to do.' And God only knew what her mother would say – for so many reasons. Yet Nora couldn't help but feel that somehow Jasmine was at the heart of all this, an impression that made no sense at all. This was the last course of action that her mother would ever have advised and that beach would be the last place she'd ever want to go, yet the feeling persisted, irrational and worrying.

Jennifer was still looking thoughtful. 'And how have you been feeling since you resigned?'

They exchanged a wry smile. They had shared a little joke, that first day in June, about the cliché of counsellors asking 'And how does that make you feel?' Jennifer agreed it was a dreadful question – yet sometimes unavoidably useful.

'Disbelieving! I mean, me without my job . . . what *is* that? And also, I feel like a little kid playing truant. I'm scared someone will find out and shout at me.'

'Someone?'

'Someone in authority. A teacher or something.'

'But there are no teachers, Nora. You're not a child and your decisions are your own. The only person you're accountable to in this situation is your boss, Olivia, and you've already told her.'

'All right then, my mother.'

'And what do you imagine she'll say?'

And just like that, Nora found herself tongue-tied. Predicting anything about her mother had become impossible lately. A distance had somehow grown up between them over the last twelve months. Nora would never have imagined that could happen, close as they'd always been, but she could remember noticing it vividly last Christmas. She'd asked Jasmine repeatedly what was wrong but Jasmine had told her she was just being oversensitive. And Nora's own troubles had started around the same time.

Then Jennifer did look at her watch. 'We need to stop now, Nora, so perhaps that's something you can think about for next time. Meanwhile, just a quick question. Did you recognise the beach? Is it imaginary, or somewhere you know?'

Nora gave a bleak laugh. 'Oh, I know it. Thank you, Jennifer.'

She gathered her things and headed out, back to the dark street that led, as all streets must, to Starbucks. She really needed a latte. Oh yes, she knew where that beach was. And she'd be more reluctant to tell her mother *that* than anything.

# Chloe

## July 1953

'Joy has a colour! And it's bright blue, like this summer sky!' cried Chloe, spinning around, her face tilted up to the sun, her palms outstretched.

Her new pleated skirt – mint-green and grey check – lifted about her legs and spun with her. It wasn't new really, she'd inherited it from Margaret Matthews (who was seventeen now, and gone away to Swansea) but it was new to *her* and quite the most grown-up piece of clothing she possessed. Her mother said maybe she should save it for best, but Chloe could think of no 'best' that could better this, the start of her annual summer holiday to Tenby.

Tenby! The very name filled her with elation. It smacked of adventure, of endless sunny days on the beaches, of romance and hidden treasure . . . She would see her glamorous Aunt Susan and her Uncle Harry – as they were calling him now. She would see her cousins, Megan and Richard, who were sixteen and eighteen. Their ages alone conferred upon Chloe a vicarious glamour that she wore like new gloves when she went home. She would see Mr Walters in the ice cream shop and Mrs Isaacs in the paper shop. She would go to the Fountains Café and the picture house and the caves and the bandstand. And above all, oh! Above all, she would see Llew.

'Chloe Samuels! You stop that twirling now!' the repressive voice of Auntie Bran cut across her spirals. 'Enough to make the cat dizzy you are! Come and sit down nice, now. What would your mam say?'

Chloe did not retort that there *was* no cat, since they were waiting at the bus stop in Carmarthen. The very mention of her mother was enough to turn her happiness to homesickness. Before she had even left the county! Her parents had put her on the bus in Nant-Aur and, fifteen miles later in Carmarthen, here was Auntie Branwen to meet her off it and make sure she caught the Tenby bus. *Oh Mam, Dad*, she thought, *how can I leave you for three whole weeks?*

Chloe and Auntie Bran subsided into side-by-side silence. Auntie Bran was satisfied that, by invoking Chloe's mother, she had effectively quashed her thirteen-year-old niece. But the truth was that Gwennan was as excited as anyone about Chloe's holiday. If she had been here, she would have been twirling too. She had packed her daughter's suitcase, layering tissue paper between the worn jumpers, skirts and blouses as carefully as if they were the finest Parisian silks. There was nothing Gwennan would not do for the happiness of her first-born child and only daughter, but she and her husband, Daf, had little to give. So they made do with this: parting with Chloe for three weeks every summer so she could have the time of her life in Tenby.

The red Tenby bus arrived in a puff of dust and a crunch of wheels. Chloe's aunt swung the battered brown case (another Margaret Matthews cast-off) up the steps and gave Chloe a quick, sharp kiss on the cheek. She stepped back as the bus ground into motion again and then, without a wave or further glance, she trudged away.

The three sisters were completely different, thought Chloe, watching her aunt stump off down the road. Branwen, the eldest, had never married and lived alone in her little cottage in Blue Street. This situation might have lent itself to all kinds of fun and adventures, had not Auntie Bran been the kind of person who chased away fun and adventure with a stiff broom. Pale and unbeautiful, with eyebrows that sprouted where eyebrows really had no business to go, Auntie Bran, it was safe to say, was Chloe's least favourite.

Then there was Susan, the 'middle child', a designation that seemed to imply all sorts when Chloe heard it muttered among the neighbours. She was tall, rather glamorous and had almost gone to university! In fact, Chloe had not known she even *had* an Auntie Susan until four years ago – there had been some sort of family feud during the war, when Chloe was a little one. But in 1950 Auntie Susan had 'mended fences'. She wrote to Gwennan, the softer-hearted of her sisters, saying it was a new decade; they should put the past behind them. She wrote that she was settled in Tenby now, and that if Gwennan was happy for Chloe to visit, they would look after her very well.

Gwennan, the youngest of the sisters, was Chloe's mother . . . but no. Chloe loved her mother so much, and it was too soon in her holiday to be able to think of her without crying. It would be worst tonight, she knew, when she spent her first night in the camp bed at the foot of Cousin Megan's bed. Then she would remember her mother's worried expression as she checked and checked that Chloe had everything she needed. Such love . . . A parting, even for just a holiday, made such love a double-edged sword.

But tomorrow she would wake to the screaming of gulls and the promise of long, sunlit days of liberty. The days would pass and Chloe would be happy, writing home in instalments, posting the letters once a week; the *hiraeth* would ease. She knew well the pattern of the days now, for this was to be her fourth summer holiday with the other branch of the family, the 'posh' branch.

And this would be the *best* holiday yet because she was thirteen! And *that* meant – her stomach turned over just thinking about it – that this year, for the very first time, she, Chloe Samuels, could attend the Tenby Teens summer dance! How could a person stand this much excitement and *live*?

Forcing herself to sit still, she dug in her coat pocket for a gob-stopper.

*Enjoy, now, cariad! Enjoy every minute!* The memory of

Gwennan's kind, lovely voice made Chloe miss her mother all the more, so she thought about Llew instead.

Chloe had met Llew that first summer in Tenby, three long years ago now, and he was her best friend in all the world. Of course, she didn't say that to Bethan Hill, who was her best friend in Nant-Aur. She didn't want to hurt anyone's feelings. BUT.

Llew was special. He was two years younger than Chloe, the same age as her brother Clark. If he had been anyone else, Chloe would have considered him a child. But he had an 'old soul', Auntie Susan said, not necessarily meaning it as a compliment. Chloe agreed, though; she could see it in his greeny-browny-yellowy eyes, and when he talked she felt as if she were with someone older, not younger. He was as tall as she was, too, and everyone knew boys grew slower than girls. Then again, Chloe had never been tall – she followed her mother like that. She worried she would end up stout like her too. No sign of that yet, though. Chloe was as slender as a daisy stem.

Llew thought a lot, and read poetry. Chloe teased him for this but secretly she was impressed. He was going to be a famous photographer when he grew up and take pictures of all the famous people of the day – the actors and actresses, the writers and dancers and inventors. He was never seen without his Box Brownie slung around his skinny neck. He was completely unafraid to accost fishermen, holidaymakers, lifeboat men, usherettes at the picture house . . . and ask them to do this, that or the other that he thought would make an interesting photograph. Even when Red Sam the lobsterman roared at him and chased him off, Llew was undaunted. Red Sam scared Chloe with his hands and feet like anvils, the drinker's complexion that gave him his name and his beard thick as a blackberry bush, but Llew danced away over the rocks and laughed at him.

Red Sam was a dramatic exception, though. More often than not people seemed flattered, or at least amused, and Llew got his picture. Occasionally they swore at him and told him he would be a waster when he grew up, like his old man. Chloe couldn't have borne being rejected like that but Llew only shrugged.

'They'll be sorry one day,' he always said. 'They'll be begging me to take their picture, but they won't be able to afford me.'

Llew would take Chloe's picture in the future, he said, because she was going to be beautiful. He said it quite matter-of-factly, the way you might say that a ladybird has spots or a butterfly has wings, but Chloe was thrilled. He was the first person besides her mother ever to say so, and she badly wanted to be beautiful because then, when she grew up, men would fall in love with her and she would have a magical life . . . Chloe was determined to have a magical life.

It was hard, in Nant-Aur, to imagine how that could ever happen. Not that Chloe didn't love her home; she did. She adored her parents, tolerated her brothers better than she let on (she would never, ever admit that she loved them) and she couldn't imagine surviving for any length of time without waking up to the sight of the mists wreathing the bryn.

But Nant-Aur was a village. She knew everyone in it and, if there was greatness in her, no one *there* was going to see it, apart from maybe her mam. To everyone else she was just 'the Samuels girl', too flighty by half, but a pretty enough little thing, if only she filled out a bit.

As for men . . . besides her brothers the village boasted only twelve boys close to her in age. Even allowing for great improvements in their looks and manners when they grew, Chloe couldn't see herself falling in love with a single one of them. They were unimaginative souls, dense as lumps of coal. Whereas Chloe wanted . . . well, in truth, she didn't know *what* she wanted, and that was part of the problem with Nant-Aur. Apart from the piano teacher and the church caretaker, both of whom were spinsters (a word that caused Chloe to shiver), all the women were mothers, wives. They kept house, they did laundry. They didn't present a wide range of options for Chloe to choose from.

An excited chant rose from the children on the bus, rousing her from her reflections.

'Oneby, Twoby, Threeby, Fourby, Fiveby, Sixby, Sevenby, Eightby, Nineby, TENBY!' they hollered, voices rising with every count, before collapsing in gales of giddy laughter.

Some of the old people tutted, others smiled indulgently. Chloe raised her eyebrows as Megan might have done. In previous years she had joined in, but she was a Tenby Teen now! No need to be childish like the little ones.

It wasn't that she didn't *want* to get married and have children;

it was just that she didn't want to do it Nant-Aur style. She didn't want to wrap herself up in an old pinny six days a week and wear a patched dress to church on Sundays, then hurry home to cook a massive roast with all the trimmings while her family snored by the fire. She wanted . . . something else, as well.

It was only in Tenby that she glimpsed alternative ways of arranging things. Aunt Susan, for example, had a husband and children, but she wore beautiful clothes from her London days. She frequently lunched with female friends and spent a great deal of time gazing at the sea, tapping her cigarette holder against her teeth and painting her nails a gorgeous holly-berry red. Chloe felt that if *she* had nail polish and pretty things to wear and time to giggle with friends, she could be happy. Her own mother had none of these things yet Gwennan was always happy, and Chloe couldn't think why. The only person she could talk to about such things was Llew, and he said that there were as many different ways to be happy as there were people in the world or pebbles on the beach.

'How do *you* know?' she had demanded, looking at him askance. 'You're ten!'

But whether he was right or wrong, Chloe liked the thought of finding her own way to be happy. She didn't want to be like her mother, nor *quite* like Auntie Susan, and she certainly didn't want to be like Auntie Bran! So she would just have to blaze a new trail. One thing she knew for sure: if there was magic to be found anywhere in the small, ordinary life of Chloe Samuels, Tenby was where she would find it.

# Nora

The anxiety was as bad as ever. At least it was Saturday, so she didn't have to go to work. So far, the big achievement of Nora's day had been getting out of bed, making a mug of tea and transferring herself to the armchair by her bedroom window. She hadn't managed to dress yet but thanks to the hot radiator, a fleecy blanket and a pair of purple bedsocks, she was warm. Even so, she couldn't stop shivering. Jennifer said when this happened to 'sit with it' and 'breathe through it' and to 'watch it with curiosity and compassion'. Mindfulness. Nora was trying. Not so much because she had faith in it as because this felt so bad – *so* bad – that she would entertain any technique, any perspective, that might one day make this cold grey paralysis go away. If the people in work could see her now, they wouldn't believe it.

Nora was – for another four weeks anyway – the office manager for the Faculty of History in the School of Humanities at the University of Greater London. She oversaw a team of nine administrators (a little faculty joke: why employ one person to do a job when three can do it half as well?) and supported eight academics, making sure their working lives ran like clockwork. She used to think of the morass of university procedures, paperwork and protocol as a dense jungle and herself as a mighty explorer slashing a way through with a machete. Because of the unflinching way she rampaged through a to-do list that would make lesser mortals quail, Simon used to call her the Achiev-o-meter. It wasn't exactly the sexiest thing a man had ever called her.

But it was true that Nora was a consummate professional. She was never seen with a hair out of place. She had *never* known what it was to cower under a blanket. But about a year ago, vague, unspecified fears had started to plague her. She'd begun to wake up crying from nightmares she couldn't remember and, sometimes, from erotic dreams so sharp and insistent, so at odds with her waking life, that she found those the most unsettling of all.

The view from the back of her one-bed flat in Kingston was a jumble of roofs and corners of buildings, a couple of drainpipes and a cracked gutter with lavish weeds springing forth like some kind of deconstructionist hanging basket. Nora sat and stared, the mug cooling between her hands.

What was she going to tell everyone at work on Monday? She had been there *nine years*; she was 'part of the furniture', as Dr Menna Brantham (Gender and Narrative 1765–1857) often said. (She meant it as a compliment.) She wasn't remotely ready to answer the questions that were sure to follow. Like, *Why?*

Maybe Simon was right. Maybe she was losing the plot. It

was a moment of pure impulse, brought about by the contrast of the image of the beach with those green-painted doors and that damn plastic fern. A sudden vehement rejection of everything they symbolised about her life. But she couldn't say *that* to her colleagues.

Her brain kept telling her that she had just made a catastrophic mistake; her job really could be worse. *But*, some rebellious, unacknowledged part of Nora whispered, *it could be a lot better, too*.

What would she do when she finished? Spend every day like today, playing dead to an invisible predator, shrinking from life? Would she go really properly crazy? The possibility had never been anywhere on Nora's radar before. She was clever. Practical. Dedicated. 'A very together young woman,' Dr Wendham Windsor (Twentieth-Century Politics and Sociology) had commended her, once.

Her mug was now stone cold. Nora set it down on the windowsill and the roofscape before her eyes reconfigured itself into the beach. Long and clean, sparkling like champagne, it was edged by froth and floodlit by a winter sun. Nora groaned. Did she now have to add hallucinations to her list of difficulties? It was just a place in Wales that she'd visited once as a child.

Nora and Jasmine had been staying with Gran, who suggested a day out in Tenby. Jasmine wouldn't go, of course, so Gran took Nora. Nora probably hadn't thought about that day in twenty years – until the beach, improbably, flashed into her mind in the office yesterday.

And why that beach specifically? Tenby had two or three lovely beaches if Nora remembered correctly. It was only briefly, at the end of the day, that they'd gone to see the South Beach. When Gran asked her if she wanted to go down there to walk, Nora shook her head; she was tired. So they went back to the car. It had been a pretty place, a happier time, but nothing remarkable had happened there. It didn't hold any special significance for her. It was ridiculous. You couldn't be haunted by a beach. But the more Nora tried to push the image away, the stronger it grew. And the strangest thing was, whenever she saw the beach, the anxiety faded.

The worst thing about having a nervous breakdown, or whatever she was having, was how disconnected it made her feel. Last night, on her way home, she had seen Glen the homeless man outside the train station. He was clutching a lead with no dog attached to it. When he saw Nora he seized her arm.

'Have you seen him?' he asked, his eyes wide and imploring.

'Seen who?' asked Nora. 'Your dog?'

He frowned at her. 'No, I don't have a dog. My *self*. I can't find my self. Have you seen him?'

Nora had bought him coffee and cake from a nearby café and sat with him for a while. She felt the same way, as though all the things that had once made up 'Nora' were coming apart and floating off. It was scary and very lonely.

Nowadays the slightest thing could rattle her. Like the prospect of this evening: she had to go to her mother's for dinner. Well, she didn't '*have to*' – Jennifer was forever pulling her up on vocabulary like that. Her mother had simply issued an invitation that Nora had been free to accept or decline, Jennifer insisted. So, Nora had *chosen* to accept her mother's – forcibly worded – invitation, hoping that this time it would be the way it used to be.

It was an effort to haul herself into the shower, get dressed and blow-dry her hair. But her mother would have a fit if she saw Nora sporting her blanket and bedsocks look, so it had to be done.

'OK, OK,' muttered Nora to Jennifer-in-her-head. It didn't *have* to be done. But she *chose* to make herself presentable to avoid getting grief. It was probably a good thing: sitting unwashed in a chair all day was hardly uplifting.

By the time she left the flat, Nora looked pale but almost normal in black jeans, a purple shirt and flats. She fastened on crystal earrings and a bracelet. Her brown hair gleamed around her heart-shaped face, neatly styled in the 'Rachel' cut that had been popular all those years ago. Nora had always loved *Friends*. She brightened up her wide grey eyes with a lick of mascara and gave herself a quick spray of La Vie Est Belle. She put the perfume bottle back, next to her mother's old hourglass. It was pretty, with a mahogany stand and duck-egg blue sand. She had loved playing with that thing as a child. Now it stood neglected among the clutter, the glass dimmed by a film of dust. Feeling oddly guilty, Nora gave it a quick swipe with her sleeve.

She felt a little better as she stopped to buy pink roses – her mother's favourite – and caught the bus. And if she was seized with a great urge to stay on the bus to the end of the line at Richmond, well, that didn't have to mean anything, did it? You couldn't always be in the mood to visit your mother, could you? Except that once upon a time Nora always had been.

Her dad, Steve, had run out on them when she was small – on Nora's first birthday, to be exact. Jasmine had never remarried. It was just the two of them and they hadn't wanted anyone else. They were close as close; that's what Jasmine always said when people expressed admiration that she coped so well.

'We're close as close,' she would smile, shaking her head. 'We're just fine, aren't we, Nora?' And they were. Their best-friendship had thrived even when Nora went to university, then went to live with her first boyfriend. Until last year they had still been each other's favourite person to spend time with, close as close.

Nora didn't know why it had changed. Nothing dramatic had happened. Nora's fault? Jasmine's fault? Or completely natural and inevitable? Perhaps no one stayed that close with their mother forever. Things were still *OK*, it wasn't as though they didn't speak or anything, *but* . . . There seemed to be constant tension between them, aggravation. The simplest conversations became landmines of misunderstanding. They were *too* close perhaps.

On the top deck of the bus to Petersham, she muttered affirmations under her breath. This wasn't Jennifer's suggestion; Nora had got the idea from one of the self-help books she had accumulated over the last few months. They did calm her down a bit.

*All my relationships are harmonious and satisfying. I am a confident, capable adult. I am free to make my own choices.*

Jasmine's house was a tiny eighteenth-century cottage at the end of a lane that now led off a modern housing estate. Nora found herself hesitating on the doorstep. She would certainly tell her mother her news. That's what Nora and Jasmine always used to do. Nora would come home from school and tell her mother every last detail of her day over hot chocolate and Jacobs crackers. Jasmine would come home from work and tell Nora about her day at the office while she sipped a glass of wine. Nora wanted it to be like that again. So she had resigned for no discernible reason and with no job to go to. She should still be able to tell her mother, shouldn't she?

*All my relationships are honest and open. I am a strong, independent adult.*

The door flew open and Nora jumped. 'Are you going to stand there all night talking to yourself?' her mother demanded. 'I've been watching you from the upstairs window. Anyone would think you didn't want to come in!'

'Of course I want to come in!' Nora flushed and thrust the flowers towards her mother, whose eyes gleamed with pleasure.

Jasmine had long dark hair, as she had ever since Nora could remember. Of course, now that Jasmine was in her seventies, the colour was bottle-assisted, but it was beautifully done and the colour still suited her, with her striking blue eyes and elfin bone structure. Her skin was soft as silk, and she was annoyingly petite – it made Nora, who was five foot nine and curvaceous, feel rather giantesque next to her. Apparently she took after her father.

'Thank you, darling, they're beautiful. You are good. Now come in, come in. What's that awful mess on your shirt?' She brushed at Nora's arm none too gently.

Nora looked down at a smear of dust from the hourglass. 'It's just dust.'

'Honestly, darling, it wouldn't hurt you to pay a cleaner once in a while. Oh! I think the soup's boiling. It's not supposed to boil!'

She hobbled off and Nora followed her mother to the kitchen. It was small and warm with oak cupboards and a terracotta floor. The sweet smell of parsnips billowed through it like a cloud. She leaned against the doorframe, watching as Jasmine fiddled with the flame on the hob and stirred the soup. She was elegantly dressed, as ever, in black silk trousers and a cream chiffon blouse. Jasmine didn't hold with aprons. For a moment she looked exactly as she always had. It was only when she moved around that you saw her age – her stiff joints and awkward bending and reaching. Nora savoured the illusion that she was a child, and her mother in her forties, and they could pour their hearts out to one another over parsnip soup.

'Sandy's joining us for dinner,' said Jasmine while Nora filled a jug and cut the rose stems.

Nora's heart sank. It had become hard enough talking to

Jasmine at the best of times. With social Jasmine it was impossible. 'Oh.'

'What's the matter? You like Sandy.'

Nora did. Another roving septuagenarian, Sandy always stayed in the cottage when Jasmine was out of the country on one of her increasingly frequent jaunts to Thailand or Canada or Malawi. Did this mean her mother was going away again?

'Will you be here for Christmas, Mum?' she blurted. Surely she wouldn't disappear over Christmas, now that Nora had left Simon?

Jasmine turned from the stove to frown at her. 'Well, of course I will!' she said, in a tone that was nothing short of impatient. 'Don't get silly now, Nora.'

'I was only *asking*.'

'Well, don't ask pointless things! Oh, there's Sandy. Go and let her in, will you?' Jasmine bent down with some effort to open the oven door, releasing the stomach-teasing tang of garlic bread. In her giant oven mitts she looked like a child wearing her father's shoes. Nora bit her lip, torn between love and frustration, then, hearing the crunch of Sandy's walking stick on the gravel, she went to the door.

Nora found herself relaxing as the evening progressed. Perhaps it was good that Sandy was here. She didn't really need to tell her mother her latest development *tonight*. It could wait.

'Nora's still seeing that counsellor woman,' said Jasmine, over lemon meringue pie. 'It bothers me. All that digging around in the past, and the waste of money. We didn't do it in our day, did we?'

'Don't forget, Jasmine,' said Sandy, 'times are different now. Young people are under a lot of pressure these days. Sorry, Nora, I don't mean to sound patronising. I do know you're quite grown-up. It's just that anyone under sixty seems young to me these days.'

Nora laughed. Sandy was wiry and strong. Her thick grey hair was pulled back in a ponytail and she wore her usual jeans and a polo neck. She was lively and interested in people. She was a good advert for seventy-something.

'So everyone says,' scowled Jasmine. 'You should hear them all on morning TV. Moaning on about noise pollution and time pressure and social media bullying . . . Everything has to be a big deal.'

Rather than start a row in front of Sandy, Nora excused herself and went upstairs. Jasmine used to pride herself on being so open-minded. How on earth had she changed so much? In the bathroom, tea lights flickered on the windowsill and the boiler hummed. Nora felt nostalgic. She missed living here, young and optimistic, catching the bus along the river to school. She missed her *mother*, for heavens' sake! Quite how she could miss someone who was sitting downstairs at this very moment she didn't understand. Especially when that someone had been driving her mad for the last two hours. It was how her mother *had* been that she missed. How it was between them in the old days.

On the landing she saw that the loft ladder was pulled down – Jasmine had mentioned that the annual exhumation of the Christmas decorations was in progress. Nora felt a sudden hankering to look through her mother's old photo albums. When Nora was young, and utterly in awe of her beautiful, adventurous mother, she had spent hours poring over them. Jasmine sat with Nora on many a winter's evening, turning the pages and telling the stories behind the pictures.

Nora had been mesmerised, believing her mother to be the woman that anyone, surely, would want to be. But now, with her mother so changed, Nora found herself wondering what life had really been like for Jasmine, behind the bright images.

'Mum,' she called, 'I'll be a few minutes. I need to look through my old books.'

'OK,' her mother called back. 'Do you want me to cut you another slice of pie for later?'

'Yes please.'

'Really? I thought you were trying to lose weight?'

'Well, why did you offer it then?' muttered Nora, rolling her eyes and refusing to answer.

Quickly she climbed into the loft and switched on the light. Boxes of Christmas decorations were piled in the middle of the floor, tinsel tails straggling out. Nora picked up the torch that lived next to the loft hatch and shone it on the various objects – her school reports and projects, suitcases, the guitar that neither of them had ever learned to play . . .

She spotted the ornamental chest that held the albums and

opened it. There was no mystery to uncover; she knew she would find no secret letter, or previously unnoticed inscription on the back of one of the photos, because she knew those albums inside out, back to front, cover to cover. She just wanted to look at them again. She pulled out the top album and opened it at random. Nora smiled. She hadn't seen these pictures for *years* . . . First, there was Jasmine's go-go girl phase. She'd been a model in London in the sixties, and the photos showed her with sooty eyelashes, mini-skirts and clunky, knee-length boots, her long dark hair backcombed high on her head.

A hippy phase in the seventies had followed – flowing tie-dyed skirts and crocheted ponchos, hair loose and longer than ever. That was the phase that had resulted in Nora.

Then she'd had what Nora always thought of as her Melanie Griffith phase in the eighties, after Steve left. With bills to pay and a child to support, she'd trained as a paralegal and then become a solicitor, succeeding as a single mother in a tough field where women were still a relative minority, then. But if she resented this further lifestyle change that had been thrust upon her, she never showed it. The photos from this time showed her with huge, *Dynasty*-esque hair, lashings of blue eyeshadow and gold power jewellery.

Nora had never known go-go Jasmine and she only had dim, rather angelic memories of hippy Jasmine – the brush of soft fabrics, the smell of incense. It was 'working mother' Jasmine that Nora remembered, was influenced by.

But Jasmine had made being a career woman look sexy,

fascinating, dynamic; Nora couldn't help but compare herself at a similar age. *A very together young woman. The Achiev-o-meter. Part of the furniture.* They weren't the sort of compliments that made a girl glow. Nora had once told Jennifer that she felt as though her mother's life was made of large, colourful building blocks, and all that was left over for Nora were the cramped, dusty spaces in between. She felt like the negative image of a photograph, the colourless, smudgy patches left over from Jasmine Banquist's remarkable life.

She flicked through the pages for a while then shut the albums and put everything back. She braced herself to return to the dinner table. And damn it, she *would* have another piece of pie.

# Chloe

## July 1953

When the bus passed the gypsy encampment near Kilgetty, Chloe really felt she was on her way. This was her special landmark. A cluster of Romany caravans stood about on a patch of common land. Open fires flickered, kettles and pots hung above them. Horses ambled and dogs streaked through the little community; women hung washing on lines and children played in noisy gangs, their shrieks of laughter reaching Chloe over the noise of the bus's engine. Every summer, Chloe waved at them, captivated. They never saw her. But from that point on, the winding roads and high hedges held only one promise: Tenby.

As the encampment disappeared behind them, the children started chanting again: 'Oneby, Twoby . . .'

Chloe sat feeling superior until her excitement overcame her. 'Eightby, Nineby, TENBY!' she yelled. They were nearly *there*!

At last, the road curved round to the right and there was a brief flash of shimmering turquoise sea before the bus went downhill, past the grey railway bridge. Then it climbed, straining and chugging, to the Five Arches, where its magical journey reached an end. By now, Chloe was bouncing in her seat.

'Fidget,' muttered an old woman in the seat opposite, shooting her a black look.

And there, beside the railings, was Auntie Susan, looking like a colour picture out of one of her own magazines. Chloe waved frantically, knocking the hat of the gentleman in front of her over his eyes.

'Oh, I'm sorry! *Mae'n ddrwg gen i,*' she gasped, ignoring the tutting of the old lady opposite. As she clambered out of her seat Chloe frowned, noticing the scabs on her knees – she'd fallen over last week playing hopscotch. She always wanted to be elegant for Tenby and scabby knees weren't exactly this summer's must-have accessory.

She scrambled out of the bus, into sea-salt air so clear it rang like bells. Gulls screamed, a warm breeze blew and Chloe was enchanted all over again.

'I'm here!' she cried, dropping her case and flinging her arms wide.

Auntie Susan smiled and stepped carefully towards her on high heels that set off her wonderful hourglass figure and slim waist. She wore a pale blue dress with a round collar, a skinny white belt around her middle and a pencil skirt so tight it might have been moulded on. No one in Nant-Aur would ever show off their figure like that. Most wonderful were her shoes and the matching small hat that sat on the crown of her perfectly waved brown hair. They were white with dark pink flowers all over them. Chloe instantly yearned to have shoes just like that. (She wore her brown school shoes, unattractive but polished to a proud shine by her father.)

'Chloe darling, welcome back,' said Auntie Susan, bending to kiss her niece lightly on the top of her head. 'What a pretty skirt.'

Engulfed in perfume, Chloe had to catch her breath for a moment before she could answer. 'Thank you! It's new. New to me, I mean, not new from the shop. I love your shoes! I'd give anything for shoes like that.'

'When you're older a nice heel will do wonders for you. You need the height. Still, you're a pretty girl. And how is your mother?'

'Mam's very well, thank you, Auntie Susan, and she says to send you and Uncle Heinrich her love.'

'Oh, he's Harry now, dear, remember? And how is Branwen?'

Chloe hesitated. It was awkward, because Branwen refused to acknowledge the cessation of hostilities with Susan. The war was over but Branwen loved to hang on to a grudge. 'Ummm, she's all right. She's . . . as she is,' she concluded, borrowing a phrase often used among the neighbours, and nodding wisely as she had seen the grown-ups do. 'How are Megan and Richard?'

'Oh, Megan's quite the young lady. Growing up fast. She's gone out with her friends but you'll see her at tea. Richard's busy with his studies. Bookkeeping, you know. He's hoping to work in one of the hotels.'

Chloe screwed her face up at the thought of bookkeeping during a Tenby summer. And it was mean of Megan not to have waited; she must have known that Chloe would love to go with her. Megan's friends were fizzy and fun like sherbet.

They set off, Chloe craning her neck to drink in the view of the Five Arches. The old town walls were castellated and chunky against the bright blue of the sky, pink flowers springing from the cracks. They always made her feel that she had landed in a storybook: Princess Chloe of Goldenstream . . . She didn't seem to have grown out of it yet.

She couldn't see the sea from here but she could smell it; she could hear it too, in the cries of the gulls that soared past on silver-white wings like blades. She smiled as they screamed out their stories of ransack and high adventure on the waves – airborne pirates, Llew called them.

They walked past the bowling green through streets of houses until they reached number twelve Kite Hill. It was a neat, medium-sized house with a pointed porch with lacy wooden edging.

Megan may have forgotten her, but Llew hadn't. He was sitting on the doorstep waiting for her. There would be escapades this afternoon after all!

Chloe had met Llew on her first ever holiday at Auntie Susan's – thus, Tenby and Llew were forever inseparable in her mind. She quite literally stumbled upon him one night. She had been spying on the summer dance for Tenby Teens; Megan was in there, of course, with Alma and Evie and Christine. Chloe thought they might have smuggled her in but they hadn't suggested it.

Only three years too young – she had kicked the wall of the Fountains Café in frustration. Megan and her friends had talked incessantly about the dance until Chloe felt that life was completely and utterly pointless and drab for anyone who couldn't go. She watched them arrive, the boys with their slicked-back hair and the girls in the new circle-skirted dresses, pouring down the path from the Esplanade like a rainbow. When they were all inside, and Chloe outside, she trudged off into the dunes, strains of Nat King Cole and The Andrews Sisters blowing after her like bubbles. And she tripped over what she thought was a branch, but turned out to be an outstretched ankle. She went sprawling face first in the sand.

'Watch out,' murmured a dreamy voice.

'You tripped me up!' she replied indignantly, sitting up and spitting out sand.

The ankle turned out to be attached to a very thin boy lying on his front and holding what she thought at first was a pair of binoculars.

'Ah, he's gone now,' he said. 'Never mind. Are you all right by the way?' He sat up, turned round and saw her. 'Oh, you're pretty,' he added. 'Mind if I take your photo?'

Chloe saw that it was a camera, not binoculars, that he pointed at her.

'Well, not like *this*!' she said crossly, starting to brush the sand off her face and tidy her hair.

'No, don't! It's like that I want you – it'll make a great photo, trust me,' and click went the shutter.

'That's enough, I must be a mess!' said Chloe. 'What were you doing, anyway? Who's gone?' The boy was wearing shorts and a blue and white striped shirt. The cuffs were frayed and he could do with a good wash, Chloe noted. She wasn't her mother's daughter for nothing. He had quite long, light-brown hair and striking eyes, somewhere between sepia and green, like the fields at home in February.

'Who's gone?'

'Yes. Just a minute ago you said, "He's gone."'

'Oh! There was a gull on that bit of driftwood.'

Chloe was unimpressed. 'There are gulls everywhere! That's not a very interesting picture.'

'Oh, it was. Come and see.' He reached out a hand and pulled her beside him. Flat on her stomach, Chloe could see it straight away. A few tall grasses framed a low horizon and a beautiful piece of water-swirled driftwood. It wasn't a view you would normally see. It was pretty.

'There was a huge gull just in that space,' the boy explained. 'Filling it, he was. Looked like a giant bird. It was a good angle.'

Chloe could imagine. Still. 'Sorry I frightened him off, falling down like that. So inconsiderate of me.'

He grinned at her. 'That's OK. Sorry for tripping you. I'm Leonard Jones by the way.'

'Chloe Samuels. Oh! Wait there! Don't move!'

'You're going?'

'I'll be back now in a minute!'

Chloe had a half-eaten packet of crisps in her cardigan pocket. Her cousin Richard was forever getting bored of meals and treats halfway through and passed them over to Chloe, who was always hungry.

She ran to the driftwood and sprinkled a few crisps over it, then darted back. She resumed her place beside Leonard, with their sniper's-eye view of the driftwood.

'Crisp?' She offered him the bag.

While Leonard rummaged in the packet, two greedy seagulls flew down to feast on the crisps.

'Ah, clever you!' He pushed the crisps back at her and grabbed his camera. 'Move, you buggers,' he muttered, and Chloe was appalled and delighted by his language. 'Turn around a bit! No, it was better when there was one. Bugger off, you scrawny one . . .'

Chloe felt like a naturalist on safari as she lay in the sand munching crisps, watching Leonard frown and fiddle with his camera. She half closed her eyes, pretending the strands of marram were long jungle grasses and she was waiting for a lion to stalk past the camera . . .

A lion. That's what Leonard reminded her of, with his mane of tawny hair and intent eyes with their golden lights. Given the way his ribcage protruded through his shirt, he reminded her of a lion who hadn't caught a zebra in a while. She smiled. Didn't the name Leonard mean lion too? Like Llewelyn in Welsh.

'I'm going to call you Llew,' she said. 'It suits you better.'

The smaller gull flew away while the other turned right towards them and glared.

'Gotcha!' he said with satisfaction and turned to Chloe with a smile. 'Thank you, Chloe Samuels, I think that'll be a good one. What did you say just then?'

'I'm going to call you Llew. It's better than Leonard. And you look just like a lion.'

'Llew,' he repeated. 'I like that. Mind you, you got the seagull to come back so I owe you. You can call me what you like!'

Chloe giggled. 'Can I call you Toilet-Face?'

'No.'

'Can I call you . . . *Mochyn*-Chops?'

'No!'

'Can I call you . . . ?' and they carried on like that until they were both laughing so hard that Chloe's stomach hurt.

After that, they roamed around until it was dark. When the tide came in they moved from the beach to the town and Llew showed Chloe all sorts of interesting corners she hadn't seen with Megan.

He showed her round the town walls, pointing out the niches where statues had once stood, the arrow slits and oillets.

'Oillets? What on earth's an oillet when it's at home?' demanded Chloe, aghast at how many words this boy knew.

'They fired cannons through them,' Llew explained, eyes alight at the thought. 'Can you imagine? Boom!'

Then he took her to see the old bathhouse in Castle Square and the strange inscription above the door. 'What are those squiggles?' Chloe wondered.

'Ancient Greek, my dad says. Don't ask me what it means, though, I've forgotten.'

'Why did you want to go to the dance anyway?' he asked when they passed one of the fine hotels on The Croft. Through the gauzy drapes, they could see shadows dancing. 'Dancing's stupid!'

'It is *not*!' Outrage stopped Chloe dead in her tracks. Perhaps they couldn't be friends after all. 'Dancing is the most wonderful thing in the whole entire world and when I grow up I'm going to be a famous dancer.'

'Are you?' Llew looked interested. He didn't scoff and say, *Yes, and I'm the King of England*, or, *Well, you fancy yourself a treat, don't you, Chloe Samuels!* as the people back home all said. So Chloe instantly forgave him. 'What kind? One of those prancy ballet ones?'

Chloe sat on the wall overlooking the North Beach, the wind blowing her hair across her face. 'You have to train for years and years to be a ballerina, and we can't afford lessons. There isn't even a ballet school in Nant-Aur for me to spy on.' She felt sad for a moment, despite the moonlight on the water and the whispering palm trees. 'But I thought what I *could* do is be a dancing girl with a band or something. Nothing common, mind you, nothing *unladylike*.'

'Don't you need to train for that then?'

'Probably. But not as much as ballet, I don't think. See, I'm ten, so it's too late for that. But it might not be too late for the other sort. I don't even know anyone who can tell me.'

Leonard looked down at his feet and kicked his already falling-apart shoe against the wall. 'I'm eight,' he said.

'Really?' Chloe was surprised. 'I thought you were older.'

'Everyone says that. It's because I'm on my own so much. And my dad talks to me like a grown-up. I think it makes me better company for him. See, my mam's gone.'

Chloe grabbed his hand. 'Oh Llew! I'm so sorry! When did she die?'

'Oh, she's not dead. She left. My parents are divorced.'

'Divorced?' She had never heard the word.

'Yes. It means they're not married any more.'

She frowned. 'But I thought marriage was forever?'

'Yes. Well. It's supposed to be. But my mam changed her mind. When I was five. She lives in London now.'

'Oh! But . . . but . . . do you ever see her?'

'Once a year, sometimes. A little bit, yes.'

'But . . . *why* did she change her mind?'

Llew looked at her with eyes full of confusion and hurt. 'I don't know. I always wonder . . . if I did something wrong.'

'No.' Chloe was very firm, very decisive. 'You couldn't have. You didn't. I promise.'

He cocked an eyebrow at her. If the obvious retorts were going through his mind – that she'd never met his mother, that she didn't really know him – he didn't voice them. He just nodded slightly and looked out to sea.

'You know, you could have watched the dance,' he said after a while. 'There's a trellis between the dance floor and the café so people can sit and watch.'

'Oh, I didn't know that. Megan's never taken me there. I might have learned some steps if I'd watched. But if I'd done that, I wouldn't have met you.'

'That's true.' He smiled and gazed out to sea again, the wind ruffling his lion's mane and his threadbare shirt. Chloe liked his silences. Her brothers never shut up gabbing, not for one minute.

When the town clock had struck ten Chloe suddenly remembered her promise to be back by nine. She didn't want to annoy Auntie Susan and never get invited back to Tenby. So, like Cinderella before her, she fled. But that was not the last she'd seen of Llew.

He called for her the following morning, looking more like a sparrow than a lion, with his stick-thin legs and ruffled brown hair.

Auntie Susan, with her impeccable manners, invited him in while she called Chloe, who was meant to be spending time with Megan and Megan's friend Alma. In fact, she was sitting on the landing reading Megan's *Famous Five* books. The other two were curling each other's hair and talking about older-girl things. Chloe wouldn't enjoy it, they told her, shutting the door in her face.

She ran downstairs and saw Uncle Heinrich and Auntie Susan looking at her visitor with a mixture of disapproval, curiosity and pity. Llew stood with his chin in the air and his hands in his pockets, legs akimbo, hair sticking out everywhere. Chloe thought he looked rather splendid. When they escaped, with a firm injunction for Chloe to be back by three, Llew told her he had something to show her.

'Brilliant!' beamed Chloe.

'You still want to be friends with me then?' He looked at her sideways.

'Of course! Why not?'

'Because of what I told you last night.'

At once she knew what he meant. The divorce thing. Did that mean other people wouldn't be his friend because of it? She must ask her mam about divorce when she got home. She didn't really understand it. All she knew was that she ached to take Llew back to Nant-Aur with her when she left. Her mother would smother him with kisses and food. She would scrub him to within an inch of his life. She would fuss over him and read him stories till he fell asleep with his head on her leg, as Chloe did. His mother must be a bad woman to leave him. Unless his father was a horrible man. But then, why hadn't she taken Llew?

He took her to his house, which was near the railway bridge. They went down a narrow lane between houses, echoes of their footsteps bouncing around them, and in through a peeling side gate. In a long, weedy garden, a tatty old shed creaked next to a dilapidated greenhouse with weeds running rampant inside it. The green, tangy smell of tomatoes rose on currents of sunny air.

'This is my darkroom,' Llew explained as he unlocked the padlock on the shed door with a key he wore inside his shirt on a piece of string. 'I've developed the pictures we took last night.'

They stepped inside and the shed rocked slightly. Chloe wrinkled her nose at the spiders and cobwebs, and the cloying smell of chemicals overlaying the musty air. Rectangular white tubs sat to one side and there was a line made out of string fastened to nails in the wood. Squares of paper hung from it, held in place with clothes pegs. Llew gestured for her to step closer and Chloe grinned in delight for there, pegged to the line, was last night, all over again.

There was the sea, rolling endlessly towards them, and there was the couple they'd seen kissing outside the dance. There was an upturned lifeboat and there was the gull on the driftwood, a proud gull-king on a plinth, framed by long grasses.

'That's a *wonderful* picture!' said Chloe. 'I don't know what it is about it – it's only a gull – but it makes me want to keep looking at it.'

He hardly allowed himself a smile, but she could tell that he was pleased. 'This is the best one,' he said, passing her the last photo, holding it gently by the edges.

Chloe held it the same way and looked at her own likeness. She was sitting in the sand dunes with her skirts all messed up, covered in sand. Sand crystals glinted on her face and there was sand in her long hair, which was snaking every which way. Her eyes looked clear and bright and her hair was the colour of sand too – the dry, pale sand at the top of the beach. He was right, it was a far more striking photo than if she had tidied herself up and smiled for the camera, like the girls in Auntie Susan's magazines.

She remembered that he was only eight. Amazing. There wasn't a single boy of any age in Nant-Aur like him. Even Bethan wasn't half so interesting and she had won a prize for recitation in the Eisteddfod. 'Did you do all this yourself?' she asked, waving a hand at the plastic tubs, the old blackout curtains at the window, the teetering shelf.

He nodded. 'My dad helped me. He put the shelf up. He got me my camera too, for my birthday last year.'

Chloe heard the warmth in his voice when he spoke of his father.

'That was good of him,' she said, not knowing how to ask what she really wanted to know: *What kind of man is he? Could it be* his *fault your mother ran away?*

Of course, that was ages ago, when Chloe was ten. Now that she was older, and knew Llew better than anyone, they could talk about anything. She knew his father was a kind, highly educated man who loved his son and missed his wife. He had never really recovered from losing her and, soon after, had lost his job too. Llew said he couldn't stop his mind wandering off after her and started making lots of mistakes. Their household was tainted with regret and that was why Llew was like an adult in miniature. His mother wasn't a bad person, Llew assured Chloe, just not really interested in living in a remote seaside town with a vague, sighing academic and a small grubby boy.

'You have to find your own happiness.' That was the first time she had heard him say it. 'She's happy in London. I just wish *I* could have made her happy,' he added with a tiny shrug as though a puff of wind had tugged him.

And now, here was Llew again, his camera around his neck as always, a big lion-grin on his face when he saw Chloe.

'Leonard Jones, what *are* you doing cluttering up my doorstep like a tramp?' demanded Auntie Susan. 'You really are the most outlandish boy.'

'Sorry, Mrs Schultz. I was waiting for Chloe.'

'Well, can't you knock on the door and wait inside like a normal person? Richard is at home. He would have let you in.'

'I don't like to be inside, Mrs Schultz,' Llew explained.

He was eleven now, longer and thinner than ever. He was a little cleaner than when Chloe had first met him but never truly gleaming and *never* seen in a tie! Chloe stole a glance at her aunt, who was rolling her eyes. Something about Llew always made her roll her eyes. She grinned at him and dropped her case. They exchanged a quick, bright hug and Chloe looked at her aunt hopefully.

'Oh, very well,' said Auntie Susan. 'I suppose you want to be outside too. I suppose you don't want the boiled egg sandwiches and chocolate cake I've prepared for your lunch . . . ?'

Chloe hesitated, biting her lip. She *loved* boiled egg sandwiches and chocolate cake. It was a question of loyalty. Llew or food? Llew or food . . . ?

But Auntie Susan laughed. 'Oh, all right, I'll pack a picnic for you both. You look half starved, Leonard. Isn't your father feeding you?'

Llew looked fierce. 'He does his best. He's not too good at cooking, though . . . Nor am I,' he admitted.

Her face softened. 'Of course, it can't be easy for him, a man alone. Well, can you bear to sit in the kitchen while I pack up the sandwiches?'

Llew couldn't, so he went to wait for Chloe on the bench on the corner, where he amused himself by snapping passers-by. Inside number twelve, Chloe was greeted by the sight of fresh pink roses on the hall stand and the smell of baking.

'It's lovely to be back,' she sighed. 'Thank you for having me again, Auntie Susan.'

'You're very welcome, Chloe, we enjoy having you. Now, I want you to be back by five o'clock at the latest. Megan is bringing Alma for tea and Richard has a friend coming too so I want us all sitting down at a sensible time.'

Chloe's heart sank a little. Alma. The meanest of Megan's friends.

When Chloe had changed into shorts and an old blouse she went to say hello to Richard, who blinked at her in a distracted sort of way, then she flew down the stairs and took the satchel that her aunt handed her. It was bulging with sandwiches and cake, all wrapped up in greaseproof paper. There appeared to be enough for ten children. Whatever the differences between the three sisters, they all had this in common: they could never be accused of underfeeding guests.

'*Thank* you, Auntie Susan!' Ecstatic to be back, she threw her arms around her elegant aunt. Susan patted Chloe on the back and pulled away, smoothing her perfect hair. That was one way in which Susan and Gwennan were very different: *cwtches* and kisses were trademarks of the Samuels household, but in Tenby things were more formal. Auntie Susan might *look* perfect, with her lovely clothes and painted nails, but Gwennan *felt* like a mother should feel, and nothing could change that.

'So you're a Tenby Teen at last!' Llew teased when she joined him. He hefted the picnic satchel over his shoulder and they walked without discussion to the South Beach. It was where they started every holiday. The Fountains Café sat right on the sand and Chloe's stomach gave a roll when they passed it. One night very soon, she would be dancing in there with Megan and Alma, Evie and Christine and Pam . . . Even though, if she were honest, she was no more a part of the gang now than she had been that first holiday.

'I am. And just you wait till you see me dance, Llew Jones! I'll make you tired just watching me. I'm going to dance to every song. I'll dance with anyone who asks me, even if they're fat and sweaty, just to get the practice.'

'What if no one asks you?' he demanded, fixing his greeny-amber eyes on her.

'Pfff.' Chloe shook her silver-blonde hair over her shoulders. 'Of course they'll ask me. And if they don't, I'll dance on my own and make them wish they had.'

'*Duw*, there's vain, you are, Chloe Samuels,' he teased, in a quavery, old lady voice.

She thumped him on the arm and threw herself onto the sand. 'Oh blast, I forgot my Astral!' In her hurry to get to this exact spot, the spot she dreamed of the other forty-nine weeks of the year, she had left the cream in her suitcase. 'I can't get sunburnt, not with the dance coming up!'

'Oh yes, life or death, your complexion,' commented Llew. He unbuttoned his shirt and threw it over her head. 'There you are, you won't burn now.'

'Piw, you stink, Llew Jones. Get your nasty boy-shirt off me!' squealed Chloe, wriggling free and throwing it back at him. 'I was wrong, you *aren't* any better than my brothers. Give me that cake!'

Of course, it was well past five before Chloe remembered the time. But by now Auntie Susan knew how it was when Chloe went out with Llew. Chloe left the beach reluctantly but it was a happy sort of reluctance because she knew she could come back tomorrow, and the day after, and the day after that . . . That was the magic of holidays: only three short weeks, but they felt never-ending, every time.

# Nora

～

*January 2015*

Here it was: the end of an era, a landmark occasion, the doorway to the Great Unknown. Nora's leaving party.

So this is what nine years of service got you: sausage rolls and falafels, cheese and pineapple on sticks and cheap plonk, in a boardroom overlooking a concrete square with some concrete benches on it. There was a chocolate cake from the campus mini-market and speeches from the various academics, who took it in turns to stand up and 'pay tribute' (actually, to do what they loved best – hear themselves talk).

It was so underwhelming Nora wasn't quite sure it was really happening. Perhaps she had just imagined that she had given nine years of her life to this place and was now about to leave it forever. Perhaps it had all been a rather odd, uninteresting dream. Dr Elsie Fletcher from the School of Economics down the corridor wandered past and was drawn in by the lure of free snacks.

'Hello, Nora,' she nodded, cramming a sausage roll, whole,

into her mouth. 'Is it someone's birthday?' Flakes of pastry showered down her crimplene blouse.

'Leaving do, actually.'

'Oh.' She paused with her mouth open, the sausage roll in full view. Nora was reminded of boa constrictors dislocating their jaws to eat large animals. 'I didn't know anyone was leaving. Who?'

'Well, me as a matter of fact.'

Her eyes grew round then she swallowed the sausage roll and laughed. 'You! Ha ha. Very good, Nora, very good. You leaving. A likely story!' She wandered off, chuckling.

The four weeks of her notice period had passed with very little fanfare. And of course, Christmas had swallowed part of it. Now she was starting a new year – and a new life. She had absolutely no idea what either would hold.

Christmas. Nora sighed. It had started well enough. It had been so lovely to be away from the office that Nora was briefly hopeful that leaving her job might not be an act of self-destruction after all. She still hadn't been able to bring herself to tell Jasmine what she'd done, though.

Sandy joined them for Christmas dinner; various combinations of neighbours came for drinks; all was festive and fun. And in the mornings it was just the two of them again, pottering round together, walking over the fields, coming back and draping the house with armloads of holly and ivy. In the evenings they watched films. With the Christmas tree dressed in decorations gathered over the years, and the smell of mulled wine and mince pies, it felt just the way it used to feel.

Until Nora, eventually, told her mother that she had resigned. And Jasmine told Nora that she was going to Italy for six months . . . then things hadn't been so good.

Jasmine had told her that she was being stupid and irresponsible – Nora's worst fears verbalised. In italics. 'In *this* economy!' she cried. 'What were you *thinking*? *Why*? This midlife crisis or whatever you're having isn't *funny* any more, Nora. You need to pull yourself together!' It felt like a kick in the stomach to Nora.

'It never has been funny, Mum,' retorted Nora. 'Not to me, anyway. I'm glad I've provided *you* with a bit of amusement but I've been going through hell and it's not like I've had a lot of sympathy from you.'

'But why *sympathy*?' demanded Jasmine, glaring at her daughter in blatant incomprehension. 'There's nothing *wrong*! Oh, I know, I know, you're having nightmares, terrible anxiety. I know it's all the rage these days to find a counsellor and wallow in self-pity. But in my day we just had to get on with it. In my day we had *real* problems.'

Nora's mouth fell open in disbelief. She thought she'd never heard anything quite so unsympathetic in her entire life. And from her own mother! Of course, there were insensitive people in the world who might well think like that. It was just that Jasmine had never been one of them. All Nora's life she had been a constant source of support and solace. Maybe her supply had just run out?

Nora had stormed out, across the frosty fields, until she

was so cold she could no longer feel her face. Then she warily returned to the cottage, half inclined to pack her bag and go back to Kingston. But Jasmine was waiting for her with two gin and tonics on a silver tray. Perfectly twisted lime slices perched on the rims and a determined smile trembled on her pretty face.

It was understanding and unconditional support that Nora craved, not gin. 'You can't solve problems with a cocktail and a bright smile, Mum. It's not the bloody 1950s!' That's what Nora *wanted* to say. But she did recognise a peace offering when she saw one. So 'Thanks, Mum, this is lovely,' was what she actually said . . . At least *she* had some awareness that harsh words could *hurt* people!

But then Jasmine had told her that in February she was heading off to Italy. For six months. Apparently she had an old friend out there.

'It'll be wonderful, darling,' she had said. 'Faith has a villa in Tuscany. Blissfully remote – and luxurious, I'm sure. Faith has never denied herself the finer things in life, as you know.'

But Nora *didn't* know. 'Have I even *met* Faith?' she had snapped, and immediately hated herself when her mother's face fell.

'I'm sure you have, darling. Well, perhaps you haven't, I can't remember. Anyway, her husband's died and she's lonely but she doesn't want to come back to England and tout herself round the family as a babysitter just yet. And I really feel I could do with getting away from . . . things . . . so this will be marvellous for both of us.'

'But, *Mum*! I'll be forty in March! You'll be out of the country for my fortieth birthday!'

'Well, I thought you could come along for a while, have a holiday! Then you'll really have to get a new job, you know. Faith would love to have you. You could celebrate your fortieth in *Italy*! Imagine! And you sound as if you need a break.'

Nora probably did. At any other time in her life, she would have leapt at her mother's offer. But when she closed her eyes and imagined a refuge, it wasn't orange and purple fields under a Tuscan sun that she saw . . .

'I was hoping we could go to Tenby for a few days,' she said.

Jasmine looked comically blank, as if she had never heard of such a place. 'Tenby?' she repeated in a dull voice, frowning.

'Yes, Tenby!' Nora's voice was impatient again. 'You know, near Gran's? West Wales!'

'I know where Tenby is, Nora!' snapped Jasmine, and Nora rolled her eyes. This was how it always was now: strange, disconnected conversations that didn't flow. There was a pause.

'So?' she prompted.

'What?'

'*Tenby*! Would you like to go with me? And why are you looking so *shocked*?'

'Well, I just wasn't expecting that, that's all. What on earth has put it in your mind now?'

'I don't know.'

'But *Italy*, Nora! Why *Wales* when you could be in Italy? Why choose sheep and rain when you could have glorious

sunshine and opera? Why choose beer and chips over a delicious, healthy salad and a perfect glass of wine? Why surround
yourself with short, fat, elderly men when you might meet an
*Italian*? Oh no, Tenby's not my cup of tea at all.'

'Mum! God! Talk about stereotypes. We have good wine in
the UK, you know. *And* men above average height, as far as
I can see. Couldn't we do both? Tenby for a couple of nights
and then maybe head out to Italy together for a bit?'

'No.'

'Why?'

'You know how I feel about Wales, Nora. I didn't leave
when I was nineteen because it was so wonderful, did I? I just
don't *like* Tenby.'

'But wouldn't you do it for me?'

'You're asking too much, Nora. I don't *want* to.'

*My mother. Seventy-five going on seven*, thought Nora. They
had parted ways in the new year crackling with disappointment.

*So this is what it's all been for*, Nora thought again, turning away
from her thoughts about her mother and from the little crowd
in the boardroom to stare out at the paved square below. *All
those late nights in the office, all that banked-up flexi-time that I never
took, all the work I took home . . .* a two-hour slot in the boardroom with snacks out of packets and a lot of hot air. There had
been job security too, of course, but suddenly this seemed an
awfully strange lifestyle to have wanted to sustain and protect.

'So!' boomed a voice in her ear, making her jump. 'Still no
idea what you're going to do with yourself, Nora?'

It was Dr Barry Brannigan (Celtic History and Myth, Britain and Brittany). He had made a hilarious speech – in his opinion – comparing Nora to a swan on the loch at Closeburn Castle. 'In days of yore, they came from and departed to no one knew where. Whenever one of these mysterious swans appeared, one of the family in the castle would die.' Indulgent academic chuckles rippled around the table.

'Well, we do know where she comes from – Kingston,' he joked, 'so let's hope that saves us from the curse! For her leaving is entirely mysterious, with no purpose, no destination and perhaps no common sense at all!' The chuckles continued. What a boy Barry was!

'Actually, Barry, your research is faulty,' said Nora now, turning away from the window. 'You should check your sources, you know. I do have a destination.'

'I hadn't heard. Got a new job then? Easy to get admin posts, I should imagine.'

Nora ignored the unintentional snub. 'No, I'm going away for a while to work on a little project of my own. In Tenby.'

'Tenby, eh?'

She didn't know what had made her say it. She almost felt as though something was speaking through her. The minute the words were out of her mouth she braced herself for a quotation. Barry prided himself on having a historical reference for any conversation. It was a useless yet irritatingly impressive accomplishment.

'"If Tenby be not the Queen of Welsh watering places, she

*must* be crowned Empress"!' Barry boomed, eyes twinkling. 'Ascot R. Hope. Italics my own.'

'Really?' Nora smiled weakly. 'I can't believe you even have a quotation for Tenby, Barry.'

'"Such varied attractions for the lover of old-world associations and time-worn architecture." Henry Thornhill Timmins.' Barry nudged her, quite hard, in the ribs and winked.

'Excellent, very impressive.'

'"The most agreeable town on all the south coast of Wales – except Pembroke." Daniel Defoe if I remember right. See there, Nora, you should be going to Pembroke instead!'

'Perhaps I should,' she agreed faintly. When he went in search of cheese and pineapple, Nora sagged with relief. How long did you have to stay at your own leaving party?

# Chloe

Chloe could feel the muscles in her legs pulling as she climbed up Kite Hill to number twelve. Bits of sand scratched her skin under her shorts and, of course, she could feel the beginning blaze of sunburn.

In the cool hall she paused to smell the roses. Voices came from the front room. She sighed. At home, the boys always teased her for being a princess and a priss, ruffling her hair and throwing things at her clean frocks. But here everyone was so immaculate she felt like a ragamuffin in comparison. She just couldn't see the point of worrying about how she looked all day long when she was on holiday and she didn't *have* rollers or lipstick or perfume.

'*There* she is!' cried Megan as soon as she stuck her nose into the front room, as if Chloe was a cat who'd gone missing for a couple of days. '*Do* come in, Chloe, it's so *lovely* to see you!' She rushed over in a whirl of burnt orange skirts that set off her dark hair to perfection. She gave Chloe a friendlier hug than Chloe had expected, then looked down in consternation and brushed sand off her pretty dress.

'Hello, Megan.' Chloe was always shy when she saw her cousin. Megan was tall and curvaceous with shoulder-length mahogany hair. Chloe thought she looked like a brunette Marilyn Monroe. She always wore lipstick and eye pencil and gorgeous clothes.

Alma was next to greet Chloe, on best behaviour in front of Mr and Mrs Schultz, though Chloe had never forgotten the time she had called Chloe 'a shabby little country girl, a boring little *child*!' Alma was very pretty too (all Megan's friends were pretty), with coppery-red hair, grey eyes and clear, pale skin. Today she wore her hair in a high ponytail that swung as she kissed Chloe, and she wore a grey dress with white polka dots. The colours were cool and crisp with her bright hair. Alma sniffed at Chloe and made an expression of distaste that no one else could see. Chloe was more than ever conscious of her beach-encrusted shorts and salty hair and wished she had gone to clean up first.

''Ullo again, Cuz,' called Richard from the window seat, lifting a languid arm, and Uncle Heinrich – Harry – came to shake her hand. He was extremely tall and wore glasses and had a curly grey moustache. Chloe liked him. He had lovely manners and sometimes talked to her about the film stars.

'And *this* is Richard's friend, Iestyn, from Cardiff,' bubbled Megan. 'Do say hello. Iestyn, this is our little cousin Chloe from Nant-Aur.'

She drew forward a slender young man with russet hair like a fox's that almost matched Megan's dress. Chloe even wondered if Megan had chosen it especially for that reason. He had a handsome face, brown eyes and an easy smile.

'Hello, little cousin Chloe from Nant-Aur.'

'I'm not so little now,' she said, shaking his hand. 'I'm thirteen, and I'm going to the Tenby Teens dance next week.'

'Her first dance!' cooed Megan, her hand still on his arm. 'It's so sweet. So exciting when you're that age, isn't it? You must excuse the state of her, Iestyn. She's been on the beach. She loves the beach. She runs wild all summer with her friend Leonard Jones, a little boy from around here. Awful thing, his parents are divorced, the mother left them . . . poor little dab.'

'Llew isn't a little boy!' said Chloe indignantly. 'He's . . . eleven!' She subsided again. Eleven didn't sound very old. Llew *was* a little boy, she supposed, she just kept forgetting the fact. For a minute she felt quite cross with Llew for not being older and therefore more impressive.

'Eleven, eh?' Iestyn laughed genially. 'I bet he's a great lad. Maybe I'll meet him while I'm in town.'

'Oh, no doubt you will, Iestyn, no doubt you will,' said Megan. 'He's round here *every* day calling for Chloe. Sometimes I feel as though I've *two* brothers. Mind you, one's enough. Richard has been quite grumpy since he started the book-keeping. But then I always say—'

'Chloe, go and get changed now,' said Auntie Susan. 'It's time to eat.'

'Yes, Auntie Susan.'

Chloe was relieved to get away from handsome Iestyn, whom

she couldn't possibly have impressed looking so bedraggled and beachy, and prattling Megan, who *would* insist on speaking for her and treating her like a child. In the bathroom she looked in the mirror and gasped. It was worse than she'd feared. Her hair hung in crispy rats' tails and her face was scarlet. There was sand in her eyebrows and a smudge of chocolate icing on the corner of her mouth. Why hadn't Llew told her? Not that he would care about something like that. Not that he'd even *notice*, probably.

'Well, you are a sorry sight, Chloe Samuels, and no mistake,' she muttered in her mother's voice as she washed her face and tugged a brush through her wind and wave-tangled hair. Guiltily, she went into the bedroom and used Megan's Mason Pearson brush. It was much softer than hers.

Her mother would never let her wear her best clothes after being on the beach before having a bath. But she must have made such a bad impression . . . so she put on her new check skirt and the cream blouse with the Peter Pan collar. Why was she even bothering? Iestyn would never notice her with Megan and Alma fluttering around him like beautiful doves. But he was so good-looking and so *nice* it had created a sort of longing in her. Sometimes it felt as if there would never be a lovely young man like that for her. She craved to be grown-up and beautiful. But Megan was never going to see her as an equal and, around her, Chloe was always going to feel like a child.

# Nora

At last Nora understood why she had put up with the punishing pace and excessive demands of her job: without it, she barely knew who she was. Even when she started temping she felt adrift. She wasn't used to uninterrupted evenings, had forgotten the concept of free time. So when Simon rang to ask if he could take her to dinner at her favourite pizzeria she said yes, even though she knew it was a bad idea.

Simon ordered for both of them, drank two glasses of wine rather quickly and then, when pizza, parmesan, black pepper, dough balls and rosemary butter had all been deposited on the table, he got to the point.

'I'm worried about you, Nora,' he said, pushing his glasses up the bridge of his nose, then reaching across the table for her hand. 'You've been acting strangely for months now. And just because we broke up doesn't mean I don't care about you. I really think you should consider seeing someone. You know, a counsellor.'

'I am.'

'Oh! Not the same one you were seeing when you dumped me?'

'Well, yes.'

'Oh God. Well, she's clearly no good, is she, or she would've talked you out of that one.'

Nora nearly choked on her dough ball. It was the first impulse to laugh she'd had in ages. After four months she'd forgotten the extent of Simon's . . . Simon-ness. 'I don't think it's her job to talk me into or out of anything,' she said tactfully. 'That's not what they do.'

'I know *that*. But when someone starts making *such* bad decisions, so *clearly* not in their own best interests, don't they have a duty of care or something, to stop you going off the rails?'

She snorted. 'Does choosing not to be your girlfriend qualify as going off the rails?'

'Leaving your partner, then leaving your job, then going to do the same work for half the money might.'

Nora considered her tomato salad. It was a fair argument. But . . . 'How do *you* know what work I'm doing?' she demanded, withdrawing her hand.

'That's not the point, Nora. The point is, I'm worried. I care.'

'No, that *is* the point. Are you checking up on me? Four months after we split up? I find that a little bit creepy, Simon.'

'It's not like that. I just rang your mother last week, that's all. It's not like I've been following your progress daily or anything.'

'Oh, that makes me feel so much better! Why the hell did you ring my mother?'

'Because I wanted to know how you were and I didn't trust you to tell me.'

'And you didn't think that might be because I'd prefer you not to know all my business?'

'Well, yes. That's why I called Jasmine.'

Unbelievable. 'And she told you? I can't believe she told you. Actually, that's not true. I can.'

'She's worried about you too, Nora! I know you've had your differences lately, but she's a lovely woman, doing her best.'

Nora rolled her eyes. 'In other words you're under her spell, just like all men.'

Jasmine could be unrelentingly charming when she wanted to be and this, coupled with her fragile beauty and genuinely warm ways, meant that men fell at her feet left, right and centre. Everywhere – men tumbling. Not that there had been a string of men throughout their life. There had been Raymond for a while, Oliver for a couple of months, a brief spell with Tony and another with Jonathan, who preferred to be called 'Jonath'. It had been hard for either of them to take him seriously. Four boyfriends in forty years. It wasn't a high tally for someone as beautiful as Jasmine.

But then, Jasmine had never set much store by romantic love and had urged Nora to follow her example.

*Never trust love, Nora. No matter how beguiling an idea it might seem, it's just an idea, not reality. No matter how well meaning a person might be, no matter how much they love you, they can always let you down.* Nora had heard these messages all her life. Any romantic notions she might once have had as a teenager had been trained

64

out of her. And they'd been dealt the death blow when Seth, her partner since university, left her ten years later.

'We did agree that you've become a loose cannon lately,' Simon went on. 'It's not *you*, Nora, to be so flaky. *And*, you're nearly *forty*!'

Nora sighed. 'I don't think being forty qualifies me for Alzheimer's.'

'Of course not, but—'

'If you say "midlife crisis", Simon, I swear I will pour this balsamic vinegar all over your grey cashmere sweater. And your head.'

Simon looked nervous. 'You see, this is the sort of thing I'm talking about.' He moved the vinegar bottle away from Nora. 'All I'm saying is that I understand these things happen to women. You're not the only one. Angus at work was telling me the other day that Claire went completely doolally when she hit the menopause. She's a few years older than you, of course, but the point is, life can be tough for women when they're facing losing their looks and—'

'*Stop!*' Nora pushed her plate away from her rather too hard. It slid across the table to bump into Simon's, which in turn slid towards him, the rim coming to rest in the bulge of his softening belly – *talk about losing your looks*! He repositioned it correctly on the table, not noticing the line of red tomato paste it had left across the front of his immaculate sweater. Nora smiled.

'Telling me that I'm hormonal and losing my looks is not likely to win me over,' she pointed out, fixing him with her addressing-the-boardroom expression. 'Furthermore, I do not appreciate being discussed by my mother and my ex-boyfriend,' she said more quietly. 'As you rightly point out, I am nearly forty – therefore, an adult. My mother should have a bit more respect for me than to go talking about me as if I'm a problem child. As for you, you are my *ex*. My life is not your business any more. I didn't break up with you to have to carry on listening to you banging on about what's good for me and what I'm doing wrong and why you're the best thing that ever happened to me! Because you're not!'

She took a deep breath. Simon looked shocked. Just for a moment, despite the designer specs, the receding hairline and the cashmere, he looked like a hurt little boy. 'I'm sorry, Simon,' she muttered. 'That was harsh. I know you mean well. It's just that it's not your place, any more.'

He hesitated, noticing the stain on his sweater at last. He dipped his napkin in his water glass and dabbed at it precisely. The people on the next table were watching them with interest.

At last Simon looked up. 'I suppose that's what I'm saying,' he said. 'Even though you broke up with me, I do see that there's obviously something going on with you. I don't take it personally. Even though you're not being very nice at the moment, it *could* be my place. I am prepared to take you on again, Nora.'

'Take me on?' *What was she, a lame racehorse?*

'You know. Take you back. Try again. I do love you, Nora, and you seem so unhappy now. It's not as if you left me and then felt happier. I honestly think if we gave it another go, it

66

would be a good thing for you. And for me, of course. What do you think?'

'No, thank you.'

'Well, don't just say it like that! Think about it at least!'

'Simon, there's nothing to think about! I made my decision months ago. I still feel the same about it. You're right, I'm not especially happy at the moment and I do want something to change, but this isn't it.'

He muttered something as he ground some more salt over his salad.

'What was that?'

'I *said*,' he replied, looking directly at her, 'that you're not getting any younger. What do you expect to find out there that's so much better than me?'

Nora rubbed her hands over her face. Then she ate another dough ball. Suddenly, she felt happier than she had in weeks. Leaving Simon had seemed an impulsive thing to do at the time. Yet now she could see as clear as day that it was the right thing. The vindication felt like sunshine. Perhaps then, in time, leaving the university would seem the same way. Perhaps she should trust her impulses after all. And if that were true . . . then shouldn't she also trust the sudden appearance of the beach in her mind's eye? Shouldn't she go there and see for herself why it mysteriously beckoned her? Oh, she'd have to finish her current temp placement – she couldn't leave them in the lurch – but as soon as that was done she would go, she decided, beaming at a confused-looking Simon; she *would* go to Tenby.

# Chloe

Chloe woke to that wonderful first-day-of-holidays feeling. She always slept soundly with the sea air. She sat up in bed and hugged herself; she loved these first few moments when she was all alone and anything could happen. Megan was still asleep, her beautiful thick, dark hair strewn across the pillow, her plump rosebud mouth slightly open.

Chloe pulled a sweater over her nightie and went to the window. From the window she could see the small yard at the back of the house where Susan grew herbs in pots and hung her washing on a line that traversed the length of the yard. Runner bean canes stood against the back wall and there was a redcurrant bush in one corner. A painted wooden gate gave onto a paved narrow lane and beyond that were the gates and yards and backs of other houses on nearby streets. It wasn't especially beautiful as views of Tenby went, but it was interesting, Chloe always told her mam. In Nant-Aur there were no other houses in sight. When they looked out of their windows the Samuels might have been all alone in the world – the last of men.

The grey and white cat from next door appeared over the

wall and tiptoed along it. Suddenly it froze, green eyes glaring down into the runner beans. Pretty but deadly, it reminded Chloe of Alma. Its eyes narrowed and its striped tail twitched. Almost in a trance it reached one dainty paw down into the foliage then withdrew it again. Then its body slid sideways, even while all four paws stayed where they were. A baby rabbit crept out of the bean patch, unaware that death was lurking above its soft brown head.

'Don't you dare!' whispered Chloe under her breath.

The cat aligned itself and crouched. The rabbit took a couple of hops into the sunshine, tiny nose twitching.

The cat sprang.

'Don't you dare!' yelled Chloe, banging on the window. The rabbit hopped back into the leaves in fright; the cat landed in the yard and scowled upwards. It stuck its head and shoulders into the leaves, flattening its whole body, preparing to slither like a snake into the thicket.

'No!' cried Chloe, banging again. 'Leave it alone! Get out! Get out!'

The cat withdrew its head and looked up again, glaring at Chloe with real fury this time. *I'll have you for this, Chloe Samuels*, its eyes said as eloquently as speech.

'I'll have you for this, Chloe Samuels,' said a crotchety voice behind her. Megan, bleary-eyed, was attempting to lift her head off the pillows and falling back again, exhausted. 'What on earth are you yelling and banging for at eight o'clock on a holiday morning?'

'Oh, I'm sorry, Megan. I didn't mean to wake you, I'm so sorry. The cat from next door was hunting a baby rabbit.'

Megan gave a theatrical groan. 'Get out of my room, or STAY QUIET!' she grumbled, pulling the pillows over her head.

Fair enough. Chloe stood on one leg, scratching one sunburnt calf with her other foot. Would she get back into bed and write to her parents? Or would she get dressed and go in search of breakfast? No. She knew what she wanted to do.

She padded out of Megan's room, closing the door quietly behind her, and climbed up the second flight of stairs to the attic. Chloe loved the attic at Kite Hill. Or, more precisely, she loved the bookcase on the landing just outside it. The early morning sun poured in over the wooden floorboards and the bookcase brimmed with the colourful spines of Richard and Megan's books. Chloe was allowed to borrow whatever she wanted for the duration of the visit, provided she didn't take them to the beach. But this was her favourite spot to read. Chloe sank down in the pool of gold. Dust motes drifted in aimless circles. Utter peace. Something Chloe didn't experience at home, with two small brothers.

'Silence,' she whispered in delight, combing her fingers through the air as if silence were a tangible substance, like honey. Then she turned her attention to the bookcase. Yes! A new *Famous Five* book! Last year there had been eleven and now there were twelve. Oh, holidays were magical – magical! She pulled the book from the shelf. *Five Go Down to the Sea*. Leaning against the wall, Chloe settled in to read.

A few minutes later the attic door flew open and Chloe, roused rudely from the Five's arrival at Tremannon Farm, gave a small scream. She scrambled up and the book went flying. It was Iestyn.

He recovered before she did. 'I'm so sorry,' he said. 'I've startled you. Are you all right?'

'I'm fine,' said Chloe, laying a hand over her drumming heart. 'I'm sorry too. I didn't know you were in there. I wouldn't have sat here otherwise.' She was over her fright but now she was embarrassed. How awful to have a girl hanging around outside his door! Her embarrassment deepened when she realised that he was wearing only his pyjama bottoms. Of course, she saw Clark and Colin like that all the time but they were boys. Iestyn was a man. Chloe looked away, a little flushed.

'It doesn't matter at all. Please carry on.'

'I was reading.' Chloe picked up the book and examined it for damage. Fortunately it was fine. 'This is a nice spot, see, with the sun, and the books.'

'Jolly good,' said Iestyn. 'Please don't stop on my account.'

He went downstairs and Chloe watched him go, uncertain. A moment later she heard the toilet flush and his returning footsteps. Hastily she sat down again, not wanting him to think she was bothered by his presence.

'Lovely day,' he murmured. 'Happy reading.'

'I knew you were staying,' Chloe explained hurriedly as the attic door started to close. He stuck his head out politely. 'I just didn't know you were staying *here*. At the house. I thought they meant you were just staying in Tenby.'

'Visiting for a week,' he said, nodding. 'Looking forward to exploring. Bit more shut-eye first, though.' He yawned and smiled and the door closed again. Chloe stared at it. A *week*! That was a third of her holiday. She wouldn't be able to come up here in the mornings and read in her special spot. He would think she was trailing after him. How embarrassing! He had seen her covered in sand and salt yesterday and now in her nightie and an old sweater today. Chloe sighed. She knew she couldn't compete with Megan and her friends, but she didn't want this pleasant, good-looking young man to think she was a complete horror either. She was thirteen now, for goodness' sake. A young lady!

Chloe lasted exactly two days trying to keep herself neat and tidy to impress Iestyn. That first morning she wore her best dress to breakfast. It was the only thing she had that came even close to Megan's or Alma's lovely frocks and she had brought it for the dance. But she was thirteen! She couldn't go knocking about in shorts and old tops all the time. She brushed her hair till it swung down her back in a silvery-blonde waterfall and wore a pretty blue headband to match the dress. She even, when Megan wasn't looking, borrowed a little of her pink lipstick. Then she went down for breakfast and the boys had been and gone.

'Gone?' asked Chloe.

'Yes, they huff gone to Pembroke to visit another friend,' explained Uncle Harry in his careful accent. He pronounced it 'Pem-broke' not 'Pem-brook'. 'They vill be back for dinner, of course. All boys always come home in time for dinner. I vas the same. My brothers vere the same.' He chuckled.

Chloe was fuming. She had assumed that Iestyn's 'bit more shut-eye' would take longer than her beauty routine. She had hoped that when he came down to breakfast he would be dazzled by the sight of Chloe in her blue dress looking, she liked to think, a little like Alice in Wonderland. Now she would have to hang about all day keeping herself tidy. That meant no swimming. She was quite tempted to call off Operation Impress Iestyn altogether but when dinnertime came she was back in her blue dress, almost without deciding to do it. She even plucked up the courage to ask Megan if she could borrow a little lipstick.

'No,' said Megan. 'You're too young.'

So Chloe went to dinner without it but she still felt excited, wondering if Iestyn would comment on her dress. He didn't.

The following day, to Llew's disgust, she refused to go swimming again. She made them walk around the town looking for dropped coins in the drainage vents in the streets. This was something they often did anyway, so she didn't know what he was making a fuss about. It was fun! Every few yards, a metal bracket ran the width of the pavement with a narrow slot in the centre. The words *David and Co, Saundersfoot* were engraved in the metal. Here and there, weeds poked through. And occasionally they spotted a coin that someone had dropped. Then the challenge was to fish it out. Once they had spent almost twenty minutes chasing down one particularly awkward shilling near the theatre. They always split the money exactly half and half.

Sometimes they took it to the slot machines and if they

then won even *more* coins (which had only happened once, so far), that was a Good Money Day. Chloe and Llew lived in hope of Good Money Days. At the back of Chloe's mind was the possibility that they might find enough for her to buy a lipstick of her own.

But when she got back to find that Richard and Iestyn weren't eating at Kite Hill that evening, she officially retired in disgust. Megan was right. She was too young to catch the eye of an attractive older boy and too young for anyone to care what she wore. The next morning she and Llew went swimming.

# Nora

As unpromisingly as it had begun, the meal with Simon had proved a turning point for Nora. For several nights afterwards she mulled over his question: *What do you expect to find out there that's so much better than me?*

It had been infuriating when he had said it, of course. But in the privacy of her thoughts she realised it was quite an interesting question. She had made some big changes recently. Now, she supposed, she had better get behind them. Otherwise, he was right: she may as well have stayed with him, stayed at the university. What *did* she expect to find that was better than a well-paid, secure, bureaucratic job and a decent, steady, if annoyingly smug, boyfriend? What on earth did she *want*?

It was a question she was still pondering as she travelled to Belsize Park for her last session with Jennifer.

So many things were circling in her mind now, like gulls weaving in and out of each other. She couldn't make sense of them all yet, but she had a growing conviction that the seemingly random, unrelated preoccupations of the last months were somehow connected: why her mother had changed,

Tenby, who her mother had been behind the colourful exterior in the photo albums, why Nora found herself systematically dismantling the life she'd worked so hard to build, her mother's view of love . . .

As Nora waited for the Northern Line at Waterloo she found herself thinking about how her mother had reacted when Nora and Seth broke up. They'd met at university and Nora had never entertained a moment's doubt that they were meant to be together. When he broke up with her, years later, she thought the world had come to an end.

Her mother had been wonderful, of course. Nora had gone to stay with her and Jasmine had listened to her for hours and let her cry, watched mindless, soppy films with her and brought her endless supplies of noodles and chocolate ice cream. That's what Nora had always told everyone: 'Mum was wonderful.'

And she was. It was just that after the first two terrible weeks, Jasmine had started cautioning her against loving so completely again. While Nora's head was still spinning, Jasmine had embarked on a manifesto about how love was overrated, how there was no such thing as soulmates, how love would always, always let you down.

It was pretty full-on, Nora reflected now, sipping her take-away latte. All she had really wanted was for her mother to tell her everything would be all right and that one day she'd find someone else.

Years later there had been Andy for six months, then Mac for a year, then Simon. Nice men all, yet each relationship less satisfying than the last. Until she found herself waking up next to Simon from raunchy dreams she could never have shared with him, which left her yearning for . . . something. Was it just unfulfilled lust? Hormonal changes? She'd been too embarrassed to discuss them with anyone, even Jennifer. But now, as she bundled onto the over-full Tube, she had a sneaking suspicion that it was worse than that – that the thing the dreams had left her longing for was love.

What *was* love anyway? It was 2015; love could be explained away in a million different ways. Magazines laid out step-by-step guides to the perfect orgasm, as though sex were not that different from assembling an Ikea desk. Therapy pointed out that no one person could fulfil all your needs and warned of the fine line between healthy interaction and co-dependence. Science claimed it was all just chemicals anyway. It was depressing, Nora decided, hanging on to a ceiling strap as the doors closed and the train rattled off.

Her mother had always seemed fine without a partner. But why had she been *quite* so vehement about love? Nora had assumed it was because of Jasmine's own abandonment by Nora's father.

How must it have been for Jasmine? wondered Nora. At least Seth had given her the courtesy of a full explanation and a sincere apology – he had met someone else, he had never dreamed this would happen, he couldn't bear that he was hurting Nora. It didn't lessen the pain of the circumstance, but at least she knew the facts. Whereas Steve had merely upped and left one day. He'd written a note, apparently, saying there was a lentil casserole in the fridge. When Seth left Nora there had been a painful sense of inevitability about it.

Nora had never met her father. Well, she hadn't needed him; she and Jasmine were close as close. Nora and Steve exchanged a few letters when she was a teenager; his were entertaining, unapologetic. Nora could have felt quite warmly towards him if her own mother hadn't been the casualty of his free spirit.

Nora could tell from the photo albums that Jasmine had been happy in the seventies. They lived in a commune, in a caravan she had decorated Romany style. She adopted the name Jasmine because, she said, plants had the most beautiful spirits. That was why Nora's middle name was Sage. Nora could still remember, vaguely, the smell of food cooking over an open fire, the cries of larks in the sky. Maybe this was why her soul had, at long last, revolted against her manufactured world of bile-green doors and plastic ferns and concrete.

She didn't want to go and live in a caravan or a commune, she knew that. And she couldn't imagine what love might look like at this age. But still, when she finally reached Jennifer's office, she was able to put into words a sense that had been growing slowly but surely within her since she'd quit her job. And she didn't wait until the end of the session to say it.

'I don't want it any more,' she said. 'I don't want a life driven by the clock, a life where I have to wear tights and smart, uncomfortable shoes. I don't want to see *man-made* in every single direction I look and I don't want value to be defined by three for two offers and salary increments. That's a lot about what I *don't* want. If you're going to ask me what I *do* want, I honestly don't know. But something tells me I need to go to Tenby to find out.'

At the end of the session she gave Jennifer a white orchid to say thank you. She had been coming here every week for . . . nine months now! That time had been a blur of fear, discomfort and out-of-character actions, with these sessions floating like smooth lily pads in the middle of it all; a place for her to sit and catch her breath. Now it had come to an end, but then, so had the blur. Whatever else Tenby was or wasn't going to be, it wasn't a blur. It was crisp, bright and beckoning.

# Chloe

Once Chloe abandoned her attempt to impress Iestyn, she and Llew resumed all their usual activities: exploring, swimming, dreaming, drinking milkshakes in the mornings and Horlicks in the evenings. The long, hot summer days slid away in a golden ribbon and everything went back to normal with one small exception: *now* Iestyn was suddenly everywhere. And saw her in the most ridiculous situations.

Chloe and Llew had two ongoing quests to which they returned every summer. The first was for Llew to get a decent photograph of Red Sam who had, he swore, the most interesting face in Tenby. Chloe argued that you couldn't really see his face since it was mostly covered with a thick black beard but Llew was determined. Every year, they would scramble down the cliffs near the lifeboat house to reach Red Sam's spot, where he sat all day every day with his fishing rod and lobster pot, though he never fished and he never caught a lobster. Whatever the weather, he wore a thick, navy jumper, a pair of shorts and heavy brown boots. Every year, Chloe stood by nervously while Llew asked, in a very reasonable voice, 'Red Sam, please can I take your picture.'

'No!'

'But please,' Llew would persist. 'I'm a photographer, you see. If you don't let me, you're thwarting my project.'

'I don't care a bloody bollock about your project.'

'But Red Sam, I won't show anyone. And it'll only take a minute. I'd be so grateful.'

'Run away, boy, before I toss you into the sea.'

'But please, Red Sam. Let me just—'

'You should know,' Red Sam might say, staring at the waves, 'that the rumours about me are true.'

'What rumours?' Llew wouldn't be able to resist raising his camera.

'That I eat children!' he would bellow, patience tried to the last. Then he would spring towards them so they ran away over the jagged rocks slippery with spray. His big hairy legs in their big heavy boots would eat up the distance between them until Chloe couldn't help screaming; it was, she told Llew, like being chased by a hungry troll.

Of course, on just such a day they reached the safety of Castle Hill just as Iestyn and Richard strolled past, deep in conversation. And there were Chloe and Llew, leaping like goats, red and panting, Chloe screaming like a *girl*. At the sight of Iestyn's handsome, astonished face, mortification crashed over her like a wave on a rock. Why didn't he *ever* see her looking pretty and sensible?

The second quest that preoccupied them, on and off, was Operation Diana Castain. Diana Castain, so local legend held, had been a society beauty from London who used to summer in Tenby over a hundred years ago. Llew's father, who had been a historian before he lost his job, had a photograph of a portrait of her. Chloe was fascinated by her dark ringlets and beautiful white dress.

Apparently she had fallen in love with a local man, Owen Lloyd-Arthur, but her parents had a marvellous marriage arranged for her in London – to a man poor Diana didn't love at all. But according to legend, Owen and Diana had discovered a secret tunnel from the old house where the Castains used to stay, leading to a cave in the cliffs. They met in secret and used the tunnel to leave messages and tokens of affection for each other on little shelves in the rock.

One day, Diana's father discovered the secret and followed her to an assignation. He found his daughter clasped in the arms of this doughty Welshman and in his rage he tore them apart with a bellow. Owen stumbled and looked set to fall to his death but recovered himself just in time. However, Diana, lunging to save her lover, did fall and plunged to the inky depths below. Owen and her father watched as her silk-clad form disappeared under the surging water.

Owen was heartbroken. The Castains swore they would never return to Tenby again. And beautiful, doomed Diana was gone forever, but was said to haunt the tunnel searching for one last token by which to remember her love.

Chloe adored this story. And even though everyone – particularly Alma – kept telling her that it wasn't true, Chloe was convinced that one day she was going to find that tunnel and treasure inside it.

So Chloe and Llew hunted for tunnels, tapping wooden panelled walls whenever they found themselves inside an old building and scouring the cliffs for likely-looking caves. There was known to be another secret tunnel under Crackwell Street and Chloe knew from the *Famous Five* that one secret tunnel was very often part of a network. She hoped that if they could find that tunnel, it might lead them to Diana's tunnel. So each year they would spend an hour or two diligently jumping on the cobbles and listening for telltale variations in sound. Thus Iestyn found them one morning, when he came in from a swim in the harbour, his russet hair dark with wet and slicked back, a towel slung over his shoulder.

'What are you kids doing?' he called out, with a friendly wave.

Chloe froze. Kids! He had called them kids! And they were, weren't they, hopping around like fools, searching for treasure. While she racked her brains for an explanation that wasn't the truth, Llew spilled out the whole tale to Iestyn. 'So Chloe thinks we can find the tunnel,' he concluded.

Chloe looked at him. Was he *trying* to make her look bad in front of Iestyn? But of course he wasn't. He was just open and honest and *eleven*!

'Oh, it's just childhood nonsense really,' she scoffed. 'I don't *really* believe that but it's fun to keep looking.'

'I'm sure it is.' Iestyn lifted the towel to dry off some drops that ran from his hair down his neck. He wore a sleeveless vest and had hair underneath his arms like her father. Chloe found herself tongue-tied. 'Well, good luck, kids. And let me know if you find anything.' He sauntered off, whistling, and Chloe sagged against the wall.

'What's wrong, Chlo? Don't you want to keep looking?'

'No, not now. I think I need hot chocolate.'

# Nora

On the first of March, Nora got in her car and drove to Wales. St David's Day — very appropriate. She had booked a hotel room with a sea view for six days and would spend her birthday there. Her mother had always joked that she'd tried hard to give birth on St David's Day but that Nora had thwarted her patriotic plans by turning up late. Not that her mother was very patriotic now.

Jasmine had remained aghast at the very idea of going to Tenby though Nora had tried again to get her to join her for a few days before leaving for Italy.

'Come on, Mum. I'd love you to come. I mean, it's practically your *home*.'

'Home is a vastly overrated concept, darling.'

'But we could visit Gran. Don't you want to see her? She's your *mother*!'

'I speak to her all the time. And mothers are vastly overrated too. *You* should know that, darling, you're in therapy.'

She remained intractable, frustrating, baffling . . . classic Jasmine. At least they had parted on better terms. Nora had driven her to Stansted and they'd had a coffee together before Jasmine disappeared through security, a small figure in teal blue and gorgeous heels. Jasmine never dreamed of dressing for comfort when she was travelling. Those shoes would do nothing for arthritic knees, thought Nora, wincing as she watched. But she could understand that her mother would want to look her best for a reunion with a friend she hadn't seen for years. It would set the tone for a glamorous holiday with lots of lunches, good wine and shopping.

Nora sighed as she left the airport. Perhaps she *should* have gone with her. Perhaps Jasmine was right, and going to Wales, all alone, in not-quite-spring, was a dismal plan. This was always the way of it: whatever Nora did, Jasmine did it bigger, brighter, better.

Now, though, she pushed Jasmine from her mind. She couldn't help herself, she was excited about her trip. It might be modest but it was all hers.

She couldn't remember the last time she had gone somewhere new (well, new*ish*) alone. Simon had been a great one for weekend jaunts; it was something Nora had liked about their time together. He always drove and Nora had enjoyed sitting back watching the scenery – a pleasant contrast to her high-octane weeks at work when it was up to her to control *everything*. But now, with a CD blasting and a takeaway coffee in her cup holder, she felt oddly . . . relaxed. The satnav gave her reassuring feedback on her progress and when she chucked her toll money in the coin bin on the Severn Bridge she couldn't help but smile. The great pinnacles of the bridge soared above her and the broad river marked the entrance to Wales . . . same grey sky, same land mass as England . . . but something did feel exciting and different, whatever Jasmine might say.

She stopped near Cardiff for a burger and a Coke. Leaning her elbows on the cream plastic table, she checked her phone. Usually, by lunchtime on a Sunday, she would have about twenty texts and sixty emails, all related to work. Not so long ago, Simon would have been sitting opposite her complaining, 'Are you with me or Olivia, Nora? You do realise you're not actually *in* the office now? You do have a life, you know . . .' Then he would pull out his own phone, texting Ant and Nate and checking his Facebook page, roaring aloud at funny pictures that she couldn't see.

Today, there was just one text – from her friend Stacie wishing her a good journey. Nora wasn't sure what that absence of prods and problems actually felt like. It might be peace, she supposed, or it might be terror. Hard to tell the difference.

She looked around at the fluffy toys and garish sweets and engine coolants crammed into the display of the shop opposite. She could smell cooking grease and coffee and a whiff of toilet deodoriser. Kids high on sugar were zooming around like pinballs. Young girls and guys were serving at the counter, wearing cardboard hats and looking understandably peeved at the fact. It was only a service station: brash and utilitarian and ordinary. But it wasn't her flat or the cottage. It certainly wasn't room 407A in the Faculty of History. She had done it. She was free.

She drove and drove until she ran out of motorway and then she kept driving, following A roads through Carmarthenshire. The countryside was wide and open and she automatically eased off the accelerator a little, savouring the last leg of her journey. There must have been a lot of rain here recently; in places the river had overflowed its banks and lay on the fields like bolts of folded blue silk.

At a place called Kilgetty she turned left, past a scrubby patch of common land where two shaggy chestnut horses grazed. She smiled. When was the last time she'd seen a horse? Suddenly it seemed a preposterous thing not to have seen a horse in years.

She turned off the music when signs for Tenby started to appear at the side of the road. If all she did was sit in her hotel room for six days and walk on the beach, it would still be the most fun she'd had in a long time. She could buy a novel! When had she last read a novel? Who had the time? Horses and books should never have become such unfamiliar things.

Next morning, Nora woke to pitch dark and womb-like warmth. The bed was soft, the duvet puffy and it was completely silent. For a moment she lay still, savouring. She had worried that she might feel anxious or even bored once she got here . . . but so far all she felt was relief, a luxurious and under-rated feeling, she decided. *It's Monday morning*, she remembered.

She sat up and fumbled for the bedside light. Her watch was showing six thirty. She could hardly believe it! She had gone to bed at ten. Nora hadn't slept for eight and a half hours for . . . years now.

A high, thin cry sliced through the silence then fell away in lapping echoes. A gull. When she pulled back her curtains she would see the sea.

After an hour or so of blissful languor, she stepped out of bed onto thick, soft carpet and walked over to the window. She pulled back the heavy drapes and gasped. The tide was in, full and high. A rising sun blazed a path of gold across the water which was pellucid and calm. Palm trees waved lazily and a gull flew past her window on soundless wings. A window seat with cushions offered an invitation.

Nora started to cry.

At first, the fact of having nothing that she *had* to do in order to avert some ridiculous disaster made Nora jittery. But surprisingly quickly she adjusted, sliding into her new existence like a crocodile into a river.

She adopted a little routine of pulling a fleece over her pyjamas when she woke and setting the small plastic kettle in her room to boil. True to her vow, she had gone out to buy a good, fat novel when she arrived and she spent an hour or so each morning on the window seat, drinking tea and enjoying the adventures of her heroine in 1930s Paris. Eventually she would take a shower, delighting in the fact that she didn't have to bother to straighten her hair.

Then she would walk on that long, sweeping shore that had

haunted her for months. She would hurry down a winding cliff path, past a rather lovely-looking restaurant set right on the beach, and stumble over the dry, blond sand to the firm, toffee-coloured shoreline, studded with shells and pebbles, where she could stride out briskly.

No meetings, no agendas, no reports, no data, no strategy, no politics and no *concrete*. Only the wash of waves, the crunch of shells and the cloudlike shapes of land in the distance.

Each afternoon, she explored the town, an enchanting place where every step seemed to yield a new view: a crooked lane between tall houses; the harbour with its old stone walls and fisherman's chapel; iron railings with whimsical Alice-in-Wonderland-sized gates leading into clifftop gardens; caves, a castle, a cannon . . .

Really, she ought to go and visit her grandmother, who lived only forty minutes or so from here. And she *wanted* to see her. It was just that it had been so long since Nora had had time to let the days flow by at their own pace, in their own way. But she'd definitely visit Gran on Friday, she vowed. She'd feel terrible if she went back to Kingston without dropping in, after being so close.

# Chloe

The Tenby Teens dance fell in the middle of Chloe's last week in Tenby. She couldn't indulge her unbridled impatience, therefore, without wishing her holiday away as well.

'I *can't* go back on Sunday!' she moaned to Llew. 'We still haven't found Diana's tunnel and we haven't had a Good Money Day this year.'

Llew looked glum. 'I don't want you to go either,' he said. 'Everything seems dull when you go. But it's not over yet. There's still four and a half days left.'

'And Thursday is the dance!' remembered Chloe, cheering up. 'You will come and watch, won't you, Llew? Shall I try and smuggle you in? You're only two years too young.'

'Catch me dancing!' snorted Llew. 'Fat chance! No thank *you*, Chloe Samuels. But I will come and watch, for a little bit anyway. Take some photos.'

On Thursday morning Chloe went to watch the boys jumping off Goscar Rock, then returned to Kite Hill at two o'clock. She wanted to enjoy every minute of her first dance – at last she was to take part in the coveted ritual of hairstyling and make-up application; she wanted to savour her entry into this exclusive club. Also, she was a bit worried that Megan would make her get ready on her own, so she wanted to stake her claim on a bit of bedroom space.

But besides Megan and Chloe, only Evie and Christine were there and they were definitely the nicest of Megan's friends. And Auntie Susan was home and came to check on the girls at regular intervals so Megan seemed to have decided to embrace Chloe's presence by becoming her patron; she lent Chloe a stiff, starched petticoat to push her skirt out, a hair ribbon and even a lipstick.

'You can't use that petticoat,' said Evie, narrowing her eyes against the cloud of smoke that rose from the cigarette she dangled between two fingers. She was leaning out of the bedroom window, flicking the ash into the yard below.

'Where'd you get the Bachelors anyway?' asked Christine, eyeing the brown box sticking out of Evie's clutch.

'Borrowed my mum's.'

Megan snorted. 'By "borrowed", you mean "stole", I suppose. And what's wrong with the petticoat?'

'It's too big for the skirt. The dress isn't made to take the layers. It's more of a day dress really, isn't it, Chloe?'

Chloe was embarrassed at her ever-wanting wardrobe. 'Yes. It's my best one, though.'

'Oh, it's fine, don't worry about it. It's a pretty dress. Just not with that thing under it. Haven't you got a smaller one, Megan?'

Megan had. The petticoats were swapped and they all agreed that Evie was right.

'Much better,' agreed Christine, 'but what shall we do with her hair?'

Chloe was thrilled. She was a pet project!

'What *can* we do with it?' demanded Megan in disgust. 'It's as straight as a die, as slippery as an eel and it's so *long*! It's completely shapeless, Chloe. I don't suppose you'd try cutting it?'

'No!' said Chloe in alarm. Not only did she happen to think her hair was her crowning glory but it would break her mother's heart if she cut it and her father would flat out kill her and that was all.

'No,' agreed Evie. 'Don't do that. It's beautiful hair, Chloe, you're so lucky. I love the colour, and it *glitters*. My hair shines, but it doesn't glitter.' She patted her plump jet-black waves, glossy as Elizabeth Taylor's.

'It is long, mind,' said Christine, wrinkling her nose. 'Halfway down her back it is. Oh, pretty enough and all that, but it's not *fashionable*, is it? Don't you ever do a home perm on it, Chloe, give it a bit of shape? I suppose it would drop out with all that length, though.'

Chloe couldn't afford a home perm, or rollers. At home, for special occasions like the Eisteddfod, her mam twisted rags into it the night before. A sleepless night always followed, the rags tugging on her scalp, no comfortable place on the pillow. But Chloe loved the smooth waves around her face the next day.

'Same problem with rollers,' Megan was musing.

'Tongs, Megan!' decreed Evie, coming to the rescue again. 'We'll put it in a ponytail and then tong it. Will your mam heat them for us?'

She did. An hour before the dance, Chloe was sitting on the toy box with her hair scraped into a high ponytail while Megan wielded thick, slightly blackened tongs. Meanwhile Evie painted Chloe's nails in Passionate Plum and Christine watched their efforts critically, helping herself to Evie's mum's Bachelors. The smell of cigarette smoke was starting to make Chloe feel sick.

'It hurts!' whimpered Chloe. 'My hair. It's tight.'

'If a hairstyle doesn't hurt, it's not worth doing,' said Megan.

At last they decreed her ready. They stood her in front of Megan's cheval mirror. Evie clapped her hands in delight and Megan nodded grudgingly.

'You look older, Chloe,' said Christine. 'At least fourteen.'

'Shame about the shoes,' said Megan. 'Nothing to do, though, ours would all be too big. She's so *stunted*.'

'Never mind,' said Evie, 'it's a lot better than it was before.'

'I suppose so.'

Chloe had exchanged her usual scruffy daps for her best shoes, black patent Mary-Janes. It was true that compared with the other girls' pastel heels they looked unimaginative and sensible.

'How are you getting on, girls?' Auntie Susan appeared at the door and Christine hastily leapt away from the window, dropping her cigarette.

'We're ready, Mummy. Look what we've done to Chloe.'

'Very nice, Chloe, very pretty indeed. You'll be a heart-breaker when you grow up, you know.'

'Thank you, Auntie,' Chloe mumbled. She felt a bit uncomfortable about that. Yes, she wanted men to fall in love with her left, right and centre. But that was because she wanted to float away on the wings of love and have adventures . . . She didn't want to *hurt* anyone.

'Speaking of which,' Auntie Susan went on, 'your little friend Leonard is downstairs.'

'Oh *no!*' fumed Megan. '*He* can't come! He's too young!'

'He's only come to take a picture of you all,' her mother interrupted. 'Don't fly into such a huff, Megan. I think it's very nice of him.'

Downstairs, Llew looked more ragged than ever, flanked as he was by Richard and Iestyn, who wore smart suits, their hair gleaming with Brylcreem.

'It's all right, I'm not staying,' he said when they clattered into the front room. 'I thought you might like a picture,' he added, waving the camera like a white flag.

'Yes indeed,' said Iestyn, shaking Llew's hand. 'Very thoughtful of you, sir.'

'Crumbs, Chloe, you look wonderful!' Llew said. 'Like a real dancer.'

'Well, I wouldn't go that far,' said Megan, bustling over and tucking one arm through Iestyn's, the other through her brother's, 'but we've done what we can for her.'

They clustered in front of the mantelpiece. After a bit of fussing, while Llew waited patiently, they got into a configuration that Megan was happy with.

'Lovely,' said Auntie Susan. 'Don't you all look smart.'

'Very good,' agreed Llew. 'Smile now!'

Click. Another facet of Chloe's Tenby summers was captured forever.

'Thank you for thinking of the photo, Llew, it's such a nice idea,' said Chloe.

# Nora

On her birthday Nora woke to an eerie whining which frightened her until she realised it was the wind. The shutters were rattling, and the glass clunked in the window frame.

'Happy birthday to me,' murmured Nora, sitting up, reaching for her fleece.

Despite the weather, the view from her window seat was still mesmerising, perhaps even more so. She watched spellbound as mercurial waves charged from the horizon and the sun rose like a silver disc of ice. The wind threw back its shaggy grey head to howl. Screaming gulls wheeled and plummeted to prove they couldn't be frightened off. Nora sank into her book and devoured it right up to its climax.

It was a lonely breakfast, without the fictional escapades of Mademoiselle Clemence Aubadine de Vincent to entertain her. In fact, it was lonely altogether. The novelty and self-indulgence of the last few days were wearing off perhaps. She had never been alone on her birthday before. And she was forty. She skewered a fried tomato and contemplated its wrinkled skin before popping it in her mouth. That's what she would look like in time.

Jasmine had always done birthdays properly. Nora had never sat down to a birthday breakfast without a pile of cards and a little spread of prettily wrapped parcels. There had always been flowers and cake. The wind still moaned and sighed outside. If Jasmine had been here, they would have embraced the weather, stayed indoors, played Monopoly, drank gin cocktails . . . but it was hard to feel celebratory alone.

Nora hadn't had an anxiety attack since she got here but she wasn't going to take the risk of sitting here wallowing. She ran upstairs to grab her coat, hat and gloves. When she stepped outside, the wind smacked her hard in the chest. She gasped. Forty was not proving particularly welcoming so far!

She turned in her usual direction, pushing into the wind, heading for the beach. As the waves rolled in, the wind blew off their tops, sea foam scattering in every direction like popcorn. Within seconds her eyes and nose were streaming. After a few yards she gave up and trudged into town instead. She headed for the bookshop where she indulged in three new books, one a sequel about Clemence. Her mother rang to wish her happy birthday and between the yowling wind and patchy signal, Nora had to admit that she was in Tenby. Her mother sounded surprisingly calm.

'Well, good for you, darling, you need a break. Though why you should choose Wales at this time of year is still beyond me! Well, maybe you'll get it out of your system now. I hate to think of you being all alone there on your birthday. I'm sorry, Nora, I should have come. Oh! And I sent your present to your flat.'

Nora hung up with some reluctance. She would have to spend her birthday in the hotel lounge drinking tea and reading, she decided. The prospect wasn't as tempting as it had been recently; the loneliness was really taking hold. She turned a corner and found herself facing into a blaze of silver, staggering as the wind cuffed her, but enchanted by the brilliance of winter sun on sea. It was a comfort, somehow.

An hour later, she was savouring her second pot of Earl Grey, lost in the continued adventures of Clemence, when a young woman with bright red corkscrew curls came into the lounge. She took a table a polite distance away and smiled.

'Gorgeous day,' said Nora.

'Barbaric,' agreed the newcomer, riffling through the newspapers and rejecting them all. She pulled out her phone instead and started typing away, prompting Nora to check hers. Once, five minutes without it had felt like severing an artery but she had gone whole days here without looking at it at all. Still, it was her birthday.

She had seven emails. Seven! In the old days only the university being flattened in a nuclear disaster could have resulted in so few. And they would probably all have been telling her to sort it out.

She skimmed the names in her inbox. Happy birthday messages from her mother, Simon and her friends Stacie and Michelle. One from Virgin offering her a new tablet. One from

LinkedIn saying that Thomas Astor was awaiting her response to his invitation. Thomas Astor had worked at the university and been dead for a year. And there was one from Olivia. Fancy her old boss remembering her birthday, how lovely. Nora opened that one first.

Dear Nora,

I hope this finds you well in your greener pastures. Your replacement, Max, has spent the last two days trying to access the Starfire database without success. He's been using the notes you left him and says you must have mistyped the password or account name. In case this is the issue, can you please email him on the main university admin email confirming the correct access details? If not, there must be another problem so could you please find time to come in within the next day or two to fix it? No one else here has training in Starfire and we depend upon it to track accommodation bookings for the HistoryNow! conference, which begins on Saturday, as you know. We are at a standstill without it.

Olivia Jeffries PhD FRHist (History Faculty Head)

The sound that escaped from Nora could only be described as a squawk. The redheaded girl opposite looked up curiously. 'Sorry,' said Nora.

She read it again. 'Well, fuck *me*,' she murmured. The girl grinned.

'Sorry again. That came out louder than I thought.'

'No problem,' grinned the girl, returning to her own correspondence.

Nora's heart started galloping. 'Shit,' she muttered, shifting around in her seat looking for files, logbooks, records . . . Of course they weren't here. Olivia's peremptory summons had always driven her into a fluster as she desperately wracked her brain for what minute detail she might have overlooked.

She typed in the admin address as if she had never been away, a whole list of university email addresses indelibly inscribed in her brain.

*Max*, she typed, *Nora here. Olivia tells me you're having trouble accessing Starfire. I'm sure the details I left you were correct. I'm in Wales at the moment but I can leave early, perhaps Thursday . . .*

She stopped. She had planned to see Gran on Friday. It had been almost two years. Gran was *old*. And she'd planned to take a second, longer visit to the wonderful Tenby Museum – she didn't want to cut her lovely holiday short. Oh God, but HistoryNow! was a huge deal, six hundred historians arriving en masse from all over the country, plus the three that always came from Germany. Imagine if the rooms got double-booked! The university would look shambolic! Nora's book slid off her lap as she rummaged in her bag for her spare memory stick. Except of course it was at home because . . .

She froze. What was she *doing*? She didn't *work* there any more! Her heart was still drumming and she laid her hand over it in sudden sympathy for the poor, easily rattled organ.

This was how she had spent much of the last nine years. In this very state.

She picked up her book and placed it on the table, smoothing out a curl in the corner. She deleted her email to Max. She didn't need the memory stick, she realised as she calmed down. She had emailed the handover document to Nick and Olivia when she left. Either one of them could have checked it. Just for her own satisfaction then . . .

*I am calm and breathe deeply. I am in control of my time and my life. I am calm. I am calm. Oh God, I'm calm . . .*

She logged into her work email. Two months on, IT still hadn't blocked her access. Inefficient but helpful. She scrolled through the document to the computer access codes then scrolled through further subdivisions. A rule of thumb for any university system: any division could be subdivided. So could any subdivision.

She found the information and it was all correct. Of course. She sat back in her chair. Outside, the wind had dropped from apocalyptic to mere mayhem. The sea was still surging and silver.

The girl with the corkscrew curls was watching her with interest. Just then, a waitress came in with a pot of coffee and a panini oozing brie and cranberry.

'Here you go, Kait,' she said. 'Greg sent it up for you. Says sorry he's stuck.'

'Oh, it's no hassle for me. But I won't turn down free food. Give him a hug for me.'

The waitress looked at her in alarm. 'No chance. Remember that to everyone else but you, Kaitlin, he's absolutely terrifying.'

'Teddy bear,' scoffed Kaitlin, tucking into the panini. 'Thanks, Jamila. See you Sunday, right?'

She poured some coffee and sniffed appreciatively. 'Would you like some?' she asked Nora. 'If I drink all this, I won't sleep for a week.'

Nora's cup was empty. 'If you're sure, thank you.'

Kaitlin somehow managed to gather up the pot, her cup, her plate, her phone and her bag and convey them all to Nora's table where she collapsed in the chair opposite Nora.

She poured a steaming cup. 'So what's rattled you, if you don't mind me asking? When I came in you were looking all peaceful and blissed out, then you read something on your phone and went kind of crazy. Are you all right?'

Nora laughed. 'I'm not sure. I'm rattled, as you say. I had an email from my boss saying I have to go in to sort out this database because I hadn't left the right codes, but I just checked and of course I *did*.'

Kaitlin's grey eyes widened. 'She emailed you when you're on *holiday* and told you to go in?'

'Oh, it's worse than that. I'm not actually on holiday. I don't work there any more. I left in January. It's actually nothing to do with me.'

'So why were you so upset? I mean, it's annoying, right, but it's kind of funny too. I mean, talk about cheek!'

Nora smiled. 'Because I *forgot* for a minute, if you can believe that. I'm so used to jumping when something needs sorting, I actually forgot.'

'Like Pavlov's dogs.'

'Exactly.'

Kaitlin whistled. 'Then it's obviously very good that you left. What did you do? Half a panini?'

Nora told her about the university while Kaitlin sliced the panini in half and gave Nora the unbitten-into part. 'What about you?' Nora asked. 'Is Greg your boyfriend?'

Kaitlin laughed. 'No!' she scoffed. 'He's my dad. He's a chef here. We were meant to go shopping for my mum's birthday present. He's a big, muscly bloke with tattoos and eleven scars, but put him in a shop and he gibbers like a little baby. I have to go with him and help. But one of the sous-chefs has been taken sick or something so he can't leave for another hour . . . I don't mind waiting. Used to waitress here back in the day. Isn't it a gorgeous hotel?'

'Absolute heaven. I don't ever want to leave again if I'm honest with you. But I'm just here six days.'

'Here with friends? Husband? Parents?'

'No, I'm on my own.'

'Oh. What's that like? Quite peaceful, I should imagine. Sorry, I'm nosy. Tell me to shut up. My mum says I'm incurably curious and that one day someone's going to tell me to back right off. I just like people, that's all.'

'No, it's OK. It's been really nice being here alone, but

today . . . well, it's actually my birthday. God, I never realised how often I say *actually* before!'

'Your birthday? How old?'

Nora smiled. Kaitlin's mother was right. 'Forty.'

'Forty?'

'Yes.'

'*Forty?*'

'Yes! What? Didn't you realise numbers went up that high?'

'No, it's not that. It's just that – why are you alone on your fortieth? That's a big one! You should be celebrating with friends . . . oh, I'm sorry. I'll shut up. It's none of my business.'

'It's OK. I just . . . well, I'm at a turning point in my life. A bit of reassessment and all that. My mother's in Italy, I broke up with my ex a few months ago. My best friend is a full-time mum so it's not easy for her to get out, and the others . . .' She sighed. 'Well, I'm not sure anyone really gets what I'm doing at the moment. So I thought I'd treat myself to a luxurious few days somewhere beautiful and just do whatever I wanted.'

Kaitlin looked impressed. 'That's cool.'

'It is?'

'I think so. Easy enough, isn't it, to do what you've always done, same old same old. But to take a step back, think things through, really *choose* your life . . . I like that.'

'Well, thanks! Apart from my friend Stacie, everyone else just thinks I'm mad.'

She shrugged. 'Mad can be good. In the correct dosage. So what are your plans? What are you doing for food tonight?'

'No plans. I'll probably just grab something in the bar. Thanks for this half a panini by the way, it's really good.'

'And, tell me honestly now, do you want to be alone this evening?'

'Well, not per se, perhaps, no. But I'm OK with it and this book is great. And chatting to you has been a nice bit of company, so thanks again.'

'I could come back later and meet you for dinner if you like. Well, we can go anywhere you fancy – I mean, it's your birthday. Only, if I come here, it saves you going out in that again.' She waved a hand towards the palm trees snatching and plunging in the gale and shuddered. '*Knobblin*'. *And* we'd get a staff discount. But I won't be offended if you'd rather not.'

'I can't think of anything nicer to be honest, but I don't want to commandeer your evening because you feel sorry for me. I know I seem a bit unstuck but I really am fine.'

'*Sorry* for you? Are you kidding? You're starting an adventure! I'm inspired! I'll meet you back here at seven.'

# Chloe

The dance was everything Chloe had hoped. It was the most *glorious* night! Six different boys asked her to dance and told her that she was the prettiest girl in the room. The music was *wonderful* – Llew wouldn't have liked it; he only liked that horrible skiffle – but Chloe was in ecstasy. Al Martino, Perry Como, Jo Stafford, all her favourites. Romantic and soulful, they transported her to the world of her dreams. She felt as if anything were possible, as if Perry himself might just walk in and ask her to dance. Or a talent scout from Hollywood might spot her. Or Iestyn might tell her he loved her . . . Even sour-faced Alma couldn't spoil her mood.

Alma and Pam had met them outside the dance, Pam and Christine put out because they were both wearing green. Alma was in red, a daring choice with her red hair and white skin, but Chloe had to admit, she pulled it off. Her buttons were black and her shoes and gloves were black and her hair was loose and curled around her shoulders. Black eyeliner made her big grey eyes dramatic. Chloe was lost in admiration for a moment. 'You are *so* pretty, Alma!' she burst out without thinking.

'I know,' said Alma. There was a little pause where her film-star eyes swept over Chloe and she could have said, 'You look lovely too,' but she remained tellingly silent.

But as the night progressed she hardly saw Alma, and Evie was actually pally. Pam, too, paid her a lot of attention, and kept asking whether Chloe thought green suited her or Christine best.

'But they're such different shades,' Chloe remarked tactfully. 'Almost different colours. You look so sophisticated in that dark green.' And Pamela was mollified.

Megan and Richard kept an eye on Chloe. Chloe suspected Auntie Susan had had a word with them. Richard even went so far as to dance with her and then said to Iestyn, 'She's a lovely little dancer, Iest. Fancy a turn with my cousin?' Iestyn courteously did. Oh, it wasn't the same as if he'd asked her because he wanted to, but still, to dance with someone so tall, so handsome, was magical. Chloe closed her eyes and let herself tilt as she spun, knowing his arms would keep her upright. So this was seventh heaven.

Caught up in the dance, it was easy to forget there was a café on the other side of the trellis. But Chloe paused regularly to peer through at Llew who was nursing one chocolate milkshake that he seemed determined to make last all night.

'Well, Samuels, is it good then? As good as you hoped?'

'*Better!*' gasped Chloe, flinging her arms out and only just missing a couple waltzing past. 'Oh Llew, I do feel bad that you're not in here with us. Do you mind very much?'

'I don't mind at all! I'm only here to see you. I'll go in a bit now I know you're OK and I've got some pictures for you.'

'Thank you, Llew.' She reached through the screen and squeezed his hand. 'Oh Llew, I *love* dancing. It makes me feel all . . . all . . . *big* on the inside, like anything can happen . . .' If she couldn't find a way to be a dancer, she was sure her heart would break. But she didn't have to worry about that tonight. Tonight she was *here*. She let go of his hand and grabbed his milkshake, bringing it to the screen and taking a suck on the straw before he snatched it away.

'You cheeky bugger, Samuels! Go and dance then, and stop stealing from me!'

The next time Chloe danced past she could still make out his Fair Isle'd figure behind the screen and flashed him her best smile in case he was taking a photo. The time after that, he was gone.

# Nora

~~~

If Nora's fortieth birthday had started unpromisingly, it ended in the most astonishing way. It was good to have a reason to get ready and go somewhere in the evening. Nora hadn't brought any dressy clothes but she wore her tidiest jeans and a black shirt with the new silver necklace she had bought just yesterday. And the new silver earrings and the new silver bracelet . . . She would do.

Kaitlin made good on her promise and met Nora back in the lounge at seven for a pre-dinner cocktail. Her new friend had her crazy curls caught up on either side with white silk daisies and wore black vintage-style crop pants and a pink and white striped top. Kaitlin, it seemed, was all about the birthdays.

'I love birthdays!' she explained, raising her mojito. 'You have to celebrate the landmarks, don't you? Life's so short and so precious. Cheers.'

Kaitlin was thirty-two, Nora learned, so it was strange to hear her talk about life being short, but she was completely right, of course. They had a three-course meal in the restaurant where a bottle of champagne was magically waiting for them on their table. Nora tried not to think about how much all this would cost, given her unemployed status. Instead she thought about her leaving do and those limp, uncelebratory sandwiches. She deserved this.

Halfway through the meal Kaitlin's dad, back on duty for the second half of a split shift, came to see them. He looked, as expected, terrifying, but he welcomed Nora to Tenby and wished her a happy birthday. Nora asked if he'd had time to find a present for his wife and his craggy face softened.

'I did, thanks. The little one by here helped me. Got some of that perfume Anna likes by Marc Whatsit . . .'

'Jacobs,' supplied Kaitlin.

'. . . and a ring from that shop . . .'

'The Secret Garden.'

'Aye. By The Sail and Sixpence.'

'They sound like lovely presents.' Nora smiled. He looked all at sea talking about perfume and shops but a pub was obviously a comfortable landmark. It was funny, too, hearing Kaitlin described as a little one. Then again, everyone was little compared with Greg. As he lumbered back to the kitchen, she noted that his neck had the circumference of a small oak tree.

Nora and Kaitlin continued swapping stories. It transpired that there had been a boyfriend, Milo, who'd broken up with Kaitlin over Christmas, after five years of living together a few miles from Tenby.

'So I've decided to move into town,' said Kaitlin. 'I'm only thirty-two. It's not too late for me to live the life a bit, you know, make the most of the fact that all my friends are waiters and bar people and my dad's a chef . . . I didn't really like being stuck out there where going shopping meant a walk to the Spar, but it was cheaper and we were doing the couple thing, you know, buying furniture and all that . . . It wasn't that far from Tenby and we said we'd come in when we wanted, but we hardly ever did, you know.'

'It's so easy to get into a rut, isn't it? I broke up with my ex, Simon, last year. We never did any of the exciting things we used to talk about when we first met. In fact, we just weren't a very exciting couple full stop. Not that life has to be exciting all the time. I just think, if it's the right person, even the boring things should seem lovely, because you're sharing them. But it wasn't like that with us.'

'You're right,' mused Kaitlin. 'I'll have to remember that when I'm missing Milo.'

'But it's so recent for you. Did you love him?'

She wrinkled her nose. 'I thought so. But then, I don't seem to be that upset. I mean, five years is a long time to be together, isn't it? I should be in bits really. He cheated on me with his colleague, Jenna. He said it didn't mean anything and seemed so earnest wanting a second chance. So I gave him one. And two months later it was over. But now all I can think about is how I have this fresh start before it's too late. So I couldn't have loved him *really*, could I?'

'Maybe not,' murmured Nora, remembering the long weeks of tears after Seth left her. No, it wasn't too late for Kaitlin. But what about for Nora, at forty?

'It'll be so great to be closer to Mum again and I've already found an incredible house to rent near the harbour. I'm just going to have some fun for a bit. Get a job in a bar or something. Try to stop worrying about things.'

Kaitlin, a worrier? She didn't seem the sort to Nora. But then again, she knew better than anyone that a bright face could hide any number of private demons.

'It sounds wonderful,' she said, raising her glass to Kaitlin's new venture. 'I really envy you. I love it here. I wish it was me starting a new life in Tenby.'

'But . . . it could be, couldn't it? I mean, what's stopping you?'

'Well . . .' Nora opened her mouth to list the reasons but one by one they all dropped like flies. Relationship – over. Her mother – in Italy. Her job – over. Her friends – vanished to the Greater London diaspora, lost to lives as couples and families. Of course, London was generally considered the place to be for decent job prospects, but then again it wasn't as though she had a plan . . . Or was this just an escape fantasy brought on by turning forty and a surfeit of alcohol?

'I don't know,' she fished. 'It would be a big step. I don't know anyone here. What would I do? How do I know if I'd actually like living here, rather than just being on holiday?'

'You don't know,' agreed Kaitlin, 'but you would if you *tried* it,' she added with a grin. 'Why not come for three months, or six months, and see how it goes? A new scene might clear your head.'

The insane thing was that it felt completely right. All at once, Nora wanted to do exactly that. The knowledge was as sudden and complete as her decision to resign. Getting that email from Olivia today, actually contemplating rushing back from Wales . . . The thought of going back there now made her shiver. It was gone. It was the past.

She took another sip of champagne. 'I want to,' she said. 'I really, really want to.'

'Really? Seriously? That's so exciting! Do it, Nora, do it!'

'But could I? I mean, *could* I?'

'Easiest thing in the world. I noticed there were a few short-term lets around when I was looking. I can recommend some estate agents if you decided to go for it.'

'Well, maybe. It seems like a big step, though. I'd have to rent my place in Kingston or I'd be broke pretty soon . . .'

'Well, don't think about all that tonight. It's your birthday. I'm sorry, I'm not only nosy but bossy. Horribly bossy. It's your life, it's completely up to you. Just maybe think about it *tomorrow*.'

Nora grinned. 'I admire your restraint! You know what I might do, though? Speak to the hotel, stay another few days. It'd give me more time to think about it and I'm really not ready for my holiday to be over.'

It was true, she wasn't. The emotional pull this place had over her was surprising her daily. Just another two or three days couldn't hurt . . .

'Good,' said Kaitlin, looking satisfied. 'Good.'

The champagne, it transpired, was on the house. The staff discount was fifty per cent and Kaitlin insisted on paying half of that so Nora had basically just had the best meal she'd eaten in years for less than she and Simon typically used to spend in their local Kingston pizzeria.

They lingered contentedly over coffee for another hour, chatting about everything from men, to friends, to past adventures, to their mothers. Nora may not have believed in love at first sight but after tonight, she thought, she would have to believe in friendship at first sight. At last Greg came out of the kitchen, looking weary, to throw them out of the restaurant.

'And quiet back at the house,' he warned Kaitlin. 'Don't go waking your mother when you go in.'

Kaitlin rolled her eyes. 'This is why I'll be glad when I move into my house next week,' she told Nora, getting to her feet reluctantly. 'Don't get me wrong, I love my parents to bits, but living with them, at my age, is intense.'

'I can imagine,' said Nora with feeling. 'Well, I'd better get to bed. And I will stay an extra couple of days, Kaitlin, so if you fancy a coffee or something, you know where I am.'

Kaitlin hesitated, biting her lip. Nora already knew her well enough to wonder what she was trying to stop herself saying now.

'Look,' Kaitlin said, obviously losing the battle with herself. She started absent-mindedly stacking their plates and cups. 'I've been wanting to say this since I saw how much you love this place. But Mum says I'm too impetuous and I rush into things.'

'So you've waited two whole hours,' Nora smiled. 'Very circumspect.'

'Yes, well, I was just wondering, if you *are* thinking about staying, I mean, if you *do* decide to come and live here for a bit . . . you could come and share my place. If you wanted.'

'Really?' Nora was flummoxed. It felt like Kaitlin was three steps ahead of Nora in Nora's own life! 'Well, I . . .'

'It's got two big bedrooms – well, three, but one's locked up – and I need to find someone to take the other room even though it's *such* an incredible bargain. It's only for six months and I thought, if I find I can't afford it, I'll bail out and go and stay with Mum and Dad. Come on, Nora, don't make me live with my parents. Or a weirdo.'

'How do you know I'm not a weirdo?'

'I have amazing people skills.'

'Right. Well, I can't say I'm not tempted. I mean, if I *did* decide to come here for a while . . . I guess it would make sense. Only, you hardly know me really, Kait.'

'I know. But if I advertised, and someone came to see the room, I wouldn't know them either, would I? I'd just show them round and we'd have a chat and I'd make a judgement. I've been auditioning you for hours without you even knowing it! Come and see it tomorrow.'

It was well after midnight when Nora floated up the stairs and collapsed on the bed, her head spinning, but not from the champagne. Her eyes fell on her lovely fat new book on the bedside table. And the pottery vase she'd bought in The Secret

Garden, which she'd stood on the dressing table as if she were making this room, that was only hers for a few days, home. Books, and arty shops and a new start . . . she could have all those things in London. But not a little house near a harbour with Kaitlin. And not the beach.

She sat up and pulled her phone out of her bag. She didn't get a signal here so she ran downstairs again. In the lounge she stood by the window and rattled off a text to Kaitlin.

Yes. I want to take your second room please. Or look at it at least. Are you sure?

The reply came back immediately.

Definite. Show you the house tomorrow at eleven? Meet you at your place?

Nora texted back a smiley and switched off her phone. Then she went back upstairs and fell into the deep, healing sleep she'd become used to since she came to Tenby.

# Chloe

The time for leaving Tenby came all too soon, as always. Chloe said her goodbyes over breakfast and Auntie Susan took her to the bus.

Llew wasn't there. They'd said goodbye the night before. They'd lit a small fire in the dunes and roasted marshmallows on sticks then sat and watched the sparks hurtle through the air until the embers dwindled. Llew had given her three photos to keep, two taken at the dance and the one he had taken before the dance, in the house with the others. Chloe gave Llew a friendship band she had woven at home, over the winter, from long strands of wool and embroidery silk filched from her mother's various projects. She knotted it around his wrist and he looked as pleased as boys could ever look.

'Darling Chloe,' said Auntie Susan when the bus came, 'it's been a pleasure to have you as always. Please give my love to your mother and father and tell them you're a girl to be proud of – so pretty and natural and good-natured. I shall miss you.'

Chloe was quite overcome. Auntie Susan, whom she admired so very much, would miss her. She would be welcome next year and the year after and her Tenby days would go on and on forever. Even when she was a grown-up and living far away, London maybe, or Hollywood, she would still come back to Tenby for summer holidays – and then she would be able to afford not only Horlicks but oysters and champagne.

The journey home was never as exciting. The winding green landscape, the gypsies, the changeover in Carmarthen, overseen by a scowling Auntie Branwen, were just sad reminders that it was all over for another year. She slumped in her seat for most of the way, reliving each sunlit moment.

But when the bus neared home, Chloe shook herself. Leaving Tenby was sad. But going home was wonderful! And somewhere along that nostalgic, deflated journey the one had turned into the other. When the bus pulled up, they were all there to greet her: Mam and Dad, Clark and Colin.

Her father, stocky and dark, held an arm protectively around his wife. Not only had Dafydd survived the war, but he was one of the fortunate few to be rescued by the fishermen at Dunkirk *and* escape permanent injury. He didn't talk about it much, and now he was a guardsman on the railways, but he did say that when he lay in the bottom of that fishing boat, blood pouring from a wound in his leg, the sky full of fire, it was the thought of Gwennan and his brand-new baby Chloe, whom he'd never met, that made him hold his nerve.

Mam, her fair hair so like Chloe's, was smiling the sweetest smile. Clark was snub-nosed, freckled and as unlike his romantic namesake Clark Gable as he could possibly be – Mam must be disappointed with that, Chloe often thought. Colin, dark-haired and diminutive, like a fairy child, bounced on the end of his father's arm as though determined to pull it out of its socket. Her heart squeezed. She was home.

She traipsed off the bus, bumping her suitcase down the steps and calling goodbye to the driver, and launched herself into a cloud of hugs and kisses and hair-pulling. Then they walked the ten minutes down the country road, between hedges misted with yarrow, back to the house. Small and white, neat and dear, it nestled at the bottom of a gentle grassy slope crowned with dark woodland which bristled with secret paths and dens where the children played for hours.

Half an hour later, when Clark had chased the chickens, something he seemed to need to do three times a day for his own self-respect, and Colin had shown her the new kittens, the family foregathered in the parlour with hot tea and bara brith, which Chloe tore into as though Susan hadn't fed her feasts all the three weeks she was away. The room was shadowed and close, but in a familiar, comforting sort of way. A white china jug from Victorian times sat on the mantel and an old grandfather clock ticked the lugubrious seconds away. Chloe sat in the best chair, by the fire, though the grate was cold and empty now, in July, and the poker and tongs hung unused from their stand on the hearth.

'So how was it, *cariad*?' asked Gwennan.

'Did they treat my girl right, those posh folk over there?' demanded Dafydd.

'Did you kiss Llew yet?' asked Clark.

'Oooooh! Llew!' cooed Colin in a voice so silly and annoying that only he could produce it.

'I'd throw something at you both except we're in the best room,' said Chloe. 'Silly children. What do *you* know? Yes, Dad, they were lovely to me. Oh, it was wonderful, Mam, like it always is. I wish you'd come one summer, even for a weekend. Auntie Susan keeps saying she'd love to see you. You could come too, Dad. You can't imagine how beautiful it is.'

'We have been to Tenby, girl *bach*!' said Dafydd, sounding amused.

'You know I can't leave the boys alone, Chloe. Your father's at work six days a week and Colin's only eight. Maybe in a couple of years we can all come.'

Chloe took a dim view of the idea of her brothers in Tenby. 'Oh, just leave them with a neighbour. Leave them in the *kennel*! It could be just us, Mam. We could go to the beach and have milkshakes in the café and you could meet Llew.'

'Oooooh! Llew!' piped Colin again. Chloe shot him a vicious look.

'You'd love it, Mam. Honest you would. It can't be good for you stuck here all day every day with nothing but the animals and the boys – well, with nothing but animals then – for company.' Chloe eternally hankered for more time alone with her mother. She hated to see her sweet, pretty mother so downtrodden. Infuriatingly, Gwennan didn't seem to *realise* that she was downtrodden.

'But I'm happy here, *bach*,' she always said. 'This little

house, this life we've made. This is where I belong, see?' It was frustrating.

'How was the dance?' she asked now.

'Oh, *Mam*! It was . . . marvellous. Oh, wait there, don't move.' She thundered upstairs. Dafydd had already taken her case up. She rummaged through it for the photos and the present she had bought for her parents then thundered back down again.

'Hard to believe the noise a dainty little thing like that can make,' her father observed.

'This is for you!' she cried, handing over a blue and white striped paper bag. She and Llew had had a Good Money Day on the very last day of her holiday. She had gone straight to the gift shop, knowing exactly what she wanted to get. She'd wanted to buy one since her first Tenby summer.

Dafydd opened the bag and drew out a small mahogany hourglass, with peach coloured sand. 'Very nice, *bach*, thank you,' he said in confusion, passing it to his wife.

'Oh Chloe! You shouldn't go spending your pocket money on us! We don't expect presents, *cariad*.'

'I know, Mam, but we had a Good Money Day. I've wanted to buy you one every year. Isn't it pretty?'

'Very pretty.'

'They have them in all colours in the shop. I love to see them all lined up. Auntie Susan has one with green sand. She uses it to time her eggs.'

'I shall put it in the kitchen and we'll treasure it, won't we, Daf?'

'Oh. Aye.'

'What else have you got there, Chloe?'

'Look.' She thrust the photographs at her mother and curled back into her chair.

'Oh.' Gwennan's face grew soft. 'Oh Chloe, you look so pretty and so happy! Look, Daf, look at Chloe all grown-up and beautiful.'

'She's always beautiful,' grumbled her father. 'Doesn't need to be all trussed up for that. And only thirteen, mind. Don't forget that now, Chloe. I don't want you rushing ahead the way the fast girls do.'

Chloe sighed. She loved her father but like all Welsh men he seemed obliged to be grumpy and grudging about anything exciting or lovely or fun. Welsh women could be the same way – Auntie Bran being a case in point – but fortunately there were others, like her mother and Auntie Susan, who made the world seem like a place worth living in.

'Stop it, Daf!' hissed Gwennan. 'Chloe's a good girl. This was her special night.'

'Aye, well, I'm only saying.' But he mustered himself and passed the photos back to Chloe. 'A very pretty sight you make, *bach*.'

Clark and Colin clustered round to see the pictures, Colin clambering into her lap for a hug while Clark made retching noises to express his dislike of party clothes and dances and the posh folk in Tenby. Chloe shook her head. *How* was he the same age as Llew. *How?*

# Nora

Falling asleep was easy. Waking up, after goodness knows how much champagne, was another matter. Nora struggled to the surface of a deep, dark sleep laced with confused dreams and eventually opened her eyes to see that it was ten o'clock. She groaned and padded across the soft carpet to consider the world. The wind had dropped, leaving in its wake a world that was still and grim; pewter waves rippled beneath a slate-grey sky while hushed palm trees played musical statues. Nora had never known grey could be so intense and insistent.

Nora regarded the view with bleary pleasure. For some reason she was in a good mood again. And then she remembered.

'Shit!' she exclaimed. She was meeting Kaitlin at eleven. She dived into the shower and as the hot water pummelled her head into alertness she was seized by a mixture of joy and terror.

What *exactly* had Kaitlin said about this house? She struggled to remember, as fragrant lather coaxed her back to life.

*An incredible house near the harbour . . .* That sounded heavenly.

But hadn't she also said it was too good to be true? And . . . hadn't she mentioned something about a locked room? Oh God. There was going to be a body in the basement or marijuana growing in the dining room and they would get raided by the police and she was *forty* now and this wasn't the age to get into dodgy situations. She had to cancel.

Then she remembered to breathe. She had been so excited last night. At last here was a prospect that actually appealed to her. Or had done, until logic kicked in. It couldn't hurt to take a look. Then, if she had a bad feeling about it, she could tell Kaitlin she'd thought better of it. An impulsive late-night text wasn't a contract. She threw on some clothes and hurried outside.

Kaitlin was leaning against the Edwardian railings outside the hotel. Blue skinny jeans, navy hoodie, navy beanie and bright, bright coppery hair springing out from under her hat like a flame in the monochrome day.

'Bad head, second thoughts, a tad hungover?' she asked when Nora reached her.

'Spot on. Thanks again for last night by the way. It was fantastic. Exactly what I needed.'

'I'm glad. I enjoyed it too. Ready to see your new home?'

'Look, Kait, I was thinking about that this morning—'

'Oh God, don't come to your senses now. Come and see it at least. I guarantee you'll love it. *Guarantee!*'

Nora smiled. 'That's a bold claim. Of course I'll take a look. I just . . . don't want you to feel let down if I decide that it's not the right thing for me at the moment. I'm supposed to be sorting my life out and I'm not sure if . . . if random is the way to go.'

'I understand, I really do. If it doesn't feel right, don't do it. It's just that it will. Feel right, I mean.'

'OK, so tell me about it properly. What's the set-up? How did you find it?'

They began to walk, passing under the Five Arches in the old town walls into a street called The Paragon.

'Hold on a minute,' said Kaitlin, passing Nora her phone and posing by the street sign. 'Photo, please.' Nora snapped her pointing at herself and wearing a suitably paragon-like expression. 'Thanks. I'll send it to Mum. It's a running joke with us. It'll make her smile and that's worth the world.'

Nora grinned and handed the phone back. 'The house?' she prompted.

'Oh, yes, so I saw an ad in the local paper. There was an email address, I emailed, I got the place. It's all been very unofficial. The landlord just goes by Jones, apparently. No Mr or Dr or anything. It's one of those big houses overlooking the harbour and it's beautiful – I mean, seriously beautiful. But he's charging probably half what he could get for it. Ordinarily I'd never be able to afford to live there. I don't really get it. But I'm not going to look a gift horse in the mouth.'

Nora's heart sank. This was sounding dodgier and dodgier. 'So what's wrong with it?'

'That's what I thought too. But I can't find anything, Nora.

See if you can. I mean, it'll be good to have another pair of eyes on it.'

'Have your parents seen it? Or a friend?'

'No. Dad's always doing split shifts and my friends are mostly in that line of work too, only available at the oddest hours. And Mum . . . well, she hasn't been able to make it yet.'

'What does she do?'

'Oh, she's not working at the moment. But she's just . . . well, she has stuff, you know? Anyway, we need to take a detour this way. I don't have a key yet. He's left it with his daughter who lives over there. She's a bit . . . well, don't let her put you off anyway.'

Nora's heart sank still further.

Kaitlin rapped smartly on the door of a large terraced house. The door flew open to reveal the sort of woman for whom the term 'middle-aged' had been coined.

'Oh, it's you.' She scowled at Kaitlin. 'What do you want? Wednesday I thought you said you were moving in. You can't just chop and change as you like, you know.'

She had dark hair like a toilet brush, a pale face speckled with dark pores and wore tracksuit bottoms, carefully ironed, with an oversized souvenir T-shirt from the Lake District, equally crisp and laundered. She gripped a feather duster in her hand; the hallway was dim and dustless.

'Hello, Mrs Watkins,' smiled Kaitlin, as though she'd received the most marvellous welcome. 'Nice to see you again. Sorry to disturb you when you're busy, I just wondered if I could possibly borrow the key again? I've brought my friend Nora to see the house. She's thinking about taking the other bedroom. Your dad did say it would be fine if I found someone.'

'Hi, I'm Nora.' Nora followed Kaitlin's example and held her hand out with a big smile. 'I hope this isn't a bad time. Only I'm going back to London in a couple of days so this is the only chance I have to see it.'

'London, is it?' Mrs Watkins narrowed her eyes and ignored Nora's outstretched hand, clinging to her feather duster like a sword. 'What do you want a house down here for then? Somewhere to come and get pissed up on the weekends, I suppose?'

Nora was taken aback. 'Er, no, actually I'm thinking of living here for a few months. If the place is suitable.'

Mrs Watkins' face darkened. 'Oh, it'll be *suitable* all right, never you mind about that. *Far* more than suitable if you ask *me*! My father's house is one of the finest properties in Tenby! "Prime real estate", as those Americans call it! He should be *living* in it, not running off on some mad scheme as he is. But he's not all there, you see. Not all the sandwiches in the picnic, is it? Not all the wheels on the pavement, my father. And if he *has* to go rushing off, he could be making a *fortune* letting it out. *Executives*, he could be having in it. Instead he's letting it go for a pittance. A pitt-ttance!' she emphasised, spitting out her t's like a car tyre throwing up chips of gravel. 'To have a down-and-out with no *scruples* living in it! Because he feels sorry for her, most like, knowing him. *Twp*, he is, *twp*! Soft in the head! And me left behind to deal with the stress.'

In a pregnant pause she visibly quivered with outrage. Nora glanced at Kaitlin. If Nora were called a down-and-out and more or less accused of taking advantage of a senile old man, she would probably not want to get involved. She would probably deliver a few well-chosen words in her boardroom voice and storm out in high dudgeon. Kaitlin, however, seemed unfazed.

'Aw, bless,' she said. 'I'm sorry, Mrs Watkins, I can see it must be a pain for you when you're busy. But if you could just let us have the key now, we can get going and leave you to it.' She wore a big smile.

Nora could have sworn she saw Mrs Watkins' jowls tremble. 'Wait by there,' she said eventually and disappeared into the gloomy interior of her house.

Nora opened her mouth but Kaitlin shook her head. 'She can hear *everything*!' she whispered. So they waited side by side in the doorway, not daring to step inside and shut the door. After what seemed an inordinately long time, their nemesis returned with a key on a manly leather key fob. She held it out reluctantly to Kaitlin who swiped it with a good-natured, 'Thank you so much, Mrs Watkins. Have a lovely day now.'

'*You've* got a job, I suppose?' Mrs Watkins demanded of Nora before they could escape. 'I won't have two unemployeds living there, no matter what my father says.'

'Oh, Nora has a wonderful job!' beamed Kaitlin before Nora could answer. 'She's a historian. A researcher with the

University of Greater London. That's why she's spending the summer in Tenby, she's researching Welsh history.'

Mrs Watkins looked unimpressed. 'History, is it?' she said with a downturned mouth.

'That's right,' Kaitlin went on. 'You've probably seen her books in the bookshop. She has quite a reputation.'

Mrs Watkins looked steadily more appalled. 'Books, is it?' she said with distaste. 'Well well.'

'Anyway, thanks again!' cried Kaitlin, hauling Nora away. 'Bye now!' The door was slammed behind them.

'What a *horrible* woman!' gasped Nora as they hurried through town. 'Hats off to you, Kait, you were just so . . . *charming*. I wanted to strangle her! I don't know how you stayed so friendly.'

'Huh, well,' said Kaitlin, 'you never met my grandmother.'

'This is it,' said Kaitlin five minutes later. 'Home sweet home.'

After meeting Mrs Watkins Nora was more certain than ever that she wouldn't take the room, but even so, she was madly curious.

It was a smart-looking townhouse painted blue, amid a row of similar houses painted in vivid pastels, creating one of Tenby's many distinctive views. It looked directly over the harbour. There was a garage door next to a front door of polished dark wood with a brass knocker in the shape of a rather flirtatious-looking mermaid. A leaded lantern hung to one side. Above them, a huge bay window beckoned.

'*How* much are you paying for this again?'

Kaitlin told her again, patiently.

Nora frowned. 'That's ridiculous.'

Nora had a penchant for looking in estate agents' windows whenever she visited somewhere new so she already had a pretty good idea of what someone could expect to pay for a house like this. Mrs Watkins was right: her father was letting it for a pittance. It *must* be falling apart. Or he was.

Kaitlin unlocked the door and they stepped inside. And Nora was smitten. Instantly, wildly smitten.

The long hall had a dark-red runner on the stone floor and the walls were painted white. There were wonderful oak bannisters and a huge mirror in a gilt frame that rippled like the sea. The stairs were painted white, overlaid with red carpet. Good taste. Manly taste. A faint smell of sandalwood. Cool, because old houses were hard to heat, but welcoming. Nora felt like a nervous child being received by a wise and reassuring teacher on the first day of school.

Behind the stairway was the kitchen, square and white, with oak cupboards, a huge granite island and brass fittings. A red blind covered the window and pots of herbs bloomed along the windowsill, the green bright against the red. Did anything say 'home' more than growing herbs? Nora wondered. A vague childhood memory stirred: Jasmine in the garden when Nora was tiny, her slender hands covered in earth, showing Nora the frothy green plants and telling her their names. How strange that coming here, into a stranger's house, should evoke something of her mother that had lain forgotten for so long.

'This is rosemary,' she could hear her mother say softly across the years, 'and this is thyme. This is mint, and this is basil.'

For once, neither Nora nor Kaitlin said very much. Kaitlin led the way up the stairs. First, they went into the large sitting room facing over the harbour, with a window seat and two huge armchairs in the window recess. The rest of the room was filled with a sofa the size of a cruise liner, a massive fireplace, several bookcases and a piano. The walls were painted a soft, sage green. Ornate coving ran around the ceiling like icing on a wedding cake and five paintings hung on the walls, all in old-fashioned, heavy gilt frames. There were two seascapes, an abstract of two people kissing, a new-agey sort of starscape with constellations and the smudge of comets and, lastly, a portrait of a dog, a black and conker St Bernard with impressive jowls and a fine cravat of white fur.

Nora cried out in astonishment.

'I know! Incredible, isn't it?' Kaitlin said, grinning. 'I feel like I'm going to be living in a stately home or something.'

She showed Nora the bathroom – spotless and elegant – and the bedrooms, behind three doors ranged along a landing flooded with natural light, even on this greyest of days.

'The *light* in here!' exclaimed Nora. It was bright, yet peaceful. She had a momentary vision of her flat in Kingston, poky and cramped. This was gracious living at its very best, she thought.

The two bedrooms both had sea views. The third door was locked.

'Drugs,' said Nora.

'What?'

'He must be a dealer or something. Probably that room is full of drugs. Or there's a body in there. There *must* be something wrong with this place.'

'Or it could just be the room where he's shoved all his personal stuff that he wants to keep private, or that he thinks would be in our way. You know, like clothes and stuff.'

Nora conceded that was also likely. 'What's up there?' She pointed to a second staircase.

'More dead bodies. Well, an attic. But that's locked too.'

'Right.' Nora was struggling to accept that anything this wonderful could be straightforward. 'Kaitlin, this *house*! It's stunning! It's huge! *How* is it this price? Has it got a damp problem or crumbling foundations or something? Is it going to fall into the sea? Is there a *ghost*?'

'I thought all that too but I've been round it three times and I can't find anything. I think it's basically just perfect – a lucky, lucky break. I couldn't understand it either at first, but it's a private rental so it saves him the hassle of dealing with estate agents, and he said he needed to go away quickly and didn't want to leave the house empty. So maybe this works for him as well as it does for us. I just think he's not a particularly money-minded guy! Not everyone is. Read his emails.' She found the thread on her phone and handed it to Nora.

Nora allowed herself to be led back to the lounge where they sat in the two huge chairs in the bay window. It was too easy to imagine any number of long evenings sitting here, looking out at the view, different in every weather.

She scrolled through Kaitlin's correspondence with their mysterious landlord.

*Dear Jones (Mr? Mrs? Ms?)* her enquiry had begun. She'd given a long and endearing account of herself and attached several glowing character references. She had also queried the rent. He had written back at length signing himself *Jones (Mr, but don't bother with that. No one does)*.

He didn't *sound* senile. He sounded intelligent, generous and humorous. He'd had to leave abruptly on personal business, he explained. He loved his house and didn't want to leave it empty for months on end:

> Not only would it be bad for the house, which thrives on TLC, but it would be a crying shame. Summer is approaching. Someone should benefit from it.

They shared a running joke about having the same surname.

*Of course, this being Wales, every other person is a Jones,* Kaitlin had written. *I assure you I'm not your long-lost daughter or anything.*

*Thank God for that! The one I have is quite enough,* he had replied. *Speaking of whom, I have left the keys with her as your point of contact in Tenby. She is a good woman but something of a stranger to spontaneity thus we don't always see eye to eye. But whatever she may say, I am of sound mind and you are not to let her spoil your enjoyment of the house.*

'Well?' asked Kaitlin when Nora handed the phone back.

Nora bit her lip to try and contain her enormous grin. 'Well, I guess I should write to him and ask if he's OK with me taking the second room!'

Kaitlin squealed and threw her arms around Nora. 'No need,' she exclaimed. 'I did it last night. He's already said yes!'

# Chloe

*July 1954*

The summer after Chloe turned fourteen was the summer she felt sure that all her dreams were coming true forever and always. A dancing teacher had moved to Tenby!

As Uncle Harry carried her suitcase upstairs that first day, Megan burst out of her room and bumped into them.

'Oh Chloe!' she cried. 'I'm sorry to be out again when you're just arriving. I'm off for my dancing lesson!' And she breezed past in a rustle of peach cotton. Chloe felt dizzy for a moment as she watched her go. Dancing lesson?

Megan had always seemed to Chloe the most fortunate of girls. She didn't know if Uncle Harry was rich exactly, but he never seemed to begrudge his stepchildren any of their whims. And they *were* whims for they never lasted from one year to the next. The first year Chloe had visited, Megan had been wild about painting. The second year it had been horse riding, the third it had been singing and last year, it had been hair and make-up. It had become a standing joke in Chloe's own family.

'And what is Megan getting up to this year?' Gwennan would ask. 'Cookery? Piano? Flower arranging?'

'Pistol shooting?' Daf would ask dryly from behind his newspaper.

'Aeroplane flying! Trapeze walking! Racecar driving!' the boys would yell, excited and unfettered by realism.

And now it was dancing, Chloe's own dearly held dream.

'Llew called this morning,' said Auntie Susan, joining Chloe in Megan's room. 'He's had a chance to go and see the mother, so he's gone to London. It's all right,' she added at Chloe's dismayed cry. 'He'll be back day after tomorrow. He won't miss much of your holiday.'

'Oh.' Chloe sagged with relief. 'That's all right then. I'm glad. He doesn't see her much.'

'It's been a year this time, I think. Apparently his father had something to take care of in London, so he took Llew along and arranged it with the mother.'

Auntie Susan always said 'the mother' rather than 'his mother', as if to keep Llew at a safe distance from the woman who had run out on her son. 'Your children are your children!' Chloe had once heard her say to her girlfriends, who waved their cigarette holders about in agreement. 'You must stand by them no matter *what*.' She had sounded rather determined.

Another two days until she saw Llew. How frustrating. They didn't correspond much between summers; neither of them were big writers. Chloe usually sent a paragraph scrawled on her mother's best writing paper round about Christmas, and received an occasional postcard, usually of Goscar Rock. For a photographer he didn't have much of an eye for a postcard. For the most part they saved up all their news for when they were together.

With no Llew to entice her into the dull, drizzly day, Chloe unpacked, then went and sat in the front room with Auntie Susan to wait for Megan. There was a plate piled high with Welsh cakes, steaming slightly from the oven and scattered with glittering sugar.

'Did Megan say she was having dancing lessons?' she asked, biting into one of the Welsh cakes. Flavour flooded her mouth and the warm, gooey dough clogged her teeth in the most wonderful way.

'Yes. We have a new lady in town, Chloe, a Miss Blossom Jenkins. I'm not entirely sure of her background – she's recently arrived from Cardiff – but she seems ladylike and accomplished. Alma started going to her, then Pam, and you know how it is with those girls – where one goes the rest are sure to follow.'

'Blossom,' whispered Chloe. What a romantic name. She wished *she* were called Blossom, or Flower, or Petal . . . Lady-like and accomplished . . . She longed to meet her.

Soon enough Megan came back, full to the brim of the sugar-foot walk, the basic Lindy step, the double Lindy and the triple Lindy.

'Look, Chloe, I'll show you.' Megan started to dance ener-getically which startled Chloe a little. Megan had always been so aloof and now here she was with her face flushed, her dark hair collapsing and her impressive chest bouncing enthusiasti-cally. Chloe would have killed for Megan's bosom.

She tried to concentrate on Megan's feet instead, but Megan

kept stopping and saying, 'No, that's not it. Oh blow! Hang on. *That's* it. No! Oh, hang it all.' So it was hard to get the pattern.

In the end Auntie Susan got up and started dancing with Megan. She danced a lively, graceful Lindy which left both girls gasping in amazement.

'Auntie Susan, you're *wonderful*!' cried Chloe.

'Where on earth did *you* learn to do that, Mother?' asked Megan, half admiring and half put out.

Auntie Susan fell back into her chair laughing, and brushed a wave of hair back from her face. 'The Lindy's not a new dance, darling. It came over during the war, you know. It was all the rage a few years ago when . . . well . . . I used to dance it with your father, darling. We had such fun.'

Megan looked startled and Chloe could understand why. Susan never talked about her first husband; she was a very private person. That's what Gwennan said: 'Susan is a very private person.'

It was from Gwennan that Chloe had learned Susan's history. She'd gone off to Cardiff very young. 'Seventeen, she was, and pretty as a picture. Broke my father's heart, it did.' She found herself a job cleaning a newspaper office, where the boss had taken a liking to her and trained her as a typist. Susan caught the eye of a visiting reporter from London and a whirl-wind romance ensued. He whisked her off to London where they married in a registry office. It caused a great commotion in the family because Susan had married without asking her father's permission, and without the family even having met the groom. Worst of all, she wasn't coming back. The neighbours thought it was high-handed, uppity behaviour and that Susan Williams 'loved herself, she did'. Branwen was more put out than anyone and when Susan did come home to visit, bringing her London husband with her, harsh words were exchanged.

Susan's two sisters visited her once, in London, but it wasn't a success. Her husband loved her, but showed little patience with her two provincial sisters, especially Branwen who was all over disapproval and bristled with slights both real and imagined. She stomped home in an almighty fume and refused ever to go again. Of course, Gwennan was not allowed to go alone, so none of them saw Susan until 1943, when Roger was killed. Then Susan came home with the two children. Gwennan gathered them in with love and sympathy and cared for them for months.

In 1946, when Susan wrote to say that she had married a German, no one was more surprised than Gwennan, who had witnessed her tears and bitter railings against the nation that had killed her husband. And no one was more outraged than Branwen. She refused to see Susan and Heinrich, writing a long, vitriolic letter to her sister.

*You have done a horrible, horrible thing. I am disgusted*, she wrote.

Susan and Heinrich paid a visit to Gwennan and Dafydd and it was a little sad, a little awkward. Heinrich's English wasn't sufficient to unlock their Welsh local accent and his clipped German intonation was foreign to their ears – foreign and unsettling. Daf, too, had lost a brother in the war and whilst he readily admitted that Heinrich was not the man responsible, it was very soon to welcome into his home a man who reminded him of the worst years of his life.

They could easily see why Susan had married Heinrich: he was gentlemanly and intelligent. He hadn't believed in Hitler's policies, the war had been a torment to him, and he had stayed in London at the end because there was nothing for him to go back to – his own home and family had been destroyed. In time the families might have become friends, but many of the villagers were not as open-minded as Gwennan and Dafydd. When Susan went for a walk, she was subject to a rain of insults. Then Branwen appeared one evening, intent on reiterating her letter in person.

Dafydd threw Branwen out and told her never to make such a scene again in his home. Susan vowed they would leave the very next morning. Gwennan had cried but Dafydd had agreed.

'It might be best, Susan,' he said, not unkindly. 'You know her views are not ours. But this is hard and it's not kind to your husband to have him here. You know how folk are. We are not London. It may be a bit soon.'

'Ve knew there vould be this, my darling. Ve talked about it,' agreed Heinrich. 'Daviz is quite right. Ve vill go in the morning and think of zem fondly always.'

The rift with Branwen was complete. The break in communication with Gwennan was more resigned and philosophical. Then Susan wrote over the Christmas of 1949 to ask if they could build bridges for the new decade, if Chloe would like to come to Tenby in the summer.

*And the rest is history*, thought Chloe now, and she squeezed Megan's hand at the unexpected reference to her father. For a moment, Megan looked sad and lost.

# Nora

A week after she first set eyes on the blue house Nora returned to Tenby on a quiet, dark night. Kaitlin had warned her that the town often played host to hen or stag parties but the god of matrimony must have been slumbering that weekend. She slowed the car to a crawl as she turned down the narrow road that led to the harbour. The glorious pastel houses were muted and shadowy in the dark. She parked in the garage and went to lean on the wall that overlooked the harbour.

'I'm really here,' she muttered, drawing deep, satisfied breaths of sea air.

She had started off trying to be sensible, staying at the hotel for an extra three days to think it over and give herself – or Kaitlin for that matter – a chance to realise it had all been impetuous madness and back out. Instead, she'd found herself dreaming of her flat: of a bedroom flooded with the harsh white glare of a neighbour's security light; of the sounds of engines throbbing outside and thumping feet overhead; of her wardrobe door hanging permanently open because the hinge was broken and she'd never had time to fix it. Home. And she'd realised that it wasn't.

So she stopped trying to fight the inevitable. She drove back to Kingston and spent three days in a whirl of activity, while Kaitlin, back in Tenby, found a job in a local restaurant – waitressing and a bit of cooking. Nora put the flat up for rent, cleaned it until it gleamed and packed two cases for Tenby. She emailed the temping agencies explaining that she was unavailable for the next three months.

And then she left. At the very last minute she dashed into her bedroom and snatched up the mahogany hourglass with the duck-egg blue sand. Reminiscent of her childhood, it was the only ornament that she wanted to take with her into the future. Then she drove to Petersham, where she said goodbye to Sandy and took Jasmine's photo albums from the attic. It was a way of taking her mother with her, she supposed.

She unloaded the car and rummaged in her bag for the key that Kaitlin had cut for her the previous week. She was just fitting it into the lock when the door flew open.

'I was watching for you!' shrieked Kaitlin, giving her a hearty hug. 'This is going to be so much fun! Are you hungry? There's wine in the fridge and I've made pasta.' She hauled one of Nora's cases over the threshold.

Nora grinned. Pasta and wine: the universal language of welcome.

The sandalwood smell in the hall was overlaid with the warm smell of dinner. Kaitlin was wearing her habitual spray-on jeans, a T-shirt and a green hoodie. Her hair was loose and she was wearing glasses. She danced ahead of Nora into the kitchen where she piled two plates high, tucked a wine bottle under her arm, stuck a corkscrew in her pocket and handed Nora the wine glasses and a bowl of freshly grated parmesan. She jerked her head at the stairs.

'Let's go up to the sitting room. I've lit the fire and we can sit in the window.'

The living room looked even more opulent with the fire flickering and the night sky outside. How odd to have such a strong feeling of coming home. Kaitlin had pulled a small table between the two armchairs and Nora set down the wine glasses.

'I still can't believe this,' she said. 'Sorry, Kaitlin, I think I'll end up saying that about five hundred times a day. But I mean—'

'I get it completely. I've been here for two days and I still feel like I'm in a dream. I know this can't last forever, right? But while it does, let's *enjoy* it!'

'I'll drink to that.'

They ate and drank, and talked. Kaitlin was a surprisingly good cook. Actually, Nora was surprised when *anyone* could cook – it wasn't her own forte. They made plans for their time here in the harbour house. They drank to Jones's health. They talked about mothers: it was easy for Nora to slip into stories about her relationship with Jasmine, their old best-friendship and recent difficulties. Then she asked about Kaitlin's. 'Your dad is so lovely. I'd love to meet your mum.' She was eager to see what sort of woman had seen through the gruff exterior to the diamond in the rough that was Greg.

But although it was obvious that Kaitlin adored her mother she seemed a little reticent to talk about her, so the conversation moved on to men. They talked more about Milo and Simon, then Nora confided about Seth and how, after that, all hope of finding a real love again had pretty much disappeared.

'And now?' asked Kaitlin, looking concerned.

'Now . . .' said Nora. 'I don't know. I can see now how I switched off to all that – and I don't know if it can be undone. I'm forty. Maybe it's too late.'

'You don't mean that? Surely it's never too late? Surely any day is a day that something amazing can happen?'

'Maybe. But I think it's hard to start a relationship at this age, really open up. Everyone's been hurt, everyone's grown cynical. I don't think I'm the only one who's given up hope. And then there's the baggage. So many people have evil exes or nightmare kids by this age. We've all grown so used to looking after ourselves, to managing our own lives, that it doesn't seem worth the disruption.'

Kaitlin gave her a look. 'Loving your positivity, Nora. Well, *I* think that's just self-protection again. Next time you're tempted to play it safe remember the university – remember Simon! – and how well that worked out for you.'

Nora smiled. 'You're perceptive, Jones, but I'm too tired to think about all of that right now. I just want to enjoy settling in.'

'Quite right and so you should, no rush,' agreed Kaitlin, forking up her last mouthful of pasta. She nodded vigorously, chewed and swallowed. 'Just, you know, when you're *ready* . . .' she added after a pause.

Nora didn't want to move from that chair, in that window. Staring out at the darkness and the little winking lights that occasionally appeared out at sea, she didn't want to bring such a perfect first evening to an end – but at last tiredness overcame her.

'Don't want to move,' she murmured through yawns. 'But have to move. Bed . . . Still got to make up the bed.'

'I'll give you a hand,' said Kaitlin. 'Oh, but first, I have to show you something. It'll only take a minute, come on.'

Reluctantly Nora got to her feet. When she picked up her bag she remembered the hourglass. She took it out and set it on the mantelpiece. It fitted in perfectly among the candlesticks and beautiful ornaments, far better than it ever had on her cluttered windowsill in the flat.

'That's pretty,' Kaitlin exclaimed.

'It was Mum's. I pinched it off her when I first moved out. It came from Tenby, weirdly enough. I think Mum came here as a kid.' She felt a little start as she said it. When she'd impulsively thrown it in her bag she hadn't made that connection.

'Well, good,' said Kaitlin. 'So now it's home.' She darted across to it and turned it over. The blue sand started to trickle. 'A new phase begins.' She beamed. 'Come on.'

She led Nora up the second flight of stairs to the attic. Since the door was locked Nora couldn't imagine what was to be seen. To her surprise, Kaitlin opened the door.

'Have you been breaking and entering while I was away?'

'His daughter came round to get something from the attic on Wednesday. When I walked past the stairs later I noticed that she'd left the door ajar so I went up to shut it. Of course, I couldn't resist a little peek . . .'

'Naturally. So what do you want me to see?'

Kaitlin pushed the door wide and switched the light on. Nora stepped inside.

'Wow!' She took a long look around.

The attic was an artist's studio. It was big and airy and she could only imagine how luminous it would be in the daytime, filled with sunshine and the aqua light from the harbour. It was cool and peaceful – a good place, she could feel that at once. Finished canvases were propped around the edges against the walls. An easel stood in the middle of the floor and on it sat a half-finished canvas.

Nora didn't know much about art. She supposed plenty of artists might leave a work half done for a while, but the odd thing was that on a table to the right of the easel there was a palette, still dotted with paints. Several paint-encrusted brushes lay about and there was a glass of dirty, paint-swirled water. She turned to Kaitlin with a quizzical frown.

Kaitlin shrugged. 'Isn't it weird? I mean, he's obviously a proper artist. You'd think he'd clean his brushes! Doesn't it look as if he's just remembered he needs milk, and popped out to the Co-op for a minute? But instead of buying milk, he found himself accidentally advertising his house for rent and leaving town!'

Nora nodded slowly. 'You're right. How strange. Maybe his daughter's right and he is a bit . . . dotty. An artist – well, that explains the gorgeous house, the exquisite taste.'

'And look.' Kaitlin beckoned Nora over to the canvas on the easel. So far only the background had been painted in, roughly: long greeny-beige grasses and sky. But standing close she could see the pencilled sketch, very loose, of a figure in the foreground, a feminine figure with, judging from the sweeping pencil marks, long untidy hair and a slender frame. As she looked at it Nora felt a strange shiver go through her.

'Who is she?' she whispered. There was no photograph to give a clue. Perhaps there had been a model or perhaps Jones had been painting from memory. Probably they would never know.

'We could ask Mrs Watkins,' mused Kaitlin, 'but I'm not sure I'd like to admit I've been in here. Not that I've touched anything, but you know what she's like.'

'God, no! Let's avoid her as much as we can. Maybe there'll be clues around the house, or maybe we'll meet Jones when he comes back.'

'Maybe,' said Kaitlin, looking dissatisfied.

# Chloe

Iestyn was staying again this summer, but this time Chloe was determined to stay well away from him. Her self-respect demanded it. Besides, she had a new preoccupation – far more exciting than any boy.

Chloe was convinced that Blossom Jenkins held the key to life as she knew it changing forever. Megan had another dancing lesson two days later – her passions were always as intense as they were short-lived – and Chloe begged and pleaded to be allowed to go and watch. Megan didn't look thrilled at the prospect, but in front of her mother she couldn't say no.

Blossom was in her thirties, older than Chloe had imagined. She wore all black – capri pants and a turtle-neck sweater – with a stretchy Alice band holding back her dark hair. Chloe was at first a little disappointed – she had imagined that a Blossom would be feminine and storybook-looking, in chiffon and glittering scarves. But she quickly readjusted her ideas; Blossom was sophisticated, she decided. And best of all, she was more than happy to have Chloe there.

'Well, aren't you a pretty little thing!' she exclaimed. 'Would you like to join in the lesson?'

'She can't,' Megan answered for her. 'She can't pay you.'

'Well, perhaps just this once I could overlook it. It seems silly you just sitting there, Chloe, unless that's what you'd prefer, of course.'

Afterwards, as they crowded out, Blossom caught Chloe gently by the arm.

'You've danced before, Chloe,' she said.

'No, I never have,' said Chloe, astonished. 'I mean, I'm always dancing around at home and I went to the Tenby Teens dance last year, but I've never had a lesson before. Ever. There isn't anything like that where I live, and we couldn't afford it anyway. So thank you again, Miss Jenkins, that's why today has meant so much to me.'

'Well, that's remarkable,' said Blossom. She cast a glance after the others that showed she had already grasped how things were between Megan and Chloe. But the girls were walking away slowly, in a huddle, listening to some scandal. 'You show great promise, Chloe. You'd make a lovely dancer with practice.'

Chloe couldn't help breaking into an enormous beam. It was what she'd dreamed of hearing all her life. 'Oh, Miss Jenkins, *thank* you. How much *are* your lessons, Miss Jenkins? I have a sixpence for my holiday. If it was enough for even one, I'd keep it all for that and not have any milkshakes at all.'

'Call me Blossom, please, and I won't take your sixpence,

Chloe. You're only here for three weeks. You're welcome to come along and join in whenever you want.'

When Chloe reported Blossom's offer to the family that evening, Megan was not at all happy. Chloe wasn't a calculating girl but she had the sense to tell them when they were all gathered for high tea, rather than telling Megan on her own. Some instinct told her that if she had, lesson times would mysteriously change so that Chloe missed them.

'Oh Megan, what harm can it do?' Auntie Susan frowned at her daughter's surly face. 'I think it's very kind of Miss Jenkins. Chloe won't get in the way.'

'It's the *principle* of the thing!' said Megan in disgust. 'It doesn't seem fair that some people get favours done for them like that while the rest of us have to pay like everybody else.'

'Be grateful that you *can* pay,' said her mother sharply. 'I think you sometimes forget how privileged you and your brother are, Megan. If you want to think about "fair", remember that not everyone is *able* to have dancing lessons and lovely clothes and books. It's not how I grew up.'

Chloe fidgeted in her seat, half wishing that Blossom had never made the offer. Megan looked stormier than ever.

'Megan darling,' said Uncle Harry, whose English was excellent now, and almost accent-less. 'You enjoy your dancing, don't you?' Megan nodded, not looking at him. 'Well then, continue to do so. It is always best in life to concentrate on what *you* do, rather than worrying about what others have or haven't got. Nothing can take your dancing away from you.

And who knows, having your cousin there to share it might even increase the fun.'

Megan gave a small smile. 'Perhaps, Father, thank you.'

'There's my good lovely girl.'

'May I be excused, please, Mother? I said I'd visit Christine this evening.'

'You may.'

When she had gone, Susan turned to Heinrich. 'She's growing spoilt, Heinrich, and quite wilful. I don't like this streak in her.'

'Oh my dear.' He covered her hand with his for a moment. 'We will continue to guide her and perhaps it will fade away. It is a tender age, after all, with many changes. Let us continue to see the best in her for there is much of which to be proud.'

'Perhaps I shouldn't go . . .' fretted Chloe. 'I don't want Megan upset.'

Auntie Susan jumped as if she had forgotten Chloe was there. 'Nonsense. You've been glowing ever since the lesson, Chloe. Megan is just being selfish. You go and enjoy yourself; it's a rare chance for you. Megan will get used to it and your uncle is right, she'll come to enjoy having you there.'

Chloe wasn't sure about that but she was glad that her aunt and uncle understood. She excused herself too. Llew should be back by now and she wanted to see him. In the hall, just before the dining room door closed fast, she heard her aunt say, 'I'm disappointed in Megan. Very disappointed.'

'You know what it is, Ma,' Richard volunteered in his languid way. 'She's jealous.'

Chloe let the door click softly to. Eavesdropping wasn't right. Even so, as she went upstairs to get her jumper she wished she had heard more. Jealous? Megan, who had everything? Of what? Of whom?

'Of you, stupid!' said Llew the following day when they sat on the beach, as tradition demanded. They were dutifully eating their way through several chicken pasties apiece and lemon cake and apples and big chunks of cheddar cheese, all washed down with ginger beer.

Chloe laughed so much she choked and Llew had to whack her on the back.

'Urgh,' she groaned when she'd recovered her breath. 'That was horrible.' She sat up and breathed deeply, aware that a bit of saliva was running down her chin. She wiped it daintily.

'Well, that or let you die,' shrugged Llew. 'Up to you, of course. What's so funny anyway?'

'You are! Megan jealous of *me*. Don't be daft, Llew Jones. That girl has got *everything*! She's beautiful, she has perfect clothes, she has a million friends, she lives in Tenby. Boys like her and no wonder. She's got everything she could ever want. I'm poor, I'm too young for boys to notice and I can't afford any of the nice things she has. So don't tell me she's jealous of me. Tell me about London instead.'

Llew shrugged again. He seemed to grow more cryptic with

every passing year. 'You're wrong and I'm right,' he said, 'but I can't explain it so you'll just have to wait and see. London was whizzo. I feel like anything can happen there. My father took me to a photography exhibition. A whole gallery full of big, brilliant photographs. Can you imagine, Chloe? That's where I need to be, some day, if I'm going to make my dream come true. And I will. I could feel it in the air, in the grit under my shoes.'

'Of course you will, Llew. I can feel it too and I don't need grit under my shoes to know it. You're going to be the best.'

'Thanks, Chlo.' He gave one of his rare warm smiles.

'So tell me about your mam. Was it weird seeing her? Was it nice?'

Llew retreated into one of his customary reflective silences. 'It was *most* weird seeing her with Dad,' he said at last. 'I mean, they used to be married. And now, instead, they're just . . . two people. They were very polite to each other then Dad went off for his meeting and Mum took me to Hyde Park. We walked around the lake and had ice creams and sat on a bench. She asked me all about school and what I liked and what I didn't like. It made me think.'

'*Everything* makes you think,' Chloe teased, but only gently, to lighten the mood.

He gave her a distracted sort of smile. 'I know. But there's such a lot to think *about*! This made me think about what being a parent is. I wouldn't have to explain all those things to Dad, because he's there, every day, and he knows them. When I say to him, "Chloe and I had a Good Money Day today," I don't need to explain what I mean. It made me feel . . .'

He trailed off and Chloe knew this wasn't Llew being pensive. He looked as if he regretted saying so much and didn't want to go any further.

'What is it?' she whispered, taking his hand.

His eyes were full of confusion. 'It made me feel that she's not my mother any more,' he said. 'I don't understand it, Chloe. I've always *thought* of her as my mother, because she *is*, isn't she? But a real mother would *know*. She'd know how much I hate school and how the kids rag me. She'd know that everything looks better through a lens so I go about framing the world into little squares that I can look at one picture at a time. It's manageable then. She'd know that my best friend lives out in the country and I only get to see her for three weeks of the year . . . mothers *know* these things.'

Chloe didn't know what to say. So she nodded and hugged him and the two of them sat in silence for a long time, looking at the sea. And she thought, as she sat there, that he was right, that being a mother meant loving and knowing your child every single day for the rest of your life. And suddenly she wasn't so sure that it was what she wanted for herself. Imagine if you had a child like Llew – sensitive and clever – and then you let him down. Or imagine if you had a child like Megan, and were stuck with her! Families could be complicated, with their rifts and discords. One thing she knew for certain was that she would never, ever hurt Llew.

# Nora

On her first day in the blue house, Nora woke to hammering rain. Tenby! She sprang out of bed and looked out of the window. The harbour was grey, the boats were grey, Castle Hill and the street and the cars were all grey. So much for her plans to walk on the beach before breakfast . . .

She pulled on a fleece and padded downstairs barefoot. Finding her toothbrush last night had been the extent of her unpacking and her slippers were still missing in action. On the kitchen island was a note from Kaitlin.

Working a double but home by nine. Help yourself to anything in fridge etc. Have great day. Warning: I believe Welsh rain can melt English people xx

*Ah, but I'm half Welsh!* thought Nora, smiling. She rummaged around to find that Kaitlin had things remarkably well stocked after just three days. Maybe it came from having a chef as a dad. Back home Nora's fridge would have considered itself full with a pint of milk, a bit of cheese and a few tomatoes.

The house was quiet apart from the remorseless, drumming rain.

But the rain served Nora well that day. She unpacked and arranged her things. She prowled around the house until she knew where everything was. She made a list of what she needed to buy and another of what she needed to do. And then, rediscovering the joy of lists, she started a third: things she *wanted* to do.

*Needlework*, she wrote, remembering that she had enjoyed it at school, then chewed her pen. What did people *do* when they weren't at work? What did they do when they were embracing life, finding themselves, all that sort of stuff?

*Exploring*. This was hard. Shouldn't she be brimming over with unfulfilled dreams, all clamouring for attention now that she had the time for them? Maybe she just wasn't a particularly inspired sort of a person.

*Kayaking*.

Well, three things was a start.

When she was as organised as she could be, she phoned her grandmother. She hadn't visited last week after all, because events with the house took over. And although she phoned from Kingston to thank Gran for her birthday present, a gorgeous pashmina in all Nora's favourite colours, she hadn't said anything about Tenby. She hadn't wanted to voice it until she was actually there.

The old woman's voice lit with delight when Nora announced herself. It always did.

'Oh Nora! There's lovely it is to hear from you again. How are you, *cariad*?'

'Really well, thanks, Gran. How are you?'

'Oh, can't complain, you know, can't complain. I'll be glad when this rain lets up, mind, and I can get out into the garden again. If it hasn't washed away by then!'

Nora had a dim recollection, from a long-ago visit, of lavender and pansies around the house and old-fashioned vegetable plots to the side. 'It's atrocious, isn't it! I'm staring out of the window and I can't quite believe it's *ever* going to stop!'

'It's bad with you in London as well, is it?' sympathised her grandmother.

'Actually, Gran, I'm not in London. I've got some news.'

'Oh? What's that then, *bach*?'

Nora remembered the Welsh term of endearment. *Little one.* Even at forty, she was still her gran's little one. She liked that. Her grandmother sounded alert and interested; she was always interested in Nora. Nora felt suddenly dreadful that she hadn't kept in touch more. Then again, there really hadn't been any time in her old life. And what would she have said anyway? 'Still working. Worked some more.' Not exactly edifying correspondence.

'I'm in Tenby, Gran!'

There was a little pause. 'Tenby? Well I never! What's brought you there, *bach*? Conference, is it? Or a little holiday? Will I see you while you're there? Only if there's time, mind. I know how busy you are and your time off is very precious.'

Nora frowned, gripped with some sort of internal tremor. How awful. Her grandmother was so unassuming, undemanding, never asked for anything. And she got very little, accordingly. Nora made up her mind there and then to change that. 'No, it's not a conference *or* a holiday. I'm actually living in Tenby, for at least three months.'

A longer pause. Then a sudden rush of what Nora could only have described as joy. 'Oh *Nora*! How wonderful! Well, you've made my day! What's brought that about then? I wouldn't have thought there'd be a job there for a high-flyer like you. Oh! Have you met a nice man, is that it?'

Nora laughed. 'No, nothing like that. It's a bit random actually, but I want to come and see you so shall I tell you all about it then?'

'Yes, of course! I don't go out much so come whenever you like!'

On Monday the rain finally stopped and Nora set off for Nant-Aur. The countryside was brilliant in that way it can only be after a torrent of rain. The lanes streamed, the hedgerows glittered and the sky was bright and clean. Nora drove through big blue puddles, laughed as a low-hanging branch swiped the roof of the car, sending showers of droplets over her windscreen, and sang as she drove. It was a very long time since Nora had sung. The roads were quiet and she was there by eleven without even rushing.

She sat for a moment in the yard, looking at the

postcard-pretty cottage. She had come here with her mother a handful of times when she was younger, but only had dim memories. Her grandparents had visited them often in London and Nora couldn't remember a trip to Nant-Aur after the age of about fourteen. Her mother had spent quite some time here seven years ago when her own father had died, but Nora had been at work then and had only been able to get away for the funeral, which had been a blur. Devastating to lose her gruff, hard-working grandfather.

This was where her mother had grown up. Hard to believe, impossible to imagine Jasmine without the buzz of London just a short journey away, without concerts, restaurants and galleries – not to mention a selection of airports from which she could fly away at a moment's notice.

A striped cat strolled into the yard and stopped, affronted, at the sight of a stranger. It was very pretty, and knew it; grey, white and black, with blue-green eyes and very white whiskers. Suddenly Nora was filled with a sense of well-being.

She climbed out and reached into the back of the car for the presents she had brought for Gran. A big box of luxury chocolates, a bottle of Baileys, some artisan bread from the good bakery. A vase from her favourite shop – very beautiful, with a delicate, swirled blue and pink lustre. Her hands were now too full to lock the car, but that didn't matter here. The cat suddenly changed its mind about her and wound its way about her ankles, a sinuous, supple outpouring of love.

The cottage door flew open. 'Nora! You've come!' Her

grandmother was sheer delight, from her sparkling eyes to her happy voice. 'Ooh, she'll trip you up as soon as look at you! Rhiannon, come away now! Let me take something from you, *bach*.'

Gwennan was short and plump, with long white hair tied back in a bun and sparkling blue eyes so very like Jasmine's. Her skin was wrinkled but soft and she wore a dress, stockings, slippers and an apron, in the old way. A smell of baking filled the air. It was like stepping back in time.

'Ooh, nasty draught, for all it's sunny.' Gwennan scowled at the weather and shut the door on the spring breeze. 'Come in, *cariad*, come in.'

Twenty minutes later they were seated at the kitchen table with mugs of hot tea and chocolate cake fresh out of the oven.

'You couldn't have timed it better,' said Gran in delight. 'I thought I'd make it today, and then if you came tomorrow it would still be fresh. But warm out of the oven is best, isn't it, *bach*?'

With her mouth crammed full and already anticipating her second slice, Nora could hardly deny that it was. Bringing bread to someone who could bake like this was slightly coals-to-Newcastle, she thought, but Gran had seemed delighted with all her gifts.

'You're spoiling me, *bach*, you shouldn't have!' she exclaimed. 'Especially with you not working and the pennies being precious. But ooh, I do like a nice drop of Baileys, especially in the coffee when Winnifred pops round.' The vase was a big success too. She put it on the kitchen windowsill straight away where it caught the tremulous spring light. 'There'll be bluebells round the back in a month. Can you imagine that colour in there?'

Nora could. The kitchen was airy and full of sunshine. There was an old-fashioned black range and wooden shelves on which cookery books and implements and jars of staples like rice and nuts were lined up neatly. She also spotted a mahogany hourglass, just like her own, but with peach sand instead of blue. She smiled at the link between different times.

Gran saw her looking. 'Chloe brought us that from Tenby. They sold them in a gift shop there. Oh, I suppose it's strange for you to hear her called that. Only I can't get myself to think of her as Jasmine, even after all these years. She loved those hourglasses.'

'I can imagine. We've got one too, with blue sand. You love it here, Gran, don't you?' said Nora, seeing a woman in harmony with the place she lived.

To her dismay her grandmother's face fell. 'I do, *bach*, I do, but I don't know how much longer I'll be here.'

'What do you mean? You're well, aren't you, Gran? There isn't anything you haven't told me?'

'Nothing of that sort, no, but will I be able to manage it much longer, I wonder? Ninety-three I am now, see. A good run I've had, and better health than most, but there's a lot of upkeep on an old house like this, and the boys keep telling me I'd be better in a little flat in Carmarthen.'

'A little . . . ? No you *wouldn't*!' said Nora indignantly. 'You'd hate it! Sorry, Gran, that's a bit presumptuous. I haven't seen you for ages and I'm assuming things. But . . . would you *like* a flat in town?'

'No, *bach*, you're quite right, it's not for me. But I suppose the time might come. I hope not, though. I hope I die here. Oh, I don't mean to be morbid,' she said, seeing Nora's expression. 'You won't come back if you think I'm one of those old people always on about death. It's just that, at a certain age, well, you do think about it. I don't mind, I've had a good life. I just hope I can stay here till I go. My whole life is here in this house.'

'Well, I love it,' said Nora, 'and I think it suits you. And if you need any help with anything while I'm nearby, just let me know. I mean it.'

'Thank you, you're a kind girl. I manage better than the boys think, really. I've got Rick Evans from the village coming in once a fortnight to do the gardens – I pay him in crumpets! I can afford to pay him properly, of course, but he says no. Mad for the crumpets he is! And Sally Farrell comes and does a dust and hoover-through once a week. Winnifred brings me stews and such so I'm not cooking *all* the time. So I do manage. But try telling *them* that.'

Nora nodded. She knew that 'them' was her uncles, whom she hardly knew. One lived in Swansea and one in Manchester. She wanted to offer more, to say she would come once a week and do whatever was needed. But what would she be doing in three months' time? Where would she be?

'I don't know what's ahead for me either, Gran. If I don't let my flat, I'll run out of money in a few months.'

'But you've got *time*,' said her grandmother. 'That means more than anything, Nora, you'll realise when you get to my age, please God. You've been so busy for so many years now. Oh, it's the way of it, I know . . . well, always has been really. Young people have to go off and find their own way in the world. But time is very precious, Nora. Enjoy it while you have it.'

'I intend to,' said Nora, cutting a second piece of cake.

'Ooh, just like your mother, you are. She was always a demon for the cake. In vain I was, trying to wean her onto the Hovis. Such a skinny little thing she was, though, never had to worry about her weight like me.'

'Or me. If Mum could see me now, she'd be furious. But do you know something odd? I've been eating like a horse the last couple of weeks, and I haven't put on any weight at all. I think it's all the walking and eating proper food instead of sandwiches out of packets.'

'Well, you've a lovely figure, *bach*, I wouldn't worry about it. Lovely face too, but then your dad was a very handsome man. Now can you stay for lunch, *cariad*?'

Nora offered to help but was flatly refused, of course. So she sat at the table, just as she had done as a child, and chatted away while Gran bustled about throwing things onto plates. She told her about Kaitlin and the fabulous house with the laughable rent, their enigmatic absentee landlord and his glowering proxy, Mrs Watkins. She told her about the painting in the attic, unfinished and abruptly abandoned from the looks of things. Eventually she got to her own plans, and admitted that they were, as yet, non-existent, unless walking on the beach and going to cafés constituted a plan. Gwennan seemed to think it did.

Over roast chicken salad and new potatoes, she told Gran about London and her panic attacks and anxiety. She told her about finishing with Simon and about quitting her job purely on an impulse, because she could see the sea in her mind's eye.

'My common sense tells me I'm in a risky situation,' she concluded, 'but I can't deny that I *feel* better. And after a year of feeling dreadful, I'm not going to argue with that. Mum doesn't get it. I know I must sound flaky—'

'You're a very responsible girl, Nora, you always have been. I don't know how people today take the pace of life. We used to think we had it hard in our day, with the mines and the rail-roads and the farms – a lot of back-breaking work it was – but I think it's just as bad now except the pressure is in the mind, you know? Instead of in the body. Everyone's on contracts and there's no security. It's not right to be always rushing, always in fear of losing your livelihood, always trying to do the impos-sible to prove you care at all. Inhuman the world's becoming.'

Gran was starting to look tired. 'Let me wash up, Gran. Why don't you go and have a nap?'

'No! I don't want to miss one minute with you! I'll sleep when you've gone.' But she looked pale and Nora could see that talking was an effort now.

'I don't need to go until this evening, Gran, honestly. I'm not in a hurry. Why don't you snooze while I wash up and then I'll come and wake you up for a cuppa?'

'Really? Ooh, there's a day this is. Aye, go on then. I've taken to having a little afternoon nap in the parlour after lunch. We always kept it for best, you know, when Daf was alive, but now it seems a shame not to use it.'

So Nora washed the lunch things and then, to give Gran longer to rest, she went outside and wandered in the gardens. Rick Evans was obviously worth his weight in crumpets. The vegetable plots were neatly divided, and the sight of the patches of bare, dark earth, was somehow exciting to Nora. The potential, of course. And the self-sufficiency! To think that here, in a few months, would be things you could actually eat! Without the middleman of Starbucks or Pret a Manger. It was a very different world from Nora's. Tall stakes with pale green fronds wrapped about them were runner beans, she knew, and at some point in the year, there would be flowers. When she was little Gramps had shown her around, told her where the cabbages grew and the potatoes, but all these years later she couldn't remember.

The little flower beds around the cottage already had plenty of colour: deep blue campanula, anemones in bright pink, indigo and dark red like crushed velvet. What Nora liked best, though, was the gentle slope that swept down from the nearby woods to the cottage. It was bright yellow with daffodils, stirring in the breeze. There was a little wrought-iron garden seat facing that way, damp and covered in cobwebs. She gave it a cursory wipe with her sleeve and sat down, despite the cold, just to look, and breathe, and be. Jennifer would approve!

Rhiannon appeared, gave a small mew, and leapt onto Nora's

lap. She walked around in one, two, three circles, then folded into a benign Buddha. 'You pretty thing,' murmured Nora. 'You pretty, pretty girl . . .'

Rhiannon began purring on her lap like a tiny tractor. Blackbirds sang, urgent and joyous. In the house behind her, her grandmother was sleeping. Nora bit her lip and conjured images of her flat, her view of drainpipes, her cramped hallway, the busy street outside, and she couldn't see a single thing to tempt her. That frightened her. Had it *always* been wrong for her? Or had it just become so somewhere along the way? *Was* it even wrong for her, or was she just getting carried away on some neurotic whim?

God, imagine telling her mother she was moving to Wales for good! Jasmine had very little that was positive to say about Wales. According to her it was nothing but rain and mud and narrow-minded people who would stab you in the back as soon as look at you. Nora frowned. Why did she have to be so *extreme* about everything? In fact, it was easy to forget that Jasmine – or Chloe as she was to her family, of course – had ever come from Wales at all. Any trace of an accent was long gone and according to her, London was the centre of the universe. It had always frazzled Nora's brain to think of her mother growing up here because it seemed so incongruous – the idea of urbane, people-loving Jasmine here, miles away from anywhere much.

But now, sitting in the fledgling March sunshine surrounded by birds and flowers, she found herself wondering how she could ever have left.

# Chloe

Blossom, for reasons of her own — *unfathomable* reasons, Megan declared — took a liking to Chloe. Not only did she let her jump around at the back of the girls' classes but she invited her to tea at her house!

Chloe was completely infatuated. Blossom was that rare and marvellous creature, a dancer! *And* she was an adult woman unencumbered by family. No grumpy husband to cook for, no snotty brats like Clark and Colin to care for, no spoilt daughter like Megan to handle with kid gloves. Chloe had never met such a person before. Back in Nant-Aur, she would have been called a spinster and people would have shaken their heads behind her back and murmured 'poor dab', in sorrowful tones. But Chloe thought Blossom was marvellous.

Her little flat on Station Road was cheerful chaos. Ballet shoes and plates with half-eaten meals, magazines, books and china ornaments crowded every surface. There were a couple of notable things missing altogether, like a proper armchair, but when Chloe looked about for somewhere to sit, Blossom gestured to a mattress on the floor. On it they sat side by side, with cups of tea and a box of biscuits on the floor between them. Her mother would have been horrified.

The wall was adorned with pictures of glamorous people Chloe assumed were dancers and film stars. The only one she recognised for sure was Audrey Hepburn.

'Oh, you do look like her,' she exclaimed, 'only you're *even* prettier!'

'Aren't you adorable? What a lovely thing to say!'

Blossom told her stories of dancing in cabarets for the soldiers during the war and of her mad escapades in New York in her late teens.

'I didn't stay there long,' she admitted. 'I was good, but I wasn't so good I could make it in the Big Apple. Such an extraordinary city . . . to survive, you've got to be the best.'

'I can't imagine anyone dancing better than you,' said Chloe.

Blossom laughed. 'Bless you, sweetheart, you're very kind. Really, you can't imagine how *tough* it is there. But I never regretted it. Never regret anything, Chloe, just keep moving forward. I met Cyd Charisse, you know, in a cocktail bar in downtown Manhattan. In fact, I *danced* with Cyd Charisse!'

'Who's he?' asked Chloe, dazed by the thought of a cocktail bar. In Nant-Aur there was one pub, The Black Lion. The women never went in there. It was dark and serious-looking and when she passed, a waft of beer and pipe smoke puffed out like a farmer shooing off a trespasser.

Blossom laughed again. 'Not *he*, darling, *she*! She's a big Hollywood star now. Haven't you seen *Singin' in the Rain*?'

Chloe shook her head. She got to go to the cinema once a year, in Tenby. She'd seen all of five films in her life.

'Well, when I met her she was undiscovered but you could tell she was going to be great. Some people just have that quality about them. And you know the inspiring thing about Cyd? She had polio when she was just a little girl. She only started dance lessons to build up her muscles afterwards. Talk about turning a weakness into a strength! Always remember, Chloe, when something bad happens, it can steer you in a wonderful new direction. Imagine if she'd never had polio, she'd never have had those lessons, and no one would have realised she could dance.'

This was a story Chloe stored up to tell Llew. It was the kind of thing he loved. The teas with Blossom became a regular occurrence and getting to tell Llew all about it afterwards was almost the best bit about them. She didn't tell Megan, though.

Despite the fact that she could dance far better this year, Chloe didn't enjoy the Tenby Teens summer dance half so much. When the time came to get ready, Chloe was dismayed to find that Evie and Christine were going to meet them there. The only friend of Megan's who had come to get ready for the dance with them was Alma.

Chloe was especially dismayed as she had been counting on Evie's good nature to dispel any awkwardness over her new dress. Megan *really* wasn't going to like this.

Chloe had come to Tenby, as she had expected she would every summer of her life, with only her blue dress to wear to anything 'best'. She had been preparing herself for scorn or pity that she had to wear the same old thing again. But now she had the opposite problem.

She pulled the dress bag from where she'd hidden it under her camp bed and unzipped it almost reluctantly, even though it contained the most beautiful dress she'd ever seen. It was a show dress from a cabaret that Blossom had danced in, and never worn again since that week on stage.

'I think you deserve something special to wear,' said Blossom when she laid the dress bag in Chloe's arms. 'And not *just* for the dance, you can keep it.'

Chloe could hardly believe her eyes when she first saw it, and she couldn't believe them now as she drew it from the bag. There would be no getting away from the truth. There was nowhere else Chloe could have come by something so magnificent.

Behind her, Megan and Alma were chattering away. Alma had smuggled in a bottle of wine – which Auntie Susan would *not* have been pleased about. Their voices grew louder and louder as they talked about the boys they had their sights on. They ignored Chloe. She kept her back to them as she stripped down to her slip and pulled on the dress. She reached round and struggled to pull the zip up. Engrossed in her efforts, she hardly noticed that they had fallen quiet. Defeated, she turned to ask if one of them would do her up and saw that they were both staring at her.

Her own eyes were inexorably drawn to the full-length

mirror in the corner and she had to admit she made an arresting sight. The dress was made of shining pink satin, pale as a cloud at sunrise. It was overlaid with fine white lace like cobweb, shot through with silver thread. It had a sweetheart neckline and little cap sleeves. With her frosty blonde hair and blue eyes, the dress called to mind a wild rose, Cinderella, Turkish delight . . .

'*What*,' demanded Alma in a dangerous tone, 'is *that*?'

'It's my new dress.'

'Where did you get it?' snapped Megan.

Chloe took a deep breath. 'Blossom gave it to me. Er, Miss Jenkins.'

'She *gave* you a dress?'

'Yes.'

'Why?'

Chloe shrugged.

'When?'

'On Tuesday.'

'Yes, but *why*? Why would she *do* that?' demanded Alma, her voice rising to a screech.

'I told you!' said Megan excitedly. 'I had a *feeling* she'd been sneaking off there. I saw Leonard Jones on the beach on his own last week and again yesterday. She's wormed her way in somehow, made Miss Jenkins feel sorry for her, and now she's wangled a *dress* out of her. Disgusting, I call it! Shameless.'

'*Shameless!*' repeated Alma, like a pious church elder, a wine glass dangling from her fingers and her lips scarlet with lipstick.

'Disgusting,' agreed Megan again, running out of words.

'I didn't wangle anything,' said Chloe in a small voice. 'She offered it to me, because we're friends.'

It was the worst thing she could have said.

'Oh! *Friends*, is it?' shrilled Megan. 'Well, la-di-dah! She's *friends* with the teacher, is she? Well, she's clearly too grand to come to the dance with *us*, Alma!'

'Oh, quite right!' said Alma, pouring more wine. 'She doesn't need *us* if the dancing teacher is her *bosom* friend now. Giving her dresses and who knows what else, I wonder?'

'*Shoes!*' Megan pointed in horror. And it was true that Blossom had been unable to countenance her beautiful dress being paired with black Mary-Janes, no matter how well polished. Because her feet were bigger than Chloe's, she'd given her a pair of old pink ballet shoes. Cut smaller than ordinary shoes, the size difference was not so great and, as she said, the ribbons would hold them on.

'*Shoes!*' echoed Alma.

They were like a couple of mean old women, scolding and staring and repeating each other, thought Chloe in a hot burst of feeling. Tears started welling. No, they were like the step-sisters in Walt Disney's *Cinderella*. That was one film Chloe *had* seen. Suddenly she remembered the scene where the nasty stepsisters tore the sleeves off the lovely pink dress that the mice had helped Cinderella to make. She took a step back.

'Her usual clothes not good enough for her any more,' Megan went on.

'Trying to outshine everyone she is,' agreed Alma.

'But it hasn't worked, has it? She looks ri*dic*ulous! You look ri*dic*ulous, Chloe! Ballet shoes? What on earth? The dress is pretty enough, I suppose, though it's a bit flashy if you ask *me*! And it's a shame you haven't got a decent figure to fill it.'

'*And* you're too pale for it,' said Alma. 'Now that would look lovely on *you*, Megan, with your lovely rich colouring. It would *glow* on you, not look all washed-out like it does on Chloe. Oh, there's a string bean, she is. There's a shapeless, colourless *scrap*!'

Chloe ran from the room crying. She couldn't bear to hear any more. She didn't want to wear the dress any more. But she couldn't change into the blue one now and admit that they had beaten her down. She wouldn't go to the dance. She would hide in the attic until they were gone.

'Chloe?' She froze on the stairs; her aunt was in the hall.

'Chloe, you look *beautiful*! What a pretty dress. Where are you going?'

Chloe walked slowly down the stairs. She couldn't tell her aunt she was going to hide. 'I was going to get a book.'

'Before the dance? You funny little thing. Oh, you're coming apart. Let me do you up.'

Auntie Susan zipped up the partially fastened dress, smoothed down the bodice and set Chloe a step away from her. 'Chloe, you look stunning,' she said. 'A new dress?'

'Blossom gave it to me. She wore it in a show once. But I don't want to wear it.'

'What? *Why?* It suits you to perfection. Have you been *crying*?'

Chloe wiped at her tear-stained cheeks. 'No.'

'You have. And I can guess why. I suppose Megan's jealous?'

Chloe didn't want to tell tales on her cousin. 'Alma said it was flashy and the colour was too pale on me. I just thought maybe . . . I wouldn't go. I'm not feeling well.'

Auntie Susan's face darkened. 'Those girls are beyond the limit. Why must they be so insecure? Come with me.'

She marched her niece up to her own bedroom and stood her before the mirror. 'Now take a good look and tell me how you think you look. Honestly.'

Chloe stared at the dismayed little reflection in the glass. She did look pretty. The colour did suit her. And the dress wasn't flashy. It was just very, very beautiful. 'Nice,' she said.

'Yes, *nice*. Now go and wash your face then come back here and let me do something with your hair.'

Chloe obeyed. Auntie Susan brushed her hair till it shone, then tied it back in a loose knot with a pink ribbon she found in her sewing things. She let Chloe have a little pink lipstick and some black mascara.

'You don't need any more,' she said. 'That wonderful dress and your lovely face are quite enough. You'll be the belle of the ball, Chloe. I want you to put those comments out of your mind and enjoy yourself, do you hear?'

Chloe nodded. 'But why . . . ?'

'Why do they do it?' Auntie Susan looked cross for a minute then smiled. 'Maybe they just need a little time to get used to the idea that the little cousin isn't so little any more and is becoming a lovely young lady. Don't worry, they'll adjust.

'Girls!' she called as she led Chloe from the room. 'Are you ready? Let me see you all dressed up!'

There was a scuffling and clunking from inside Megan's room – no doubt they were hiding the wine – then Megan and Alma emerged, Megan in bright red, Alma in emerald green. Megan's hair was set in her usual glamorous waves and Alma's had been cut to shoulder length, permed and set off with a green ribbon. Together they looked a bit like a Christmas decoration, thought Chloe, shrinking behind her aunt.

'Lovely, the both of you,' said Auntie Susan calmly. 'I like your hair that length, Alma. Megan, that colour is splendid on you. You are both such pretty girls. And what do you think of Chloe? Isn't she growing up fast?' She gave Chloe a little push. 'And hasn't Miss Jenkins been kind? I bet you two can imagine better than anyone how Chloe feels, since you've both had such lovely dresses for years. Do you remember your yellow dress last year, Megan? And your navy and lilac the year before?'

'Mmm,' said Megan.

'Well, I think you're all ready.' Auntie Susan bundled them down the stairs and out of the door. 'Off you go and have a good time. And when you get back I want to hear that you've all had a wonderful night, *every* one of you. I want to hear *everything*.' It was her way of warning them that she wouldn't stand for moods or meanness.

Nevertheless, it was uncomfortable. They walked to the

dance in silence and even the magic of the beach couldn't ease the sting of feeling so unwanted.

But Llew was there at the door, with a pink rose in his hand. 'Dad said girls need things like this for dances,' he said, giving it to Chloe as if he was thrusting an old hanky at her. Chloe tucked it into the ribbon in her hair. 'Thank you,' she said quietly.

'What's wrong?'

'Nothing's wrong. I . . . I just wish I could be with you tonight, instead of at the dance. Let's just go somewhere, Llew.'

'You want to prowl around Tenby dressed like that? It's them, isn't it?' Llew tilted his head after the others. 'They've been at you again. It's the dress, isn't it? I knew that would happen.'

'Oh, I can't bear it, Llew!' she burst out. 'All I've ever wanted was for Megan and her friends to like me. But they said horrible things. Auntie Susan said I look beautiful but . . . It doesn't feel the same now. Am I stupid? For wanting—'

'For wanting them to like you? Yes.'

Chloe scuffed her pink ballet shoes against the doorstep.

'Excuse me, young lady.' A stout man with a walrus moustache wheezed past and Llew pulled her to one side. They giggled.

'*He's* not a Tenby Teen,' Chloe whispered.

'Definitely not! Look, Chlo, I don't know why you care about those girls. You have friends at home, you have me and Miss Jenkins. I know none of us can be with you tonight but next year I'll be a teen, and then look out! You'd better get in there and start practising because you'll need it to keep up with me!'

177

'Oh yes, Llew Jones! A regular Fred Astaire you are!' Llew only ever danced to make Chloe laugh. He looked like a stick insect jerked around by a one-handed puppeteer.

'Aye, well . . . but still, Chloe. You've had all those lessons, you have a special dress. This is what you've wanted all holiday. Don't let *them* spoil it.'

But she'd been running after Megan a long time and habits, especially bad ones, were hard to break. 'I just wish . . . they *wanted* me. Megan's so *beautiful* . . .'

'Megan's not beautiful!'

'Oh, you're just a little boy, you're *twelve*, you don't know *anything* about girls.'

'Yes I do. You're beautiful and she's jealous because no amount of make-up and posh clothes can change the fact that she's not a patch on you. Her eyes are too small and her mouth is too thin.'

'Llew! I'm shocked at you! She looks like Marilyn Monroe!'

'You're the only one who thinks that.'

'I think it because it's *true!*'

'Chlo. This is a stupid thing to argue about. Are you going in or what? Look, shall I come and sit in the café again? I wasn't going to torture myself this year – I was just going to give you the rose, take your photo and go. But if you want, I'll have a milkshake and wait around until you're enjoying yourself.'

Chloe looked up at him dolefully. 'Would you, Llew? Oh, *would* you?'

He rolled his eyes and took her hand. 'Come on then.'

# Nora

Nora's visit to Nant-Aur left her reflective – and very puzzled. She turned off the tunes on the return drive; it had been a long time since she could bear to hear herself think but now it felt safe again. The purr of the engine was reassuringly mundane.

When she got home, Kaitlin was cooking up a storm. Some sort of elaborate veggie stew with about seventeen ingredients was simmering on the stove and on the counter was a ton of fresh coriander and a mountain of peel. *A whole compost heap, right there*, thought Nora, dropping her bag in the corner.

'Are we expecting a large family for dinner, or will you be eating that for a week?' she wondered. Having been, until recently, a wrap-in-a-packet kind of girl, she was in awe of proper home-cooked food, and a little intimidated. The few meals she had cooked for herself since arriving in Tenby were modest: cheese on toast, mashed banana on toast and avocado on toast.

Kaitlin looked round with her customary grin. If she was devastated about her break-up with Milo, she didn't show it. '*We'll* be eating it for a week. You're just in time. Or have you eaten?'

'Just lunch. And a ton of cake. But Kaitlin, you can't keep feeding me all the time, I can just have some—'

'Beans on toast?' Don't be daft. I love cooking and it's nice to have someone to share it with. Milo wasn't really interested in food – he'd quite happily have eaten frozen pizza every day – and at home no one can get near the oven except Dad. You'd think he'd have enough of it at work! This is my favourite cold weather stew. Plenty of chilli. Wine? Window? Debrief?'

Nora couldn't resist.

They settled into what had already become their respective chairs, Kaitlin's angled more towards North Beach and Nora's towards Castle Hill. They talked about their days; Kaitlin had had a busy shift considering it was out of season, but she liked earlies, she said, because they meant that she had a bit of a day to herself afterwards. She had finished at four, gone to see her mum, had a drink with some friends then come home to make stew.

'I love making stew,' she said, 'it's so comforting.'

Nora wondered why she needed comforting. Maybe she was more upset about Milo than she seemed. She was casting about for a tactful way to broach the subject when Kaitlin asked about her trip to Nant-Aur and once Nora started talking, she couldn't stop until she'd recounted the whole day and all its mysteries.

After sitting in the garden until she was so cold she could hardly move, she had gone indoors and loaded up a proper, old-fashioned tea tray. She had made tea in a teapot, with cups and saucers and milk in a jug. Then she had cut two more slices of cake – as though either of them needed it – and found some napkins in a drawer. Then she carried it through to the parlour, which she didn't think she had ever been inside before. But as Gran said, when Gramps was alive, they kept it for best.

It was overly warm in there, especially after the fresh breeze outside, but her gran was lying on the small sofa with a crocheted pink blanket pulled over her, looking content in her sleep. When Nora set down the tray she woke up with a smile.

'It was lovely spending time with her,' said Nora to Kaitlin. 'I feel sad for her that she's so alone when she obviously loves spoiling people. There's a huge piece of chocolate cake for you in my bag by the way.'

'She sounds like a doll. You seem really thoughtful now, though. Are you worried about her?'

'Well, only a little bit. She's fine at the moment, you know. I'm just thinking about my mum. But I won't bore you about her *again*.'

'You can if you like. Maybe one day I'll tell you about mine.'

'I thought you and your mum were really close?'

'We are. I thought you were with yours?'

Nora laughed. 'We are! I guess there's more to the story, though.'

Kaitlin rolled her eyes. 'There's *always* more to the story with mothers!'

It was a comforting thought. Maybe, with mothers and daughters, there was always *stuff*. As Jennifer had said, it was a complex, profound relationship. How could it be straight-forward?

'It's just that today, being where Mum grew up, was so *odd*. And I found something out today. Or perhaps I already knew it, but if I did, I'd forgotten. For as long as I can remember, right, my mother's had dark hair. Really beautiful, long, jet-black hair. I remember once I came home from college one weekend to surprise her and I found her dying it – but she was in her fifties then so I didn't think much of it. And she *said* – I'm sure she said – something about assisting nature. Which added to my impression that she was dying it to cover some grey.'

'OK, so?'

'Well, she used to be blonde! I'm not sure I ever knew that. I mean, I must have, mustn't I? Or maybe I didn't. We visited my grandparents a few times when I was little, but the parlour was never used then – I don't know that I'd ever been in there before. We sat in there this afternoon. It's a proper old-fashioned parlour, with a mantelpiece covered in framed photos, and there was Mum as a girl. And she was blonde! I was so astonished!

'When I remarked on it, Gran said, "Well, yes, you knew that, didn't you, *bach*?" as if it was completely obvious, so I just said yes of course and that was that.'

'Terrible Welsh accent by the way,' commented Kaitlin. 'Really bad. But OK, so your mum used to be blonde then she went dark. Is it that weird really? I mean, lots of people dye their hair. My Auntie Bea's getting blonder with every decade.'

'I know. It's just that with changing her name as well . . .'

'Wait, what? She changed her name?'

'Oh, see to me, that's not the strange bit. I *have* always known about that. Her name's Chloe by birth. My gran loved the name. And my uncles are called Clark – after Clark Gable – and Colin.'

'Chloe, Clark and Colin,' murmured Kaitlin. 'Nice. All my elderlies are called Phyllis and Doris and that sort of thing. Why on earth did she change *Chloe*? It's a lovely name.'

'Well, she was a hippy in the seventies. Oh, not like you say about someone, "they're a bit of a hippy" just because they've got a felt handbag and they like crystals. A proper, proper hippy. In a caravan, in a commune, washing in a stream, bells on her skirts, all of it. A lot of them changed their names back then, you know, to symbolise a new identity, a turning-away from everything they were before, a rejection of society and all that. She's had such an interesting life my mum, done so many different things. Anyway, so her best friend Bethan became Beryl, like the crystal, because she was into crystals, and Mum became Jasmine. She's mad about flowers and plants. My middle name is Sage.'

'Wow! That's so cool! And weird. I mean, I get why they did it, but still, imagine if you just decided tomorrow you were called Liz. It'd be so hard to get used to calling you that. And I've only known you a couple of weeks. What did your gran say?'

'I don't know. That's one of the things that struck me as odd today. Shouldn't I *know* what Gran said about her only daughter changing her name? But if Mum's ever told me, I've forgotten. The stories she told me over and over, the ones I know by heart, none of them are to do with her family, or her childhood. So, Mum not using her birth name, well, I'm used to that. But realising she doesn't even *look* like she used to either . . . I mean, she *does* of course, she's so beautiful she's unmistakeable, but still, to change your hair from really pale to really dark is quite radical, isn't it? And for more than fifty years now.'

'You're right, that's not a phase,' Kaitlin reflected. 'I'd love to meet your mum. Any chance she'll come to Tenby when she's back from Italy?'

'Exactly what Gran asked. I don't even know if I'll still be here when she gets back, do I? She's out there for six months. I'm only here for three – as things stand.'

'Uh-huh.' Kaitlin smiled and looked out of the window.

'What's that supposed to mean?'

'Nothing.'

'No, what?'

'Well, I just get a feeling you'll be here a lot longer than that, one way or another.'

The worrying thing was the way Nora's heart leapt when she said it. A leaping heart meant she hoped it was true, and she didn't want to hope, in case it couldn't happen. She didn't want to admit to Kaitlin, or Gran, or even herself how much she was starting to want to make a completely new life for herself here in Tenby.

It was very unlikely to be viable, she told herself sternly. Much more realistic to go back to London and everything she knew.

'What?' asked Kaitlin in turn. 'Go on, admit it, you know you're going to stay.'

'No I *don't*!' scoffed Nora. 'Of course I don't! Salaries are lower here and I can't live in a luxury home with sea views at a knockdown price forever. I'm far better off thinking of this as a three-month sabbatical to get my head straight, and then getting back to reality.'

'Mmm hmm,' said Kaitlin. 'You're *in denial*!'

'You sound like Jennifer!'

'Have you talked to her lately?'

'Actually, yes. We had a phone appointment this morning, before I left.'

'And what does she think about your latest adventures?'

Nora grinned. Kaitlin was annoying. 'That I sound really happy. That it obviously agrees with me being here.'

# Chloe

By the time Chloe got home to Nant-Aur, she had deliberately forgotten any bad memories of the holiday.

The dance had ended in triumph for Megan – which meant that she had been much nicer to everyone for the rest of the week. Megan's triumph consisted of dancing with, flirting with and, finally, being kissed by eighteen-year-old Michael Everley.

All the girls at Megan's school called him Heavenly Everley, the handsome Teddy Boy with the perfect quiff and the dark, dreamy eyes. Chloe agreed that he looked like a rock 'n' roll singer, but she didn't even allow herself to dream. The consensus all summer was that he was out of even Megan's league, so Chloe didn't stand a chance. But then Megan's wildest dreams came true.

Chloe, along with Evie, Pam, Christine and even Alma, had watched as Megan and Michael – they even *sounded* good together – swayed, wrapped around each other, to 'Blue Moon'. Chloe felt vindicated. She was right and Llew was wrong. Megan *was* beautiful; this proved it.

*Now* Megan wanted to talk to Chloe; *now* she sought her out.

At last she seemed like the cousin Chloe had always wished for. But Chloe was tired of being at the mercy of Megan's moods. She spent her last few days with Llew, enjoying all their old pastimes and recapturing that carefree holiday feeling, which only faded at night, in Megan's room. Still, life was easier with Megan happy.

So by the time she was enjoying her traditional welcome in her family's parlour, she remembered only the good bits. She relished showing her parents the dress and the ballet shoes, and the ribbon that Auntie Susan had let her keep.

'Does everyone think our girl needs charity?' blustered Daf in his growly voice. 'What's wrong with the clothes *we've* given her, I'd like to know?'

But Gwennan steered him fair with a sharply muttered, 'Hush, *cariad*!' Her face lit up at the sight of the glistening, gorgeous dress.

'*Duw*, there's a frock!' she murmured, stroking the fabric. 'You must have looked like an angel in it, Chloe *bach*. Put it on for me to see you in it after.'

Even stupid Clark and Colin were quite impressed.

Chloe always loved the first week after coming home. It was *even* better than the last week before going. Anticipation was exciting, but whenever the goodbyes approached, Gwennan and Chloe grew teary, Dafydd grew silent and Colin and Clark ran around giving celebratory war whoops, singing 'Goodbye, Chloe Samuels, farewell for three weeks!' to the tune of 'It's a Long Way to Tipperary'. By the time Chloe left, her emotional radar would be thoroughly confused. Whereas reminiscing and telling her stories was sheer pleasure.

She loved the feeling of worldliness that her Tenby travels gave her. Never mind that when she was actually in Tenby she felt distinctly *un*sophisticated. When she came home, the things she had seen and done, the people she had met, set her apart. It was a realm of experience all her own. Even her father listened to Chloe with interest then, and he was determinedly uninterested in anything outside Nant-Aur, beyond the railway and the union and the village.

He shook his head in wonder when she spoke of such things as New York and photography and film stars who had had polio. And Chloe loved feeling important in his eyes. He was very much a man's man was Dafydd, and according to his nature found it easier to relate to his sons. So for much of the year Chloe felt secondary in his attentions. It was frustrating to be the first child and only daughter in a family such as theirs. That was why she always took care to make her summers by the sea sound as tempting as possible. It was one of the reasons she liked to forget anything about them that wasn't perfect.

Even so, Chloe looked up from her magazine one evening a year later to find her mother watching her with a frown.

'What, Mam?'

'You're off to Tenby next week, Chloe.'

'I know.'

'Aren't you looking forward to it?'

'Yes, of course I am. Why?'

'Because usually by this stage in the proceedings you are jumping around like a grasshopper. You're talking about nothing but Llew this and Megan that and Tenby Teens the other. Instead, you're sitting there reading *School Friend* like the meek young lady I know you're not. Is the novelty wearing off, is that it?'

'No! I *love* Tenby!'

'But something's bothering you, *bach*, I can see it.'

'No, Mam.'

'Is it Llew? Have you two had some sort of falling-out?'

Chloe snorted. The very thought of it was impossible. 'Of course not, Mam! It's not *Llew*!'

'So there *is* something then!' crowed Gwennan. 'I knew it. If not Llew, then who?'

Chloe sighed. Her mother was too bright for her own good. She folded her *School Friend* neatly open on the story she was reading, *The Silent Three*. It was Chloe's absolute favourite series in the whole magazine.

'It's Megan,' she admitted at last. 'I don't think she likes me very much. Last time I was there she said some unkind things. By the time I left we were on good terms again but now that it's nearly time to go, it's coming back to me.'

'Oh *bach*, I'm sorry. I can see that would upset you. But how could anyone not like *you*? You're so kind and sweet and lively. Well, this cottage seems like it's fallen under a cloud when you're gone.'

Chloe frowned. She had thought about this more than she liked to admit and had some ideas, jumbled and confusing though they were.

'I've always admired her so much, Mam, always wanted her to like me. I kept thinking that if I was nice enough to her then one day she would. But it's only got worse. Llew says she's jealous. I keep telling him she can't be. I mean, she looks just like Marilyn Monroe, only dark. Although Llew says she *doesn't*. But anyway . . . I don't know, but I think maybe me being pretty and nice and all that *annoys* her. Or something.'

'Megan is a handsome girl, yes. But that's not all there is to it, is it, *bach*? You are very special. You have a light about you that a lot of girls don't have. Megan must see that and perhaps she wishes she had it too. Does Susan know any of this?'

'Yes. I think she's cross with Megan. She said Megan was spoilt and wilful.'

'Susan said that to you?'

'Well, not to me, to Uncle Harry. Then I overheard Richard say she was jealous. So that's two people,' she realised. Maybe there was something in it after all.

'Well, try not to worry about it, Chloe. I know it's easier said than done and I'm cross with Megan for upsetting my girl. But I'm sure Susan will have had a word with her and it'll go back to how it was before. Not perfect, maybe, but fair enough, you know? Just normal.'

'Yes, Mam, I hope you're right. Thank you.'

Chloe climbed off the sofa and gave her mum a hug.

Gwennan held her tight and Chloe could smell the fragrance of baking in her hair, the fresh air on her clothes – she had just brought in the laundry – and the indefinable Mam smell underlying it all. Her mother's curves squashed against her and she felt herself to be a little stick in comparison. Her mother hugged her with so much love that everything felt all right, everything in the world.

'Mam,' she murmured.

'Yes, *bach*.'

'Do *you* think Megan looks like Marilyn Monroe?'

'Not really, *bach*.'

# Nora

Nora was sitting cross-legged on the sofa, frowning at her laptop. She was trying to write an email to Jasmine. Despite everything, she missed her marvellous, maddening mother, and wanted to be able to share her amazing experiences with her. But she had decided not to, not just yet. It was frustrating, not to mention upsetting, that things had come to this between them. She had her mother's address in Italy and wanted to send her little presents and postcards with gorgeous views. But so far she was sticking to emails.

Nora didn't like lying. She had never needed to. She had always believed in telling the truth and if other people didn't like it, so be it. But this was different. She didn't want her mother's disapproval and bizarre reactions to spoil her budding happiness. It was new and tender as a seedling and Nora didn't want it flattened in the wrath of Jasmine. It wasn't as though Jasmine would suddenly jump on a plane, drive to Tenby and haul Nora bodily back from the land of short men, rain and misery. *Probably* she wouldn't. But there would be angst. Anxiety and angst. There would be emails, phone calls, texts.

*Are you sure you're doing the right thing, darling?*
*Your mental state is obviously worse than I had thought!*
*What on earth are you doing about money?*
*In my day we didn't run away from our problems, we faced up to them.*

Nora didn't need any of that right now. She was figuring things out her own way. She reread her mother's latest email.
*Darling*, Jasmine had written,

The weather here is simply gorgeous. Unusually fine even for Italy, Faith says. I feel almost guilty languishing in the sun, gazing out over the hills, and thinking of you in that cramped little space in Kingston. Come out, won't you? We went to a fabulous little market yesterday. I bought THREE pairs of jewelled sandals in different colours. Excessive – but they're so comfortable and you know that comfortable sandals are as rare as free parking in London! I shall attach some photos with this message if I can figure out how this paperclippy thing works.

How are your 'issues', darling? I do hope there's been some improvement. I know I may not have said all the right things but I hope you know I love you and I don't like to think of you struggling. Faith says her granddaughter went through a very similar thing at your age and she's fine now. So you're not the only one and there is hope.

Tell me your news! I want to know everything,

Love, Mum xxxx

There were no photographs attached.

Nora sat for a long time with her fingers resting in the starting position. She remembered learning to type long ago, determined to have a great career like her mother. She'd even started to study law at one point but dropped out after a term and a half. Those tomes of cases and precedents, of tort and family and corporate law, had a strange effect on her; she'd never slept more than she did during those months. Even Jasmine, excited though she was at the thought of Nora following in her footsteps, had conceded that it wasn't for everyone. So Nora had changed to business and economics and after uni she had taken a secretarial course. Typing had seemed so alien then. She used to sit with her fingers just like this, hovering over asdf and ;lkj, bracing herself for all the mistakes she was sure to make. For years now her typing speed had been close to a hundred words per minute. It was a basic life tool like breathing. But it wasn't helping her now.

Hi Mum,

I'm so glad to hear you're having a lovely time and please don't feel guilty. I really am fine. Not sure how or why but I'm just going with it. No pictures came through. Try again, I'd love to see your sandals. I'm attaching a pic of a beautiful vase I bought the other day.

Then she realised that she couldn't send the photo she had meant to send, of the vase in its place on the bookcase in the corner of her room, with the light falling in on it from the window above, because her mother would see that it wasn't in her flat. Jasmine had a mother's keen powers of observation. Should she put it on the floor? No, because then Jasmine would see polished oak floorboards and/or a gorgeous Indian rug in pale and dark blue and gold, instead of good old hard-wearing grey carpet. She nearly deleted the sentence about the photo. Then she sighed. There would be nothing left to say at this rate. She hopped off the bed, put the vase on the duvet – her bedding was her own – and took a photo.

*I've made a new friend called Kaitlin. She's very cheerful and positive and good company, so we've been hanging out a fair bit. You'd like her. Hope you can meet her when you come back.*

Which was true. Although *where* would they meet?

*I've spoken to Gran a couple of times lately.* Also true.

*She seems well, it's been lovely talking to her. She sent me a lovely pashmina for my birthday.*

She added that so her mother didn't wonder why she was suddenly talking to her grandmother so much. And because it made it a bit longer.

*I know I've thanked you before but thanks again for your presents, Mum, I love them.*

There were only so many times she could pad her email out reiterating thanks but she would get her mileage while she could.

*Incredible to think Gran's in her nineties. She looks so great –* no, delete that. How would Nora know how Gran was looking if she was still in Kingston? Avoid all that.

*I've been getting out and walking quite a bit.* She stopped again. She couldn't say anything about the sea air, or the diamond-bright light or the tossing palm trees. This was a nightmare! *I think the exercise is doing me good, keeping me in a better frame of mind.*

*Thanks for the ongoing offer to visit. It means a lot. Maybe in a couple of months (*like, three!*) I will. Keep in touch, Mum, and keep enjoying!!!*

*Love, Nora xxxx*

*Send.* Phew! Nora sat back and blew out a big sigh of relief. She hated that she had to be so restrained in what she told her mother.

Her life was growing increasingly full. She had impulse-bought a luxurious notebook from a local shop selling Indian goods: thick handmade paper bound between covers of cream linen embroidered all over with little feathers worked in silver thread. Into this, she transferred all her lists; it seemed a more fitting repository for her growing sense of what she wanted her life to be than her battered 99p notebook with a plain black cover from some generic stationer. And Nora's list of things she wanted to do was getting longer the more diligently she worked her way through it. She haunted community noticeboards and began turning up to classes: yoga, zumba, baking . . . It still fell to Kaitlin to cook anything vaguely nutritious but Nora loved splashing about in batter, making cupcakes or blueberry sponge . . . Best of all was when Gran showed her how to make Welsh cakes. It was a time-honoured family recipe, passed down through generations.

'I showed your mother how to make them in this very kitchen,' she said, spreading the mouth-watering dough on the plank and passing Nora the bowl to scrape out. Nora felt intoxicated by the sense of history. In some ways, she felt closer to her mother than she had in a long time. To the part of her mother she had never really known: to Chloe. She felt as if she was looking backwards and forwards at the same time – creating her own future and learning about her mother's past. It was magical – yet she wasn't telling her mother a thing about it.

Gran also taught her a bit about the garden. Rick had gone to Thailand for three weeks and she wanted to keep on top of it while he was gone.

'I'll help if you give me instructions about every minute detail,' agreed Nora. 'I'm not kidding. I know nothing about plants unless I buy them ready-cut and wrapped in plastic. It's embarrassing.'

'Nothing to be embarrassed about,' scoffed Gwennan. 'You've just had a different life, that's all. If I was in London today, I wouldn't be able to use computers and Oyster cards without you showing me, would I?'

'I suppose not.' Nora smiled and gave Gran a kiss. She'd always liked this sweet, easy-going woman. Now, she realised, she really loved her. At first, she had treated Nora like visiting royalty, showering her with food and little gifts, spending hours facing her over the scrubbed kitchen table, refusing to be distracted as they caught up on what amounted to a couple of decades. But now they'd fallen into a pattern of just being together, doing whatever needed to be done. It was as if Gwennan had stopped fearing Nora's presence was a brief, one-off flash of brightness. And Nora loved behaving as if that were true.

She grew to love, too, the winding drive from Tenby to Nant-Aur. The primrose bank outside Kidwelly was dying back to grassiness now, but the woods at the last bend before Nant-Aur, which had been green-black for the last month, had begun to shimmer with a haze of bluebells. In London, journeys had been nothing more than opportunities to catch up with emails. This was the first time she had *bonded* with a journey, she thought.

She jumped when her laptop pinged with a new email. Surely her mother wasn't writing back *already*? But no, it was from Sarah at the lettings agency. Nora opened it incuriously, expecting a weekly update.

'Oh my God!' exclaimed Nora. She read it again. Was she imagining this? They had let her flat. The couple (a couple? In that space?) would be moving in on Friday. They were paying the full amount without query. Sarah outlined again her fee and what this meant Nora would receive every month. But Nora already knew. She had gone over and over every conceivable variation since she had put it on the market. This was amazing news. This was better than she had hoped! It meant she was living rent-free. Which meant that she would be spending her savings far, far slower than she had feared. Which meant that she had more breathing space. More time to figure out what she wanted. More *time*.

'Oh!' she whispered, hardly daring to believe it. *And* it meant she had six months before she could go back to her flat. Of course, there were other places she could go: Jasmine's cottage. Stacie's. But she already knew she would stay here. She texted Kaitlin.

Flat rented! Looks like I'm here till September! x

A reply flashed back. How could she text and wait tables at the same time?

Fanbloodytastic! I don't want to say I told you so or anything but I could be psychic? x

Nora smiled. September. Oh! That meant that when Jasmine came home from Italy . . . Nora would still be here. At some point between now and then she should probably mention to her mother that she had moved.

# Chloe

*July 1955*

Chloe loved the bus ride to Tenby as much as ever that summer. All the landmarks – the gypsy camp with the skewbald horses, the first sight of the sea, even changing buses at Carmarthen and Auntie Bran's surly eyebrows – seemed reassuring and magical. It was only as the railway bridge came into sight that her heart sank a little. Tenby, Llew, Blossom, three weeks of freedom, yes, she wanted them all. But as for Megan, and Megan's moods, those she could do without.

Her first sighting of Auntie Susan increased her nerves. She met the bus as always, looking elegant as ever in a brown suit and a white blouse with a frilly collar and gold polka dots. But her face was drawn and she wasn't peering through the bus windows to spot Chloe, the way she usually did. When the bus pulled up with a puff of brakes and smoke, she gave a little start, as though she had quite forgotten where she was.

Chloe's heart sank. Was she wearing out her welcome? Had Auntie Susan decided that having her there was too much trouble? Megan was her daughter after all and if having Chloe there made her miserable, it must be very difficult.

But Auntie Susan's face lit up when she saw her. 'Chloe!' she exclaimed. 'How good to see you, my dear. My, how you're growing up. I do like your coat. Welcome back.'

Chloe slumped with relief. If anything was wrong, it was clearly nothing to do with her. 'Hello, Auntie Susan,' she said, hugging her aunt before remembering that she wasn't a very huggy person. 'It's so lovely to be back. The coat's second-hand again, but I think it goes with my eyes.'

'Margaret Matthews or Patsy Jones?'

Chloe relaxed further. 'Margaret. She was home from Swansea for the weekend last month. She's engaged now, you know. It's good of her to think of me.'

'Very nice, dear. Llew's already been round once; he got the time of the bus wrong.'

Chloe grinned. Her scatter-brained, wonderful, reliable friend.

She fell into step beside Auntie Susan. She still envied her aunt's long legs, but as Auntie Susan's glamorous skirt was tight, she couldn't walk very fast so the two walked comfortably together. Gulls swooped low and the old stone arches watched them pass. The click of bowls on the bowling green drew Chloe's eye to the white-clad players, like figures in a painting.

'It's wonderful to be here,' she sighed.

'I'm glad, but I'm afraid I do have two pieces of bad news for you, Chloe.'

Chloe tensed. 'Is it Llew?' she asked at once. 'Is he all right?'

'Bless you, he's fine, dear, everyone's fine. It's nothing like that. It's just that I know how you look forward to spending time with Megan and her friends, but Megan's not here.'

'Today?'

'Not at all during your visit, dear. She's gone to stay with her friend Charlotte in France – the family have very kindly invited Megan for the summer. It's a wonderful opportunity. She'll be able to brush up her French and of course she's looking forward to meeting some lovely young French men. So you won't see her this year, but she sends her love.'

Chloe's stomach twisted. She felt guilty, as if she had made it happen by wishing for something like this. Did Megan dislike her so much she was avoiding her?

'Is it me, Auntie Susan?' she couldn't help asking. 'Is she still cross about the dancing and the dress? I'm very sorry.'

Auntie Susan frowned hard, as if something was upsetting her very much. Then she stopped to face Chloe. 'It's nothing to do with that, dear, I promise. She's forgotten all about it. No, she's gone for nearly four whole months! You can see why she jumped at the chance. Harry is very generous, but this isn't something we could afford otherwise.'

'Oh, that's all right then, that's lovely for her. Maybe I could write her a letter or a postcard.'

'She'd like that. Well, the good news is that you'll have the room all to yourself! You can sleep in Megan's bed instead of that old camp bed. Heavens, when I put it away after your last visit I noticed there's a stray spring in it. You poor thing, you shouldn't have been sleeping on that!'

'It was fine, Auntie Susan, I didn't notice it.' That wasn't strictly true, but it was polite, so Chloe didn't mind saying it. Now it was starting to sink in. No Megan! Three weeks not only in Tenby but with a room to herself and sleeping in that big soft bed with the pretty rosebud cover . . . Chloe tried to stop herself looking too happy.

It wasn't until Chloe was unpacking that she remembered Auntie Susan had said there were two pieces of bad news. 'What else did you want to tell me, Auntie?' she asked.

'Oh yes, I quite forgot. I'm afraid you won't be able to continue your dancing lessons this year. Miss Jenkins has gone.'

'What?' Chloe sat heavily on the bed.

'I heard she went back to Cardiff, but Muriel Dennis swears it was Birmingham and Sheila Shears is convinced it's Aberdeen. Anyway, I meant to write and tell you only there was the difficulty with Megan – getting her all packed, I mean. It was just such a whirlwind it slipped my mind.'

She did look very tired; Chloe hoped she wasn't ill.

'I hope you're not too disappointed, dear. I was worried that with Megan and Miss Jenkins both gone it might not be very lively for you this year. Even Richard is living in at the hotel so I do hope you won't be bored with just the three of us in the house.'

'Not a bit. I'll love having you and Uncle Harry to myself *and* I've got Llew! It'll be a lovely holiday, Auntie.'

That much was true, but Chloe was crushed about Blossom. She took her pink dress out of her case and hung it up. She had been dreaming all year of Blossom teaching her new steps, inspiring and encouraging her. She had even learned to knit over the winter and made Blossom a scarf for a thank you present. The glamour was gone from her life again. She should always have known that it couldn't last.

The next day, Chloe and Llew asked all around but Auntie Susan was right: there really was no consensus about where Blossom might have gone, though rumours, of course, were rife. Eventually Llew had the bright idea to ask at the post office whether Blossom had left a forwarding address. But she hadn't. Chloe penned a note to Blossom in her best handwriting and popped it through the door of Blossom's old house in Station Road, just in case whoever lived there next might somehow know where she had gone. Chloe knew it was futile, but she had to try everything she could think of. It was her first experience of losing someone who lit up her life.

'Why didn't she leave me a note?' she despaired. 'Didn't she *want* to keep in touch?'

'I don't think that's her way,' said Llew. 'I think she was just the restless sort, Chlo, not too good with roots and ties. You know, I never had the feeling she was going to settle here very long. But it doesn't mean she didn't care about you. It was obvious she did, very much. It's just her nature.' It helped a little.

Despite this bruising disappointment, it was a lovely holiday. Chloe and Llew spent every day on the beach except for three days in the middle when it poured with rain. Then they spent hours in Llew's darkroom developing pictures and in the attic at Kite Hill reading. One day they went to the cinema. Llew was excited because it was a Western, and Chloe was reconciled because Auntie Susan had given them a bag of fudge which they devoured before the main feature started. They emerged giddy with the delight of being entertained.

Blinking in the daylight, they pretended to have a shoot-out, cannoning into each other and earning more than one reprimand. Then Llew bumped into someone who grabbed his arm and shoved him against the wall.

At first Chloe thought it was a man, he was so much taller and broader than Llew, but a second look showed a boy of around her own age, with a fashionable navy cardigan with cream lapels, sharp brown winklepickers and slicked-down hair. None of these measures disguised the fact that he was meaty, spotty and had a nose like a blob of chewed-up gum.

'Sorry, Will, didn't see you there. Hope I didn't hurt you.' Llew spoke mildly, as if it were the usual thing to have a conversation with a hand gripping his throat. He sounded so unruffled that Chloe thought for a moment that it was a friend of his, playing around.

'You couldn't hurt me if you tried, you weedy little runt. I could hurt you, though, couldn't I? Remember what happened in March?'

'Of course I do,' said Llew in the same reasonable tone but Will's face was a mask, his tone vicious. 'Well, no harm done so you might as well let me go,' Llew added. 'We are in the middle of town in broad daylight after all.'

Will looked round, still pinning Llew by the neck. The cinema crowd had dispersed quickly, hurrying from the rain. Where *was* everybody? wondered Chloe, panicking a little.

'That's true,' said Will, 'but it won't always be, will it, Jones? Weirdo. Crazy boy. No wonder with *your* father. My father says he's got his head in the clouds and you haven't got a fighting chance. You hear that, Jones, you haven't got a fighting chance.'

He threw a punch to Llew's stomach, and Llew crumpled. Chloe flew at them. 'Llew! Llew! Are you all right? You! Cardigan Boy! You leave him alone, you disgusting ugly monster. Take that!' She kicked him hard on the shin and he gasped.

'You little cow! Who's this then, Jones? Your girlfriend? You don't mind slumming it, do you? Where did you drag her in from? A pigsty? Run along home, little pigsty girl. This is men's business.'

'Men!' exclaimed Chloe scornfully. 'You're not a *man*. You're just *fat*! Pick on someone your own size, you *turnip*!'

Llew straightened up, his hand on his stomach, his face paper-white and streaked with rain. 'Don't speak to her like that, Will Slocombe.'

'Who's gonna stop me? You?' taunted Will.

'Is everything all right here?' A gentlemanly-looking fellow with glasses, a large umbrella and an old-fashioned hat stopped and peered at them.

'Perfectly all right, sir,' said Will, at once the picture of innocence.

'No!' Chloe declared. 'This boy has just attacked my friend and punched him in the stomach. He's a bully.'

Will laughed. 'She's joking, sir! I wouldn't do that. Me and Leonard are friends from school, always joking around, aren't we, Len?'

'It doesn't look that way to me, young fellow,' said the man. 'I think you'd better head off home and keep away from these two youngsters. Off you go now.'

Will turned tail, to Chloe's relief.

'Are you all right, boy?' asked the man.

Llew winced and nodded. 'Yes, sir. Thank you very much. I'm grateful.'

He nodded and left them, muttering something about 'not in my day' and 'whatever is the matter with young people today?'

Chloe turned to Llew. 'Llew, are you all right? Do you need a doctor? What can I do?'

He shook his head but she was shocked to see his eyes burning with tears. 'I'm fine, Chlo, don't worry about it.'

'Are you mad? He punched you really hard! He could have done some damage.'

'I said I'm *fine*.' He said it in the tone that made him sound so much older than her, so much wiser. 'I've had worse. Damn,

I keep forgetting how fast he can throw a punch. He moves fast for a lumbering oaf.'

'How often does this happen? Who is he?'

'He's in my form at school.'

'He's *thirteen*? Are you serious?'

'Actually he's fourteen. He's behind a year because he's really stupid. Come on, Chlo, let's go. Let's go and play on the slots. I've got a couple of pennies and I'm feeling lucky.'

'Oh yes, I can see it's *your* lucky day,' she snorted. 'No, not the arcade. It'll be crowded and noisy and I want to talk to you, young man. Let's go to the Seashell. Horlicks on me,' she added recklessly.

'Young man,' echoed Llew in disgust, but he followed her, limping.

When they were settled by the window, two mugs of steaming Horlicks between them, Chloe began her interrogation. Llew took a long time to answer but she was used to that. They stared out at the rain rolling down the window panes, the sand soaked and dark like beeswax, the sea dull as pewter.

'He's always been around,' said Llew at last. 'He was in my old school and now he's in the grammar – I've no idea how. He's a bully. His parents drink. He's unhappy.'

'Well, that's very sad but it doesn't mean he can bully *you*,' said Chloe, feeling like a lioness. 'You're special and you don't deserve it. Well, nobody deserves it but you know what I mean. You *especially* don't deserve it. He can't have any friends at all!'

'Chloe, he's got lots of friends. I'm the one that doesn't.'

'But *why*?'

'Because they want to be on the right side of him. They don't want him punching *them* in the stomach, do they? He's big and he's rich, so.' He shrugged eloquently. 'And they think I'm weird because of how I talk and the photography and, of course, I'm poor, and Mum's gone and Dad's not much like other dads . . . It's just how it is, Chloe. But you don't need to worry, I've got it under control.'

'Didn't look like that to me,' Chloe muttered. 'And what happened in March? He said something about March.'

'That was the last time they beat me up, Will and his cronies. So it's been a while, I've done quite well this year.'

'Oh *Llew*! You've never even *mentioned* it before.'

'Look, Chloe, some things are private. It is frightening, of course it is, but it's not my real life, it's just a stupid situation I'm in because I'm a child. But I'm waiting, Chloe. I'll get older, I'll grow, I'll leave school. I'm cleverer than they are and I've got bigger dreams than any of them. One day I'll be rich and famous – and tall. They'll all want to be my friend then. But I'll remember. I won't get revenge or anything like that, but I'll know what they are. I'll leave them all behind and have a better life than any of them.'

'But it's *years*,' said Chloe in a small voice. 'Years and years before you can leave school and change everything.'

She understood now why his tawny lion's eyes were so often far away. He was waiting for a far-off day. Chloe had dreams too, but really she knew she would never be a dancer and she'd probably never have lots of glamorous clothes and men falling at her feet. Maybe someone would love her, one day, but there was nothing she could do to *make* that happen. Whereas Llew knew exactly what he wanted and he *was* going to make it happen. She scraped her spoon around the bottom of the mug, scooping up the thick, treacly lumps at the bottom.

'Thanks for sticking up for me,' said Llew with a sudden grin.

'You're welcome.'

'You called him a turnip. And . . .' – his lips twitched – 'Cardigan Boy!'

Chloe smiled. 'Cardigan Boy,' she repeated. Suddenly nothing had ever seemed so funny in the whole long history of name-calling. The pair of them laughed until they wheezed and Llew clutched at his tender stomach. Chloe reached for his hand.

'Friends forever,' she said.

'Friends forever.'

They wandered off into the rain. It was warm and splashy and somehow cheerful after the revelations of the morning. The sun simmered behind the clouds and a rainbow arched over the harbour, mirroring the colours of the houses. Naturally they had to look for the pot of gold – now *that* would be a Good Money Day! The rainbow vanished somewhere around the Assembly Rooms, leaving them with nothing but puddles.

'That used to be a photography studio, you know,' said Llew. 'In the last century. My dad told me.'

Chloe looked sideways at him and could see that although he was talking about the past, he was thinking about the future.

'You'll have one,' she said, 'a studio all of your own. I don't suppose you've remembered what that means, have you?' She pointed at the inscription in ancient Greek above the door of the bathhouse.

'No, sorry.' She could tell he was still thinking about photography.

Chloe shrugged. 'Every year I keep meaning to ask Auntie Susan, every year I forget.'

# Nora

April came with a burst of bluebells in the unlikeliest places – walls and hidden corners and pub gardens. For once the old adage 'March comes in like a lion and goes out like a lamb' held true. Gone were the fierce, shipwrecking winds, the iron-grey skies and the punishing rains. In their place were soft, dusky evenings, warm afternoons and birdsong everywhere, bubbling like champagne at every turn.

Nora found that she could breathe, properly breathe, for the first time in over a year. A massive weight had been lifted now that her flat was let and the wolf no longer at the door. She walked around Tenby, gulping down fresh air as if it were the elixir of life. She seemed to be thinking in clichés; but clichés became clichés, she supposed, because they had their own truth. She dispensed at last with worries that the capricious Jones would rethink his generosity and hoick up their rent or throw them out. She had come to accept that there were no bodies hidden behind the locked doors and that the dreaded Mrs Watkins wasn't going to put a curse on them. Now, at last, the coast was clear, the world was her oyster and she certainly wasn't going to look a gift horse in the mouth.

She had decided to give herself three months without worrying about work at all. She had found the contact details of several local temp agencies so that she was poised and ready. But for now there was no immediate financial imperative. She would think of it as a sabbatical.

If her silk-covered notebook full of lists directed her life, then her guide to Tenby's history, bought in the local bookshop, explained it. She was rediscovering her love of history. She adored stepping outside her front door into a medieval harbour, threading her way through lanes that had been trodden by Tudor merchants and gentleman engravers. It was a delight to live so close to the only fisherman's chapel in Wales to be built on sand, a thrill to see a blue plaque on every other building.

One bright, brisk day, finding herself at the bathhouse, she stopped and looked up at the ancient Greek inscription. A couple in anoraks were standing next to her.

'Do you know what it means?' asked Nora.

'No, sorry,' said the man in a broad Yorkshire accent. 'We don't know Welsh.'

Nora gave a quizzical smile as they walked away. Would her bible be able to help? She pulled her history book from her bag and looked it up. Yes, there it was. Euripides.

*The sea washes away the ills of men.*

She felt a little thrill. It was certainly true for her. Ever since she'd arrived – in fact, even when she was still at home and only hallucinating the sea – it had started to do just that.

She had taken to haunting Tenby Museum at least once a week. She loved the peaceful space built into the castle walls, crammed with art, fossils, clothes, videos of Tenby as it had been in her mother's day. There was something about the ever-elusive nature of the link between past and present that compelled her and she remembered that one of the reasons she had taken the job at the university was because it was in the history faculty. She'd planned to read the history journals and go to some of the talks. But she'd never had time.

She started going out in the evenings, joining Kaitlin after work in the local pubs, meeting her friends, having fun. Kaitlin's best friends were Danny, a Jamaican guy who had come to London when he was ten, then moved to Tenby when he was twenty, his sister Lilian, and Portia, whom Kaitlin had met at uni and who ran a café in Pembroke but seemed to spend all her evenings in Tenby with the others. Danny was an accountant by day, a fact that caused Lilian to laugh uproariously whenever he mentioned it because it was so at odds with his flamboyant personality. He DJ'd at a local club on Saturdays and hosted the best, friendliest, most fun parties Nora had ever been to. *Cuban salsa*, she added to her list.

Lilian was a fashion designer, zipping off to London every couple of weeks for business, otherwise existing in a riot of colour and fabric in her flat-cum-studio and somehow making good money despite Kaitlin's incessant demands for free samples.

'Why?' demanded Lilian every time. 'All you ever wear is jeans and hoodies! It's wasted on you.'

'Beauty needs no justification,' Danny would argue, running for the world's most charming man award.

'Lil, can you make me something for my fifth anniversary party?' asked Portia. 'Business, not marriage,' she explained in an aside to Nora.

'Only if you don't let that dog jump all over it. I have some taupe raw silk that would be perfect on you but I don't want claw marks in my creations.'

Into this comfortable, close-knit little group Nora was welcomed with ease and warmth. At first she was careful not to cramp Kaitlin's style, and refused some of her invitations. She didn't expect just to step into Kaitlin's life; she needed to make one of her own. But Kaitlin was an inclusive sort of person. Her long work shifts and Nora's increasing number of activities meant they couldn't live in each other's pockets anyway, so Nora stopped worrying. When she first decided to live with Kaitlin, she had truly hoped that they could co-exist harmoniously as housemates. Memories of less-than-enjoyable flat shares in her twenties had led her, if not to *expect* the worst, at least to entertain it as a distinct possibility. But they were more than housemates. They were friends.

One evening, when a thick drizzle congested the harbour, Kaitlin asked Nora to show her Jasmine's photo albums. 'Do you mind?' she asked. 'Tell me if I'm being too nosy again or if you're not in the mood.' But Nora was only too happy to go through them again. What better way to try and explain her maddening, marvellous mother? How else could she even begin?

So Nora brought the albums to the lounge. Curling up on the sofa next to Kaitlin, she prepared to revisit the history of Jasmine Banquist, née Chloe Samuels.

'Do you want random order, or shall I start at the beginning?' she asked.

'The beginning,' said Kaitlin at once, like an excited child.

'Very well, then let me begin.' Nora did her best *Listen with Mother* voice. She picked up the navy blue album with *Memories* sentimentally etched on the cover in gold foil. The spine creaked as she laid it open and turned to the first page.

'Wow!' said Kaitlin at once. 'She's stunning! Nora, your mother really was a beauty.'

'Wasn't she? I used to wish I looked just like her when I was little. It broke my heart that I was so big and clumpy when I wanted to be a Tinkerbell like her. Doesn't bother me so much now, though.'

Kaitlin eyed her with exasperation. 'There's more than one way to be beautiful, you know, Nora, and you are very gorgeous. I wish *I* had your cheekbones, my God! And those huge eyes! Don't waste time thinking you're plain. Life is too short and you need to count the blessings you have.'

'How old are you?' asked Nora, amused. 'Ninety?'

'Don't knock words of wisdom, even if they come from the

young and nubile as opposed to someone in your decrepit state at forty,' said Kaitlin mildly. 'I know what I'm talking about, Nora Sage Banquist. Get on with my story.'

'So these are my mum's London days, right after she left home. She's nineteen here.'

'I can't imagine how ballsy she must've been to leave Nant-Aur for the big city, and all alone,' mused Kaitlin. 'Talk about culture shock.'

'I know. But she'd always dreamed of the bright lights. When she got the chance to try out as a model she leapt at it.'

Nora turned a page and smiled at one of her favourite photos – Jasmine in a bright red mini-dress with her then-boyfriend Marco, a ludicrously handsome Italian with long wavy hair and a Vespa.

'It's like a scene from an Audrey Hepburn movie!' gasped Kaitlin. 'I can't believe that was her real life!'

More photos of Marco followed, more of Jasmine in a variety of outrageously short skirts, sassy boots, wide hairbands and cute little pillbox hats.

'I would *kill* for that wardrobe,' groaned Kaitlin. 'She didn't keep the clothes, did she?'

'Sadly no. When Mum moves on, she doesn't look back. You'll see.'

Another page displayed Jasmine in a floor-length silver gown, her hair piled up in a beehive and decorated with a tiara. She wore long earrings like icicles and long satin gloves over her elbows.

'Blimey!' exclaimed Kaitlin. 'What happened next? Did she marry a prince or something?'

'No, it was for a fashion shoot. Though she did date a Lord Something-or-other for a while, not to mention a couple of aspiring actors and a fellow model or two.'

'And Marco?'

'Went back to Rome. Now, a lot of these are seconds from her photo shoots.' Nora flipped through a couple of pages but Kaitlin stopped her and turned back to look at them properly.

'There aren't many pictures from her personal life, are there?'

Nora shook her head. 'She said that for a while modelling *was* her life, that between the shoots and the parties it became one big whirl and she forgot everything else.'

'Well, *yeah!*' exclaimed Kaitlin. 'She's in London, with a cool career, in one of the most exciting periods in history. She's young and probably a bit silly and vain – I know I would be if I looked like that! I'm not surprised she forgot everything else.'

Nora smiled at Kaitlin's avid expression as she turned the pages. Jasmine in hot pink. Jasmine in psychedelic, acid-coloured prints. Jasmine in white, with daisies. Jasmine with a young Lou Reed. Jasmine in a bar, David Bowie in the background. Jasmine grinning with Jean Shrimpton, their arms around each other's necks.

'Is that . . . ? And is that . . . ?' gasped Kaitlin.

'Yes. And yes.'

Kaitlin was right. The life Jasmine had led in her twenties was the coolest life imaginable. Anyone would want those experiences. Nant-Aur was absolutely the sort of place you left when you were young, then returned to when you were getting on a bit and the city had broken your spirit, she thought to herself with a little snort of amusement. Except that Jasmine never went back.

'Wow, wow and double wow,' said Kaitlin when she reached the end. 'Give me the next instalment immediately!'

Nora obliged. 'That's a girl called Melody – not convinced that was her real name either – who introduced Mum to *this* guy, who was the one who started the commune in Devon in 1968. A year later Mum joined him. By then she'd hooked up with her old friend from home, Bethan Hill. Look, here's Bethan.'

She pointed to a dark-haired girl, wide-hipped and square-jawed, with a stern expression softened by a lovely glint of humour in her dark eyes. 'They ran into each other in Soho one day after losing touch for years. Anyway, Bethan went with her and now we see the second incarnation of Jasmine. The flower child, with her flower name and, eventually, her baby.'

'*You!*' breathed Kaitlin. 'Well, if you're up for talking me through the seventies, I'll get us both a beer.'

'Perfect.'

Nora sighed contentedly as Kaitlin scampered off. She loved having locally brewed beers, freshly caught fish, vegetables from the organic farm three miles away and herbs picked from the pots in the kitchen. In the evenings she went out to hear local bands. Satisfaction was becoming an almost constant experience.

Kaitlin came back with the beers and a china plate laden with Welsh cakes Nora had made earlier, still warm and delightfully stodgy. 'I took the liberty,' she said.

'Mind reader.' Nora still couldn't get her head around how good things tasted when you'd made them yourself, when your mother and grandmother had made them in the exact same way before you. The sweet, buttery taste, with the wonderful squash of sultanas, filled her mouth and the dough clogged her teeth.

'These are really good,' mumbled Kaitlin. 'Now show me the next one.'

The third album was brown with a red spine. It was bigger than the others, more of a scrapbook really, and alongside the photos were bits of ribbon, recipes for elderflower wine and pressed flowers of all varieties. Jasmine was transformed. She still had the long, straight hair but the sooty eyelashes and pale, shimmery lipsticks were gone, along with the sassy fashions. At thirty she was fresh-faced and natural, with crowns of flowers in her hair, flowers threaded between her toes, and bells on her long skirts that dragged in the mud. More beautiful than ever.

There were plenty of pictures of Jasmine with Bethan – who became Beryl. Beryl's hair grew throughout the pages, Nora noted with a smile. Photos of Jasmine strumming a guitar, photos of Jasmine by a campfire wrapped in the arms of different long-haired young men.

'Were they . . . ?' asked Kaitlin delicately.

'I think so. Free love and all that, you know.'

'I wonder if there was anyone really special to her,' mused Kaitlin. 'Anyone different, who really touched her heart?'

Nora shrugged. 'My dad, I guess? But Mum's always been funny about men. She *loves* being adored but she doesn't really let anyone get close. She brought me up telling me that romantic love wasn't all it's cracked up to be, that you can't rely on it, that people always let you down. I used to be *such* a romantic when I was a teenager, you know, but she kind of schooled me out of it. Probably just as well, now.'

'Nora, would you *stop*?'

Nora was startled. 'What?'

'Always talking as if you're some washed-up old has-been! It's ridiculous. You're a gorgeous woman, you're only forty. Why shouldn't you be romantic?'

'Well, it's not that easy, you know. I mean, it's not like deciding you need a new pair of shoes. You can't just go out and try them on and take them home. Well, I suppose you *can*, but it doesn't mean you're going to find the ones you *need*, the ones you really, really want to . . . wear. Some shoes are just . . . *wrong*.

'On which note, here's my father, the very first photo of him. It's the night they met.'

As a photograph, it was unremarkable. Just another grainy shot of hippies round a campfire. But for Nora, it was the beginning of her own story. There she was, literally a twinkle in her father's eye.

He was leaning against a tree, beer bottle in hand. He was tall, like Nora, and watched Jasmine across a crowded field. If she was aware of him, you couldn't tell. But as the pages turned there were more and more photos of Jasmine and Steve together. And then, a broken-down brown gypsy caravan wheeled to the edge of the field. Photos of Jasmine up a ladder, hair under a scarf, painting it. Somewhere along the years the photos had become somewhat muddy polaroids with random flashes in the corners like Christmas decorations. The poor quality didn't disguise how bright and quaint the caravan became, especially when pots of flowers and herbs appeared in clusters around its wheels.

'That's where my mum and dad lived together. And here's the wedding.' Her parents and their friends looked ragged and colourful in the conventional church setting, though Jasmine, of course, looked exquisite in apple green with a crown of white jasmine in her dark hair.

'And here's Mum pregnant. Doesn't she look proud? Dad looks a bit scared, though!'

'You do look like him, Nora. His height, his colouring, his bone structure. He was a looker too, wasn't he?'

They did look good together, yet Nora had never thought they looked quite right somehow, even on their wedding day. Maybe it was just because she knew how the story ended, so she was looking through the filter of impending separation.

'He looks nice,' said Kaitlin.

'I think he was. Look, no photos for a while. Almost as if she got bored with recording it. Anyway, then we move on . . . to *this*!'

Nora reached for a green album and flipped it open with a flourish.

'Baby photos!' exclaimed Kaitlin with relish. 'Oh my God, is this you? Really? Hilarious!'

'Thanks! I thought you said I was gorgeous.'

'*Now*. Then, not so much! Bald, dribbly . . . I'm not really a baby person. Why were you so *red*?'

'I think I was a perfectly normal shade, thank you. Here's Mum, even making the exhausted mother-of-newborn thing look good.'

It was true. Jasmine was pale and straggle-haired, but her look of absolute love made her luminescent. She gazed down at Nora with a doting expression, her profile delicate, her lips slightly parted as though she couldn't believe the miracle of it.

'She loves you,' said Kaitlin.

'I know.'

Various pictures followed of bald, red Nora, recognisable only by her huge grey eyes, which were always staring steadfastly at her mother. 'You can tell she's the centre of my universe, can't you?'

'And vice versa. Oh look, you're a bit older here. Look at your little dungarees! Oh, thank God, you've got hair at last.'

Nora endured a photo-by-photo analysis of her cuteness quota until they reached the end of the green album and decided to take a break to eat.

'I'd love to meet your mother,' said Kaitlin as they went downstairs. 'You've *got* to persuade her to come here when she's back.'

'I'll try. And I'd love to meet yours. I've been here weeks now. I see your dad whenever I go to the hotel and he talks about Anna all the time – I can't believe I haven't met her yet. It was such a shame she couldn't go to the cinema with us last week. Is her cold better?'

'Oh, you will. Yes, she's fine now thanks. We'll sort it soon.' Kaitlin began to slice halloumi, then paused. 'You know, all that stuff your mother said about not believing in romance . . . I don't think that's your dad's fault.'

After wafting round the kitchen for a while Nora sank onto a stool at the island. She propped her chin in her hands.

'Why do you say that?'

'Well, it's obvious from the photos that they weren't soul-mates. I think they fitted each other's idea of what love should look like, but the reality didn't match it.'

'I agree. Yes, he was handsome, she was beautiful, but it takes more than that, surely?'

'And then the way the photos just ran out. I mean, she's got pictures of *everything* else. She's got the time when they got together . . . well, everyone always likes that bit. The wedding, of course. And the bit where they're setting up home, expecting you. But everyday living together . . . nothing. Then you're born and the photos start up again, loads of them. Obviously she was excited about that. I don't think he can have broken her heart, do you? Dented her ego maybe, but nothing else.'

'I know what you mean,' Nora admitted. 'I think you're right. And yet I can't shake this feeling that there's *something* else. Something happened. You saw how she was with me in the beginning. Well, it was like that for years and years. We adored each other. We still do, I think, but it's not *easy* any more.'

'Should it be? I mean, she's your *mother*.'

Nora laughed. 'Everybody says that! But it used to be, even when I grew up. We were like the freakin' Gilmore Girls! Oh well, the answers aren't going to appear in the pages of a photo album, are they?'

'Probably not,' agreed Kaitlin, chopping courgettes. 'Apart from the obvious, of course.'

'What's the obvious?'

'Well, you know, the glaring omission.'

'What? My father?'

'*No!* Has it really never occurred to you?'

'*What?*'

'Well, the beginning.'

'The beginning?' Nora wracked her brains for clues in the glamorous London days. That bit had always felt quite straightforward to her. 'What about it?'

'Well, it's *missing!* What about her childhood, her teens, her visits to Tenby? Why aren't there any photos of those?'

# Chloe

After the Turnip Incident, as they referred to it, the holiday passed without further mishap. Early mornings glittering with promise led to long, scorching days. Hearing Llew talk about the future with such certainty made Chloe realise that adulthood wasn't that far off. These summer days, with everything just as it had always been, were precious. So she made the most of them: she had never laughed so much and every night she slept deep, refreshing sleeps, exhausted after walking, swimming and climbing all day. She luxuriated in having a whole room and a large double bed all to herself.

Not only was Megan in France but Richard now had an assistant manager position at the Sea Breezes, a hotel on the other side of Tenby. It was a live-in post so his room, along the corridor from Megan's, was empty. And the attic room remained empty too, now that Richard's visiting friends could stay at the hotel; there was no more handsome Iestyn to tempt and frustrate Chloe, though she thought of him sometimes. Chloe's relationship with Richard had always been cordial but distant – but now, excited about his new

226

life, he invited Chloe and Llew to have afternoon tea at the hotel, on him.

It wasn't a particularly lovely hotel. The toilets smelled a bit and the other customers were mostly very old. The food wasn't half as good as Auntie Susan's. But it was a novelty to go to a hotel – any hotel – and it made them feel very grown-up. Chloe always took care to look tidy, *just* in case she should catch a glimpse of Iestyn – but she never did.

Richard seemed more animated than Chloe had ever known him. Being a hotelier obviously agreed with him. Well, to each his own, as her mother would say. Chloe was already looking forward to getting home and telling an envious audience at school.

'We go to *hotels*, do we, Chloe Samuels?' Bethan would say. 'Too *grand* for the likes of us now, I expect.' And Chloe would tell her she was being silly but she would toss her hair a little and ooze sophistication.

The final highlight of the summer of 1955 was, of course, the dance. It was momentous this year for two reasons: it was Llew's first year as a Tenby Teen *and* . . . Chloe received her first kiss!

Llew dressed in a suit, with his springy brown hair flattened against his head, was the funniest sight Chloe had ever seen. However, she bit her lip and refused to tease him – it had taken all her powers of persuasion to make him come at all.

'I don't see why I have to,' he had moaned for the past two and a half weeks. 'You've managed perfectly well without me till now! And I don't like dancing. I should think you'd be *glad* to go without me.'

'Now don't be silly, Llew Jones!' scolded Chloe, sounding uncannily like her mother. 'You're a Tenby Teen at last, so you can go to the Tenby Teens dance!'

'Just because you *can* do something doesn't mean you *should*,' muttered Llew.

But now here he was, looking sheepish, his lion's mane tamed and gleaming. He even handed his precious Box Brownie to Uncle Heinrich so that he could take a photo of them together, in front of the mantelpiece. The year before last he had been the little boy on the other side of the lens, now he was growing up too. Time was passing, thought Chloe with a dart of fear.

They walked along the Esplanade, the undulating silver alter ego of the full moon shining in the ripples of indigo sea. It was so warm that Chloe carried her wrap and her frosty pink skirts rustled against bare legs. She might want to be sophisticated but she couldn't bear to grapple with stockings when her own legs were so brown and smooth.

It was the best dance ever. Megan wasn't there to snip and chip away at her confidence. Llew told her in his usual matter-of-fact manner that she was beautiful and she just decided to believe him. And the girls, with the exception of Alma, all looked pleased to see her.

'We weren't sure if you'd come, with Megan away. We should have gone to Kite Hill and checked,' said Pamela, looking dismayed. 'Have you had enough to do?'

'Of course! Llew and I have been up to our usual tricks. Llew, come and meet Megan's friends.'

'Leonard Jones,' said Alma. 'Never mind.'

Chloe hated her more than ever. *You don't know how brave and clever he is,* she thought furiously at Alma's retreating back. Alma had grown her hair again and it once more snaked down her back in a bright copper ponytail.

'Never mind *her*,' said Evie. 'She's like a bear with a sore head this summer. At a loose end, see, with Megan gone.'

'Her partner in crime,' put in Christine, with a roll of her eyes. 'Nice to meet you properly at last, Leonard. Come and sit with us and tell us things about Chloe.'

With a ruffle of skirts they ushered him off to a booth and plied him with lemonade in exchange for gossip. Chloe had to laugh. Llew had never been the focus of so much female attention! And he looked as though he was handling it better than she would ever have expected.

'Come on, Chloe, you too,' called Pam. 'We want to know what it's like staying at Megan's without her. Is it peaceful? Have you found any love notes under her pillows? Any skeletons in her closet?'

Chloe felt part of the gang more than she ever had when Megan was there. She found herself wishing that Megan could go to France every year – then felt guilty for thinking it.

Llew kept them all in stitches with his attempts at dancing. They took it in turns to coach him but he looked less like a lion than a scrawny chicken bobbing up and down. He was a good sport, though, and shrugged when he sat down, out of breath.

'It's more fun than I thought,' he admitted.

Alma's brother Graham asked Chloe to dance and he was the first of many. Chloe was fifteen now and her dainty, ethereal prettiness was blossoming into something altogether more alluring. With her white-blonde hair and her dancer's dress of rosebud and cobweb, she was, as Llew had said, truly beautiful. Without Megan's repressive presence, her habitual diffidence eased; she became freer and more open. It was like a pretty, timid whippet emerging as an exotic borzoi.

'You look like a . . . candy cane!' said Dan Watkins, pressing his mouth to her ear as they danced.

'You look like a seashell, all pink and shiny,' said Albie Myers, somewhat more poetically.

But Ron Lewis, seventeen and handsome, with hair the colour of corn, didn't say anything at all. He just fastened his clear brown eyes onto her face and held her, as they slowly swayed to Al Martino's 'Here in My Heart', which was Chloe's absolute favourite song.

Ron was the best-looking boy Chloe had ever danced with. He looked a little bit like Tab Hunter. None of the boys Chloe knew bore any resemblance to the men in the films – apart from Michael Everley and she didn't really know him. When Ron squeezed her hand, still wordless, Chloe nodded, not even quite knowing what she was agreeing to. But he had the most melting, expressive eyes she had ever seen. And he was seventeen! Just *wait* until she told Bethan and the others.

Ron led her outside. The tang of salt on the air, the wash of the sea, the brilliant moon silvering the dunes, were all impossibly romantic. Chloe shivered, and Ron put his arm around her. Ron sat down on the sand and she sat beside him. Then he fixed her with that intent gaze once more. He smelled of caramel. He held her for a while then he kissed her.

The kiss lasted a minute or so. It was warm and pleasant and when he ran a finger along her cheekbone she shivered. The night was charged.

When Ron pulled away from her, he smiled at Chloe. But still he didn't say anything and she started to feel awkward. Was this normal? Was he mute? But no, he had asked her to dance. Was it the girl's job to make conversation? Or perhaps he was very shy.

'It's a lovely night,' she said at last.

'Yes,' said Ron.

'You're very handsome,' she said, more boldly. 'You look like Tab Hunter.'

He smiled again, looking a little incredulous.

'You can say something back to me if you like.'

He looked at her.

'You know, like, do you think I'm pretty?'

He frowned and blushed. 'Pretty?' For a moment Chloe thought he was going to say no. Then he continued, 'You look like a . . .'

Candy cane? Shell? Mermaid? Please don't say candyfloss.

'Like a *goddess*,' he ended fervently. 'Don't you know? You look like a goddess. You look as if you should live in that moon!' He pointed upwards to leave Chloe in no doubt as to which moon she should inhabit.

'Golly!' said Chloe. 'Thanks!'

They lapsed into silence once more and held hands while other couples kissed and moaned around them. Chloe saw Pamela come outside with someone Chloe didn't know. Pam waved at her and gave her a hasty thumbs-up before turning towards her companion.

Ron was staring very hard at the sand and Chloe realised that he was nervous. And it was because of her. He thought she was a goddess; he couldn't believe his luck in being here with her. It was a sudden reversal and Chloe understood that his feelings were in her hands. This was how it felt to have power over someone. She had always wanted to feel like a siren, like the beauties in the films. But now that she was experiencing it she wasn't sure if she liked it. It was a lot of responsibility.

'Would you like to go back inside?' asked Ron.

Relieved, Chloe nodded and leapt to her feet. Ron followed like a shadow. He fixed her with those big eyes again and this time Chloe felt a little frightened. Not *of* him, but *for* him; of this whole matter of boys and girls and hearts and kisses. She brushed down her skirts and they went back in to the dance.

The girls were all locked in slow dances. Llew was sitting alone looking all around.

Chloe turned to Ron and smiled. 'Thank you very much, Ron,' she said politely, as if he had made her sandwiches for tea. Then she went over to Llew.

'Have fun?' he asked.

'Ron Lewis is terribly shy. He hardly said a word to me.'

'He's not very bright. But he's nice enough.'

Chloe felt a bit awkward. She didn't know how to talk about this with Llew. It was the first time romance had intruded upon their friendship, from either side.

'You don't mind, do you, Llew? Only, I am fifteen. And we are growing up.' For once she found his slow response maddening, and grew anxious.

'We *are* growing up,' he said at last, 'and you're running ahead of me as always. But I don't mind. Just don't go so fast I can't follow.'

Almost at once Evie and Christine joined them, bursting over with high spirits. 'Where's Pam?' they wanted to know.

'Outside with some boy,' said Chloe.

'Paul Preece!' exclaimed Christine. 'We'll have to go and find her now in a minute or he'll eat her alive. You know what Paul Preece is like!'

Evie obviously did for they both burst into fits of giggles.

'What about you, Christine?' asked Llew. 'You look cheerful.'

'I danced *five* dances with Andrew Thomas and *do you know* what he said to me at the end just now?'

All three heads leaned closer. Chloe hoped it wouldn't be something naughty; she'd be embarrassed with Llew there.

'He said, "See you on Monday!"' whispered Christine.

Llew and Chloe looked at each other, bemused.

'Don't you see?' Christine sounded impatient. 'He *never* says that. It's always just "So long, Chris!" He's never said a *day* before. He wants to see me again!'

Llew raised his eyebrows. 'It doesn't take much to keep you girls happy, does it?'

Christine swatted him on the arm. 'You don't know anything about it! You're just a little boy. I tell you, it means something!'

'That's marvellous, Chris,' said Evie, sounding unconvinced. When the girls blew off to reclaim Pam, Llew and Chloe looked at each other.

'What a night,' said Llew. 'I never thought you'd persuade me, Chloe Samuels, but I'm glad you did.'

Chloe beamed. 'I'm glad I did too.'

When the time came to leave, Chloe looked through the door, over the beach and suddenly felt reluctant to step outside, into the end of another year's dance, into the future. Then Llew grabbed her hand. 'Hey, Chlo,' he said urgently.

'What?'

He fixed her with a parody of a romantic stare. 'See you *Monday*!'

They laughed so hard that they could hardly walk.

# Nora

———

Over the following days, Nora couldn't stop thinking about her conversation with Kaitlin. She was right. Again. Nora had always assumed Wales was missing from the albums because life there had been dull. But now, spending time with Gran, she realised that wasn't right. Nant-Aur may not have had the bright lights of London, but life had been rich and warm. And someone like her mother? There was no way that nothing exciting had happened to her in nearly *twenty years*. The question was, what? Why didn't she want to remember it? And could that possibly be what was affecting her relationship with Nora all these years later?

Why on earth had she never asked these questions before? But really, Nora reflected, how much did any child think about their parents' lives other than in terms of how it related to *them*? Jasmine had said this was her life story, and Nora had accepted it, never mind that two decades were missing. It was the story of their lives *together* that Nora had loved the most, with all the self-centred fascination of a child. Even when Nora grew up she had still never thought it strange that there were no photos of her mother's childhood. She'd supposed they hadn't had a camera, and that if photos did exist, they just didn't interest Jasmine.

Sophisticated, raven-haired Jasmine Banquist was her mother – but so was white-blonde, Welsh Chloe Samuels. Nora was having trouble even reconciling that they were the same person.

She was startled from her reverie by a hammering at the door.

Glenda Watkins stood outside. Above her unlovely face, a shock of hair was teased by the breeze into standing straight up like a mohawk.

'Sorry to disturb you,' said Mrs Watkins, scowling. Translation: *I'm sorry you're here, getting in my way.*

'No trouble,' said Nora. 'What can I do for you?'

'I'm after something of mine that my father's locked in the spare room, daft apeth. Would it be a bother if I come in to fetch it?'

'No bother at all. Come in. Lovely day, isn't it?' added Nora as she closed the door behind them.

'For those of us who have the leisure to sit around thinking about the weather I'm sure it is.' She looked all around. Kaitlin's pink hoodie was hanging off the bannister. Nora's colourful Indian handbag was sitting at the foot of the stairs. Down the corridor through the kitchen door, a jumble of unwashed dishes could be seen. 'It feels wrong, mind,' announced Mrs Watkins. 'Coming into my father's house, seeing you here, strangers, making yourselves at home.'

'Well, that *is* what we pay rent for,' said Nora mildly, then bit her tongue. Why had she mentioned the rent?

'*That's* not rent. That's a farce. But you know my views on that. I've written to my father again pleading with him to see sense but will he see it? No. He won't.'

Silently Nora cheered the eccentric Jones and fumed at Mrs Watkins for being such a meddling killjoy. 'Well, it's just a short-term arrangement,' she said. 'I'm sure he'll be back soon enough. Do you know where he is? I hope he's well.'

'Aye, you would,' muttered Mrs Watkins darkly and rather cryptically. 'Well, I'd better have a look for this thing now. I'll go on up.' She drew a key from her pocket and stumped up the stairs.

'Would you like a cup of tea?' Nora called after her.

'No thank you,' came the reply.

Nora couldn't resist following Mrs Watkins and waiting in the landing. She wouldn't put it past her to nose into the other rooms too. Mrs Watkins threw her a look of dislike as she went into the spare room and pushed the door behind her. It didn't click, though, and silently opened a few inches. Nora could see her broad backside in the air as she bent and rummaged through some boxes. The room was, as Kaitlin had surmised, full of all the personal things that Jones had just wanted to get out of their way. She saw a heap of men's clothes thrown over a chair, a mass of boxes and files, some fishing tackle, wellington boots and, stacked against the far wall, more canvases.

'Lurking by there, are you?' Mrs Watkins said, her red face

appearing in the gap. 'Having a good look at what doesn't concern you? Well, I've got what I came for and I'm locking up again now, mind.'

'Just wondered if you needed any help.' Nora and Kaitlin had planned that the next time they saw Mrs Watkins they would tell her the attic door was unlocked. On the spot Nora decided not to. 'But you've obviously found what you wanted so that's good. A . . . teddy bear!' she ended in surprise.

'Aye, well, my son is down with my granddaughter. And the *wife* of course,' she added, as if reluctant to admit the existence of such a person. 'The little one is having the upsets in the night. I thought Wendy might soothe her.'

'Wendy's the bear,' guessed Nora, smiling.

'Aye. She was mine when I was small. My father used to say she was a special bear.'

'That's lovely,' said Nora. Perhaps there was another side to Mrs Watkins after all.

'Oh, daft as the day is long, my father is, always talking rubbish. But it might help the child.' Perhaps not.

Mrs Watkins pulled the door firmly to, locking it with an unnecessary degree of rattling that suggested she was making a statement. But not before Nora had glimpsed a painting hanging on the wall. She frowned and craned her neck but all too soon it was out of sight.

'There!' said Mrs Watkins, looking at her with petty triumph.

'Are you sure you wouldn't like a cup of tea?' asked Nora

sweetly but Mrs Watkins went on her way, square hips rocking, anorak zipped tight, teddy bear in hand. Nora watched her go, shook her head then closed the door.

In the hall, she paused. The painting in the spare room had been of a girl, she had seen that much. Nothing unusual in that. But something in the tilt of the head and the fall of long fair hair had been familiar. It reminded her of the photographs of her mother in Gran's parlour. Nora shook herself. Artists the world over had always painted blonde, beautiful women. She was just seeing mysteries where there were none; she was too preoccupied with her mother. And there was no time to ponder now, with her first patchwork class starting in half an hour; the next activity on her wish list.

Later on, sitting in a small community hall with seven other ladies, all stitching away, Nora had to smile. It was like a scene from a Jane Austen novel. The other women were mostly older, around sixty. Margaret Lloyd-Wynn was seventy-two. And Grace Wells, who was forty-five, came with her youngest daughter Anwen, who was seventeen. Molly Davies, who took the class, was around Nora's age and gorgeous, with sleek dark hair and a husband and two children whom she talked about constantly. *There's someone who loves her life*, thought Nora.

When Nora had phoned to make enquiries, Molly explained that she taught patchwork the old-fashioned way – drawing round templates, cutting out and stitching by hand. 'I feel I should tell you in case you're expecting a super-modern approach with cutting wheels and grid boards and all the fancy equipment,' she said. 'Are you a big patchwork buff?'

'Not at all. I haven't picked up a needle since school. But I always fancied having a go.'

'In that case, this approach is probably better for you. It means you don't need a massive outlay on equipment before you start and then, if you decide it's not for you, you haven't wasted money. Also, we work our way through quite small projects, so hopefully you'll get a sense of achievement early on. Those are the practical reasons I teach the way I do. The other reason is that I think it makes a nicer class. We can sit closer together, we can chat more easily, and I like the sense of history. We basically do patchwork the way our mothers and grandmothers did.'

'It sounds wonderful,' Nora said. 'When can I start?'

Now here she was, making a cylindrical sewing caddy. Most of the ladies had brought old clothing to cut up and use; fashions from various decades were strewn over the table, evoking amused or admiring comments from the others. Margaret had brought a buttercup-yellow silk dress from the 1950s. Rachel Beynon had a blouse from the eighties that provoked hoots of laughter with its shoulder pads the size of sofas and its nipped-in waist.

'My daughter says if I ever think about wearing it again, she'll disown me,' said Rachel sadly.

'The power silhouette!' Nora reflected. 'My mother was that shape for an entire decade.'

It made Nora wish that she had some sort of heritage to cut up and weave into a new life. Instead she'd gone to the haberdashery in Haverford West where, following Molly's instructions, she had bought a metre and a half of a light pattern, the same of a dark pattern and the same again of plain. Maybe she would ask Gran if she had something she could use for the next project.

It was peaceful in the hall, with its Formica tables, big tea urns in the corner and wide bands of sunlight falling through the windows. When her neck grew stiff, Nora looked up at the women around her, their expressions of concentration, the dust motes circling in the sunshine, and smiled.

Nora was watching Molly demonstrate how to make a Suffolk puff when the door of the hall crashed open and banged against the wall, making everybody jump. A man staggered through with an armload of boxes obscuring his face.

Margaret laid her hand over her heart. 'Oh, my pacemaker!' she moaned.

'Sorry!' came a voice from behind the boxes. 'Elbow slipped.'

He came weaving towards them, blinded by boxes.

'Wait, Logan! Hang on a minute,' called Molly, laying down her puff (failing to tuck the needle safely into the fabric as she had instructed). She reached up to take the top box from the pile. 'These are so heavy!' she exclaimed.

'It's the china for the vintage tea. Thanks, Mol, I can see now.'

He carried the pile to the back of the hall and set them

gently on the floor. Nora couldn't help noticing that his dark blue T-shirt clung to a very muscular back and his jeans pulled a bit as he flexed his legs to bend. Meanwhile Molly was still teetering and swaying with just the one box so he quickly rescued it.

'Sorry for the interruption, ladies,' he said, looking over at the group. Nora felt something in her stomach curl. He had short, neat dark hair and blue eyes. He was tall and undeniably good-looking. He had an accent too, something Antipodean. She'd always been a sucker for an accent. Hastily she started stitching like mad, pricked her finger and looked up again. It wasn't every day you saw such serious eye candy.

'Thank you for bringing the china, Logan,' said Anne Lewis. 'Did you hear anything about the glasses?'

'Not a thing.'

Anne tutted. 'Delphine Carter trying to organise anything is like trying to organise a . . . well, a function in a brewery, if you get my meaning. Everything half done. Never mind. Not your fault, Logan.'

'*Duw*, there's strong you are, *bach*,' said Margaret, gazing at Logan.

Nora grinned at the endearment. *Little one*. He was six foot two if he was an inch. He noticed and smiled back. 'We haven't met,' he said and walked over to shake her hand. 'Logan.'

'Nora,' she said, horrified at being singled out. She was sure she must be blushing all over the place. How predictable. How embarrassing.

'New to patchwork? Or just to the group?'

'Both. Can you tell?' She laughed, holding up this morning's effort which was sadly skewed and had one patch somehow dangling from a long thread.

'It's looking lovely. Um, whatever it is. Well, I'd best be off. Nice to meet you, Nora. Good to see you, ladies, and sorry again for the heart attacks.'

And just like that the impossible happened. At least, Nora had always thought it was impossible but clearly it wasn't. She fell in *something* with Logan. Whether it was love or lust, or deeply in like, she wasn't clear, but there was something, and she was floundering in it. It felt stronger because it was so unfamiliar; she had never thought she would find herself smitten all in an instant. Wow. This guy was *gorgeous*.

Logan went over to Molly and drew her warmly to him with one arm, kissed her cheek. 'Bye, Mol, see you at home.'

'Bye, gorgeous, see you later.'

Nora looked down at her sewing again. Of course. Logan would be Molly's husband. Her heart plummeted. She remembered what Kaitlin had told her last week: 'All the men in Wales are either married, over sixty, under twenty or in gaol.' Admittedly she'd had a couple of pints of cider and was becoming slightly morose about Milo at the time, but of course a man like that wouldn't be single. He and Molly looked amazing together. Nora didn't let herself watch him walk away. No point indulging the feelings that had unexpectedly blossomed. He wasn't available. Life was good. She hadn't been looking for a man and her reaction had taken her totally by surprise. Now she just needed to forget about it.

Amazing the depth of the disappointment, though. She felt somehow chillier, as though she needed a cardigan, whereas a moment ago she had been perfectly warm.

# Chloe

*July 1956*

Finally, it was Chloe's sweet sixteen summer. Last year she had been kissed and had taken high tea in a hotel. Who knew *what* tales she would have to tell when she went home this year?

In the end, it could be summed up in just one word: chickenpox.

She had looked forward to Tenby more than ever after Auntie Susan had promised she could have the attic room all to herself.

'You and Megan are both young women now,' she had written. 'We don't have to keep a room for Richard's parade of friends now he's at the hotel, so it can be your room whenever you're here.'

The thought of having that lovely, sun-washed attic all to herself, with the brimming bookcase just outside the door, was a delicious prospect.

She'd been feeling a bit scratchy and swimmy before she left but everyone put it down to excitement and the unusually hot

245

weather. She had her monthly curse too, and was just feeling horrible in general, so there was no need to look for further explanation.

She'd been in Tenby only a day when she got up from the dinner table and staggered, scorching and light-headed. Auntie Susan suspected heatstroke and insisted on putting her to bed, only to find, when she handed Chloe a light cotton nightdress, that Chloe's slim body was covered in a nasty rash. The doctor was called, the diagnosis pronounced.

'But . . . how long will it take?' cried Chloe. 'How much of my holiday will I miss? Not . . . a whole *week*, surely?'

'Chickenpox can take two weeks, or sometimes even longer, to clear up, child,' said the doctor, looking over his spectacles at her.

'But that's my whole *holiday*!'

'Well, don't look at *me* like that! I didn't give it to you.'

'But the dance!' Chloe pleaded, catching Auntie Susan's hand. 'I'll be better in time for that, won't I?'

'Perhaps a dance won't be exactly what you'll feel like after a dose of the chickenpox,' said Auntie Susan vaguely.

Megan, when she came to wish Chloe goodnight, was more direct. 'You'll have scabs all over you,' she explained, 'and when they drop off they leave scars, horrible scars. It's a terribly disfiguring disease.' Chloe wished her cousin was still in France.

'But *you* don't have scars. Auntie Susan said you could only come and see me because you've had it, so you can't catch it off me. It hasn't disfigured *you*!'

'Not on my *face*,' Megan conceded. 'I was lucky, all my scars are out of sight. You might not be so lucky, though. Look, you've already got a nasty scab on your chin. I bet that'll scar. And the one on your nose definitely will.'

Chloe had never felt so horrified in all her life. When Megan left, she cried into her pillow, her poor, itching body wracked with sobs. She would be disfigured! She'd only just started to believe that her mother and Llew *weren't* biased, that she really *was* beautiful, that her dreams of love and a remarkable life were possible. Now they were over, snuffed out before they had begun, just like the time she had started learning to dance, then Blossom left. She was blisteringly aware of each and every sore that tormented her. There were *hundreds*! She would look like the lepers in the Bible. Little children would scream when they saw her coming. She wouldn't be beautiful. She wouldn't even be plain. She would be hideous!

The next morning she heard footsteps thundering up the attic stairs and cringed, not wanting to be seen. Thank goodness Iestyn wasn't staying so there was no danger of *him* seeing her like this. But it was only Llew. He flew to her side like a startled duck bursting from a riverbank.

'Oh Chloe, your auntie's told me. Do you feel very horrible?'

'Yes,' sniffed Chloe, her eyes filling with tears. 'You're not supposed to scratch them but they itch like . . . like *hell* . . . and I'm hot and so uncomfortable. I can't sleep and I'm bored.

It's ruining my whole holiday. We only had a day! And . . . and . . .' She started to cry in earnest as it sank in all over again. There was no guarantee that she'd ever be able to go out in public again.

'And what?' asked Llew, after waiting patiently for some minutes.

'I can't even tell you.' Chloe turned her face away, panic welling up inside her. 'It's too terrible!'

'Well, what's the point of a friend you can't tell the terrible things to? That would be as useless as a friend you can't have any fun with. Tell me, Chlo. It won't seem so bad then, I promise.'

She looked at him again, and drew a shaky breath. 'Llew, I'm going to be scarred. Chickenpox leaves *scars*! I'm glad you've got all those photos to remember me by. I'm going to be *disfigured*!' Then she started to bawl and couldn't stop.

Llew looked at her incredulously, and gathered her into a hug, holding her until the crying eased. Then he laid her gently down on her pillows again. To Chloe's utter astonishment, he sniggered.

'What's funny?'

Llew chuckled.

Chloe was thoroughly confused. He had been so tender, so sympathetic. 'Llew! *Stop it!* It's not funny to be ugly, and have children running away at the sight of you!'

Llew guffawed so much he couldn't speak. At last he composed himself, with visible effort. 'Chlo, that's not *true*! You won't be disfigured! You're not going to be ugly. What are you talking about?'

'It *is* true! Megan told me!'

'Oh, *Megan*! And you believe everything she says, do you? Because she'd never want to upset you, would she? Chlo, it's *chickenpox*! Every other person has it at some point. And how many hideously scarred people do you see walking around? None! Because it's not *true*!'

A shimmer of hope started up in Chloe's heart. What he said made sense, as usual. But would Megan really tell her such a cruel lie? Although, what *had* she said, really, and what had Chloe imagined from her words? She couldn't quite remember now.

'Really?' she asked in a small voice. 'Is that really true, Llew? Oh! Does that mean I can scratch them after all?' She lifted a hand to her face.

'No! Megan's right that they can scar if you scratch them. So you mustn't. But even if you did they'd only be tiny little scars, the same colour as your skin, no one would even notice. That's the absolute worst you'll be left with. But you won't, because you won't scratch.'

Chloe lowered her hand. 'But you *promise* me I won't be ugly?'

'Cross my heart and hope to die!'

'Really?'

'Swear on my Box Brownie.'

'Oh.' Then Chloe knew he was telling the truth. 'Well, that's not so bad then. I can bear anything as long as things go back to normal at the end. But, oh Llew! Our lovely holiday. Completely spoiled. I'm sorry.'

'It's not your fault, you goose. And it won't be *completely* spoiled, just a bit. I'll come and see you every day and we'll have some laughs, you'll see. All right, we wouldn't choose to spend three weeks in the attic, but we'll be together, that's the main thing.'

'But Llew, you *hate* being indoors. Just because my summer's spoiled doesn't mean yours should be too.'

'I'll manage. I can be outside after you've gone home. It wouldn't be the same without you, Chlo. Nothing's the same without you.'

Chloe was touched, her eyes welling up all over again. Chickenpox must make you very emotional. 'Nothing's the same without you either,' she whispered.

More footsteps on the stairs and Auntie Susan came in with the calamine lotion. 'Llew, would you go and wait on the stairs a minute? I need to take Chloe's nightie off and put this on all the spots. It'll help with the itching, dear,' she added to Chloe.

Chloe winced as she lifted the nightdress over her head and it brushed her skin. She couldn't bear to look at herself and shivered as Auntie Susan dabbed the cool pink lotion here and there.

'Thank you,' Chloe murmured. 'I'm so sorry to be so much trouble. Perhaps you'd better send me home.'

'Nonsense. You're not well enough to travel and it's no trouble. Megan and Richard both had it, I remember the drill well enough.'

Chloe gasped. 'And Llew? He's had it?'

'It was the first thing I asked when he tried to come barging in. I've never seen him so keen to come into this house! He had it when he was seven.'

'Oh good. He says he's going to come and see me every day and read to me. Isn't he a lovely friend, Auntie Susan?'

Auntie Susan looked at her for a minute, then nodded. 'He is. A very good friend.'

# Nora

On Nora's next visit to Nant-Aur she took her sewing roll, almost finished now, to show Gran. Gwennan loved to see things from Nora's life. Nora had taken new books, containers of Kaitlin's exotic cooking and, of course, they spent ages poring over her phone looking at photos. Mostly they were pictures of her Tenby life, but she also showed her Stacie and her boys, Simon ('hmmm, nothing special,' was Gwennan's verdict) and obviously Nora and Jasmine at various occasions.

Nora remembered to ask about fabric for her next patchwork assignment. 'I'm going to make a quilt,' she explained. 'Not a huge one, just a sofa blanket. If I buy *all* the material, it'll be a bit impersonal. I'd love to make something with a bit of history in it.'

'Well, it's funny you should ask. I was going to ask a favour of you as well. I've got some old crockery up the attic. Mair Hughes is after it for this teashop she's starting. What do they call it now? When they make everything look like it did seventy years ago?'

'Vintage?'

'Yes, that's it. A vintage one she's doing. Apparently the

252

crockery's to be all mix and match – now that's something we would *never* have done in the old days but there you are. I was going to ask would you mind very much going up there for me and bringing it down?'

Involuntarily Nora thought of Logan's muscles flexing under the weight of a tower of boxes. *No!*

'Of course, Gran. Shall I do it today?'

'I don't think there's a rush with Mair, but there's a bag of old clothes up there, lots of your mother's and some of mine as well no doubt. You can see if there's something you'd like for your quilt.'

When all the china and a big bag of clothes had been stowed on the landing, Nora had a thought. 'You don't have any old photos of Mum, do you?' she called, sitting on the edge of the hatch, legs dangling. I'd love to see some of her as a girl.'

'Bless you, Nora, photos of your mother? I've got dozens! Not up there, though. Come down and I'll show you.'

So Nora closed up the attic and followed Gwennan into her room, which had an old-fashioned pink coverlet over the big brass-framed double bed she had shared with Dafydd for sixty years, an old-fashioned cheval mirror, a matching hairbrush, hand mirror and comb set on the dressing table and a number of crystal ornaments sitting on crocheted doilies. Nora laid her hand over her heart. It was unbearable, the thought of sharing life with someone for so long and then having to go on alone. How did anyone bear it? Perhaps she really *was* better off single. At least she was used to it.

Her grandmother opened a wardrobe in which a small number of clothes hung neatly and pointed to a white shoebox on the floor. 'Will you pick it up for me, *cariad*? Save me bending.'

She hobbled downstairs to put the kettle on while Nora raced up and down carrying everything into the parlour. Then with tea and cake as the inevitable accompaniment, they went through everything.

There were five different china sets in all and Gran asked Nora if she wanted one.

'I know it's not the sort of thing the younger people buy nowadays,' she said. 'It's not dishwasher-safe or microwave-proof or anything like that. If you'd rather not, I won't be offended—'

She got no further for Nora's burst of enthusiasm. 'I'd *love* one! Are you sure? Oh, thanks, Gran, it's beautiful. I don't *want* modern things any more, I want gorgeous meaningful things . . . Oh, which one shall I have?' Eventually she chose a candy-pink set with gold edges and little bluebirds painted on the side.

'Present from my sister Susan on my tenth wedding anniversary, that was. She always did have lovely taste, Susan. That's four sets for Mair Hughes,' commented Gran. 'She'll be satisfied with that.'

Then they moved on to the clothes. Gwennan unfolded one garment after another, stroking them gently as if reliving all the memories they carried. There were a few of her old dresses but mostly they were Chloe's things. Cute little toddler dresses, a Sunday-best pinafore, some old kilts and plain blouses with

Peter Pan collars. There was a blue dress that Gwennan said she had worn to every smart occasion for about five years. 'Not that there were many of them, mind! Just the occasional wedding in the village and the Eisteddfod. And of course the Tenby Teens dances she was wild about.'

'Tenby Teens?' laughed Nora.

'Aye. When Chloe turned thirteen it was all she talked about for months! Months beforehand and then months after.'

Nora smiled. Her mother did get enthusiastic about things. She stroked the blue fabric, soft as butterfly wings. It was a sweet dress, an innocent dress.

'Oh!' smiled Gran. 'Here's why she stopped wearing the blue one.'

Nora watched, spellbound, as she shook out the frosted pink dress with its full skirts, silver-threaded lace and scalloped neckline. 'Wow! It's like a film-star dress.'

'There was a dance teacher in Tenby one year. Used to dance on stage she did, and this was one of her costumes. She gave it to Chloe as a gift. Very kind it was. Her father always said it's what started her off on her glamour and fashion, but I told him, she wanted those things long before. She'd always wanted them. This was just the first chance she had to wear them.'

'Mum had a really glitzy lifestyle in London, didn't she?'

Gwennan sighed. 'Aye, she did.'

'You've got photos from that period, have you? Because I've got loads. I've always just assumed she sent you some?'

'Yes, she did. But those aren't the photos of her that I love,

255

proud as I am, of course. Only, she was gone away from us, see. I wouldn't have minded that – I always knew Nant-Aur was too small for Chloe – but it was so *complete*. One minute she was here, helping me round the house, telling me her dreams, hugging me every five minutes; the next minute she was gone, and she hardly came back. And of course, Chloe modelling in London was dark-haired, and lovely she looked. Only, she didn't look like my girl.'

Nora frowned. The girl who had worn that sweet blue dress, who had gone crazy about a summer dance and adored her mother, didn't seem like the girl who had shaken off the dirt of her small village and never looked back.

'Why did she . . . not come and visit more?' she asked, not wanting to stray into difficult waters. 'I know everyone leaves home and goes off to do their own thing but . . . why didn't she keep in touch better? And lately. Now.'

'I don't know, *bach*. I've often wished, you know, that it could have been different. Round here, lots of the young people do stay close to home, close to family. Then again, lots of them don't. Mair Hughes's son is in Australia and her daughter's in France. They Skype and all that, but it's not the same. So I'm not the only one. Only Chloe was always so . . . well, we were close.'

Nora frowned. Gran was echoing what Nora had said about herself and Jasmine so often. She didn't quite know how to ask Gran if something had happened, back in the day, to coin Kaitlin's phrase.

Gwennan lifted the lid off the shoebox of photos. 'This is

*my* Chloe,' she said. 'This is how I remember her. This is when she was happy.' She handed Nora a sheaf of photos.

Nora's jaw dropped. There were so many! She had assumed photographs weren't a luxury many working-class families had in the 1950s. But here was Chloe in her blue dress with a group of other spiffed-up young people, all in 1950s clothes, posed stiffly before a fireplace. Here she was at a dance. Here she was on the beach, the wind wrapping her long hair across her face as she tucked into an almighty sandwich. That one made Nora smile. It wasn't flattering; she could almost feel the amusement of whoever had taken it.

No pictures of Gwennan or Dafydd or the boys. Apart from the more formal group shots, they were all of Chloe and only Chloe. And she wasn't in Nant-Aur. 'These were all taken in Tenby?'

Gran nodded.

'Who took them?'

'That was Llew. He always gave her some to take home for us, bless his heart.'

'Who was Llew?'

Her gran looked incredulous. 'Who was *Llew*? You're not telling me your mother's never told you about Llew?' Her amazement was such that for a moment Nora wondered if she'd made a mistake and simply forgotten. But no, she'd remember a name like that. She shook her head.

'Who was he? Some Tenby photographer who set her on the path to being a model?'

Her gran looked more confused than ever. 'No, *bach*! Llew was Chloe's best friend!'

Now Nora was confused. 'Bethan was her best friend.'

'Until your mother started going to Tenby she was. But that first summer she met Llew and that was it. Fast friends. She used to say to me, "Mam, Bethan's still my best friend in Nant-Aur, but Llew's my best friend in the whole world!" Oh, they were inseparable for those three weeks every year. Chloe loved Tenby, that was for sure, but there's no doubt Llew was the heart of it for her.'

'I've never heard of him,' murmured Nora, lost in thought. Could this be the mystery Kaitlin had guessed at?

'Lovely lad, he was. Well, from everything your mam said to us anyway. We never met him, shame that was. His mother had left his father – a big disgrace back then. But he wouldn't let it affect him. Worked hard in school, bright lad. I thought I might meet him that chickenpox year but in the end your mother recovered well enough to come home on the bus as usual while I was minding the boys.'

Chickenpox? Nora was starting to realise that Gran was a regular treasure trove of her mother's untold stories.

'So . . . she went *every* year? To Tenby. And she loved it?'

'Well, yes, *bach*!' Her unflappable grandmother was starting to sound slightly stressed, as though Nora were being deliber-ately obtuse, or *twp* as they said around here. 'The highlight of her year that holiday was. She stayed with my sister Susan. She went when she was ten the first time then every summer until she went to London. That life swallowed her up, it took my Chloe. Oh, I shouldn't say it, it's up to the young ones how they live their lives. But how can a kind-hearted girl who loves the sea and her family and her best friend, who had dreams, yes, but who had her two feet firmly on the ground, just turn into this . . . *other person*?'

Now Gwennan had tears in her eyes. Nora dropped the photos and put her arms around her. 'I'm sorry, Gran, I didn't mean to upset you. It's just . . . I had no *idea* . . .'

'It's not you, *bach*. I miss her, that's all. You think you come to terms with things, you think you accept them, but I've been missing her a long time, to tell the truth. Oh, she's a good girl. She phones me twice a week and it's not as if I haven't seen her over the years – she loved Daf and me visiting the two of you in London. I always enjoyed that. I never expected her to stay in Nant-Aur, like Daf did. *He* thought she would marry some local boy – live in the village and pop in every day. Thought it because he wished it, of course; that's how the world is for men. But I knew Chloe would leave. I just never thought she'd leave so *completely*.'

Now more than ever Nora felt sure that something had happened. But she couldn't ask Gran. Not today anyway, while she was this upset. She was very old. Her sons were already concerned. Nora didn't want to give her a heart attack.

'Oh Gran. Mum loves you so much. That's something she *has* told me, over and over. Life just sort of . . . carries you along sometimes. Like me and my job. It's a funny old thing, isn't it?' she finished limply.

But Gwennan appeared comforted. 'Aye, *bach*, it is. Well, fancy me getting upset then. Not like me to have a cry.'

'Crying's cathartic,' said Nora, echoing Jennifer's words to her some months ago. 'Shall I make you another cup of tea, Gran? This one's gone cold.'

It was only driving home that she remembered what Gran had said as she passed Nora the photographs. *This is when she was happy.*

Was she suggesting that in London, in the sixties, she *hadn't* been happy, the radiant, dazzling young woman posing in all those photographs? Although, who knew *what* she had been thinking or feeling deep down? In a way, they were all professional photos; she had to look that way. Underneath the facade, had she missed the woods and fields of home at all? The bright beaches of Tenby? Her motherless best friend? *Had* she been happy?

# Chloe

For the first week of Chloe's chickenpox Llew was as good as his word and read her *Famous Five* stories every day. Because Chloe was sleeping a lot, he went out roaming with his camera in the early morning before calling at ten o'clock. Auntie Susan would give him lunch, which he would eat at Chloe's bedside, devouring enough for both of them while she picked at chicken salad or sipped a little soup, then fell asleep. Then he would go off again to do Llew things before returning at four to sit with her for another couple of hours. He'd go home for tea with his father and in the evenings, he developed the photos he'd taken during the day to take to show Chloe the following morning. That way she still got to see Tenby even though she couldn't leave her bed.

On the second Tuesday she woke feeling a little better. Her head felt clearer, and she was sure the spot underneath her left elbow was getting smaller. She couldn't wait to tell Llew, but he didn't come.

Nor did he come the next day. Auntie Susan was concerned, Chloe was beside herself imagining worst-case scenarios: Will

Slocombe had beaten him up; Llew had slipped on the rocks and fallen; Red Sam had finally eaten him. Uncle Heinrich had a hunch and set off to Morris Street to enquire. A harassed-looking Mr Jones answered the door. Llew had chickenpox.

'But I thought you couldn't get it twice!' exclaimed Chloe. 'I'd never have let him come if I'd known this could happen.'

'He told me he had it when he was seven,' frowned Auntie Susan. 'Is Mr Jones sure, Harry? I know he's a doting father but he's not the most practical man . . .'

Uncle Heinrich perched at the foot of Chloe's bed, his blue eyes smiling behind his glasses. 'I called up to see the boy myself. It is the chickenpox. I'm afraid that Leonard has told to you a – what do you say in English? – a pale lie?'

'A white lie. Oh.'

'Yes, a white lie, so that he could come and see Chloe.'

'But I *told* him it was highly contagious! I made it perfectly clear!'

'I am certain you did, my dear. But he was determined, no? It was foolish of him, perhaps, but very gallant. No man of stout heart can be kept from the object of his affections.'

'Oh,' sighed Auntie Susan again. 'That poor boy. That silly, silly boy.'

The days that followed were unspeakably tedious without Llew. Apart from her aunt and uncle and Megan, her only visitor was Evie, who came twice. She brought Chloe a sherbet fountain, a magazine and good wishes from Pamela and Christine. Chloe was touched.

Megan was confusing. One day she brought Chloe some flowers, fresh from the garden; she arranged them in a jar and placed them where Chloe could see them. But when Chloe thanked her, she shrugged irritably, saying, 'It was Mum's idea.'

She looked different too. Chloe hadn't noticed at first because she'd been in a chickenpox haze, but as it lifted she could see that Megan had lost a lot of weight. She'd always been voluptuous but now she was downright slender and it didn't especially suit her. Her face had a drawn look that dulled her shimmer. Chloe tried asking her if anything was wrong, but Megan just rolled her eyes and said, 'Super compliment, Chloe, thanks! I look better than you do anyway,' and flounced out of the attic. Chloe wondered if it was because Michael Everley had thrown her over. Maybe she missed him. Maybe he had broken her heart – but she had learned her lesson and didn't like to ask. Megan was so proud. She wouldn't want anyone to think she couldn't get the boy she liked.

Chloe was completely better by the end of the week. The doctor was delighted with her progress and said she was an exemplary patient. There were still some small scabs here and there but they would soon be gone, he said. None of the others had left any mark at all. He gave her a clear pass to go outside and enjoy the rest of her holiday as she pleased.

There was almost a week left. It was more than Chloe could have hoped at the start. But now Llew was ill, so there was only one thing to do. She went first to the paper shop where Mrs

Isaacs inspected her for damage, holding her face between her chubby fingers and turning it this way and that.

'No marks at all,' was her verdict. 'I had to put mittens on my Sheila to stop her scratching and even then she rubbed at them with the wool. But you've done very well, fair play.'

Then Chloe spent her holiday money on Llew's favourite comics and set off to Morris Street. She would read to Llew every single day as he had done for her. The sea was sparkling and happy shrieks drifted up to her from the beach. The summer breeze was intoxicating after being cooped up for two weeks but Chloe was determined. If she never saw daylight again, she would visit Llew every day until he was better.

# Nora

'What is that *face*?' demanded Kaitlin, walking into the kitchen and bringing a waft of fresh air with her.

Nora was sitting at the kitchen table, frowning over her mother's latest email. She looked up from the laptop.

'What face? How's the weather?'

'Beautiful. Perfect for your purposes. That face like a cornered skunk.'

'Oh, *that* face. Just reading an email from Mum.'

Kaitlin grinned. 'How is she?'

'Good, she's good . . . but she's asking *questions*! So many questions, and they're getting harder and harder to answer. Like, will I pop in to see Sandy, and when am I getting a job and where am I doing all this walking and why did I send her a photo of my lovely vase lying on the bed and can I please stand it up on the table and take another one so she can see it properly without the pattern on the bedspread distracting her . . . ?' Nora ran her hands through her hair. An interrogation squad would have *nothing* on her mother.

'I've been trying not to lie but I've got to decide. Either I start lying or I tell her where I am.'

'And I'm guessing you don't want to do either.'

'Not really . . . I feel I'm this close to figuring something out. I just don't know what it is.'

'But how would telling her stop you finding out whatever you need to?'

'It wouldn't, I suppose. I just feel superstitious. She's *never* given me the impression that Tenby was important to her. She's always acted as if she didn't really like it. But Gran said she lived for her time here. Oh, I don't know what to do.' She closed the laptop with a bang. 'I'll think about it while I'm walking.'

Today was the day Nora was trying out the Tenby Ramblers. Her list was flourishing. As she ticked things off, she thought of other things to add. Now it covered two whole pages of her new notebook, a far cry from the three ideas she had squeezed from her tired brain three weeks ago.

Last week she had rung the Ramblers and this morning she was to meet them outside the church (inside if it was raining) where they would organise carloads. They would walk two and a half miles of the Pembrokeshire coastal path then turn around and go back again. Nora had deliberately opted for a shorter walk in case the company wasn't good. She'd never previously fancied being one of a large number of anorak-wearing, stick-brandishing hikers crowding along a cliff path, talking about haemorrhoids, but she was longing to get out there and Kaitlin wasn't interested.

An hour later she was getting out of a car at Angle with three other women, all very friendly and not a haemorrhoid between them, she dared to hope. There was only one other carload, carrying three white-haired, hearty-looking men. They were all tightening bootlaces and patting pockets for tissues and energy bars when a blue Fiesta came hurtling into the car park. It pulled up beside them in a spatter of gravel and a cloud of dust.

'Dear dear,' said Elizabeth Fellows, waving a hand in distress.

'Sorry about the dust!' cried Logan, jumping out of the car. 'Hadn't realised how fast I was going, didn't want to miss you. Tenby Ramblers? Oh, hello, Nora, how you going?'

Nora was so surprised to see him that all she managed by way of reply was, 'Um, yeah, good.' What on earth was *Logan* doing here? Making his second dramatic entrance in as many encounters. She'd done quite well at not thinking about him over the last few days; she didn't want her inconvenient attraction to him to mar her walk.

'I got to the church late,' Logan continued. 'Nightmare with the kids this morning. Sarah said I'd only just missed you and reckoned I'd catch you. Is that OK?'

'Of course!' said Alex, who was in charge of the ramble. 'The more the merrier. Alex Chambers. Good to meet you. Just a gentle one today, that suit you?'

'G'day, Alex. Logan. Sounds ideal. I just want to get to know the coastline better, you know.'

'Excellent. It's stunning, Logan, you'll be glad you did. So

267

that's two new ramblers with us today, troops! Let's make sure they want to come back. Walk with me, Logan, tell me about yourself.'

Logan shot Nora a warm smile and fell into step with Alex, followed by Sid and Arthur, then Fliss and Bev, and then Nora and Elizabeth.

For ten minutes Nora couldn't concentrate on a word Elizabeth was saying; she was flustered that Logan was there. She was content to bring up the back of the group, as far from him as possible. Not that he didn't have a perfect right to be there, of course; she didn't have the monopoly on the Tenby Ramblers. It was just that he was very, *very* attractive and very unavailable and she was wearing an old pair of unflattering walking trousers with a rip in the right leg and a yellow vest which clung to her tummy bulge. Over the top she wore a blue body warmer with the stuffing escaping from it, so it looked a bit like a cloud-studded sky. No make-up, hair pinned up anyhow just to keep it off her neck . . . *Not* that it mattered, since he was *married*.

But gradually she settled down. The landscape was, as Alex had promised, stunning. Glimpsing it from the car was completely different from feasting her eyes on the never-ending dazzle of turquoise that sparked with golden darts, from feeling the breeze on her face, or from seeing baby rabbits, nodding pink thrift, plummeting seabirds . . .

They walked more slowly than she would have done alone, but there was something rather soothing about that, a gentle rhythm, an easy stride, on and on around curve and bend, steady and mesmeric. Because the path was fairly narrow they stayed in their twos most of the way so Logan wasn't really an issue. And besides, thought Nora, ozone and sunlight restoring her perspective, the world was full of good-looking married men. She didn't have to be silly about it. He seemed like a friendly, interesting guy. It was fine that he was there. It was great.

As she walked, she pondered the issue of how to reply to her mother. Emails composed themselves in her head: *Guess what, Mum! I'm back in Tenby for a bit . . . Pics attached! Lovely weather and it's great to be out of London for a while.* Yes, that was it; edge closer to the truth without any need for full disclosure. Of course, there would be further questions – *How long is a bit? How are you paying for it?* – but she would deal with them later.

Before she knew it an hour had passed and they were sitting on a grassy clifftop, opening flasks of coffee and hot chocolate.

'Getting on all right, Nora?' asked Alex.

'Wonderful, thanks. This coastline is amazing. I can see how people become addicted.'

'That's it! We do! Well, I hope you'll come again. We're starting at Amroth next week if that's of any interest. On holiday, did you say? Or with us for longer?'

'A sabbatical of sorts, so I'll be around a while.'

'Splendid, splendid,' said Alex, moving off to check in with the other walkers.

'How long is a while?' asked Logan, sitting on the grass beside her. He seemed very large and very solid.

'You sound like my mother,' said Nora, without thinking. It was just that Jasmine was always so present with her.

He pulled a face. 'I wasn't about to judge, just wondering.'

Nora smiled. 'I don't know is the answer. At least six months. Probably six months. Six months is the plan. Although actually, wow, I've been here a month already!'

'So five months then,' teased Logan. 'Are you sure it's five? Cos I need to know.'

'Shut up.'

'No, seriously, I'm glad it's a while, that's all.'

'Well, thanks.' Nora felt warmed by his interest. 'I love it here to be honest. Not sure I ever want to go back. But I expect I'll have to. You know, jobs, real life, common sense and all that,' she added in response to his querying look.

'Yeah, real life,' he sighed, looking pensive for a moment. Then after a pause, 'It *is* gorgeous here, though, isn't it? We've got scenery to die for at home, of course, but this . . . it's kind of magical to me. Reminds me of childhood, though I never came here then.'

His words touched a precise chord in Nora. That was exactly how she felt. She had presumed it had something to do with connecting with her roots, her grandmother and, ever so imperfectly, her mother.

'I know exactly what you mean. My flatmate keeps saying I should just stay. But I can't bring myself to believe that would be possible. I worry that if I tried to make it solid and permanent, it would just dissolve, like a mirage.'

He looked at her intently. 'At the risk of parroting you, I know exactly what *you* mean. It's like sometimes, out of all the great places there are in the world, you light upon one where you just feel *right*, you know? Like, it can give you everything that's really important to you. And then it seems too good to be true.'

'Is that how *you* feel about Tenby?' She wondered if it was the place or Molly or both that made him happy to be so far from home.

'I'm coming to. Fast.'

Nora nodded. Tenby did feel like that for her, she realised. There was a pleasing sense of fit between herself and the place that made her not want to quest further for a sense of home. It did offer everything that was important to her. But did it offer everything she *needed*? Like a good job, for example, a sustainable income? She sighed. It seemed intolerably jarring to think like that here, on top of the world, looking down at a swathe of ocean so blue she could drown in it. Not literally, of course. That wouldn't be good.

'That wasn't a good sigh,' observed Logan.

'Just thinking about jobs. I'm in between at the moment.'

'Ah! So when you say sabbatical, you mean you're a bum!'

Nora grinned. 'That I am, Logan, that I am. But although that's obviously a highly desirable state, I can't be one forever.'

'What did you do, before?'

'Office manager in a university. Admin at a super high level. Keeping the world turning, you know?'

'Ah, little things like that. And is that what you'd do again, d'you think?'

'I really, really don't want to. But it's what I'm qualified for, it's where all my experience is. I'm having such a great time here, trying out so many things that I love, but I'm not sure I can make a living out of walking and patchwork and eating cake.'

'Come on,' he laughed. 'Think outside the box! There has to be a way. I'll help you draw up a business model if you like.'

'What about you? Um, I hate to ask this but . . . where are you from? I know Aussies and Kiwis hate getting mistaken for one another but I really can't tell . . .'

'Kiwi born and bred, but my dad was Welsh, hence the surname. He died when I was a kid, God bless him. When I came to a . . . crossroads in my life, I came over here to see where he grew up, discover my roots.'

*And met Molly, obviously*, thought Nora. *I wish I'd met him then.* She pushed the thought away. No good could come of that.

'Funny,' she said. 'In a way I'm discovering my roots too – my mum grew up near here but I've never spent much time here at all.'

'Is your mum still alive?'

'Oh yes, very much so. She's in Italy at the moment, living it large with a friend for six months. And how many children do you have? Two, right?'

He looked startled. 'Yeah! How did you know? Oh, I guess Mol told you. Yeah, two kids, Sylvie, twelve, and Brendan, sixteen. They're great, you know? Worth every bit of trouble. Do you have kids?'

'No.'

'Married?'

'No.' The monosyllable hung on the tangy air, heavy and awkward. Why did it always carry that resonance? So many people were perfectly happy being single. For years Nora had never even questioned it – work had kept her so busy, so blind. After being with someone who was sweet enough but just *wrong* for her, like Simon, being single was a blessed relief! But even now that she was starting to open up to the idea that maybe she wasn't done with all that . . . love stuff . . . it was hardly a tragedy, was it? Some people were coupled up and others were not. It was 2014 after all! So why this perpetual expectation of blame, or pity? Worst of all, it wasn't just her. She could have sworn he looked slightly uncomfortable.

When Alex called them to order, Nora looked longingly in the onward direction. Now that she had a taste for it she wanted to go on and on and discover everything there was to see on this magical coastline. Yes, magical, Logan had chosen the right word.

He caught her glance. 'That'd be nice, wouldn't it?'

'*Really* nice. I'm definitely going to do more walking while I'm here.'

'Good on ya. Hey, we should go sometime. Without the group, I mean. Go at our own pace, go on for miles. What do you reckon?'

Nora was caught. She'd love it. Of course she would. But was it wise, given her crush on him? It *was* a crush. She wouldn't dignify it with any weightier vocabulary. Then again, he wasn't the only attractive married man in the world. She couldn't avoid them all and only ever make friends with women or ugly men, could she?

'Only if you want to,' said Logan, obviously misunderstanding her hesitation. 'No worries if you don't. Kiwi fault, we instantly think everyone's our best friend. Molly could come with us maybe, how about that? I don't want to push you. If you fancy it sometime, let me know. Otherwise I'll shut up.'

'No, I'd love to. It's a great idea. And Molly too, lovely! She's so nice.'

'Yeah,' he grinned. 'I'm pretty partial to her myself. She's not the biggest walker, I have to warn you, so I may not be able to talk her into it. I'll do my best, though.'

'OK, well, either way. I'll look forward to it.' Nora was relieved to have been decisive. His manner was so open and direct there was no way this was a pick-up. Besides, he clearly wasn't going to have designs on her in her too-snug vest and ancient walking gear, when he was married to gorgeous, svelte Molly who looked like something out of *Call the Midwife*. He was just being friendly. Which was a good thing. Of course it was.

# Chloe

What heaven to be here again after what was effectively a two-year break, for all she'd seen of Tenby last year. Gazing out at the Labrador-coloured sand and sparkling turquoise sea, Chloe took a long suck of her strawberry milkshake. At last, she had been invited to join the girls on an outing. Actually *invited*. She hadn't had to ask or plead to tag along. It had only taken eight years.

Admittedly, it wasn't Megan who'd invited her, it had been Pam and Evie, but still. Chloe was squashed into a booth with Christine, Pam, Megan, Evie, Alma and a friend of Christine's, Iris. Iris, visiting from Saundersfoot, was squeezed in next to Christine, just about falling off the end. Chloe was cramped and uncomfortable, her bare legs sticking to the red vinyl banquette. And, she was a little bored.

Alma was engaged. She kept waving her hand, with its minuscule splinter of diamond, and talked ceaselessly about her fiancé. That's what she kept saying, 'my fiancé', as if he

275

didn't have a name. He was James Jones, Chloe knew – no relation to Llew – and he 'had prospects'. Alma was like a very pretty ginger cat who had licked up every last drop of cream. No room for Evie to talk about *her* fiancé, and she had become engaged two months before Alma. So much had changed while Chloe was away.

Of course they were all older than Chloe, twenty and twenty-one now. Chloe had always thought Megan would be the first of their crowd to get engaged. For one thing, she was still, in Chloe's eyes, the prettiest of them all. For another, she had always said she would. But as far as Chloe knew, she hadn't dated anyone since Michael Everley and was still the slimmer, more subdued Megan that Chloe remembered from Chickenpox Summer.

It was hard for Chloe to concentrate as Alma droned on. Just before she left her father had given her some food for thought.

'When you come back, *bach*, we'll have to talk about your future,' he said awkwardly. Heart-to-hearts weren't his strong suit. 'Next year you'll be eighteen. I'm in no hurry for you to leave us but your mother says it's a modern world and girls are going and doing things now . . . I suppose she's right but I must have final approval on your plans. I am your father.'

'I don't have any plans yet, Dad, but I'll come up with some just to shock you,' she had laughed, kissing his cheek.

'There's a girl you are,' he said.

It made Chloe smile, the way he always looked so bemused by her. But she loved him, oh she did, and he was right, she did want to go and do something. Or she would, when she thought of what it was. For she had accepted that she wouldn't be a dancer.

Leaving home would be hard. It was hard enough leaving for three weeks in the summer, even now she was seventeen. Honestly, every time she got on that bus, she felt the tug of the emotional umbilical cord. How would she manage when she had a job? She would have pre-arranged days off and she wouldn't be able to go home in between, no matter how homesick she was. She'd always dreamed of London, or at the very least Cardiff. Now even the distance to Swansea seemed too great. Perhaps she should think about Carmarthen . . . but wouldn't Bethan scoff?

Well, she didn't have to think about it now. *Shouldn't* think about it now, on holiday. No matter what, she decided, she would always come to Tenby for her summers. Even if it was just two weeks, or one, nothing would ever stop her.

Then Iris giggled and said, 'Well, he's a little bit delicious, isn't he? Who's *that*, girls?'

Her tone of breathy wonder caught Chloe's interest and she looked up. She couldn't see anyone eye-catching.

Then Iris added, 'He's coming over! Do you know him, Chris? Will you introduce me?'

That was when Chloe saw Llew. But this wasn't Llew as she knew him. For one thing, he seemed to have grown about ten inches. For another, he was dressed in a shirt and trousers. And what's more, the camera slung around his neck wasn't his tatty old Box Brownie, but something altogether larger and more complicated-looking.

For a minute, she felt a little shy. She could see what Iris saw: a tall, tawny-haired young man with something assured and set apart in his manner, a certain lanky grace to his walk and intense amber eyes that rested on the group of girls as he walked over.

For an instant it was as if all the summers when she and Llew were outsiders, scruffy and poor, had never been. He no longer looked like a little boy her brother's age – although Clark had gone to work with their father now, come to that. Instead, Llew was a young man, and Chloe was a popular girl, and she had a strange feeling of somehow being in another dimension. But then he reached them, grinned and said, 'Chlo! Welcome back!' His voice belonged to the old Llew and her heart melted with relief.

'Llew Jones! There's a beanpole you are! What happened, did your dad leave you in fertiliser over the winter?'

'I shouldn't be surprised,' murmured Alma, making a delicate show of sniffing the air, but Llew didn't hear and Chloe didn't care. All she wanted was to be out of here, Chloe and Llew again, in the sunlight, on their own.

Llew beamed at Chloe then remembered the other girls and said hello to them all, one at a time. Alma was rude, Megan was stiffly polite, and Pam and Evie were maternally fond, exclaiming over his height, his clothes. Christine introduced Iris and Llew shook her hand with perfect manners.

'Leonard Jones, delighted to meet you. Are you here for long?'

As always, he sounded older than he was, and had a sort of old-fashioned charm; much of his father's manner had rubbed off on him. Clark might be working now but he still thought a fart was the funniest thing that could happen on any given day and his idea of greeting a girl was, 'Orright, lovely? 'Ow's it goin'?' He would bellow his advances in a deep voice, copying the men of the village. Then he'd sneak behind the pub for a fag so that none of his mam's friends would see and tell on him.

Iris was gazing up at Llew, asking if he was a photographer. *With that great big camera hanging round his neck? What gave you that idea?*

He smiled and explained that he had a summer placement with the *Tenby Times*, which was news to Chloe. That was a big deal!

'If you'll excuse me, Iris, ladies,' Llew was saying now, for all the world like some debonair film star of twenty years ago, 'I'd like to steal Chloe away. I have to go back to the office this evening so I've only got a couple of hours.'

The office? A couple of hours? Is this how it was going to be now?

Chloe stood up but Iris and Christine and various cardigans and bags were in the way. Iris seemed particularly slow to get out of the way. In the end the new beanpole that was Llew reached across to take Chloe's hand and pulled her up onto the table. Then he hooked an arm around her waist, swung her down and off they went. For a moment – *just* for a moment – Chloe felt as though she were in a film, whisked off by the leading man while the other girls watched her go. But of course, it was only Llew.

Once they were out of the café they exchanged their usual bear hugs. 'You look so different!' exclaimed Chloe. 'How are you so *tall*?' She realised that last year they had only seen each other horizontal and covered in scabs.

'Different good?' asked Llew.

Chloe considered. Iris might think he was a hunk and a dreamboat, and she could admit that he would certainly seem striking if you weren't used to him. But to her he still looked like the same old Llew, and that was the main thing, after all.

'Different good,' she agreed and he smiled. 'But what's this about a summer placement? News to me, Llew *bach*! Forget there was such a thing as a stamp, did we?'

'No. I deliberately wanted to surprise you when you came. Oh Chloe, there's so much to tell you and I've been saving it all up. In May, Mr Aspell from the *Tenby Times* came up to me in the street! He said he'd seen me round about taking photos and making a nuisance of myself. He asked me if I thought I was up to making a nuisance of myself on a regular basis and I said I'd certainly never had any trouble doing it so far. He asked me about my camera and my photography and I told him I was going to be a famous photographer someday. He smiled a bit, you know how grown-ups do, and said, "Is that so?" and I told him yes, it was. Then he asked if he could see some samples of my work. So I went to see him the next day. I took loads of pictures with me, Chlo, put them all in a folder that my dad gave me. And Mr Aspell asked if I'd be interested in getting some work experience. Unpaid, he said, but I'd have assignments and my work would be published in the paper if it was good enough. Of course, it means the chance of a job when I'm older. And a reference. It's a really big opportunity, Chloe!'

'It is! Oh, it is, Llew! I'm so *happy* for you! Are you enjoying it? Are you learning? And how have you got new clothes and a new camera if he's not paying you?'

'The camera's borrowed from work. But he pays me expenses! That's what he calls them anyway. He gave me money for trousers and two shirts, and I have money for a sandwich and a pop every day and money for bus fare. Of course, I don't take a bus, I walk, but he says it's a standard arrangement. So I have a few pence left over every day. And yes, I love it. I feel more . . . solid, because I've always said I'm a photographer and now I am. People don't laugh at me quite as much. They still laugh, but not as much. I feel as though what I've always known, and what's real, are coming closer together now. Oh, I wouldn't choose all the assignments he gives me, but that's the point of it, isn't it, to do something different, to meet a brief, as he calls it. One day he sent me out with Dai, the paper photographer, and I watched everything he did. Shadowing, they call it. He's a bit of a twerp really, and I don't think he liked having a kid hanging around, but I'm learning! I'm on my way, Chloe!'

Chloe gave him another huge hug. This was tremendous!

Now *this* felt like Tenby again, her and Llew, strolling along, spilling their hearts to each other, no one else around . . .

'Hello? Chloe! Leonard!' They turned at the unfamiliar voice. It was Iris, chasing after them in the sunshine. She had waved, shoulder-length blonde hair, not frosty pale like Chloe's but gorgeous and golden. Chloe loved that colour. She had blue eyes too, but they were quite close together and her teeth were really quite large. Nice figure. All this Chloe somehow noted in the space of two seconds, having noticed none of it before. What had come over her?

'Chloe, you left this in the café.'

Iris was brandishing Chloe's little purse with the long gold string. She carried a few coins and a comb in it.

'Thanks, Iris.' She hooked it round her neck and over one shoulder. 'That's kind of you. Enjoy your afternoon.'

'Oh. I wondered. Where are you two going?'

Chloe and Llew looked at each other. No one ever joined them on their rambles. But then, Iris wasn't from around here. She didn't know how it was with them.

'We don't know yet,' said Llew.

'How silly you are! Then how will you know when you get there?' asked Iris, not looking at Chloe.

Llew frowned. 'It's just what we do.'

'Well, can I join you? If you haven't got any special plans? I'd like to walk around the town a bit.'

No special plans! This was their first day together in a whole year! And last year hardly counted. But how could they say no to someone who had asked, and who was looking at them now with big raindrop eyes and a face like a hopeful hamster?

Llew looked at Chloe. Chloe shrugged crossly. Llew might have lovely manners when it came to hellos and goodbyes but he was only fifteen and he was like every other man on the planet when it came to dealing with women who were happy to push themselves in where they weren't wanted: useless.

'All right then,' he said, sounding very unenthusiastic. 'If you think you won't be bored.' Chloe almost laughed. Surely Iris would get the hint.

'Not me! I never get bored. Mother says I'm very resourceful,' said Iris, tucking one arm into Llew's and one into Chloe's so that she was walking between them.

*I bet you are*, thought Chloe.

'My two new friends,' cooed Iris. 'I *love* making new friends. Now you must tell me all about yourselves. Leonard, tell me more about this newspaper!' And off she went, leaning against him as he ducked his head to explain. Chloe was towed along like a lagging child.

After wandering around for an hour with Iris showing no signs of tiring, nor any interest in Chloe at all, Llew had to go back to the office. He pulled his arm free from Iris and stared at Chloe beseechingly.

'I'll see you after?' he checked anxiously.

'Of course.'

'Oh! What are you doing after? Where are you going? What time?'

But Chloe was ready for her this time. 'We're going to visit Leonard's old auntie who's very, very sick. Terrible, the lungs on her. Always coughing, poor dab, and the phlegm flying everywhere, but she's so kind we love her dearly. Would you like to come?'

Llew looked astonished. He had no auntie, sick or well, but if Chloe said so, he wasn't going to argue. 'Green phlegm,' he added.

Iris looked crestfallen. 'Oh, no thank you. I've said I'll do something with Christine. But I'll see you tomorrow, I hope.'

'Bye, Chlo.' Llew sloped off, a dashing newspaperman no longer, a boy again, unsure how his much-anticipated reunion with Chloe had been sabotaged by forces beyond his control.

The two girls stood looking after him.

'Oh, you are good, to wait around for him like that when he's obviously too busy for you, and to visit his relatives when you could be having fun,' said Iris. 'But then, as he's your boyfriend I suppose it's only right.'

'He's not my boyfriend,' said Chloe automatically, then kicked herself.

'Oh, isn't he? Well then, you wouldn't mind if he took me out? I rather like him.'

'I'd never have guessed. It might depend on what *he* wants, though.'

'Oh, men don't know *what* they want. It's up to us to tell them! Don't worry about me, Chloe, I'll have Leonard Jones wrapped around my little finger in no time.' And off she scuttled.

# Nora

One night in the pub, after Danny and Lil went home, Kaitlin and Nora were talking about the locked room in their house. Well, Jones's house. Nora was possessed with a greater and greater longing to see that painting on the wall properly, and Kaitlin wasn't far behind in the curiosity stakes.

'Why are we so curious?' wondered Kaitlin. 'Well, I know why I am, it's cos I'm nosy. What's your excuse?'

Nora had no idea. So many things were preoccupying her lately. Her mother, their relationship, Jones's paintings, Logan . . . 'I feel like it's important somehow . . . though I might just be barking,' she said. 'It's a very real possibility.'

'Cheers to that,' said Kaitlin, clinking her pint of Autumn Gold against Nora's bottle of Corona.

'Tell you what, Kait,' interjected Darren, a twenty-something regular in The Hope and Anchor. 'If you likes, I'll come round one day and fiddle the lock.'

Darren had done a bit of time as a teenager for breaking and entering, as well as 'a bit of violence, like, but not *bad* violence', as he put it. He'd learned the error of his ways now and started a 'new life'. His new life seemed to consist of haunting the Tenby pubs and drinking most of the day and night. But at least there was no crime. 'I don't do that no more, mind,' he reminded them sternly, 'but the skills don't go away, like. I'm not proud of it, but you've been nice to me, so if it 'elps, I'll do it.'

Kaitlin had explained to Nora that people were understandably sceptical about Darren. 'Waste of space,' was one of the nicer comments he regularly received. 'Fuckin' crim scumbag,' was often heard when the other young men were beered up and feeling invincible. 'I'm not saying he's a great role model for . . . well, anyone,' Kaitlin had said, 'but he's doing better than he was and that's not something everyone can say. Plus, kindness is free.'

'That's nice of you, Darren,' said Kaitlin, 'but it's OK, thanks. I don't think it's the way to go. You know, generous landlord gives us the run of his gorgeous home at a knock-down rent . . . breaking into his private space is *not* how we want to repay him.'

Darren frowned for a minute, digesting her rationale, then nodded. 'Aye, fair play, like,' he agreed eventually and wandered off to play pinball.

Kaitlin grinned at Nora. 'Can't say I'm not tempted.'

'Me too. Don't suppose he'd be able to lock it up again after him, would he?'

'I don't think thieves' skills lie in locking things up securely,' mused Kaitlin.

'Hey, Kait, do you know a guy called Logan Davies?'

Katlin shook her head. 'No, why?'

'Just wondered if you knew him. He's Molly's husband.'

'Your patchwork teacher? I don't know her either. Why?' she asked with a wicked twinkle. 'Is he fit?'

'Well, yes, as a matter of fact. Drop-dead gorgeous actually. But married, and I don't do that, so there you go.'

'Aren't we paragons? We don't hit on married men and we don't break into private rooms.'

Nora sighed. 'Our haloes must be dazzling. They'll probably name saints after us.'

'Stick a memorial on Caldey. Saint Kait . . . ooh! But you know what we *can* do?'

'What?'

'We could look in the attic again, couldn't we? I mean, if our own lives are so sad and boring that we need to go nosing into someone else's? I mean, it's open. We've been in before . . .'

'It wouldn't be prying or snooping,' agreed Nora, excited. 'We'd do it in the spirit of respectful interest.'

'Respectful interest,' agreed Kaitlin, downing the last two inches of her drink. 'Let's go.'

They belted home through the chill, salty night, hurried up to the attic and switched on the light. Nora went straight over to the large canvas on the easel, examining the faint pencil outlines. It remained vague, a fall of hair, a suggestion of bare legs perhaps. Oh, it was hopeless. How could Jones bear to leave it like this? If she had any artistic talent at all, she didn't think she'd be able to tear herself away from her creations until they were finished. Then again, how did she know she didn't? That was something else for her list.

Meanwhile, Kaitlin had carefully turned five canvases around, one at a time, and gave a low whistle. 'Come and see, Nora.'

Two were seascapes, with light streaming through the waves, gulls arching above them and far-off horizons only faintly visible. The rest were portraits and they were uncanny. One was a lobsterman in a navy cable sweater and gumboots, a fierce expression on his red face and a huge beard. He looked like an ancient Celtic warrior transported to a different time and place. Although it wasn't a lovely painting in the traditional sense, it had that Tenby quality to it – *magical*, thought Nora. That word again. You felt you could see or sense the man's whole tragic story in his burning eyes and wind-tugged clothing. One was a slender dark-haired woman in black slacks and sweater, very Audrey Hepburn, ankles crossed and a teacup dangling from her fingers. And one was of two young women on a bench on Castle Hill. Their faces were hidden, heads bent together as though sharing some delicious gossip. One had thick dark hair in a Marilyn wave and one had a sleek red ponytail that fell across her half-turned face.

'They're *incredible*!' breathed Nora.

'God, Nor, he's seriously talented. All this time we've been speculating, we should just have looked him up on the internet! He's bound to be famous!'

'You know what? You're right. Look, Kait, there are plaques on the frames. These have been in an exhibition!'

They sat on the floor in the dust to read the tiny lettering, black on pewter. The seascapes were called *Sea Dream* and *Sea Dream 2*. *Red Sam*, it said underneath the lobsterman. The Audrey Hepburn lookalike was *Blossom*. And the third portrait was entitled *The Cats*.

'He's right,' chuckled Kaitlin. 'Look at those two! They're having a right old bitch about everyone! Let's look at some more.'

She jumped to her feet and Nora followed, brushing off dust. They turned another three paintings around. All were different views of Tenby – the harbour, the North Beach with distinctive Goscar Rock and the Caldey Island boat launching from Castle Beach. They were contemporary, but still had that enchanted quality – Tenby as a storybook town, somewhere that had somehow endured and retained the glow of the past.

'It's like a whole world here in the attic!' murmured Nora.

'This is agony,' groaned Kaitlin. 'I need information.' She tore downstairs and reappeared a minute later with her iPad. She perched on the windowsill, a kind-faced moon showering silver light over the harbour behind her. *Jones artist Tenby* she typed into the search engine, bringing up a mass of entries. Nora perched beside her and they read avidly.

His name was Leo Jones. There were several obsolete sites for old exhibitions and there was an instructional blog for beginner artists. There was a whole website devoted to his landscape photography – he was multi-talented, it seemed – and there were a number of reviews and articles about his work.

But the bios focused on his work and gave very little personal information at all. There was nothing to give a sense of him as a man – nothing to match the accomplished artist with the 'daft apeth' of Mrs Watkins' description, nor with their astonishingly generous, doubtless eccentric landlord.

'It doesn't even mention that the Wicked Witch of the West is his daughter or *anything*!' frowned Kaitlin.

But they did find one exciting bit of information. At the end of June, a gallery in London was to show an exhibition of his previously unseen works. It would open on the twenty-eighth and run for five weeks. Kaitlin and Nora looked at each other.

'Yes,' they said in unison.

# Chloe

Llew was freed from the newspaper office shortly after nine. Chloe was waiting for him outside.

'Have you been there long?' he asked, hurrying towards her, looking very important with his sensible clothes and reporter's camera around his neck. 'I thought I was meeting you on the beach.'

'You were, until Iris Evans told me her plan to wrap you round her little finger. I decided I'd better hang around to warn you. I wouldn't put it past her to lie in wait for you, you know.'

He grinned. 'You mean, like you're doing? Ow! All right, keep your hair on. Let's go. Now what's that about Iris? She wants to do *what* with me?'

Twenty minutes later they were sitting in the sand dunes, thick jumpers protecting them from the late evening's chill.

'*Duw*, there's a wind this week!' commented Llew, taking a swig from the ginger beer bottle. Chloe had saved all the money she hadn't spent during Chickenpox Summer so they could have an extra luxurious summer this year to make up for it. She had brought crisps and ginger beer for them to enjoy.

She noticed with fascination how his Adam's apple bobbed as he swallowed, and how a tiny prickle of beard was starting to show on his chin. Llew was growing up! Well, what did it matter? She was no stranger to growing boys. Voices dropping and squeaking, hair sprouting, brains getting even stupider. She had two brothers for heaven's sake. But Llew! The friend of her childhood, her favourite person, about to step over that threshold and become a man. How strange.

She told him Iris's plans to show him what he wanted. 'As if you didn't know yourself!' she huffed. 'As if you're not ten times cleverer than *she* is. The cleverest person in Tenby, as a matter of fact.'

He just laughed and said, 'I suppose it's flattering really.'

'Flattering! Oh, I suppose you're going to tell me you're interested now, are you? That you're quite happy to be wrapped around the finger of some scheming little—'

'Of course I'm not interested, don't be *twp*. She looks like a squirrel and that voice would get on my nerves after five minutes. Even if I was, I wouldn't start going out with someone while you're here, would I?'

'Wouldn't you? Why?'

'Well, stupid, because you're only here for three weeks and I want to make the most of my best friend!' He said it in a 'that's obvious' tone.

'I know,' said Chloe, but suddenly she felt afraid. Yes, she was his best friend – the person he liked the best. But wasn't the point of a girlfriend or boyfriend that *they* were the person you liked the best? When Llew got one, she wouldn't come first with him any more. Even if he didn't like Iris, other girls would look at him the same way. He was still only fifteen but it was older he was getting, not younger. Blast, it would be very inconvenient if her best friend turned out to be a heart-throb. How would they get a minute's peace?

'Llew,' she said hesitantly.

'Chlo.'

'Everything's changing, isn't it?'

'Everything's always changing, Chlo, that's life.'

'I know. But . . . sometimes you don't *see* it changing, so you can pretend it isn't. Like all the summers we've had. But now . . . you've got a job, sort of, and my dad wants me to make a plan. I'll be eighteen next year. We can't afford college, of course. I'll need to get a job. What if . . . what if this is my last summer in Tenby?'

'What? No, it can't be. You won't stop coming, just because you're growing up? You'll still come to Tenby.' And he sounded like a child, like her brothers, for the first time since she'd known him.

'I want to. But what about when I'm working? I don't expect they give you three weeks off every summer, do they? And what about . . . ?' Chloe trailed off.

What about when she was dating someone? Engaged? Married? Suddenly all the things she had dreamed of for so long seemed within reach, but they would change her world as she knew it. How could she spend her summers with Llew then?

Iris had thought they were boyfriend and girlfriend. As they got older, more and more people would think it, she supposed, and no fiancé would like that. But somehow she couldn't say it. She didn't want to spoil their precious time together. More precious than ever if it was running out.

'Of course you'll come,' said Llew, frowning into the wind, his shoulders hunched inside his thick sweater. Chloe waited, knowing that with Llew whatever else he was thinking might follow in a minute or in a few days. The pesky wind kept wrapping Chloe's hair across her face like seaweed and ruffled Llew's mane so that it stood up all peaks and ridges like the top of one of her mam's meringues.

'Are you cold?' he asked.

'A bit.'

He held out one arm for her to snuggle up to him and she did. His arm lowered about her shoulders and they shared their bodies' warmth, although it wasn't *that* cold. No one was going to die of exposure. It felt as though they weren't huddling against the wind, but the future, with all its unknowable threats and promises.

*This is my life*, thought Chloe. *Beaches in Tenby and fields in Nant-Aur. Summers and winters and ginger beer and crisps. School and books and swimming and dancing and dreams . . . are any of those dreams going to come true? Are any of them meant to?*

She closed her eyes and laid her head against Llew's shoulder. She felt the solid warmth of his shoulder, the rough wool of his jumper under her face. She felt the sand cool underneath her legs and heard the whisper of waves and grasses. She relaxed. She was here in the dunes, where she belonged.

Suddenly Llew pulled her to her feet. 'Come on then, let's get you properly warmed up.'

'What do you mean?'

'Let's have a swim. Nothing like a nice bracing swim to get the circulation going.'

'But I haven't got my cossie!' she protested.

'That's never stopped us before!'

It was true, it hadn't. Llew was tearing off his jumper, his shirt, his new long trousers and stood in the moonlight shivering. 'Come on, girl! I'm freezing here! You haven't gone all ladylike on me, have you? You're not turning into one of those girls that's all, "Oh, my hair! Oh, my lipstick?" You're not *chicken*?'

'*No!*' Chloe hotly denied this shameful accusation and yanked her jumper over her head. Then she unfastened her dress. She stepped out of it and stood next to him in her bra and pants, chin jutting.

'Well now. I'm not chicken, am I? But *you* are if I beat you to the sea!' And she ran hell for leather over the sand, her hair a silver ribbon streaming behind her. A shell or a crab spiked her foot, causing her to lollop as she ran, making Llew roar with laughter behind her. But she got there before him, just. The lacy froth licked at her ankles, and she plunged on. *Duw*, it was cold! Cold like a sledgehammer. But she wasn't a chicken; just let Llew Jones say she was.

\*

Later that night, Chloe lay in bed, staring at the moon through the attic window. She couldn't stop thinking about the future. She knew everyone grew up but she didn't want anything to change. Despite the minor inconveniences of being poor, of being unable to learn to dance, of Megan and Alma, who had a happier life than she did?

Perhaps she and her husband could live in Tenby. That would be a dream, wouldn't it? Llew could get married too and the four of them could visit each other and have dinner parties and go on trips on the weekends. She and Llew's wife could be best friends and help each other adjust to their wifely responsibilities and have fun together. The men would have their jobs and come home in the evenings and they would talk about their day together, all four of them. Well, they probably wouldn't eat together *every* night. Sometimes they would want time alone, as couples, a romantic evening in front of the fire, holding hands; perhaps a whisky for him, a gin and tonic for her.

She imagined herself some years from now looking at the clock and exclaiming, 'Good heavens, is that the time?' She would run to change into a pretty frock and brush her hair and put a little make-up on. She would have filled the house with vases of fresh flowers and she would have baked. And when Llew came home, he would look around and say . . .

Wait, *what*? Llew?

*Don't be daft, Chloe, he's married to the other one*, she scoffed to herself. There's absent-minded she was. So Chloe's husband, let's call him . . . Tab, like Tab Hunter – now *there* was a dream-boat – would look around and say . . . But try as she might she couldn't really imagine how Tab might look or what sort of thing he might say.

# Nora

— ❧ —

'Help me decide!' moaned Nora. 'This is impossible!'

Kaitlin surveyed the scene with interest. Nora was sitting in the middle of the sitting room floor with clothes spread out all around her.

'Is this a new kind of wardrobe?' asked Kaitlin, stepping over some skirts and sitting cross-legged on the sofa. 'A wardrobe that in all things resembles a floor?'

Nora cast them a rueful glance. 'I've got to choose what to use for my quilt! They're all so gorgeous and they all have these great stories behind them. But Molly says no more than five.'

'Molly with the gorgeous husband?'

'Molly with the gorgeous husband. He texted me this morning by the way. Got my number off Molly. Wants me to go for a walk with him next week.'

Kaitlin raised one eyebrow.

'Stop it! He's just friendly. He's a Kiwi.'

'Even so. I'd like to see this Logan for myself. And his sultry needleworking wife. There's something off with this scenario and I can't figure it out from the information you're giving me.'

'I think so too,' sighed Nora. 'I don't *want* anything to be off because not only do I like *him*, I really like Molly. I think we could be friends – but not if there's some weird dynamic with her husband.'

'When's patchwork?'

'This afternoon at three. How will I pick just five of these by then?'

'My friend, I know nothing about patchwork and I couldn't care less. But I *will* meet you from class, check out the siren and only be twenty minutes late to work.'

'Don't get fired on account of nosing into my life, will you?'

'No better cause.'

Nora arrived early and, as she'd hoped, found Molly alone, setting out the chairs.

'I'll give you a hand,' said Nora, starting to unstack them.

'Thanks.' Molly beamed at her. 'It's lovely you're enjoying the classes so much, Nora. You must come round for dinner one night. If you'd like to, that is. I realise two screaming kids doesn't make for everyone's dream scenario.'

'My best friend at home has three. I'm hardened to it.'

'Perfect. I'd suggest something like the cinema – I love films – but it's so hard to get away with the children. I'll check the calendar and get back to you.'

'I'd love that.'

It was partially true. All other things being equal, Nora really would have liked to be friends with Molly. But this thing with

Logan was bugging her more and more. She took a deep breath, hoping she wasn't making a mountain out of a molehill.

'Can I ask you something, Molly?'

'Sure.' Molly started unpacking needles and thread from her sewing box. She took out the sheets of sandpaper they used to make templates because it gripped the fabric.

'Logan mentioned a cliff walk next week—'

'He did? I'm so pleased.'

'Really? Oh good. Well, I just wanted to check, he said you weren't really up for going and . . . well, I didn't want you to miss out. I mean, it doesn't have to be next week.'

'Oh, don't wait for me. If I had some spare time, I'd much rather go to the cinema. Walking's Logan's thing. And yours too I gather.'

'Yes.'

'Brilliant! So you should definitely go.'

Nora started unpacking her own things. So now she had no reason to say no and she would be invited to dinner too. God! Were they after a threesome? She glared suspiciously at Molly, but she looked so wholesome and happy, with her blue floral hairband and dangly blue earrings, that it hardly seemed likely. It was clearly Nora's own issue. She'd grown more used to working than socialising. They were just normal, friendly people. They had a strong marriage with no jealousy or suspicion to mar it. That was good.

True to her word, Kaitlin appeared outside the community hall at half past four. Nora was last out, walking with Molly, listening to her chatter about Johnny Depp. She introduced her two friends and they chatted for a while, Kaitlin and Molly finding three mutual connections in five minutes. It was the Welsh way, Nora had learned.

When Kaitlin finally remembered she had a job to go to, Nora walked her there. Kaitlin shrugged her shoulders. 'I don't get it, I freely admit. She's lovely. I get why you like her, I get why she's married to a gorgeous guy. Maybe you're right. Maybe it's a Kiwi thing. Maybe he just really is that friendly.'

Nora frowned. 'Wait a minute, say that again? Did you just say *maybe I'm right*? I couldn't have heard you properly.'

'Oh, shut up. It has to happen sometimes.'

# Chloe

'What was it like kissing Ron, Chlo?'

Chloe looked up in astonishment. She and Llew were lying on their fronts on the sand. She was reading *Girl's Crystal*, a pot of Astral beside her. The picnic was between them, singing a siren song, but they'd made each other promise they'd save it till at least half past twelve. They always dived into their food too soon and went hungry in the afternoon.

Llew had been reading. Now apparently he was on one of his strange trains of thought that started from who knew where and led to somewhere even odder.

'What on earth made you think of that now? I've barely laid eyes on Ron these two years. If you're thinking of trying it, I don't think you're Ron's type.'

'Ha ha. No, I was just wondering . . . if kisses are different with different people?'

'Why are you wondering that? You're too young to think about that.'

'I'm fifteen. You were fifteen when you kissed Ron.'

'It's different for girls, we mature quicker.'

'Is that right?'

'*Yes*, it's right! Why? You haven't kissed anyone, have you?'

'Yes. Sandra Sharples last Christmas.'

'Never! Well, there's a quick starter you are! And what became of Sandra Sharples?'

'Oh, nothing. She was only here for a week. She went home again. To Llandeilo or Llandovery or somewhere. Pretty girl.'

'Oh. And do you miss her?'

'No. So have you kissed anyone besides Ron?'

'No, I haven't. Llew, why are you thinking about all this?'

Llew shrugged. She'd grown used to his new height and sophistication over the last two weeks. He was still too thin, thought Chloe, assessing him with a motherly eye, but he was a good-looking boy now, very nice indeed.

'Iris came round last night. Wanted me to kiss her. I said no. It made me think.'

'Iris . . . ? How did she know where you live?'

'I suppose Chris told her. It's not a secret.'

'So she just knocked on your door and said, "Leonard Jones, I want you to kiss me"?'

He grinned. 'No, not like that. Dad answered the door and she said "Good evening, Mr Jones. I'm Iris Evans. I've come to see if Leonard would like to go for a walk."'

'She never! She's a fast piece!'

'I said no. I said I had pictures to develop. She asked if she could watch and I said no, I never let anyone in my darkroom – which is true, except for you of course – and then Dad offered her a cup of tea! So I had to stay a bit. Then he went out to do something and she leaned across the table all stare-y and weird and said, "Leonard, would you like to kiss me?" So I said no.'

'Just no?'

'Yes.'

'Not, "I'm sorry, Iris, I'm very flattered but I don't think it's a good idea"?'

'Just no. Then she said, "But *I'd* like to kiss *you*. You won't be ungentlemanly and say no, will you?"'

'Ooh, cunning! So what did you say?'

'I said it would be ungentlemanly to kiss her as I didn't want her to be my girlfriend. She looked a bit surprised, then my dad came back and I went to the darkroom.'

Chloe rolled onto her back, laughing. 'Oh Llew, you are funny. I wish I could've seen her face. I don't want her to be hurt but you are *so* straightforward!'

'Isn't that a good thing?'

'Yes! But maybe it doesn't *feel* good to Iris. I bet she's so embarrassed now, poor dab.'

'I don't think so, look.'

Chloe twisted her neck and saw Iris's distinctive pink shoes step-stepping over the sand towards them. She groaned. 'Oh *no*. She's going to want to stay for lunch—'

'Hide the cake,' said Llew, fumbling in the bag. 'Quick, shove it under your towel.'

'Is that all you can think about? Our lovely afternoon's going to be spoiled and all you can say is "hide the cake"?'

'Dig a hole under your towel. Put the cake in. Cover it up!'

'Llew, don't be silly! Stop it, get off!' He was shoving the cake, wrapped in greaseproof paper, towards her and she had no time to dig a hole. She flipped the towel over it and sat with her legs curved around the bump.

'Hello, sun bunnies!' shrilled Iris. 'What a lovely day! Mind if I sit down for a minute? I've got all this nasty sand in my shoes.'

'That's because it's a beach,' said Llew.

'Why don't you take your shoes off, Iris?' Chloe asked politely. 'You might find it more comfortable.'

'Well, silly Chloe! Then I'd have sand all over my feet, wouldn't I?'

'But you can just brush them off after.'

'Well, I'm not lucky like you. I don't have a big strong boy to carry towels and such for me. Oh! Is that a picnic? Oh, you *are* lucky things. I'm starving and I don't have a penny spare after going to the cinema with Christine last night.'

'Where is Chris?' asked Chloe, hoping to divert her.

'Helping her mother with something. She'll be along in an hour or two. Aren't I lucky to run into you? I do hate being on my own, don't you? Although I don't know why you two are always on the beach. I prefer a nice shop, me. What sandwiches have you got? Oh, do say ham! That's my favourite.'

'Egg,' said Chloe, 'but we haven't got very much, actually—'

'Oh nonsense! Look at the size of this bag! Shall we tuck in then? It's twenty past twelve.'

Iris plumped herself down between them and started unwrapping sandwiches. Chloe looked at Llew and Llew looked at Chloe.

*Hurry up, Chris*, thought Chloe, and surreptitiously dug a hole in the sand behind her with one hand. Then she dropped the cake into the hole and covered it with her towel. Llew gave her a wink of approval.

# Nora

---

The following Monday, Nora's walk with Logan was rained off. When she pulled back the curtains to see grey lances plunging into the sea, she didn't know whether to feel relieved or disappointed. Certainly a walk would have been lovely. As for seeing Logan . . . well, that was complicated of course. But she was geared up for it and wanted to get it over with. She just wanted to feel reassured that his intentions were strictly honourable and find her own attraction to him vanished. At least one of those things seemed unlikely.

Her phone buzzed. Logan cancelling, probably. Yes, Logan.

Hey Nora, lovely day for it! Not that I'm a fair weather walker or anything but shall we take a rain check?! Can I take you to lunch instead so I can still see you and stay dry? x

Oh, for heaven's sake! This was ridiculous! A walk was one thing. Two people with a genuine shared interest. But lunch? Just for the sake of seeing her? That was a date, right? He'd even done the thing where he went to the trouble of changing the capital X that automatically appeared after a question mark to a small one, so it didn't seem so . . . so *kissy*!

If he were single, she'd be over the moon right now. But he wasn't. He was married. To her new friend, who was lovely. And suddenly Nora was angry. This wasn't fair on her and it wasn't fair on Molly. She grabbed the phone, all sorts of furious responses running through her head. Then she paused. Went to make a cup of coffee before replying. She didn't want to say something she'd regret later.

She stared out of the kitchen window while she waited for the kettle to boil, wafts of basil and coriander dancing about her. The tiles were cool beneath her bare feet. This really *was* ridiculous. She was forty, not fifteen. But that was the problem with being out of the dating game so long: you forgot how to handle things like this.

*I am equal to every situation. I always handle things well.*

Nora firmly believed that honesty was the best policy, in love as in all things. Not that this was *love* of course . . .

She couldn't go another week or more with this uncertainty. She marched upstairs before she lost her resolve and set her anger aside. Facts, not feelings. That was how she'd dealt with her job all those years.

Hi Logan. Not quite comfortable with lunch. It feels a bit datey and you are married. I hope you understand.

Halfway down the stairs another buzz made her stomach swoop. That was quick! Had she made things worse? She ran back up.

I didn't realise you knew. I'd like to explain. A quick coffee at least to clear the air?

He didn't realise she *knew*! Did he suppose it made her feel better that he had been trying to pull the wool – or rather the patchwork – over her eyes? What a piece of work! How long could he hope to continue a deception like that in a small town? And how *could* he explain? She'd seen the obvious affection between them, the way he helped out with her projects, was hands on with the children . . .

Nora had found herself wondering, after the fact as usual, why Molly had talked about her 'screaming kids'. Hadn't Logan said they were twelve and sixteen? Why *couldn't* Molly leave them to go to the cinema at that age? But perhaps the kids had behavioural difficulties. Perhaps they were slightly autistic. Or maybe they were just really spoilt. Maybe that put a strain on things. Not that *that* was an excuse.

Still, a quick coffee to clear the air . . . It would be good – if nerve-wracking – to hear his story, and make her own position plain. Then her conscience would be clear. She wasn't going to hide from him.

Good idea. 11 as planned? Where?

'Well done, Nora, well done,' she muttered, then went downstairs again. She heard another text come through but drank her coffee and washed up the cup, before checking her phone.

To her relief, the café was central, crowded and slightly smelly thanks to a large, damp Labrador. However, when she walked in and saw him, her heart swept right through her chest. He looked so handsome in a navy jumper and jeans. He was wearing glasses to read something on his phone and he looked very serious, almost nervous. On such a big guy it was somehow endearing. And the glasses made him look, if possible, even sexier . . .

But that was not the point! She had come here to put the record straight. He might be unbearably gorgeous, but if he went about making moves on his wife's friends he was also arrogant and uncaring, which were *not* attractive qualities.

Even so, she faltered in the doorway. She watched as a waitress offered him a top-up. She was only about eighteen but Nora could tell by the way she looked at him that she thought he was handsome too. A sort of shy admiration, all confused by the fact that he was old enough to be her father. And Logan smiled at her kindly as he shook his head.

*All my relationships are straightforward and happy. I always know what to say. I am equal to any situation.*

She took a deep breath and pulled back her shoulders. Now or never.

'Hi,' she said as she approached his table, kicking herself

because her voice came out husky. It was nerves, of course, but she sounded like a bunny girl.

'Hi,' he said, with a brief, self-conscious smile. 'Thanks for coming. I hope we didn't get off on the wrong foot. I haven't intended any harm, truly.'

Nora sat down. She had already decided not to jump in with the accusations but it was hard . . .

'I accept that,' she said, doubtfully. 'I don't want to make a mountain out of a molehill. I just . . . wanted things to be clear . . . I didn't want to jump to the assumption that you . . . that you . . .' It felt impossibly vain to say, *that you fancied me.*

'I thought you just wanted to be friends,' she tried again, 'you, me and Molly. I thought that would be . . .' *weird, complicated, difficult* '. . . nice. But then I got your text today and it did seem as though you might want a little more than friendship.'

'And you obviously don't.'

'Well, *no*! God! Of course not!'

He recoiled a little. 'Jeez! All right. You don't mince your words, do you?'

'Well, no. But I thought it would be better than having a misunderstanding. So where do we go from here?'

'Again, to the point! I don't know. It doesn't have to be a big deal, does it? I mean, I'm a grown-up, I can handle it.'

Nora frowned. This was bizarre. It was as though he were perfectly entitled to ask her out!

'Can I just ask you one thing, though?' he went on, tapping his fingertips on the table. 'Is it *just* because I'm married?'

'Well, of *course* it's because you're married! Not *just* because you're married! That's a pretty big deal, wouldn't you say?'

He gave a small shrug. 'Well, yes and no.'

'Yes and *yes* in my world. Or do you have an open marriage? In which case I still wouldn't be interested by the way, call me old-fashioned.'

'I do! I call you very old-fashioned. I mean, it's not like it means anything any more. It's only a marriage in name now, as a matter of fact.'

'Oh, that old chestnut. I suppose in a minute you're going to say, "My wife doesn't understand me."'

'Well, I wasn't going to say that. But she doesn't. I don't understand her either. That's what's been so sad the last few years. But these things happen, and we stay friends for the kids. It hasn't been easy but I don't see how we could have handled it better under the circumstances.'

'Well, I suspect going out looking for an affair won't help, for a start.'

He looked at her incredulously. 'An affair? That hardly seems the right word.'

'Well, OK, I know it was only lunch but still. And what about *me*? Didn't it occur to you that this might be the last thing *I* need? But of course, you don't know anything *about* me!'

He spread his hands in a plea for peace. 'You're right. I don't. But . . . forgive me . . . that was sort of the point of asking you to lunch. So we could get to know each other.'

Nora raked both hands through her hair, feeling like a fly

bumping into glass. Why was he making her feel as though she were somehow the one being inconsiderate?

'I don't know what to say, Logan,' she said at last, wishing he wasn't so desperately handsome. And *endearing*. 'We're obviously not going to see eye to eye on this. Can we just leave it, please? Altogether.'

He curled a hand around his glasses and tucked them into a coat pocket. 'Sure. If that's what you want. No worries.'

'Good.'

'Good.'

'Right then. I'd better go.'

'Yeah. I suppose Molly told you?'

Nora snorted. 'I suppose she might feel entitled to mention it.' Although Molly *hadn't* actually told her, she realised.

'Only she's normally so good about minding her own business, that's all. I just wish I could've explained it to you myself.'

'Minding her own business? Are you kidding? Logan Davies, you're outrageous. Why *should* she make it easy for her husband to hit on other people?'

'What's Andy got to do with this? He wouldn't . . . Oh!'

Nora saw light dawning on his face. She was just one step behind him. *Oh.*

'Who's Andy?' she asked in a small voice.

Logan laughed. 'Oh Nora, in about five seconds you are going to feel so embarrassed. I feel really bad for you. Andy is Molly's husband.'

'I thought *you* were Molly's husband!'

'Er, no. I'm her brother-in-law. Andy's my brother. Step-brother actually but we're really close. I'm not Logan Davies. I'm Logan Parry.'

'Oh God.' Nora buried her face in her hands. He was right. She was mortified. She'd just said to him that . . . she'd basically just accused him of . . . but wait, he *was* married. He'd said as much!

'So who's *your* wife?'

'OK, so now we're back to the conversation I'd hoped to have with you over lunch. My wife is Naomi. She's in New Zealand, with our kids. We're halfway through a divorce, expecting the papers to come through in a few weeks. It's all very amicable, though sad, like I said. We've been separated a year and a half and I came to Wales a month ago, around the same time as you, I gather. She's been dating for a few months now. I haven't seen anyone else since we split. This was my first date in a long time. Would have been.'

'Oh.' Nora's face flooded with heat. 'Do I look like a beet-root?'

'Yeah. It's pretty funny.'

'Oh God. I thought you wanted to cheat on Molly or that you had an open marriage, or that you were a sociopath. Oh. I *wondered* why Molly said she had screaming kids, when you said they were twelve and sixteen.'

'Mine are. Molly's on the other hand are six and three.'

'I'm so embarrassed. I'm *so* embarrassed. I'm sorry, Logan. Obviously you'll never want to speak to me again because I'm clearly a mad person. I'll just leave you to get on with your day – and your life – in peace . . . I'm sorry about the divorce by the way, and I'm glad you're doing OK, and, um, I wish you all the best. Truly. OK, bye.'

All this while Nora had been standing and putting her coat on and fumbling in her pockets for change only to realise that in her state of high tension she'd come out without any money at all.

'Um, I don't have my purse. I don't suppose you could . . . just until I can pay you back? I'd give it to Molly. You wouldn't have to see me.'

Logan roared with laughter. 'Wait!' he gasped, reaching out and grabbing her hand. 'Wait till I can breathe again! So you want me to pay for your coffee?'

'Yes. Unless they trust me to come back with it. They probably will. I've been in here a few times.'

'No, that's fine, I'm happy to splash out.' He looked at the menu. 'Two forty on you. Only . . . isn't it a bit . . . *datey*?'

'No!' fumed Nora. 'This was not a date!'

'As you made very clear.'

'I mean, this isn't what I'm like on a date!'

'I'm relieved to hear that! For the sake of men everywhere.'

She sank back into her chair, realising that she didn't actually want to go anywhere. But Logan had his arms folded across the table, his face on his arms and his shoulders were heaving. Such broad shoulders. Such broad *single* shoulders. And she had just called him a sociopath.

'Stop it!' she said. 'Logan, stop laughing!'

'I'm *crying*!' he wailed through his arms.

'You're crying? Oh no! Logan, sit up, look at me. What's wrong?' Oh God, maybe he had a personality disorder.

'I said, I'm *trying*! Not crying, you lemon. You startle easily, don't you?'

'I'm from London! What do you expect?'

He took a deep breath and grinned at her. 'Nora?'

'What?'

'Can I please just take you to lunch?'

# Chloe

'Chloe, will you go to the dance with me?'

They were crabbing on the rocks at the near end of the South Beach. Chloe was bent over, backside in the air, frowning in concentration. Her face was red, her net poised over a clear amber pool. She could see movement in there, definite wavy movement in the shadows . . .

'Hang on,' she said. Here it came . . . here it was . . . and swipe! Down went her little red net and the crab was caught.

'Look, Llew, look! It's a big one. Oh, look at all his eyes! Doesn't he look furious?'

'Not sure crustaceans experience emotions, actually.'

'Look at his little claws going! Oh, I can't bear it, I'm going to put him back. Hang on.'

'I'm hanging on.'

'There. Back in the water. Nice to meet you. Bye, Mr Crab!'

'Chloe, are you sure you're going to be eighteen next year?'

'Well, I like to see them. They're so interesting, aren't they? What were you saying?'

'Will you go to the dance with me?'

'Well yes! I mean, I'll be there, you'll be there, we'll be together.'

'I mean, as my date.'

'Your date?'

Chloe sat on the rocks and looked up at him, puzzled. Standing between her and the sun he was a long leggy silhouette. 'What do you mean? We're friends. So how can it be a date?'

He came to sit next to her. 'Iris has asked me, so I told her I already had a date. So I have to take someone or I've lied to her. There isn't anyone else I want to go with. Can we just *call* it a date, at least?'

'Well, if you like, if it's to save you from Iris.'

'Thanks, Chloe.'

Chloe was looking forward to the dance more than ever this year. Compared with last year, when she had missed the whole thing, when she had been covered in pox and feeble, she felt tanned and strong and full of life. She hoped calling Llew her date wouldn't give people the wrong impression. In practice it wouldn't make any difference. He'd still call for her at Kite Hill. They'd still walk down with Megan and whichever of her friends were around.

Richard wouldn't be with them this year for he was no longer a Tenby Teen. He'd been promoted from trainee manager to assistant deputy manager and was suddenly very much the man about town. Whenever Llew and Chloe bumped into him, which was surprisingly often given that he had a full-time job, he handed them a coin. 'Buy yourselves an ice cream,' he would say, in parody of a jolly uncle.

'Shift work,' he said, when Chloe asked him cheekily whether he was ever actually in the hotel. 'Something rather nice about going to work when others are heading home, going out when others are just starting work. A fish against the tide, a bird against the breeze.'

Chloe and Megan got ready by themselves this year. When Chloe asked Megan about the other girls, she shrugged. 'I wasn't in the mood,' she said. 'They're so childish they make me tired. I'll see them there.'

Chloe was a bit worried. How had Megan gone from being the social queen of her little world to someone who'd rather prepare for a dance alone? Perhaps Tenby seemed like a come-down after France. At least Megan was still *going* to the dance, thought Chloe, stepping into her pink dress.

'Same old thing again,' said Megan.

So when Llew knocked on the door at a quarter to seven, he found he had two ladies to escort. If he was rattled, he didn't show it.

He handed Chloe a bunch of flowers: a gorgeous-smelling haze of buddleia and oleander with ragged stems, and even two or three pink roses, of a very distinctive shade which she recognised as coming from Mr Dodd's garden – the scratches on Llew's hands testified to nefarious flower acquisition.

'Oh Llew, thank you, they're wonderful,' she said, burying her face in them and breathing deeply.

'I do apologise, Megan,' Llew said. 'If I'd known I had the pleasure of escorting you as well, I would have brought you some but I assumed you'd be with your friends.'

'I will be, soon enough, and you're not my escort,' she retorted, then added, 'but thank you for the thought.'

The photograph that Uncle Harry took that night showed Chloe glowing and clutching her flowers, Megan scowling and Llew between them, just one lock of his slicked-back hair sticking up in an early bid for freedom.

As they walked to the dance, Llew took out his old-fashioned manners, polished up for the occasion. He was attentive to both girls and Chloe was touched by the effort he made with her cousin, whom he'd never particularly liked.

Outside the Fountains, they found the whole crowd waiting for them in rainbow dresses. Only Alma was already inside, glued to her fiancé, in case anyone should fail to realise that she *had* one. When Iris saw them she muttered to Chloe, 'So you and Leonard *are* an item after all?'

For Llew's sake Chloe said, 'I suppose so, yes,' running her hand up and down his arm possessively – and rather daringly she thought! Perhaps she had it in her to be a femme fatale after all. Llew smiled down at her and she thought they were doing a very good impression of a couple.

Perhaps too good. An hour or so before the end of the dance Chloe realised that although she had danced with almost every boy there, no one had asked her for a date, no one had asked her to go outside. As she had feared, everyone had the wrong impression.

Then again, she wondered, who would she *want* to date? She'd already kissed Ron and whilst it had been all right – sort of – she didn't long to repeat it. He was a nice boy but imagine a lifetime of silent dinnertimes! No thank you. Graham was out of the question because he was Alma's brother. If he were the greatest catch in Wales, there was no way she was having Alma Pendle as a sister-in-law. Michael Everley was handsome as ever but she'd never really felt comfortable around the older boy and besides, she wouldn't like to find out what Megan would say if Chloe had designs in that direction! Even though Megan never so much as looked at him any more. Brian Walters was too short, bless him. Oh, Chloe was short enough herself, but that didn't mean she wanted a husband who scurried to keep up with his friends. Owain Hughes was sweet but stupid. He still thought Bristol was in Wales and no one could disabuse him of it. Chloe had no wish to do all the thinking in her marriage; half would be just right. Well, who would have thought the choice would be so poor in Tenby? Then there was Rhys Jenkins, laughing with his friends. Chloe watched him critically. He was clever in school, according to Llew, he was decent looking and generally good humoured. She wouldn't want a grumpy one. Rhys then . . . was *he* her best bet?

She could walk over there right now and say, 'What's so funny then, Rhys Jenkins?' He would ask her to dance again . . . and then what? Did she want to kiss Rhys Jenkins? No, she did not.

Did she want to *marry* Rhys Jenkins? She sighed. Surely love couldn't be arrived at by a process of unenthusiastic appraisal like this? (Although looking at Alma she wouldn't be surprised if that turned out to be the case.)

She was hopeless. She would never get a husband if Llew was the only boy she ever wanted to be around. Honestly, anyone would think that they . . .

A thought struck her. She swallowed. If love couldn't be measured out like ingredients for a pie, if it couldn't be controlled and chosen . . . if she only ever wanted to be with Llew and he only ever wanted to be with her . . . what did that *mean*?

A strange feeling crept over her, half dread, half delight. He had looked so proud tonight, arriving as her date. Acting coyly with him in front of Iris had come naturally to her. It was as if he . . . as if they . . . but that was impossible! He was like a little brother to her. Except, he wasn't. She had spent their entire friendship reflecting how he was nothing like her brothers. They always compared unfavourably with Llew. *Everyone* compared unfavourably with Llew. But that didn't mean that . . . it wasn't the same as . . .

Chloe grew very hot and yet icy at the same time. This was no good! She couldn't marry *Llew*! He was fifteen! And even if she waited – *years* – for him to grow up, what then? A romance? What if it went wrong? What if it ruined their friendship? If that happened, it would be the end of the world. She *mustn't* fall for Llew because she couldn't bear life without him; couldn't *bear* it.

# Nora

They went to the restaurant on the South Beach that was called, appropriately enough, the South Beach Bar Grill. Nora had walked past it many times but never gone inside. It was all panoramic glass windows and scrubbed wooden floors, surrounded by sand and sea. She had always felt it was a place to save for a special occasion.

In the pouring rain it was very romantic. They sat in the window, looking out at sand that had darkened to the colour of beeswax and an ocean like a heap of tarnished swords.

'Do you have plans later? Me neither. Good,' said Logan.

Over pre-lunch cocktails Nora lost some of her embarrassment about the mix-up and Logan explained why he had come to Wales.

'Naomi and I tried really hard for a long time to pretend that everything was OK. When the strain of pretending finally got to us, we became monsters. I'm not kidding you. All the small ways two people can torture each other when they're under the same roof but not in love any more? We found them. When we finally decided to throw in the towel, it took another year

*The Hourglass*

to really get behind our decision because we didn't want to tell the kids. We did it last year. Brendan was fifteen and Sylv was only eleven . . .' he shuddered. 'Worst thing I've ever had to do, by far. But at least by then Naomi and I were united in the relief of ending it. So we did a good job of explaining, I think. All the nasty things we said were only between ourselves, they never heard them.

'I moved out and I've been living in an apartment in Wellington Harbour for the last eighteen months – it's great for work, I run a sailing school there. Naomi and the kids are still in Porirua but it's only half an hour away and I'd head up there most days to see them. Things were working pretty well, but I needed a break. Apart from the fighting and the divorce, I'd been working really hard building up my business for a decade. I was exhausted, to put it simply. So I discussed it with the kids and they gave me permission for a holiday!' He grinned.

'I came over here for a few months, to visit my bro and Mol. It's great. Andy works on the rigs – the oil rigs – so he's away for days at a time. I can help Molly with the children and when he's back we make the most of family time. In between I just kind of . . . wander about and hit on women. Well, you.' He smiled. 'The kids are coming over to spend August with me then we'll fly back together. This trip is the best thing I ever did, Nora. It was getting hard to remember who I was underneath the whole dad, work, divorce thing. Being with Andy, getting out on the coast, it's better than a year of therapy. Why are you smiling? You think I'm a wreck, don't you? You're not going to stay for lunch. You're going to finish that mojito and run.'

'No, I'm going to finish this mojito and order another one. I'm smiling because you sound like me. Oh, I don't have kids, or a divorce going on. But I've come here to recover from my life too. I'd buried myself under a pile of paperwork this high.' Nora raised her hand as high as it would go, way over her head. 'I *was* my job! Then I started having all kinds of anxiety so I had therapy and it helped, but only so far . . . Then I came here and . . . well, it just went away. I never would have thought it could be that simple but maybe sometimes things are!'

He considered. 'Yes. Maybe we're just not used to considering what we really want so we're taken by surprise when we do, and it works. So why Tenby? Oh, because your mum comes from here, right?'

'Nearby, yes, but the real reason is . . . well, it's a bit strange really . . .' But Logan was listening, and he'd been so open, so she told him about the day she resigned and the unprompted vision of a beach that appeared, then persisted in beckoning to her until she paid attention. 'It was *this* beach, actually,' she ended, looking out at the view and frowning. 'And now here I am having cocktails on it. Life can be very mysterious, can't it?'

'Hell yeah. Life has some fun with us all right.'

When the waiter came over, Nora ordered hake; Logan ordered risotto and a bottle of Sauvignon Blanc. 'I don't usually drink this much,' he said, 'but you make me a bit nervous.'

'I'm not really surprised after this morning,' muttered Nora, feeling a little light-headed herself, not being accustomed to the daytime cocktails.

'Not because of that, because I like you. It's nice to be with a beautiful woman again, even if it's not a date,' he teased. 'Cheers.'

Beautiful? Her? Then again – she caught her reflection in the glass – her hair was wet and plastered to her head, emphasising the heart-shape of her face, her eyes were big and bright. Why not?

'It could be a date if you want,' shrugged Nora offhandedly, clinking her glass to his. 'Now I know you're not married to Molly.'

He grinned. 'Aw, if I'd known it was a date I wouldn't have told you all the gory details, I'd have impressed you with tales of sailing my boat around Wellington Harbour and all the cool people I know and what a great guy I am!'

Nora smiled. 'True, and neither of us would have mentioned therapy yet—'

'Exactly! Though honestly, it's something I'm quite proud of. Everyone hits a wall at some point. It's what you do when you get there that matters, don't you think?'

'I do actually. So, Logan, tell me about your boat, tell me about your business . . .'

For two hours they sat and talked. Nora made him laugh with tales of her job, which turned out to be far more entertaining in the telling than it had been at the time. She told him about her amazing stroke of luck in meeting Kaitlin and moving into Jones's beautiful house. And about patchwork and yoga and the paintings in the attic and her gran. After lunch they shared a chocolate hazelnut tart and a pot of tea. They left half the wine.

'Too ambitious at our age maybe,' shrugged Logan. 'Do you want to take it home for your housemate?'

'I think I will.'

Nora gazed through the window. The rain made wrinkled worms on the glass and blew in soft clouds about the beach. A black dog raced across the sand, barking, its owner huddled into a red anorak. It was wonderful here. It was wonderful being with Logan. She didn't want to leave the restaurant but she supposed it was time.

'So, Nora, I know we haven't actually finished this date yet, but what are my chances of getting another? Do you still fancy that walk when the weather clears?'

She felt suddenly happy. 'That would be good.'

'Good.' He looked pleased and paid the bill. Since Nora didn't have her purse he didn't really have much choice.

The lacerating rain had eased and they stepped outside into a soft, cobwebby drizzle. Without debate, they started wandering along the beach.

*He's only here for a couple of months*, Nora told herself. *He lives on the other side of the world. He has children there and an important job and a life*. But still. She knew that this would seem the most romantic place in the world forever after this. She couldn't remember feeling this comfortable, yet this alight, with any man since . . .

But of course, there was no point comparing him with

Seth because when she had met Seth she had been so young, a different person. At that age you took love as your due, she reflected, expected it to drop on you like an apple from a tree. But to feel like this at forty, after years of disappointments, heartache and cynicism, to feel yourself coming alive again . . . there was a poignancy and a power to that. All those years of thinking that love didn't exist, or wasn't important, that men were bastards and women didn't need them, and games and rationalisations and armour . . . all swept away in a wash of rain and emerging light.

He tucked her arm through his and they meandered, quiet for the most part, looking at shells and driftwood, watching scrapping birds, taking in the sweep of the horizon and the shape of Caldey Island, only barely visible in the misting rain.

'Been out there yet?' he asked.

'Not yet,' said Nora. When she had arrived it wasn't the season; the ferry ran from April to September. Now, somehow, suddenly, it was May. Time was passing faster than she liked.

'Fancy going sometime? Andy says it's worth a visit.'

She nodded. 'Kaitlin said it's special. Yes, let's go.'

She liked the height and breadth of him next to her. She liked the solid tread of his footsteps beside her and tucking herself against the navy blue shape of him. She liked the scent of his skin that reached her when the breeze blew the right way, the occasional bright-eyed glances he threw her. In fact, she liked Logan Parry very much.

When the tide turned, they walked back, unhurried. By

the time they reached the cliffs; the beach had narrowed to a buttermilk ribbon between the dunes and the frill of the white and grey sea. Logan stopped. Nora's hand slipped from his arm. He took both her hands and smiled at her.

She smiled back, tentatively. The soft rain blew about them and silvered his dark hair. He was giving her the look. The Look. She hadn't seen it for a long time but she knew what it meant. This tall, gorgeous man to whom she'd been madly attracted from the first minute was going to kiss her.

Their lips met, cool and damp with rain, soft and warm underneath. Nora's arms floated up of their own accord to wrap around his broad shoulders and he held her close. How long did that kiss last? Nora never knew afterwards. It felt as if they had stepped out of normal time. Eventually he stepped back and said, 'Wow.'

'Wow,' echoed Nora, not trusting herself to say more.

He took her hand and they walked back to town. Nora was relieved when he started pointing out the shops and bars he liked, normal little things that returned her feet gently to the pavement. Then they were back at the café where she had stood in the doorway that morning, watching him and wishing with all her heart that it might be different. And now it was.

The church clock struck four. Surely that was long enough for a first date? Except, it didn't *feel* enough. 'Do you want to . . . ?' said Nora at the same moment that he said, 'I don't suppose you want to . . . ?'

'You first,' he laughed.

'I was going to say, do you want to come in for a coffee or something? I only live two minutes from here. But you must have lots to do.'

'I have nothing to do. I was going to suggest another coffee in here, if only to erase the memory of the last one . . .' Nora grimaced. 'But your place is a much better plan.'

The wonderful thing was that he didn't seem to have any agenda. Nora remembered so many dates with men where they barrelled into her home and started an in-depth conversation about something dull like insurance, or looked around the flat assessing, like a builder, what needed to be changed. On one memorable occasion, her date just launched in and started a thorough snogging before she could so much as put the kettle on. This had quickly led to swift one-handed bra removal, a skill the man in question was clearly proud of and liked to utilise as often as possible. (As Jasmine always said, just because you *can* doesn't mean you *should*.)

With Logan it wasn't like that. They just stood in the hall for a minute looking around, a sense of possibility trembling between them. *Here we are*, it seemed to say. *We have this time together – how wonderful*. Wonderful irrespective of what they did or drank or talked about.

'It's really something,' he said at last.

She nodded. 'Come and see the rest of it. Tea? Coffee? Juice? I guess not wine,' she smiled, leaving the half-full bottle on the kitchen table.

'A juice would be great. Whatever you've got.'

Nora set a tray, the way she did for Gran, with napkins and biscuits on a plate, a glass jug of apple juice and two glasses. Logan smiled when he saw it and touched her arm. 'Nice. Thank you.'

He carried it upstairs and nearly dropped it when he saw the lounge. 'Holy shit! You've struck lucky and no mistake. What I wouldn't give to know this guy's story!'

'Me too.' Nora sat down in her customary seat at the window, scene of so much girl talk. It was funny having Logan's manly bulk in the chair opposite instead of Kaitlin's slender form and riotous red curls. After a while they moved onto the sofa where he kissed her again and they slid further down until she was almost lying on top of him and the rain furred the windows, obscuring the harbour. Nora hadn't snogged like this since she was a teenager!

They were interrupted by the sound of the front door opening and Kaitlin's voice in the hall.

'Hello? Nora? Anyone home?'

Nora sat up, panting slightly, and pushed her hair off her face. 'Up here, Kait!'

'I'm coming up. Just got to get these . . . boots . . . ouf . . . off! So guess what?' she carried on, her voice carrying easily. Kaitlin never saw being in different rooms as any deterrent to conversation. 'I ran into Molly in town and *guess what*?'

Nora and Logan exchanged a smile. 'What?' called Nora, mischievously.

'She was with this bloke, right, and it wasn't her husband. I mean, he looked nothing like the guy you've described. He had kind of light-brown shaggy hair and he wasn't that tall. They were holding hands and nuzzling. Yes, *nuzzling*!' Kaitlin's words were breathless as she ran up the stairs and burst into the lounge.

'So what do you make of *that*? Oh! Hello. Who's this? *Oh!*' she concluded, taking in two sets of ruffled hair and two flushed faces. 'You must be—'

'Logan,' said Logan, standing up to shake her hand. 'Molly's brother-in-law.'

Kaitlin looked at Nora.

'Yes,' Nora confirmed. 'It seems I got things a bit muddled.'

'The shaggy hair guy? The nuzzler? That's my bro, Andy.'

Kaitlin covered her face with her hands. 'I am so embarrassed!'

Logan grinned at Nora. 'It's like déjà vu,' he said. 'Kaitlin, it's a pleasure to meet you. I've heard a lot about you and I hope it's largely accurate.'

Kaitlin nodded. 'I can see why she likes you. Is that wine in the kitchen for me?'

# Chloe

School was over forever. Her exams were all finished. She was eighteen years old. Each of these facts seemed equally impossible to believe. It was 1958. She was old enough to become engaged, to get a job. When her mother was her age, she had given birth to Chloe!

Chloe still didn't know what she wanted to do with her own life. But at least the summer was taken care of. She was going to Tenby – not for the last time, she truly hoped. Then she would go home and spend the month of August working in a shop in Carmarthen. The shop was owned by a Mr Adams, a friend of her father's boss. Through the chain of news-sharing – some might call it gossip – that was the lifeblood of the area, he had heard that Daf Samuels' girl had grown up presentable and sensible and was looking for something to do with her life. He had several staff wanting time off in August and having Chloe there for a month would solve his difficulty. At the same time Chloe would gain some experience – and a little pay. Mr Adams was fond of solutions that helped all parties.

Chloe was glad to have a short-term plan that wasn't too drastically different from life as she knew it. She could live at home and go to work every day on the bus, and things wouldn't change *too* much, just yet.

*You baby*, she chided herself. *Where's that adventurous spirit you thought you had all those years ago when you dreamed of London and Hollywood? Now it comes to it you're frightened to leave home!*

It was a big world, Chloe knew, full of wonders and entice-ments. She just found it hard to imagine loving anywhere more than Tenby and Nant-Aur. But it was good to realise that she was lucky; that her life wasn't one she could leave without a backward glance. Yes, she was lucky, and loved.

Loved. Inevitably her thoughts turned to Llew. He did love her, she knew, and she loved him. She just didn't know exactly *how*. The dance had ended quite as normal last year, Llew walking Chloe and Megan home and saying a polite goodnight on the doorstep. The holiday too came to a typical close and Chloe returned to Nant-Aur with nothing more significant than his usual bear hug and a parting gift of a pretty shell bracelet to remember him by.

Even so, over the long months apart she had thought a lot about last summer. Somehow, while she helped her mother in the house and her father in the garden, then returned to school and went to her lessons and gossiped with Bethan and studied for her exams, the idea that there might be more between them than friendship had circulated and settled in her system.

*Might* be. She wasn't prepared to admit to more than that. But you heard the phrase 'childhood sweethearts', didn't you? It must exist for a reason. She still stumbled over the fact that he was younger, but it was only two years after all. Now it might feel funny but when they were twenty and twenty-two, or twenty-eight and thirty – ancient! – it would seem like nothing. Chloe shook her head in disbelief. That she was even entertaining the idea! On the one hand it felt terrifying. On the other, the thought of spending the rest of her life with Llew was the happiest prospect she could conjure – happier even than dancing in a Fred Astaire film.

Well, nothing could happen this year. Llew was still a boy, and she was only eighteen. Yes, girls her age were getting engaged, but plenty weren't. She just wouldn't hope so hard to meet someone else, that's all. What was meant to be would be, as her mam always said.

Auntie Bran saw her onto the Tenby bus at Carmarthen as always. Chloe was old enough to catch a bus on her own now, of course, but part of her enjoyed the tradition. And then she was off again, quite the young lady of the world.

The bus pulled up in Tenby with its familiar puff of brakes, the doors jerking back to let in the gull cries and ribbons of sea air. Chloe felt utterly contented. It was always summer in Tenby, she was convinced.

But her beaming smile fell when she saw Auntie Susan.

'What's wrong?' Chloe cried before they greeted each other. 'Is Llew all right?'

'He's fine, Chloe. Dear me, I must not have put on enough make-up! I wanted to give you a fine welcome!'

'Oh, you look lovely,' said Chloe. She did. She was wearing a smart navy suit, with a turquoise blouse and cream high-heeled shoes. 'You just look . . . worried. Are *you* all right?'

'We're all fine, dear, you mustn't worry. It's just that we've had a little . . . bother with Richard. He had a spot of trouble at work but it's all sorted now. Come along, dear. It's a cloudy day so I have hot chocolate waiting for us at home. Llew asked me to tell you that he'll call at six. He's working at the paper today.'

'Hot chocolate will be lovely, thank you.' Chloe was unsettled. Auntie Susan looked even more upset than she had when Megan was acting up. Being a mother really couldn't be easy, though Gwennan almost always seemed contented and calm. And surely Megan and Richard were a dream compared with Clark and Colin . . .

'We have a friend of Richard's staying this year, Chloe, I hope you don't mind. He'll stay in Richard's old room so you can still have the attic of course. It turns out that when he let his friends stay at the hotel these last two years, he shouldn't have.'

'Is that why he got into trouble?'

Auntie Susan hesitated. 'That's part of it, yes.' Chloe thought of Richard swanning around Tenby, always seemingly at leisure and attributing it to shift work. She'd always felt there was something funny about it. Perhaps he would work a bit harder now.

'Anyway,' continued Auntie Susan, 'Harry and I were rather hard on Richard, but he seems to be toeing the line now so we thought it might cheer him up to have a friend here.'

'That's a nice idea. I'm sure it will. What's his friend's name?'

'Iestyn Morgan. He was here a few years ago. Was that before you started coming to us?'

'No, I remember Iestyn. How . . . nice.'

A score of embarrassing memories flooded back. Meeting him for the first time covered in sand and scabs, her face smudged with chocolate. Fleeing, shrieking, from Red Sam. Hopping about like a fool, looking for secret tunnels. Reading outside his bedroom in an old nightie . . . Just as well she'd decided not to try to impress anyone this year.

A few minutes later she was sitting in the front room, hands wrapped around a pretty china cup, while Auntie Susan asked her about the exams and her job-of-sorts with Mr Adams in Carmarthen. While they were chatting they heard the front door open and voices in the hall.

'That'll be Megan and Iestyn,' said Auntie Susan, pausing with her cup raised halfway. 'Megan's been entertaining him while Richard's at work.'

*I bet she has*, thought Chloe with a smile. For once it didn't bother her. Megan was probably much more Iestyn Morgan from Cardiff's type anyway.

'Darlings! We're in here!' called Auntie Susan.

Megan came in first, looking even more drawn than her mother. Her hair was less bouncy too and her skin was pale. But she greeted Chloe with a hug and a kiss that were possibly the warmest they had ever shared. Chloe squeezed her hand and hoped they'd have a chance to catch up properly later on. After all, they weren't girls any more; perhaps, at last, they could properly be friends.

'Chloe, here's Iestyn,' said Megan. 'Iestyn, I don't suppose you'll remember my—'

'Little cousin Chloe from Nant-Aur!' finished Iestyn with that same warm grin and easy manner. He was as lovely as ever, and even more handsome. His russet hair had grown and fell in luxuriant waves to his shoulders, and he wore dark-rimmed glasses, which Chloe thought made him look breathtakingly intelligent. 'Of course I do. Hello, Chloe, wonderful to see you again. Goodness, you're all grown-up. And so *beautiful*!'

# Nora

May danced past and turned into June. Nora started to see the summer Tenby that her mother had known. Roses ballooned in the gardens. The town bustled with tourists; the beaches were no longer bare but crammed with happy people groaning in the relief of sun and salty air. The ecstatic screams of children plunging into icy water, darting in and out of caves, rang through the air. Those things must have been the same in the fifties, Nora thought.

Nora and Logan decided to see each other only every other day so that they could catch their breath between times and remember that this was, despite the fact that they were both in their forties, essentially a summer romance. They were both experiencing something they had long since ceased to expect out of life, something that surpassed even old, buried longings. It was intoxicating and it would have been easy to make this time all about the passion, they acknowledged. But they had to be mature and sensible. That plan lasted half a day.

It was wonderful, exhilarating, terrifying. Regular debriefs with Kaitlin were called for. The beginning stage of a relationship, though euphoric, was scary once you'd been burnt, they agreed. There were so many hopes and fears and you couldn't see clearly through the fog they created. And the lust! Well, that didn't help with keeping your head straight.

'Jennifer said it's all projection,' Nora remembered. 'We see what we want to see, at the beginning. I went out with this guy once, and all he wanted was sex. *Nothing* else. When I ended it he looked really let down and said he'd only asked me out because I looked so "up for it". The guy after *that* ended it because he heard me swearing one day. He said he'd thought I was very ladylike but clearly he was wrong! Two guys, two months apart. The same me. I asked Jennifer what they were seeing and she said, "What they wanted to see." I suppose we're the same, though. I looked at Seth and saw my forever person. I looked at Simon and saw . . . actually, I don't know *what* I saw then.'

'It's true,' agreed Kaitlin. 'I met this guy once and I was drawn to him because he was so different from me, you know. He wore suits and seemed really structured – I never saw him drunk like the other guys I knew. I guess I saw stability. But it got a bit scary really. He turned out to be this awful rigid person who raged every time he saw that I had a flaw. When I ended it he said he'd obviously been very wrong about me – he'd been attracted to me because I looked so *biddable*. That was his word.'

'*Control freak!*' said Nora in horror.

'Exactly. I'm so glad I got out fast. But *biddable*! Me! Would *you* say I look biddable?'

'About as biddable as a force-ten gale. See, this is what I mean. What if Logan thinks I'm biddable? Or perfect and ladylike? Or slutty? How do I know *what* he's thinking?'

'You don't. You just have to go forward blind for a while and trust your instincts. But if it's any comfort, he seems pretty sorted to me. I think he's a nice bloke.'

'Yeah,' sighed Nora. 'I think so too.'

One day when they'd been seeing each other about two weeks, Nora and Logan caught the boat to Caldey Island. They wandered hand in hand like two enchanted children between the peacocks, past the turreted Cistercian monastery, the ancient churches, the massive white lighthouse. They were helpless to resist the sweet clouds of air outside the chocolate factory and left with pockets bulging with white paper bags. They lay in a meadow of long grass and ladybirds, feeding each other chocolate and fudge.

In the middle of bliss, always a good time to start second-guessing everything, Nora remembered her conversation with Kaitlin and started to worry. *Surely* this was too good to be true?

'Logan?' she said, sitting up and fighting her desperate need to ask him if he thought she was biddable. There had to be a better way to phrase what she wanted to know.

'Yes, Nora?' He smiled, reaching up and gently removing a spider from her fringe. *Oh, so handsome. Please don't be a psycho.*

It took Nora a while to find an appropriate question. 'What

do you see when you look at me?' she asked. Her voice trembled a little.

Logan didn't scoff or make a flippant reply. He lay in the long grass, hands behind his head, and stared at the sky. Somewhere in the distance a horse whinnied. Nora stroked some red spikes of sorrel.

'That's a good question, isn't it?' he asked at last, rolling onto his side to look at her. 'It's a strange thing when you feel so drawn to someone you don't really know at all. When I look at you, Nora, I guess the first thing I see is a beautiful woman. I'm a man, what can I say? And I see a person with this whole history of achievements and joys and suffering that I'm only just starting to learn about. I see an enigma. And I see integrity, warmth and a real sparkle for life. That's what makes me want to keep getting to know you.'

Nora looked out to sea so he wouldn't see the tears in her eyes. What a beautiful answer. He saw her. Through the limited view their short acquaintance had given him, he saw her as clearly as he could.

'Is that OK?' he asked.

'Good answer,' she said in a muffled voice, still unable to look at him. She held her hand out behind her. 'Fudge, please.'

As the weeks went on they got to know each other better. It was Logan who pointed out to Nora that if she was looking for a future career direction, her passion for history might be a clue.

'I've never thought about history,' he marvelled, 'but you're even making me love it! You keep telling me these little things about everywhere we go and you make me want to learn. You could be a teacher, or a historian, or something.' And Nora again remembered applying for her old job because she thought history would be a nice faculty to work in. She thought of her well-thumbed local history, even now weighing down her bag. And she smiled.

Although it was hard to stay apart, the threads of the rest of her life weaved in and out of her time with Logan. Nora finished her sewing caddy and started on her quilt. She gave up on yoga forever but started a life-drawing class that she loved despite being astonishingly bad at it. She still hadn't met Kaitlin's mother, Anna – plans kept falling through – but Nora just assumed she was as laid-back as her daughter and it would happen when it happened. Danny turned thirty and celebrated with a Jamaican-style garden party, with a barbeque and curried goat and dancing. Stacie came to visit, looking vaguely stunned by her emergence from Life as Mother for three days.

Twice Nora went to Nant-Aur in the morning, drove Gran to Tenby, then drove her home in the early evening. On Gwennan's first visit, Kaitlin cooked for them in the house. The second time they had lunch in the hotel and Greg came out to say hello. Both times Logan joined them and Nora had never seen her grandmother so excited.

'He's wonderful, Nora, a real old-fashioned gentleman,' she whispered when Logan went to the loo.

It was the final straw for Nora. That both Stacie and her grandmother had met the man who was so important to her, while her mother didn't even know he existed, felt all wrong. The last months and years in London, her anxiety and lack of conviction, her nightmares and the tension with Jasmine, didn't seem real any more. She knew they had been, she knew she had gone through it, but she didn't want them defining the future. *Enough already*, as Logan would say. So she sat down one afternoon and wrote her mother a long and open email, at last.

Darling Mum,

How I miss you. It's been way too long.

Thanks for your last email. I loved reading the news and the photos are beautiful. Well done for mastering the paperclippy thingy! Please give my best to Faith. I'm grateful she's giving you such a great time.

Well, I've loads to tell you, so save reading this for a quiet hour on the terrazza – oh, and sit down. Mum, I'm in Tenby! I've been here a while now. You know I came for a few days after you went to Italy? Well, that's when I made friends with Kaitlin, whom I've mentioned. You'd love her. To cut a long story short, we're renting a house together. I've rented out my flat in Kingston for six months. I haven't forgotten that at some point I need to get a job again. Think of it as a sabbatical if you like.

The Kingston flat more than covers the rent here and the difference is my spending money. I don't need a lot. That said, I feel like I have more than ever before – the only thing missing is you! I've got a whole new lifestyle springing up.

Sea air and walks and hobbies and friends and time to think. I've seen quite a bit of Gran, of course. It's lovely! She talks about you a lot and seems happy to have me nearby. When you get back, please come and see us. I want to show you my life here, even if it is just a temporary one, and I want you to see Gran. I'll drive up and get you if you're tired after your travels.

I've been so worried about telling you, Mum. I've always sort of sensed that you don't like Tenby much. I don't know why and I suppose I could be wrong, but I don't think so. I didn't want to upset you. If I'm honest, I didn't want to make you angry. I've done so many things lately that seemed to. Like therapy, like quitting my job, like wanting to come to Tenby. But I'm glad I did all those things.

I'm trying all sorts, Mum. Lots of walking, like I told you. Yoga (NOT for me), patchwork, life-drawing, cooking (also not my strong suit . . .) and more.

Even that's not everything! Brace yourself! I have met a man! But before you get too excited I have to tell you it's unlikely to be a long-term thing. He is over from New Zealand, staying with family. He has children (two) in NZ so will be going back in September. My life, my loved ones, are here, so it's hard to see a future but after all, we've only been an item for a few weeks so that hardly seems the point. The point is, he's lovely, Mum!

As it stands, I'm here till September. I'm assuming that I'll then return to London, get a job and pick up where I left off.

That said, I would miss this place like crazy – and Kait and Gran. Logan too, of course, but he'll be on the other side of the world, so that's that.

Well, there's so much more I could tell you, about the amazing house I'm staying in, and Kaitlin's exuberant cooking, and so many things, but this may be a lot for you to take in. I hope you're not angry with me, Mum. I don't know why you should be. But I've always felt I'm treading on eggshells with you when it comes to Wales and I hope you won't think it's disloyal of me – somehow – to be happy here. I love you, Mum. Write back and tell me you'll visit in September, when you're back, before I leave. I've been wanting and wanting to share my impressions of this beautiful place with you. So here are some pics at last.

Love, Nora xxxxxxx

# Chloe

The harder Chloe tried to hold on to childhood for this one last summer, the more the magic formula eluded her. She felt like a toddler clutching a slippery bar of soap. The tighter she grasped, the more it popped up and shot away in unexpected directions.

Beautiful Megan was less beautiful. Poised Auntie Susan looked fraught. Smiling Uncle Harry smiled less, and Richard was nowhere in evidence, even though his friend was staying at Kite Hill. Most surprisingly, Megan seemed actually glad to see Chloe and confided the full story about Richard. He had skipped work countless times, blaming a mix-up on the rota, when in fact he had altered it himself; he had let his friends stay there for free, unauthorised; he had been found helping himself to the expensive gin or the best wines more than once, a small glass stashed away behind the bar. He had even, Megan whispered, looking unhappy, been implicated in the disappearance of some money, though there had been no proof that he was responsible.

'That's why he still has his job,' she admitted. 'If that had been traced back to him, he would've been out. But he's explained everything else away through ignorance or confusion and he's promised on his life to go straight from now on. He's on his last chance, though, we all know that. I worry for him. And I can't stand the gossip. You know what people are like.'

She shuddered, as if she had too much experience of unkind gossip. Megan had always been so bouncing and brazen, had rebuffed Chloe so often, that it had become hard for Chloe to think of her as someone with problems and feelings. Megan was always just her big cousin – glamorous, popular, *lucky*. But nowadays her eyes didn't sparkle as they used to and had faint brownish patches underneath them, so Chloe braved another rejection to ask if Megan was quite all right – apart from this business with Richard of course. For a moment Megan's face darkened in the old way and Chloe braced herself for a lashing of scorn, but then Megan sighed.

'I'm fine,' she said, 'just angry with Rich for getting himself in this pickle and not thinking about how it reflects on his family. On Mum and Dad. They deserve better.'

Even with Llew, Chloe felt awkward. Her musings about their relationship made her self-conscious around him for the first time. With every year he seemed less of a boy; his wise pronouncements and pensive air no longer seemed at odds with his age. He made no mention of their 'date' at last year's dance, nor gave any sign that anything might change between them. Which made Chloe work hard at being normal, when normal was exactly what you *shouldn't* have to work at.

Then there was Iestyn. His presence made the house at Kite Hill feel different too. As hard as she tried not to, Chloe found herself making an effort with her appearance. She didn't want to flirt with him, but pride made her want to look her best before someone so attractive and different.

Iestyn and Chloe were the earliest risers in the mornings, aside from Uncle Harry, who left early for work. They fell into conversation over toast and cereal or while they made tea and coffee. Iestyn dressed like no other young man she knew. His long legs were always clad in black jeans and ankle boots – unusual in the height of summer, though they somehow suited him. He wore loose shirts, usually cream or grey, always in some almost-sheer fabric through which the contours of his chest made themselves known to Chloe as she spread marmalade or lit the gas on the stove.

Somehow they fell into a routine of sitting together and talking at the start of the day. He asked about Chloe's life – a story quickly told, she felt – and told her about his own. Last year he had gone to America to stay with distant relatives. He talked a lot about the Beat Generation and enlightenment. Now he was at college in London, studying law. Chloe couldn't help but be impressed: think of all that learning! Think of being a channel for justice! One morning, he asked if he could buy her a milkshake sometime when she was free.

Chloe was nonplussed. She was *always* free – always or never, depending how you looked at it. The whole point of the holidays was freedom, freedom just to be. Long, blank days to fill up with Llew as they saw fit, moment to moment. Even his boss, Mr Aspell, fitted Llew's placement more or less around the time that Chloe was here. But how could she explain that she was promised to Llew for three whole weeks? It sounded silly as soon as it popped into her head. Nevertheless, she tried.

'I see a lot of Llew,' she said. 'I mean, that's what the holidays are for, really. I don't see much of anyone else.'

'No, Megan did mention that,' he said thoughtfully. 'I think she'd love to see more of you too. I don't want to disrupt your plans, only can't you spare even an *hour*? *One* day? I'd love to take you out, Chloe. Nothing heavy, just a milkshake. You're impossibly pretty, you know.'

Of course, Chloe felt instantly guilty at not being available for her cousin, then indignant as she remembered all the times she'd *longed* to spend time with Megan and been snubbed. How was she supposed to know Megan had changed her mind? Then she felt illogically annoyed with Llew for getting in the way of something so simple. It was only a milkshake; it wasn't, as Iestyn put it, anything *heavy*. So why did she feel so guilty?

Lastly, she melted at his compliment. *Impossibly pretty.* She could see the admiration in his eyes. Chloe dazzled a little at the idea of being seen with this stunning young man who talked about someone called Kerouac and lived in London and wanted to be a lawyer.

'I could probably manage tomorrow,' she said. 'About three o'clock?'

Later that day she told Llew, without much thought to his

response. On the rare occasions that Megan or Richard had included her in something, if Auntie Susan and Uncle Harry wanted her, and of course the summer that Blossom was there, Llew had never batted an eyelid.

So when she mentioned that she was going to have a milkshake with Iestyn the next day, she was expecting his usual cheery 'Right-oh, Chlo'. Instead he froze and looked at her as if he had been shot. They were meandering from shop to shop at the time, collecting a pleasing little trove of magazines, gobstoppers and crisps. Since Llew's job, with its generous 'expenses', little luxuries like these were more affordable for them. Right there outside the paper shop he stared at her with an expression that made her bristle.

'You're not starting all this again, are you?' He sounded peeved.

'All what?' she demanded.

'Running around after Megan and that crowd, trying to be something you're not.'

Chloe was astonished. 'What on earth do you mean? This is nothing to do with Megan! Iestyn is Richard's friend and he's asked me to have a milkshake with him. What's the matter? It's nothing heavy!'

'*Heavy?* So you're talking like him now. Don't waste your time, Chlo, you're far too good for all of them.'

'You've got a nerve! Don't tell *me* who to spend my time with. I'm not trying to be anything. He just asked me and I said yes.'

'So you're not remotely impressed by the fact that he's at college in London and he's older than you?'

'Well, so what if I am? It's OK to admire people, you know.'

'He's not worth it.'

'You don't even know him!'

'I know enough.'

'Then what? Tell me.'

'It doesn't matter.' Llew turned away, his lion's eyes clouding over.

'There isn't anything, is there? You're just jealous.'

'Jealous? Of *him*? You think he's more impressive than me, do you, so I *must* be jealous of him? Why? Because he's richer? Posher? Better looking? Is he cleverer than me? Funnier? Is he a better man?'

Chloe was at a loss. 'I don't know what's got into you, Llew Jones,' she said, hoping to raise a smile as she usually did when she used his full name. Nothing. 'You're not a man, anyway, you're a boy, and of course he's *not* a better person than you, but why does it have to be a comparison? It's only a milkshake.'

'That's right,' sneered Llew. 'It's nothing heavy.'

'*Llew!*' Chloe was close to tears. What had she done wrong? How could she make it right? She wanted more than anything to be friends with Llew again; it certainly wasn't worth losing that for a milkshake with Iestyn. But now she couldn't back down. There was no way she would change her plans just because he didn't like them.

'I'm sorry, Chlo.' Llew looked sober. 'I don't mean to be a

bore. Of course you must do what you want. It's just . . . well, I want to make the most of you in case you can't come next summer. And also I just . . . I think you're special. And I get frustrated when you try to be as good as people who aren't half as good as you.'

Chloe didn't understand. That wasn't what she was trying to do, was it?

'And I don't want you getting hurt,' he went on. 'I've watched you all these years running after Megan, how you tried and tried. I don't want you doing the same with this Iestyn.'

'But *he* asked *me*!'

'Yes, for now. But he's only here a short while. What then? He'll go back to London and forget you and you'll have wasted our time for nothing. But it's not our time, of course. It's yours, and you must do what you want. I'm sorry.'

'Why would he forget me? So you're saying that a boy like that couldn't really be interested in a girl like me? That you can't see me fitting in in London, with students and sophisticated people and all of that?'

'Well, not really.'

Chloe stared at him. A fury rose within her. How dare he? They had always supported each other's dreams. Always! Nant-Aur was the place where she had to contend with her brothers telling her that every idea she had was stupid. Tenby was the place where she had Llew, and they believed in each other. Now, all of a sudden, he didn't.

'Not because you're not good enough, Chlo,' he went on.

'Just because . . . that's not who you are, Chloe. It's just not who you are.'

The fury erupted. 'Yes it *is*,' she bawled. 'Yes it *bloody is*!'

He looked at her with round eyes and an awestruck expression.

'To you I'll always be just a kid with scabby knees and sand in her hair,' raged Chloe, 'but I'm not! I'm a grown-up now! I'm a . . . a *woman*! *Other* people think I can go places. *Other* people think I'm beautiful. I thought *you* did but I seem to be wrong.'

'Chlo!' Llew said, a little plaintively she thought later. But it was too late. Chloe was crying and she didn't want him to see her crying and she didn't even understand *why* she was crying.

'I'll see you later,' she muttered and stormed off, not even noticing that she had dropped her copy of *School Friend*. She just wanted to be alone.

# Nora

'Where is it? Where's the damn suitcase? Oh. There. Bugger. Where's my phone? There it is. Now where are my black tights? Oh, for fuck's sake! Is it too much to ask to find a pair of tights? And my pink dress. Where is it? Where is it?'

The sounds of Kaitlin packing drifted along the landing. She had hung her pink dress from the bathroom door last night, a pair of black tights draped over the hanger, so the creases would fall out. Nora smiled and took them to her. Kaitlin was standing in the middle of her room, face as red as her hair.

'Nora, have you seen my . . . ? Oh! Where were they?'

'Bathroom door.'

'Now I remember! Thank you.'

Kaitlin folded the dress in such a way that Nora couldn't help but question the use of hanging it at all but who was she to add to the angst? She zipped up her case and looked at Nora, her eyes shining.

'I'm ready! Big city, here we come!'

The journey was easy. No nightmarish traffic except for one

hold-up just past Newport. They chatted and sang along to the radio and stopped twice, not because they needed to but because they could. They rolled into Petersham at two thirty and Nora followed the road through the new estate and out the other side to her mum's cottage.

'It's like the gingerbread house!' said Kaitlin in delight.

Nora parked on the gravel next to Sandy's VW Beetle and the cottage door flew open.

'Nora!' exclaimed Sandy, hurrying out to meet them. 'How lovely to see you, darling. And you must be Kaitlin! My goodness, you're pretty. Look at that hair!'

'Thank you for having us to stay, Sandy,' said Kaitlin, submitting happily to a hug. 'We're so excited.'

They bustled their things indoors while Sandy put the kettle on.

'It's such a lovely day I thought we might sit in the garden,' she suggested.

'Perfect,' said Nora. 'Can't think of a nicer start to the trip. It's good to be back.' And it was. All the angst around her mother, work, *everything*, seemed to have dissolved like mist. Here was where she had lived as a teenager, and in her twenties. Here she had been happy.

They spent a lazy afternoon in the garden, moving in and out of the shade of the magnolia tree as comfort dictated. It was one of those brilliant days where the sun was strong but a soft breeze stopped the heat becoming stifling.

'We had day after day like this when I was a girl,' sighed

Sandy. 'That's not just nostalgia, the seasons used to be more defined. Still, silly to moan about that on a day like today.'

Nora tilted her face up to the sun. 'Sandy, you met Mum when you were both in your forties, didn't you?'

'That's right. We were paralegals at the same firm. The only two female paralegals, in fact. I was at your fifth birthday party, Nora.'

'And when you were getting to know Mum, did she ever talk about Wales? About her childhood?'

'Not that I remember. We talked a *lot*, but there was so much going on in the present. We existed in a state of perpetual outrage at the sexism we were dealing with most days. Family, career – they gave us plenty of food for thought. I knew she'd been a model, and I knew your father had left . . . that's as far back as we went really.'

'Mmm, I suppose that's normal. It's just that sometimes I feel like Mum's whole life started at twenty when she went to London. Being in Tenby and spending time with my gran makes me realise that of course she had a whole life before that. I'm hearing stories from Gran now and I wonder why Mum never told me them.'

'I honestly don't know, Nora. Any ideas?'

'Maybe something happened, something bad. It's hard to imagine Mum would keep something big from me all these years but it just doesn't add up. They were poor but she *loved* her parents. They grew their own food and she had friends and brothers . . . Apparently she was crazy about Tenby and went every year without fail . . . She was *happy*. But now when she talks about Wales she makes out it's this awful place that she can't bear to think of. Oh, and has she ever told you about Llew?'

'What's Llew?' Sandy struggled to get her tongue around the unfamiliar consonant.

'Exactly. Me neither. Turns out he was her best friend in the world. He lived in Tenby and they were inseparable apparently. Why has she never mentioned *him*?'

Sandy looked thoughtful. 'I don't know, Nora. It is a little strange. But you know, it almost doesn't surprise me. I've always thought that deep down your mum is—'

'Unhappy?'

Sandy frowned. 'I don't know that it's as strong as that. But there's *something* . . . She's so warm and generous and loving. Yet, at times she can be quite brittle, almost harsh. And she's always held men at arm's length to a degree I've never really seen anyone else do before. Of course, being so beautiful, that always took quite a bit of doing. I never really felt it was about your dad – she was always so philosophical about him, you know? "Men come and go," she used to say. "He gave me Nora. She's all I need."'

'She said it to me too. I can't help wondering if it's something to do with this Llew character. Whether he broke her heart. But they were so young! Children really. I suppose something *might* have happened then. But what?'

'Have you heard from her lately?'

'Yes, last week. She sounds good actually. I told her where I was and she didn't freak out, surprisingly.'

It had been a huge relief. Nora hadn't heard from Jasmine for a week after her email. She'd started to worry that she'd caused some irreparable rift between them, without even understanding why. When the reply came, Nora had opened it with a hammering heart. It was short, but generous.

Darling,

I'm sorry I've been such a grumpy cow that you've been afraid to tell me where you are! I never wanted it to be like that between us. I have been a bit difficult, I suppose. Well, you try dealing with arthritis and memory loss and wrinkles! Ha ha. I'm glad you've told me now. And glad to hear that you're happy and finding your way and that you've made good friends there. I suppose I've been worried about you, and wanted you to get back on track, when what you needed was to spread your wings and try something new. Give my best love to Gran and yes OF COURSE I will come and see you both when I get back. I miss her and you very much. I'll keep this brief. Faith has house guests and there's always something happening. But I'll write longer soon. Meanwhile, please feel free to tell me anything you want to and trust me not to be so unreasonable in future. I LONG to meet Kaitlin and your Logan . . .

I love you xxxxxxx

Nora's relief was immense. Anyone who said you didn't need your parents' blessing over a certain age had clearly never been the only child of a strong-minded single parent. The force of that bond never, ever went away. Hearing from Jasmine had cleared another cloud from her sky. And it had come in time for her to enjoy the London trip without worrying. All was well in her world.

The afternoon drifted by. Kaitlin had drawn up a detailed timetable of all the things she wanted to do in London; that afternoon was scheduled to explore Richmond. By five o'clock the first part of her plan was already derailed.

'But it's hard to care,' Kaitlin yawned, stretching her arms over her head, brushing a cloud of gold and magenta honeysuckle and dislodging a couple of gorging bees. 'It's so lovely here. I'm just gonna go with the flow.'

Nora laughed. Kaitlin rarely did anything else. She could give *lessons* in flow. The schedule had been uncharacteristic and wildly optimistic.

The days flew. From a long walk by the river in Richmond and dinner in a cute Mexican, followed by margaritas in the courtyard, to meeting up with Stacie the following day for lunch and the theatre, to ticking off two of the eight things Kaitlin had scheduled for the next day, they enjoyed every minute.

Then it was Friday, and Jones's exhibition had opened the night before to a wonderful review in the *Evening Standard* and another in the *Times*. They read the reviews over brunch before heading into central London to see for themselves.

The exhibition was housed in a small gallery in Kensington. With bow windows over a cobbled street, it looked charmingly old-fashioned from the outside. Inside, it had been extended at the back and the roof converted, so that it was spacious and airy. The walls were long and white; it was spotlit and subtle and hushed.

Nora and Kaitlin exchanged excited glances. Jones was basically a stranger yet they felt a thrill of proud anticipation, like parents at a school play.

'Look!' whispered Kaitlin, waving at an A4-sized notice in a frame. *About the Artist*, it said at the top.

There was a photograph of Jones, with statistics underneath: Leo Jones. Born 1942, Tenby, South Wales. Started painting 1959. Twelve exhibitions. Various residencies, teaching posts and awards. He was successful, Nora realised, really successful.

The black and white photograph showed a handsome, angular older man, with a shock of white hair and clear, penetrating eyes. He was wearing a fisherman's jumper and his expression suggested that sitting for promotional photographs wasn't high on his list of preferred activities.

'Impressive,' murmured Sandy, and Nora wasn't sure whether she was talking about his appearance or his credentials.

'That's our *landlord*!' observed Kaitlin with a frown.

The first section was seascapes. But they weren't just any seascapes. Already they could see what the exhibition blurb termed 'the deeply personal, meditative nature of his work'. Five were of the South Beach, painted from the same angle, but in different moods at different times of day.

'They're so *real*!' gasped Nora, staring. She was sure that anyone would find them powerful. But knowing the place as she did, she was astonished by how truly he had captured it. Looking at them was like being there – they invoked such a strong feeling, the feeling she'd had in those early days when she stumbled to the beach from the hotel in the mornings, exhausted and wondering how on earth she'd washed up there. She remembered staring at the waves, feeling that if she just stood there long enough her life might start to make sense again.

*The sea washes away the ills of men*, she remembered.

'Why do I feel that these are all about loss?' wondered Sandy, looking confused. 'It's just the sea!'

Kaitlin pointed at the titles. '*Missing*,' she read. '*Missing you. Still Missing. Still Missing You*. And *Missed*. Ha! Mist. Because it's misty. Even when he's sad he's a little bit funny. You're right, Sandy, they are.'

The second section was portraits. The farther they walked the farther they travelled back in time. From a contemporary figure of a woman in the rain with a small child, to a pair of eighties-looking lads with skinheads, Doc Martens and cigarettes, to a well-padded matron at a sweetshop counter, to the same fiery lobsterman they had seen in the attic, this time leaping over the rocks with a face like fury . . . these were real people with real lives and real stories.

'There's Red Sam!' said Nora, feeling as if she had just bumped into someone she knew.

'They're incredible,' said Sandy. 'How does he capture a whole history like that? Well, he's a very talented man, your Jones, very talented indeed.'

'I know,' said Kaitlin proudly, as if she had taught him to paint herself.

Next they passed through lush Welsh landscapes and bustling street scenes of Tenby. 'It's like showing you photos of where I live!' said Nora to Sandy. 'Look, that's our house!'

And then they moved on to the last section, hung on the largest stretch of wall. There were just four paintings, but they were enormous, filmic, captivating. Nineteen-fifties youth captured in all its brightly coloured innocence and hope. Sandy moved rapidly from one to the next before coming back to study them all properly. But Nora couldn't get past the first one.

Her mouth dropped open and the strength drained from her legs. She looked, and looked again. It was one of her grandmother's photos, larger than life and in full colour. It showed a self-conscious, excited-looking group of teenagers clustered in front of a mantelpiece. She knew from Gran that Chloe was about to go to her first ever Tenby Teens dance with her cousins and their friends. And it was obvious to Nora that for the artist, this picture was all about Chloe. She was painted no bigger or brighter than the others, but Nora felt that if she stared at it long enough she would eventually learn everything there was to know about her mother. It was incredible.

She turned to Kaitlin but Kaitlin had moved on to the second painting. To Nora's surprise, she was staring at the huge canvas with an expression every bit as flabbergasted as her own. Nora looked at the picture: six girls squeezed into a vinyl booth in an old-fashioned 1950s style café. There was her mother again.

Kaitlin turned to Nora, mirroring Nora's own bewilderment. 'Why are *you* looking so blown away?' Kaitlin asked.

Nora pointed at Chloe, dressed in shorts, a blouse and an unhappy expression.

'That's my mother,' she said. 'Why are you?'

'Your mother? This is like *The Twilight Zone*.' Kaitlin pointed at one of the other girls, a beautiful redhead wearing a shiny ponytail and a grey and white polka-dot shirtwaister. 'That's my grandmother.'

# Chloe

Being with Iestyn was very different from being with Llew. It lacked the years of familiarity and friendship, of shared jokes and memories, the ease of knowing the other person inside out.

But with Iestyn, Chloe felt like a lady. And she was, after all, a young lady. During that first milkshake she felt shy and stupid, but she put that down to nerves, and the fact that she was still upset with Llew. It was strange, being in one of *their* places with someone else.

But the following day he took her out for lunch and she enjoyed that more. He took her to one of the posh hotels along The Croft, with their views across to Saundersfoot. This was a whole different experience from visiting Richard at the Sea Breezes. It was so luxurious that at first she couldn't speak to any of the staff in case she made some awful faux pas. But Iestyn was so gentlemanly and relaxed that she soon felt as if she had been born to eat sumptuous lunches with oysters and sponge as light as cloud, beneath a chandelier as big as a cherry tree.

She was fascinated to hear about Iestyn's family and studies and ambitions. To her relief, he took her comments and questions seriously. This was a proper, grown-up conversation! A proper *date*. She was wearing a pretty yellow dress that was only two years old. It wasn't *very* smart but it was the most suitable thing she had. Iestyn complimented her lavishly and when she glimpsed herself in a nearby mirror, she hardly knew herself. Her hair was smooth and gleaming, not tousled and full of sand as it invariably was with Llew. Her cheeks looked peachy and smooth instead of flushed and sun-scorched. Even the yellow dress looked quite elegant in its simplicity. She couldn't deny it, she looked beautiful. Being here with Iestyn was helping her believe it. In fact, being here with Iestyn made all her dreams seem just at the end of her fingertips.

She told him about her childhood wish to be a dancer with a fond laugh she hoped made her sound like a woman of the world. He looked sympathetic.

'But it's a travesty,' he said. Chloe wasn't certain what a travesty was but she was prepared to agree with him. 'You're so beautiful and bright and lovely. You should have the world at your feet. What a crying shame that all your talent and shine should go to waste in some mouldering backwater with no opportunity and no vision.'

Chloe opened her mouth to say that Nant-Aur, although limiting, wasn't exactly mouldering, but he swept on. 'We talk about this in college, you know, about the working classes and the waste of potential. If you were living in London, you'd be surrounded by dance schools. If your father was a banker, he could pay for them. What's the difference between you and that girl? Not talent. Merely circumstance. It's outrageous. Of course, the Buddhists say that attachment is the source of all suffering. And Kerouac, Ginsberg et al reject materialism absolutely. I'm not very principled, I'm afraid, Chloe. I espouse their beliefs in theory, yet I'm glad my father can pay for me to have a good education. If I can do anything to help you, Chloe, you must let me know.'

Chloe's head swam with delight. Exactly what he *could* do she wasn't sure, but oh, to be talking to someone whose world didn't consist entirely of what was known and safe and boring!

Iestyn paid for lunch then they stood looking out to sea, hand in hand. The contact distracted Chloe from the view – the contact *and* what it meant. It meant that she hadn't been found lacking, that he liked her and probably wanted to take her out again. This was perhaps how it had started for Alma and James, for Evie and Sam. She pointed to the hazy hills across the water.

'Isn't it beautiful?' she said. 'Tenby's my enchanted kingdom.'

'It's very pretty. But Chloe, haven't you ever been to London? That truly is the place where all things are possible. You must come and visit sometime. My mother would love to meet you.'

'I'd like that,' muttered Chloe, ducking her head; she could feel herself going red. He gave her hand a little squeeze.

'Now, I'd offer to walk you home,' he said, 'but as we're going to the same place, it's a little academic! Very distracting sharing a roof with someone as pretty as you – *not* that I'm complaining.'

He kept hold of her hand as they walked through town.

Chloe felt as if their linked fingers were a glowing brand that everyone must see, that announced that they were a couple, though she wasn't sure, really, that they were, or that she wanted to be. But it seemed rude to pull her hand away. She tried not to catch anyone's eye and hoped against hope that Llew wouldn't see them like this. Not that she was doing anything wrong. However, the walk seemed twice as long as usual.

When at last they got home, Llew was waiting on the doorstep.

'Heavens, why doesn't the lad knock on the door and go in?' wondered Iestyn.

But Chloe didn't stop to explain his obsession with the outdoors; she slipped her hand free and ran to Llew.

# Nora

❦

'I wish I'd brought them,' muttered Nora. 'Why didn't I bring them? But how was I to *know*?'

Kaitlin and Sandy were staring at her.

'Brought what?' asked Sandy.

'The photos. My God, this is too weird. Sandy, that's *Mum*! That blonde girl! Mum when she was young. These are paintings of photographs Gran's loaned me. They were taken by Mum's friend Llew, back in the fifties. How did Jones get hold of them? Did he *know* Llew?'

'*Jasmine?*' marvelled Sandy. 'Yes, I can see it! The eyes . . .'

'Nora,' said Kaitlin. 'Did your gran ever tell you Llew's surname?'

'Yes, it was Jones. Llew Jones.'

'Oh my God!' laughed Kaitlin, looking incredulous. 'This is beyond belief. Jones *is* Llew! He must be! OK, if it was just the Jones, I wouldn't think so, but *Llew*? *Leo*? They both mean lion. What are the odds of that?'

'You're right,' said Nora faintly. 'I have to email him. Or Mum. Or . . . I don't know, am I *hallucinating*?'

'Let's go and find a café,' said Sandy. 'We should sit down, have a coffee, then come back and look at the paintings properly, when we've recovered.'

'Good idea,' said Nora gratefully. 'I can't take it in. I need coffee. No, I need sugar!'

In a daze, they regrouped in a nearby café. Nora collapsed into a chair while Kaitlin and Sandy queued for drinks. They brought her a large hot chocolate and a brownie for good measure.

'I mean . . .' said Nora. 'How?'

'Is your grandmother still alive, Kaitlin?' asked Sandy, clearly seeing that Nora wasn't ready to articulate.

'No, she died three years ago.'

'I'm sorry.'

'Thanks, but honestly, she was a bitch. One of those unhappy women, you know? Thought the world owed her a living, took her frustrations out on everyone around her. Dad said she was a nightmare when he was growing up. She's in that painting in the attic, isn't she, Nora? The Cats, do you remember? The red-haired girl and the dark-haired girl on Castle Hill, but her face was hidden by her hair.'

'Yes, you're right.' Sugar was slowly thawing Nora's brain. 'That must be her. What was her name, Kait?'

'Alma.'

'I wish we could take these paintings home with us and look at them in private.'

'Well, if you've got hundreds of thousands of pounds . . .'

said Sandy. 'Otherwise I suggest you get it together and we have a really good look while we have the chance.'

'Yes, of course we must. So, Kait, your grandmother knew my mum! And *Jones*!'

'Looks like it. I don't know how they all fit together. But they're all a similar age, I guess, and Tenby's a small town. Perhaps it's not *that* surprising, in a way.'

But Nora was thinking of the day she'd handed in her notice at work. Sitting at her desk, seeing Nick come in all rain-spattered and refreshed, realising something was very wrong with her life. Suddenly craving for the South Beach at Tenby when she hadn't been there for twenty-seven years. Being haunted for weeks by that shimmering stretch of sand in her mind's eye. It was as if her subconscious had suddenly jumped up and said, *This is where you need to go to sort yourself out and learn all the answers to the mystery*. And Nora hadn't even known there *was* a mystery.

'What about your grandfather, Kait? Is he still alive?'

'Grandpa James? No, he went before Gran. Honestly, I think it was the only way he could get away from her. He was a mild-mannered sort, you know, and she was so sulky and complaining. Even Dad said he was glad when Gramps died because he deserved a bit of peace.'

Nora could imagine Greg saying it. 'And did she ever talk about her young days? Her friends? Did she ever mention Chloe?'

Kaitlin thought hard. 'No. All I remember is Gran always saying she was the prettiest in her circle – had a handspan waist, she always used to say. She used to mention a Pamela, I think, and a Megan, who apparently got sent away, or the whole family left in disgrace, or something. Honestly, I tried not to listen much, it was always just gossip and grudges about people I'd never even met.'

'Megan,' said Nora. 'That was Mum's cousin. She had a brother, Richard. Gran told me Mum used to stay with them every summer.'

'Incredible,' said Sandy. 'Just incredible. What are you going to do, Nora? Will you tell Jasmine?'

'I don't know. I *want* to. But if she's kept this to herself all these years, there must be a reason. I wish she was coming home sooner. I wish I could ask her face to face.' Nora shook her head.

She looked around the café and took a deep breath. The smell of coffee, the drone of traffic outside, the queue shifting and sighing from door to counter were all very normal. It was 2015, not 1950-something. She finished her brownie, took a last swallow of hot chocolate. 'I'm ready.'

The gallerista looked surprised when they crowded back. 'Hello,' she said. 'Back for another look?'

'Yes,' said Nora. 'There's too much to take in all at once. They're just so beautiful. These last four particularly.'

'Extraordinary, aren't they? I'm happy you like them.'

Now Nora made a point of reading the summary at the start of the exhibition.

The Fossdyke Gallery is delighted to host Leo Jones's latest and most revealing collection. Here we see more clearly than ever before his sometimes satirical, always profoundly emotional response to the people and places that have formed him. His use of light to make the familiar unique has been discussed and feted. Always an artist's friend and muse, light, in these paintings, has a magical, nostalgic quality. Jones has said it is a filter through which the viewer can gaze down the lens of the years, a nod to his first love, photography. His portraits are at once novelistic and uncompromising in his fearless rendering of human frailty. Here we see his deeply personal response to the passing years, to that which is timeless and that which must inevitably change. Critic Walter Hughes has said that Leo Jones, 'alone among living artists, not only tells stories but sings arias with his brush. These arias then sing of love and loss and life, in all its splendid, gutted glory'. This is his most personal exhibition to date.

*Life in all its splendid, gutted glory.* What had gutted this sensitive, talented man? Nora looked carefully at the photograph of Jones, the distinguished face, the casual clothes, the burning expression. Those eyes weren't just the intense, brooding eyes of an artist. They were eyes that looked at life unflinchingly and refused to shy away from what he saw. 'He's courageous,' Nora whispered to herself, 'and passionate. Art is a great love, but life itself is a greater one. I *wish* I could meet him.'

'The opening must have been wonderful last night,' she said aloud. The gallerista looked up again.

'Yes, everyone involved was very pleased. A large gathering, and influential. Of course, it couldn't fail to be magical, with these wonderful works of art all around.'

'Was the artist here?'

'Yes, of course. Leo is a very private man but even he wouldn't miss his own opening.'

'Is he still in London?'

'For a few days, then he flies to Lisbon to visit friends.'

'Oh no! I mean, I see. If I had painted these, I don't think I'd be able to leave them behind.'

'Are you an artist too?'

'Oh God, no. I just love it. These. Thank you.'

Nora joined Kaitlin and Sandy in front of the last four paintings. She would write to Jones, she decided. She would come back to London before he left if necessary. Lisbon indeed. She *had* to see him before he left the country.

Then she applied herself to the pictures again. The first was the gathering at Auntie Susan's house, the pre-dance portrait. Chloe was wearing the blue dress that she, Nora, was currently in the process of cutting up to make a patchwork blanket! God, she hoped her mother wouldn't mind. She was beautiful, of course, but that wasn't news to Nora. What was interesting was that she didn't look as if she knew it. In all the photos Nora had ever seen of Jasmine, she knew it. *This wasn't Jasmine,* thought Nora suddenly, *this was Gran's little Chloe*.

The second painting was the diner scene. Although they wouldn't have called it a diner then, in Tenby, would they? That was an Americanism that probably hadn't come over yet.

'It's *Mean Girls* for the fifties,' said Kaitlin beside her. 'They're the in crowd and your mum knows they don't really want her so she's unhappy.'

Nora nodded slowly. Her mother looked younger than the others, less assured. She was toying with the straw in her milkshake. The painting was called *Strawberry Milkshake*.

'And they're better off than her,' added Sandy. 'Look at the hem of her shorts.'

It was a tiny detail, but yes, the shorts were fraying. Her shoes had been carefully mended. She wasn't wearing bangles and brooches like the other girls.

'It's extraordinary seeing her so blonde,' mused Sandy. 'Why on earth did she start dyeing it?'

The third painting was a happy one and it was breathtaking. Chloe at a dance. The other dancers were a blur; the whole canvas was taken up with this mischievous, dancing elf, ponytail and pink ribbon flying, sugar-pink dress shimmering, making her look like a Christmas tree fairy.

'She's jiving or Lindy-hopping or something,' Kaitlin laughed in delight. 'She's bewitching!'

'And I suspect Jones was bewitched,' remarked Sandy.

'He loved her, didn't he?' said Nora.

'I think so,' agreed Kaitlin.

'All those years, all those times Mum said to me, "Don't trust love, anyone can let you down," . . . was she talking about *Llew*? Is *he* why she told me never to have faith in love?'

Nora's eyes filled with tears as she remembered herself at

the age Chloe was in the painting, dreaming so desperately of love, as all people that age did, and her mother's warnings, always warnings. *Love isn't to be relied upon. Safer to make a good life without it.*

'I hope he didn't cheat on her with my grandmother,' said Kaitlin with a curled lip, 'or your mother will hate me. I look a lot like her, I'm told.'

'You really do, except your hair's curly.'

'And you're prettier,' said Sandy. 'Character always shows through.'

'Thank you, Sandy.'

They turned to the fourth and final painting. It showed a very young Chloe sitting in the dunes, long grasses all around her, her hair blowing across her face and sand everywhere – on her skin, in her hair, on her clothes, glittering and smudging but doing nothing to obscure her loveliness. Her expression made Nora smile. She was laughing, but at the same time she looked cross.

'What is that face?' wondered Nora.

'She's thinking, *Don't point that bloody thing at me while I'm covered in sand and my hair's a mess*,' guessed Kaitlin.

Nora and Sandy laughed. 'That sounds like her,' Sandy agreed.

'What's it called?' wondered Kaitlin. 'Oh, look!'

Nora squinted at the plaque. *The First Time We Met*, she read.

# Chloe

Chloe and Llew were friends again. He apologised and she apologised, then she changed into her shorts and off they went. They didn't refer to the row after that except once, when they came out of the sea, dripping and glittering, and Llew asked, 'Do you like him, Chlo?'

No need to ask who he meant. 'Yes, I do,' she said. She could only ever be honest with Llew.

'So is he your boyfriend now?'

'No, at least not yet. But I think he's . . . interested.'

'Of course he is! He's not blind. And you? Are *you* interested?'

'I don't know. Well, of course I'm *interested*. I'm not blind either and he's very gentlemanly and kind and interesting. But I don't know if I'm ready for . . . oh, I just don't *know*, Llew. It's confusing. He's everything I ever dreamed of really. But . . .'

'Just so long as there's a but!' grinned Llew, grabbing her hand. 'Come on, I need sandwiches. Just . . . do what you need to do, Chlo, but ask yourself every minute you're with him, "Is *he* good enough for *me*?"'

So she did. It was the complete opposite from how she

usually thought when she met new people. She asked it when Iestyn took her to the Playhouse to see *Peyton Place*; she asked it when he asked if he could be her date to the dance, even though he was twenty-two – not a teen at all. He would lie, he said, to have her on his arm. She asked it repeatedly and the answer she came up with was yes. Despite his unconventional appearance and flirtation with Buddhism, he was studying law and came from an excellent family. He was considerate, and he wasn't a snob. He was what her mam might term 'a decent young man'.

When Iestyn asked her one morning if they might have a picnic on the North Beach that night, Chloe said yes. She knew what a moonlight picnic meant. He would kiss her, and perhaps ask her to go steady. And she would say yes. She was almost sure she would say yes. Being with Iestyn felt like being borne along on a gentle wave.

She dressed with special care that evening in a pleated skirt with brown and cream checks and a pink blouse. She asked Auntie Susan if she could borrow her single strand of pearls for the occasion and Auntie Susan handed them over at once.

'You look very pretty as always, dear. You're seeing quite a lot of Iestyn, aren't you?'

'I suppose I am. Auntie Susan, do you mind?'

'Mind? Why ever should I? He's a nice young man from a good family. Just the sort you should be getting to know. I just wondered . . . what about Llew?'

'What about him?'

'Well, does he mind? The two of you have always been so

close. I always thought – maybe it was just my fancy – that he had a bit of a soft spot for you.'

'We're just friends, Auntie Susan. He's my best friend in the whole world . . . still . . . but we're not, we've never—'

'I just wondered. Well, have a wonderful evening with Iestyn. I offered to provide the picnic, you know, but he declined very politely. I saw him earlier with a big box from the bakery so I think you're in for a treat.'

'How lovely,' said Chloe, drawing her silky pale hair over one shoulder to fasten the pearls. She couldn't imagine anything better than one of her aunt's picnics and had a moment's nostalgia for the countless packed lunches she and Llew had demolished over the years. But Iestyn just had a different style. Llew was as free and spontaneous as the gulls scrapping around the harbour, whereas Iestyn was more like a sleek greyhound. Chloe grinned at the analogy. She shook her hair back and admired the necklace.

Iestyn did indeed have his own style. He held her hand all the way to the beach, carried an enormous hamper and when they arrived he spent some time looking for the perfect spot: sheltered, soft sand, Goscar Rock not taking up the *entire* view . . . When Chloe and Llew went to the beach, they just threw themselves down wherever they happened to be.

At last he set down the hamper and drew out a massive tartan picnic blanket. He spread it out, brushed off some errant grains of sand and invited Chloe to sit. She watched in fascination as he unpacked plates, napkins, ginger beer and a bottle of white wine.

Chloe had never drunk wine before and longed to try it. There was a box of dainty sandwiches and another of iced fancies that Chloe had often admired in the bakery window but never been able to afford. Finally, Iestyn brought forth a single red rose.

'For you, you beautiful doll,' he said, presenting it to her earnestly.

'Oh Iestyn!' she gasped, realising that she sounded like Scarlett O'Hara.

As the picnic progressed, she started to feel as though she really *were* in a film. Gradually the beach emptied and two or three people she knew called out a cheery 'Goodnight, young Chloe' as they went, casting fond, knowing looks at the couple. And Chloe was filled with a peculiar urge to call back, 'No, it's not like that! It isn't real!' But she didn't, because that was silly.

And then – she could trace it to the minute – she realised that she was bored. It was just after she finished a cucumber sandwich and was picking up a chicken one. Iestyn was telling her about the car he hoped to buy when he'd saved enough money. He went into quite a bit of detail about finish and engine capacity and other such boy-type things and Chloe suddenly saw Llew, as clearly as if he were here, going on and on (and on!) about shutter speeds and lenses and developing techniques. Equally boyish, equally foreign to Chloe, yet somehow she could listen to Llew all day. Cameras were fascinating because he loved them. And she loved him.

'Oh!' she said aloud.

'Yes, it's exciting, isn't it? Won't I be the daddy-o when

I'm driving through Richmond Park in my gleaming MG?' agreed Iestyn.

Chloe smiled and nodded. Oh no, *now* what was she going to do? Iestyn was staying for another week. It would be impossible to avoid him and very awkward to explain. If she could just get through tonight, then she could speak to Auntie Susan and ask for advice on how to handle a suitor that didn't . . . that you didn't . . . Good looks and money didn't matter a *jot*, she understood suddenly. It wasn't that Iestyn wasn't good enough for her – he was a good-hearted young man with sound aspirations. There was nothing wrong with him at all except that he wasn't the person who lit up the hours for her like the sun, like her ragged, leonine, lovely Llew.

She would get through this date and go home, then she would slip out again and run to Llew's and throw gravel at his window until he stuck his messy head out and she would tell him . . .

'It's good to see you looking so happy, Chloe.' Iestyn's voice broke into her thoughts.

Chloe blushed. Surely it was the height of bad manners to spend a date with one man dreaming of another. *How* had she got herself into this mess? She hoped Iestyn wouldn't think she had been leading him on. She truly hadn't meant to. Only, she hadn't *known*.

'Chloe,' said Iestyn, and her heart sank. He touched his finger to her chin and lifted it gently. 'You're so beautiful in the moonlight. You're always beautiful. You're a very special girl.'

'Thank you,' she squeaked.

He was looking at her in *that way* and she couldn't look away. *Look how handsome he is*, she told herself urgently, in the hope that she could somehow avoid disappointing him. He was leaning closer and closer and she didn't know how to tell him what had changed. She didn't know herself how you could be in love with someone and not even *notice* – except that it was Llew and he was so young and he had always been there and . . . oh! Iestyn's lips met hers. They were gentle; it wasn't so bad. She endured it for a few seconds, then drew away and smiled in a brisk way that she hoped said, 'Lovely, now let's eat some more sandwiches.'

But she obviously gave the wrong sort of smile because he said, 'Oh Chloe!' and kissed her again, his tongue parting her lips and his arm pulling her close. He was handsome and considerate and it was a moonlit beach and she was a lucky girl but she didn't want to be doing this. She didn't want to, she didn't want to . . .

'I don't want to!' she exclaimed wildly, aloud. Her hand flew to her mouth in horror. Poor Iestyn looked distraught.

'I'm sorry,' he said at once. 'Forgive me. I didn't mean to be . . . this is too fast for you. I get it, Chloe, I didn't mean to hurt you.'

'Oh Iestyn,' she said, tears rushing to her eyes. 'It's not you. I'm so sorry. I've had a lovely time with you this week, but I shouldn't have come tonight. Only I didn't know that I shouldn't. I like you *very* much, but I've realised that it's not—'

'When?' he asked in a small voice, staring at Goscar Rock.

'Just tonight. I wasn't sure. I thought . . . you're so hand-some, Iestyn, and I'm so flattered, but I don't . . . I'm sorry, I don't know how to do this.'

'Well, I suspect you'll get plenty of practice. You're a beautiful girl, Chloe, I don't think you realise the power you have. Is it completely hopeless? Might your feelings deepen?'

Chloe stared at him. Was he *begging* her? Was what he said true? She didn't *want* to do this to a lot of men. The sooner she and Llew were properly together the better. Oh, why was he so *young*? He was so annoying!

'I don't want to lead you on, Iestyn. I wouldn't want to keep seeing you with this difference in our feelings. As a friend, yes, of course, but . . .'

'It's that boy, isn't it? Your young friend with the camera. He had the first claim on you.'

'Well, I don't know about a claim exactly but it's to do with him, yes. It's hard to understand because we've always only ever been friends. But there's something about the two of us . . . and I'm sorry if you've been hurt because of it.'

Iestyn fell silent and Chloe watched him anxiously. Being honest with Iestyn was one of the hardest things she had ever done.

'It's quite fine, Chloe,' he said at last. 'I wouldn't like you to feel you'd done anything wrong. Shall we stay and finish the picnic? I think we can enjoy that together at least, and then head home, no harm done. What do you say?'

'Truly Iestyn? You don't hate me?'

He winced. 'Of course not, silly. Come on, try one of these cakes.'

Now that the cloud of wrong circumstance had cleared,

Chloe was able to enjoy the rest of the evening. They even had a couple of laughs and she found herself breathing more easily. Then Iestyn realised that even with all his careful planning he had forgotten the corkscrew.

'I can't believe it's not here!' he muttered, rummaging in the patently empty hamper. 'Chloe, will you hold on here while I run and get one?'

'But it'll take you ages to go home and back!' said Chloe in astonishment. 'Why don't we just leave it? Or we could go home and drink some in the kitchen,' she added, realising that this would be her only chance to try wine for a really long time.

He tilted his head, considering. 'No, that won't feel right. Kitchens are for cocoa and cups of tea.' Iestyn and his style again! 'And I do really want you to have the treat I planned for you, even though things aren't what I'd hoped between us. I could run up to that hotel where we had lunch the other day and borrow one. I'm sure they'll trust me to return it. I'll be five minutes, tops. What do you say?'

'All right then, if you insist.'

He hesitated. 'Perhaps I shouldn't leave you. Come with me. The things will be all right here.'

But after the awkwardness of earlier Chloe rather wanted a few minutes alone. 'Don't be daft! This is Tenby, not the big city. I'm safe as houses here, Iestyn, and after those cakes I'm too full to go running up and down cliffs.'

'Fair enough, you stay then, I won't be long.'

# Nora

❦

Dear Jones,

I hope this finds you well. And let me thank you – again! – for allowing Kaitlin and me to live in your lovely home. I assure you that we are loving and appreciating every minute.

I hope you don't mind me writing to you but it feels absolutely urgent that I do. Kaitlin and I went to see your wonderful retrospective in London yesterday. I can't tell you how blown away we were but I'm not writing to tell you how talented you are – I'm writing because one of the characters in your paintings is my mother. Her name then was Chloe Samuels, but I've only ever known her as Jasmine.

I don't know what the link was between the two of you – I'm sorry to say she's never told me much about her childhood – but I'm coming to suspect that you may be a friend of hers that my grandmother only recently told me about, a friend she called Llew. I truly hope that writing to you isn't stirring up any unpleasant memories and I certainly don't wish to cause any awkwardness. But I had to write. Can you imagine how I felt, standing in the Fossdyke and seeing my own mother in full colour and larger than life?!

*The Hourglass*

Mum is in Italy until September and I'd rather not ask her about this until we're together. Meanwhile, if you could find the time and willingness to let me know anything about my mother back then, I would be so grateful. If nothing else, I felt I should let you know the connection.

With very best wishes,

Nora Banquist

386

# Chloe

During those few minutes sitting alone on the dark beach, Chloe's head spun with her new knowledge. All those hours she had spent trying to dream up ways she could get married and still see a lot of Llew . . . How could she have been so blind?

She would tell him tonight. It didn't cross her mind to wonder how he would take the news. He loved her. He always had and somewhere deep down she had known his heart better than her own. She hugged herself in anticipation, savouring this last hour or so before everything changed.

Around her, the beach was satiny and dark in the moonlight, and the whispering tide was out. Behind her the cliffs, with their clinging bushes and trees, their winding paths and steps, reared up as if they wanted to touch the stars. At the foot of the cliffs a broad concrete walkway with a railing led from the harbour along the length of the beach. A gentle breeze touched her arms and she shivered. She felt lucky about Iestyn. What a nice, decent man he was. It took a big person to be a graceful loser, her mam always said.

Suddenly, a pair of strong arms wrapped around her from behind and she jumped. She hadn't heard any footsteps.

'Llew?' she said, even though she knew it wasn't Llew. But it couldn't be Iestyn because he would never grab her like that after she had put him straight.

'Guess again,' said a deep voice in her ear and she felt hot, unwelcome breath on her neck.

'Iestyn?' Her voice came out small and scared. Maybe he wasn't such a graceful loser after all.

'Not him either,' said the voice, 'though I bet you wish it was. I saw you earlier, kissing, and cuddling . . . Can't think why he's left you all alone out here. I wouldn't. But you are all alone, Chloe.'

'Who are you?' demanded Chloe, managing to inject a little anger into her voice. 'Iestyn's coming back any minute and Llew's on his way too,' she added for good measure. She struggled against the arms, which were pinning her arms against her body. 'Let go of me now, let me see you. This isn't funny.'

'Come on, Chloe, don't pretend you don't like it. I've seen you at the dances, flirting with everyone who'll look at you. And I saw you French kissing that Cardiff boy. What's wrong with a bit of home-grown, eh?'

'*Ron?*' asked Chloe, struggling even harder. This was seeming less likely by the minute.

'See, you can't even guess. You've lost count of them all. Well, I like a girl with a bit of experience myself. And if you're anything like your cousin, you'll be a right goer. Come on then,

Chloe, give me some of what you've been spreading around the other boys. I'm very good, you'll like it.'

'No I won't!' she shrieked, as he turned her to face him. She found herself just inches from Michael Everley's curling film-star lips.

'Oh Michael, it's you!' she exclaimed in relief. 'Thank goodness, I thought you really meant it then. It's not very funny you know.'

'I'm not joking,' said Michael. His dark eyes, that all the girls thought were so liquid and gentle, that they swooned over, weren't liquid and gentle now. In the moonlight they glittered like coal and Chloe was suddenly afraid. But it was all right, Iestyn would be back any minute. And she couldn't be in danger. It was Michael Everley! Everyone knew him. He was a Tenby boy.

She drew as far away from him as she could within his restraining arms, when she heard a strange and disconcerting rumble. A storm? But the sky was calm and clear. Michael was leaning in to kiss her now and his lips were hot and hard on hers, his tongue forcing its way into her mouth, his fingers digging into her arms. She could almost see the rows of round, black bruises she would have tomorrow, like spiders.

She whimpered in pain but because of his mouth, covering hers, it came out as a strangled groan.

'Yeah, you like that,' he said, pulling away to look at her with an expression that Chloe had never seen on a man before. He looked like someone in the fish market assessing a pollock and wondering how he might cook it. He looked as if he might flip her over any minute and run his hand along her underside.

'No!' said Chloe, while she could. 'It hurts! It's horrible. Stop!'

He leered at her. 'Not a chance,' he said. 'You and me've had this coming a long time. I know you're a bad girl, but that's OK, because that's how I like them. Like your cousin, she was a dirty slut and I enjoyed every minute. But now she won't talk to me, she's so hoity-toity. Let's see if you can be a little friendlier to Michael, hmm?'

He grabbed her leg and pulled it, so that her legs were apart and facing him. She almost fell backwards, only his other arm held her upright. She was mortified. She'd never been in such an ungainly position before. But her embarrassment was small compared with her growing fear. He couldn't be doing what she thought he was doing, he couldn't *possibly*. It was all just a horrible misunderstanding. But it needed to stop now. With her now-free right arm she pushed him back, or tried to, but he was solid and determined and she couldn't move him. Then there was another rumble behind them, like the first but louder. This time Michael heard it too. He looked up.

'Help!' screamed Chloe. 'He's attacking me. Help me!' Where was Iestyn?

'Shut up!' he cried, shaking her. 'What was that?'

It came again, deep as thunder, but a harder sound. Chloe looked round but he caught her face and yanked it back towards him. 'Never mind,' he said.

'Pearls,' he said, toying with Auntie Susan's necklace with one finger. 'Pretty pearls. You like to dress up for the boys, don't you, Chloe? I like that too. There's a lot I like about you. Now let me see the rest.' He started unbuttoning her blouse with one hand and the treacherous fabric slipped easily from the buttons.

All it took was a queue at the bar, or a helpful hotelier hunting for a misplaced corkscrew, and Iestyn could be a lot longer than he intended. Chloe felt a drenching terror.

'No!' she whimpered, starting to cry. 'I don't want to. Please, Michael, I really don't.'

He gave a scornful laugh.

'Well, sweetheart, I don't believe that for a minute!' Another rumble sounded, closer this time, and they both looked round to see a rock the size of a football bouncing down the cliff.

'Shit!' he said, looking up in disbelief.

*Llew!* thought Chloe wildly for a minute. He was up there throwing things at Michael to stop him. But that was ridiculous, of course. And now the rock was followed by a slow slither of earth and bushes that no one could possibly have uprooted. They watched, frozen in that awful, indecent position, as the landslide gained momentum, dropping faster and faster towards the beach and hitting the concrete walkway below with a cloud of dirt. Branches, earth and a couple of rocks scattered.

Michael turned his attention back to her blouse, pushing it off one shoulder so that one half of her brassiere was exposed. 'Very nice,' he grinned, 'very modest. Good girl, Chloe.'

Then Chloe started screaming like a demented thing. 'Help!' she yelled at the top of her voice. 'Help me! Help me!' She screamed it over and over, wrenching up the sound from her lungs by the very roots. There must be someone, somewhere.

'No one can hear you, darlin',' grunted Michael. 'No one's—'

But then, clear as day, they heard a voice. 'Chloe! I'm coming!'

'Shit,' said Michael again. 'Come on, love, hurry up.' He tugged her legs until she was underneath him and covered her mouth with a hand. But the voice came again.

'Get off her, you bastard. I'll kill you! Hang on, Chlo!'

It really *was* Llew. She didn't know where, she couldn't see him, she only hoped he was close enough to reach them in time.

And then another voice, fainter, Iestyn.

'Chloe! I'm coming! Stop! Stop!'

'Bloody hell,' growled Michael. He rocked back onto his heels, assessing.

Chloe took the chance to sit up and pull her blouse around her though her fingers were shaking too much to do it up. All along the cliff, tiny showers of earth trickled towards the beach. The dry summer and the reaching roots of plants must have unsettled everything. Michael let go of her.

She could see Iestyn high above them, hesitating at the top of the cliff path. And at the foot of the cliff, along the concrete walkway, Llew was running like hell towards them. He seemed oblivious to the earth showers, pelting right through them.

Michael bolted in the opposite direction across the beach.

'Llew!' she screamed, scrambling up. 'Llew! I'm coming!' Another slide began. She didn't want to be buried alive. Then again, she didn't want to stay here either. She ran.

Llew was nearly with her – it was all going to be all right. Nothing else mattered. Then one final heave of the cliffside sent a pile of earth pouring directly in between them.

Chloe hesitated but Llew didn't. He put his head down and charged through the dark, solid rain. The next minute his legs seemed to buckle under him and he fell. Two boulders bounced down the cliff with an ominous cracking sound and Chloe was sure one of them hit Llew, as best she could see through the confusion – did it hit his *head*? She ran to him.

'Llew!' she cried. 'Oh dear God, be alive, please be alive.' She kneeled at his side and cleared the earth off him. He had landed awkwardly, one leg twisted, but that didn't worry her half as much as the fact that his eyes were closed and he wasn't moving. She turned. Michael had disappeared into the night. Iestyn, picking his way down the disintegrating cliff path, froze.

'I'll call an ambulance,' he yelled, turning back.

'Llew,' sobbed Chloe, smoothing his hair back from his face and smearing dirt across his cheeks. Otherwise she dared not move him. She glanced up at the cliffs, but now they seemed still and as permanent as ever; the only movement was Iestyn, scurrying up the steps as fast as his legs could carry him.

'Oh Llew, don't be dead. I love you so much. Please don't be dead.'

# Nora

Nora closed her eyes and tilted her face up to the blazing sun. She took a deep breath of clear, heady air and knew that for days to come, probably for the rest of her life, she would be able to see this walk whenever she closed her eyes. Citrus-yellow swathes of gorse; a stony path unfurling at her feet; coves as beguiling as a folded-back bed; fishermen on the rocks below. The sky soared with birds – skuas and sooty shearwaters as well as choughs and gulls – and a bobbing black bead in the calm water revealed itself at a certain angle to be the head of a seal.

Perfect. No matter how much time she spent here, Nora thought, she would never take it for granted. She had wanted something different from her old life. Well, this was different.

An arm slid around her waist and she felt the solid heat of Logan coming up behind her. She leaned back. Even *more* perfect. She hadn't thought, until this summer, that there were degrees of perfection.

He kissed her neck, licking the sweat and making her wriggle.

'Logan,' she groaned, turning to wrap her arms around him, 'don't! We're in public! I don't know if I can—'

'Can't control yourself around me, woman?' he smirked. 'That's how I like it.'

'That ego!' she teased, making a face, before losing herself in kissing him. Eventually they roused themselves and carried on on their way, Logan keeping a weather eye out for dolphins and basking sharks. After a while they dipped into a wood and surrendered themselves to the dance and dapple of sunlight and leaf.

'So, Nora,' said Logan after a while.

He sounded like a schoolteacher, thought Nora. 'Logan,' she replied, equally businesslike.

He cleared his throat. 'Um, it's July.'

'It is.'

'I love our time together.'

'So do I, Logan, you know that.' Nora stopped on the earthen track. Sycamores sighed and nodded all around. Something serious was coming. Something to celebrate or something to dread?

Logan stopped too and took both her hands. 'I want you to know, Nora . . . well, I love you. I mean, I really love you.'

*Celebrate!* Nora felt joy sink through her like champagne. It wasn't the first time he'd said it. In bed they'd both gasped out the magic words. But they were old enough to know that it didn't always translate to real life. This felt real.

'I love you too,' she said, looking at him steadily so he'd know she wasn't just saying it. A blackbird chirruped somewhere nearby.

'But the thing is this,' he said.

*Dread*. 'Oh, did there have to be a but?'

'Sorry, *but* is a bad word. It's just that I've been thinking about the future.'

*Celebrate!* 'You have?'

'Yeah. Look, you probably think I'm crazy, it's only been a few weeks. I know it's still very early days and I know you're deliberately not thinking ahead right now. So I don't want to put a downer on things. But Brendan and Sylv are coming next week. And after that, I go home.'

Next week. It sounded so soon. There were actually ten days before Logan's kids arrived but still, it wasn't long. Nora looked around and, finding no convenient log, sat down on the grass at the side of the path. He joined her.

'Yeah, it's a sitting down conversation, isn't it? Now don't get me wrong, Nora, I want you to know my kids. I really hope you'll spend time with us, if you don't hate the idea. I want them to know about us. But when they're here, I won't be as free. And then . . .'

'Then you go back to New Zealand.'

'Exactly. It's a long way, Nora.'

'Couldn't get much further.'

'No further at all, really.'

'Yeah.'

They sat side by side in the grass, staring at the path. Another couple, shrieking and laughing, hove into sight. They looked at Logan and Nora strangely then disappeared through the trees.

'So what, if anything, would you like to do?' asked Nora fearfully.

'I'd like to throw you down right here and ravish you in the bushes. I'd like to kidnap you when I leave and take you back with me. I'd like to rob a bank so I could move my whole family here whether they like it or not and you'd never have to go to work again and we could just carry on walking and swimming and having rampageous sex and drinking wine by starlight . . . but realistically . . .'

'Realistically your options are a lot more limited.'

'A *lot* more. Realistically, it's this: go home, continue to raise my kids, wait until they're grown. Well, until Sylvie's grown. Which will be . . . six years if I consider her grown when she goes to uni. Or forever, if we end up having the same kind of relationship as you and your mum.'

Nora swiped at his arm. 'Very funny.'

'And by that time you'll have got entangled with some other bloke who's nowhere near good enough for you. So that's where I need your input, mummy's girl. Can you see any way of increasing my options? Like, you could come and visit. Any time. But it'd be one hell of a long-distance relationship. It'd be frustrating, tiring, stressful, unspontaneous, expensive—'

'Stop!' cried Nora, covering her ears. 'I get it, I get it!'

'Sorry. I'm telling myself, not you, because I keep having this wild thought that we can do it, y'know? That we can just do this . . . but how? And it might not be what you want. Nora, I'm serious, if you only want this summer, I would understand.'

'You think that's how I feel? That it's just some sort of holiday *fling*?'

'No, I know it's not like *that*. But you're in transition, you're working out what you want from your life. I don't want to add to your complications. If you tell me that the best thing for you is to keep this – us – here, in this summer, where it's beautiful, but part of that transition, I'd . . . well, I'd be gutted, yeah. But I'd want what's best for you.'

Nora leaned her head against his shoulder. 'You're amazing. And you're right, it's not easy to see a way forward. But you're not a complication, and I don't want this summer to be all we have, so if there is a way, let's find it.'

She felt him drop a kiss in her hair. 'You don't know how happy I am to hear that. It doesn't make things easy, but it means so much that you feel the same. OK, so we've been together two months. It's nothing, really. But I'm just going to be honest because we don't have time to be anything else. I feel like – please don't think I'm crazy – like I've met the person I want to be with. You know? Like, maybe for the next fifty years. Do you think I'm insane?'

Nora shook her head. 'I feel the same.'

'Thank God for that. But if we both lived in the UK, how would it go? We wouldn't just move in together now, would we?'

'Of course not.'

'Because we wouldn't want to rush things, right? We'd want to take it one step at a time, enjoy it? Yeah?'

'Yes. And because we'd want time for our brains to catch up with our hearts and just reassure ourselves that the feelings don't exist in a bubble. You know? I guess that's the main thing for me. I do feel we're in a bubble. I don't want it to end but it will. If you did live in this country, this summer would still end, we'd still have to go back to work and stuff, but it would morph, wouldn't it, into a new phase?'

'Exactly. And it would all happen naturally. But if we want something to happen, we have to *make* it happen. That's something that works really well for me in all other areas of life. But when it comes to relationships . . .'

'Forcing doesn't work. I know. It's like trying to make flowers open.'

'Yeah.'

They fell silent again, brooding. The blackbird, obviously considering them part of the scenery now, hopped out of the bushes to stand in the sun, yellow beak open, glossy throat trembling, pouring out his song. It was so good, thought Nora, to be with a man who could sit in silence, just holding her, and soak up the beauty of it. Simon would have pulled his phone out long ago. He would have taken a photo of the bird, looked it up on the internet, tweeted about it and given Nora a lecture about ornithology.

'Hey, Logan?' said Nora at last. 'You've been so looking forward to having the kids here. Don't let this spoil it, don't feel torn. We'll sort out whatever we need to sort out. It's all good,' she concluded, borrowing one of his phrases.

'Yeah, it's all good. Thanks, Nora.'

They set off again, emerging from the shady woodland and passing a lonely church. According to Logan, recently converted UK history aficionado, it had been as far as a band of Napoleonic invaders had made it, once upon a time. 'They'd counted on local support to overthrow the system, but they didn't get it,' he explained.

'Knowing this place, everyone was probably too laid-back to want to fight,' said Nora, thinking of Kaitlin and Danny, Portia and Lil. Darren! 'Probably they all just wanted to chill out and enjoy the weather.'

On the way home they stopped for dinner at a quaint pub they'd spotted on the way over. They took a table in the corner with a view of the garden, and watched the lawn turning grey, then violet, as evening drew in.

They were halfway home before Nora remembered to check her phone, something that would have been neurologically impossible in her old life. She fished it out of her rucksack in case there were messages from Kaitlin or Gran. But there was only a missed call from a Tenby number she didn't recognise.

Strange to get a call from an unknown number with a Tenby code. Kait, Kait's work, Molly, Danny, Lil, Portia, Mrs Watkins and even the bookshop were all stored in her contacts. Maybe it was a wrong number, or a sales call.

'You have one new message,' advised Voicemail Vera. 'Press one to listen to your messages.'

Nora did. 'Hello . . . Nora? Miss Banquist?' said a deep male

voice that she didn't recognise. It was a craggy, cultured voice
that she immediately warmed to. 'This is Leo Jones . . . that is,
Jones – your landlord, I suppose. I picked up your email this
morning and, well, I'm back in Tenby now. I wondered if we
could meet? I don't want to intrude, I wouldn't take up much
of your time. And there's no obligation, of course. Anyway,
please call me back at your convenience. My number is . . .'

Nora pressed save and hung up. Jones. In Tenby. *Where* in
Tenby? She and Kait were staying in his house! How awful.
Was he back for good? Well, he was allowed to change his mind
and come home.

'Trouble?' asked Logan, glancing from the dark country
roads at her face.

'No, yes, I don't know. Guess who that was?'

'*Strictly Come Dancing*?'

'Yes, they're crazy to have me. Actually no, it was Jones.'

'*Jones?* Holy shit. Was it about your email?'

'I guess so. He said he read it this morning and he wants to
meet. Logan, he's in Tenby!'

Logan whistled. 'Wait, what? So he read your email *this
morning* and he came to Tenby right away?'

Nora checked the time of the call. Three fifteen. 'Pretty
much. If he read it this morning in London . . . yes. He must
have jumped straight in a car, or on a train or whatever.'

'Jeez! He *really* wants to talk to you!'

'I think he does. Oh Logan, do you think he's back for good?
Do you think Kait and I will have to move out sooner than we

planned? I mean, he said six months but he's in his seventies. We can't just keep living there and leave an elderly man homeless.'

'He'll be fine,' said Logan. 'He might be older, but he's not *elderly*. Not if he's exhibiting world-class art and planning trips to Lisbon and taking off across the country at a moment's notice. He won't back out of his promise, I'm sure. I think the real issue here is that when you meet him, you'll find out an awful lot you never knew about your mother. I think your questions are about to be answered.'

# Chloe

The next two hours were a dark, desperate blur for Chloe. Iestyn joined them and tried to hold her but she shoved him away. After Michael, she didn't want anyone touching her. And if she hadn't come on this stupid date with Iestyn in the first place, if she hadn't been so vain and silly and easily impressed, Llew wouldn't be lying here now.

The ambulance men arrived. The ambulance was in the harbour; they would stretcher Llew there when they had made an assessment. To Chloe they seemed intolerably slow.

'Will he be all right?' she wailed. 'Will he be all right?'

One of the men, young, with dark hair and a rugged face, suggested that someone should take her home. Chloe recoiled like a wild animal and flatly refused. The medic took in her gaping blouse with a frown and gave Iestyn a narrow look.

'Keep her back,' he ordered shortly.

Events seemed to progress in a series of disconnected flashes. Chloe sat in the sand, crying. Somehow they got Llew onto a stretcher and carried him away. Chloe leapt up and chased them, begging to go with them. But the ambulance door slammed shut on a still-unconscious Llew.

'He's alone!' she gasped, struggling to breathe. 'He can't wake up and be alone. Someone has to go with him.'

Iestyn buttoned up Chloe's blouse and somehow got her to the nearest hotel, where he bought her a brandy and telephoned Kite Hill. All the while she couldn't stop shaking and crying.

The next thing Chloe knew, Auntie Susan, Uncle Heinrich and Mr Jones were crowding into the hotel. She couldn't make sense of the barrage of questions around her, though the looks of loathing that Mr Jones was shooting at her hit home. Nevertheless, he was insisting that she come at once. 'We can't waste time here,' he shouted, 'we must get to my boy!'

Next, they were all piled into Uncle Harry's blue Ford, swinging through the dark night, the adults muttering about Rookwood. Chloe didn't know who or what Rookwood was but she knew that if Mr Jones was there in the car, they must be going to Llew, and if Auntie Susan was there, she must be safe, so she allowed herself to detach from the situation altogether; her mind became a blank.

The next time she connected with her surroundings, she was in a hospital waiting room with her uncle and aunt. They were sitting on hairy red and brown chairs and the smell of antiseptic filled the air. The light was bright and hurt her eyes.

'Llew?' she asked in a whisper.

'His father's with him. The doctors said we must wait here,' said Uncle Harry.

'Where are we?'

'In Cardiff, at Rookwood.'

Of course, the big hospital. Had they driven all the way to *Cardiff*? She couldn't remember it.

'Is Llew all right? What do the doctors say?'

Auntie Susan looked worried. 'They haven't said anything yet. It's too soon. Chloe, can I get you anything? Can you tell us yet what happened?'

But Chloe shook her head. She couldn't remember. Didn't want to remember. She was wearing a thick jumper, she noticed. Someone must have put it on her. It was Uncle Harry's jumper. She curled her hands up inside the long sleeves. Auntie Susan put her arm around her and Chloe clung to her, as if she was her lifeline to all that was familiar, the only way back to a happy ending.

The clock on the wall showed that an hour had passed, then another. Eventually a tall doctor, with a shock of grey hair like a cartoon of a scientist, stood before them. He looked calm, which gave Chloe hope that he didn't have anything serious to impart.

'I must be quick,' he began. 'I need to get back to Leonard but I understand that you, young lady, were there and saw what happened?'

Auntie Susan's arm tightened around her. Chloe swallowed and nodded.

'Can you tell me? It can sometimes help to know what

caused an injury. It's clear that he's received a terrible blow for instance. Did someone hit him?'

Chloe shook her head. She didn't want to talk about it but if it was going to help Llew she had to . . . 'It was a rock.'

'A rock? How so?'

'We believe there was some sort of landslide,' said Uncle Harry, looking as if he could hardly believe it.

'A landslide? In *Tenby*?' He looked at Chloe.

'Yes,' she said. 'The cliffs . . . started sliding and Llew was running towards me. He got caught in a fall. Mostly they were just earth and plants but a few stones came down. He fell over and I saw . . . I saw a rock, about this big, bounce off him. I thought it hit him on the head.'

'Ah, I see. No, it hit him on the neck.'

'Oh! That's good!' cried Chloe. 'Isn't it?'

'Yes and no. We believe there is damage to the spinal cord and injuries in the neck area can affect the use of the arms and legs. It's too soon to say yet what the damage will be. We'll know more tomorrow. A lot will depend on whether any sensation returns to his limbs in the next few hours.'

'Leonard can't feel his arms or legs?' exclaimed Auntie Susan in horror.

'Not at present. But he's only been conscious a short while and he sustained a great trauma. Early days, as they say.'

'Can I see him?' asked Chloe. 'Please? I'm his best friend.'

'I'm afraid I can't allow it at this time. Leonard needs absolute rest and I have more examinations to make. Please make yourselves as comfortable as you can.'

When he left, Chloe sat up. The three of them looked at each other.

'He is alive,' said Uncle Harry. 'That is the first miracle. That is a wonderful thing. We can be thankful.'

'But what if he can never walk again?' whispered Chloe. 'Oh Uncle Harry, what if he loses his legs?'

'He will not,' decided her uncle with conviction. 'He is young and strong and already we have better news than we might have hoped. The damage will not be too great.'

Chloe ducked her head. Uncle Harry's kind blue eyes were too much for her just then. She felt she'd had a reprieve that she didn't deserve. The doctor hadn't asked *why* had Llew been running towards her, through a landslide. He was a doctor, not a policeman; he was only concerned with the facts concerning Llew's physical state. But Chloe . . . Chloe knew the whole story. She just didn't know how she could ever tell anyone. If Llew was hurt, oh, if Llew lost his legs because of her, if he could never run or swim or lope around Tenby again . . . she would want to die.

# Nora

It was too late to phone Jones back that night. 'God, I hope he doesn't think I'm ignoring him,' she fretted to Logan for the rest of the drive. 'I hope he doesn't think I don't want to meet him.'

'He'll know you're busy,' said Logan, reassuring as always. 'Relax, darlin', you'll call him in the morning.'

He was right, she knew, but she played back the message twice more on the drive – and again before she went to bed – trying to pick up every nuance of his tone. What came across clearly was his excitement. His words were polite and professional, the words of a man used to dealing with all sorts of people. But his tone was the tone of a little boy who couldn't wait for Christmas. Or summer.

Logan didn't spend the night. They both wanted to be up early, Logan to help with the kids – Andy was away – and Nora to ring Jones.

'Maybe he won't be able to meet me tomorrow,' speculated Nora. 'He must have a lot to sort out now he's back. Oh God, Logan, I'm never going to sleep tonight.'

'You'll see him tomorrow,' predicted Logan. 'If the guy came all the way to Tenby in the blink of an eye, he's not going to put anything else first. Chill, sweetheart, just chill.'

*Easier said than done*, thought Nora, letting herself into the house, his kisses still humming on her lips. She couldn't even tell Kaitlin because she was staying at her parents' tonight. Typical! She'd been doing that a lot more lately. A couple of times Nora had even thought she'd heard her crying in the night but when she'd asked about it, Kaitlin had denied it. Even so, Nora remained convinced that she couldn't be over Milo as completely as she claimed. A few months wasn't long after you'd lived with someone. And no matter how old you were, nothing was quite as comforting as being mothered.

Well, it was eleven fifteen. A sensible bedtime. She really must try and sleep. She must *try*.


The next morning was a perfect Tenby morning. Blue sky, wavy sea, bright pastel houses, gold sun. Like a child's drawing. Nora woke early and made a cup of tea. She curled up in the window seat. How soon could she ring? That generation were often early risers. Then again, he was an artist . . . that probably made him atypical. Suddenly she was bubbling with excitement. She was going to meet *Jones*! At long last she would meet the man who had made her Tenby summer possible, who had painted those gorgeous paintings, who had once been her mother's *best friend in the whole world*!

She forced herself to eat a tiny bowl of cereal, take a shower . . . and then at ten past nine, she rang him.

He picked up on the third ring.

'Hello, is that Jones? I mean, Mr Jones? This is Nora Banquist. I hope it's not too early to call. I didn't get your message until late last night—'

'Nora! How wonderful. Do you want some breakfast?'

'Oh yes! That is, I've eaten, but I'd love to join you for coffee. Would you like to come here? To the house, your house?'

'No, no, I won't intrude. How about I treat you to The Cabin? It's got the best coffee in Tenby. And if you discover an appetite and want a second breakfast, which is something I heartily endorse since watching *The Lord of the Rings*, they do great food as well.'

Nora grinned. It was like planning to meet an old and very dear friend. 'I love The Cabin. I might stretch to a bagel. What time is good for you?'

'Now? Ten minutes?'

'Perfect.'

Glad she was dressed and ready, Nora texted Logan with an update, grabbed her bag and ran. She hadn't texted Kaitlin, though she was tempted. She didn't want her worrying about the house if there was no need. And after speaking to Jones, she suspected there wasn't.

She burst into The Cabin and stared around. There was no mistaking him, even if she hadn't seen his photo at the gallery. He stood up as soon as he saw her. He was very tall, and only slightly stooped. He had a shock of white hair, sticking up at all angles and the most piercing, goldy-browny-greeny eyes. He wore jeans and a white shirt and a striped scarf – Indian cotton – was wound around his neck. He looked like someone she would want to know, thought Nora, gazing at him – in any circumstances.

'Nora.' He strode across to her and shook her hand in both of his. 'How lovely to meet you, my dear. Thank you for coming. Thank you.'

'No, thank *you*!' she protested. 'It's wonderful to . . . for so many reasons! There's so much I've been wanting to ask you, I don't know where to start!'

'I feel exactly the same. Shall we sit? Perhaps we should order, then set about learning everything we need to know?'

Nora's appetite had returned with a vengeance. She ordered croissants and granola with yoghurt and berries and a mug of coffee. Jones ordered the Full Welsh and a pot of Paned Cymreig. When that was all sorted, they looked at each other in a kind of wonder.

'I feel as if I know you,' he murmured, looking moved. 'You're so like her.'

Nora laughed. 'I'm not! I'm ten times her size for a start!'

He shook his head. 'The part of your hair and the way it falls, your dainty chin, the sweetness of your smile. I want to jump in and ask you a thousand questions,' he said, 'but that would be very ungentlemanly. You first.'

'OK. Well, first of all I want to say thank you, again, for being so generous with the house.'

'Nora, you've thanked me. Many times! You both have.'

'Yes, but you don't understand. We've both had so much . . . well, we both really needed a stroke of luck, you know? And you've given us one. It means the world. But you're home now and you must want to reclaim your house. And we'll completely understand . . .'

'Lord, no, Nora! Please rest assured. The last thing I want to do is renege on our arrangement. You must stay until whenever we agreed.'

'The nineteenth of September,' Nora reminded him. The date was burnt on her awareness.

'There then. I am *not* throwing you out.'

'But . . . it must be so inconvenient to be home but not home! Where are you staying?'

'There's a room above The Three Bells. Oh don't, it's fine,' he added, seeing her dismayed expression. 'I'm unusual, Nora, always have been. Trust me, I'm used to an itinerant lifestyle. What I really want is . . . well, this. Just to talk to you. Your mother . . . is she well?'

'She's fine, Mr Jones. She's having a ball in Italy with a friend of hers.'

'And your father? Is he with them?'

'Oh no, my father left us when I was one. We haven't seen him for thirty-nine years.'

'What a fool. I'm truly sorry, Nora.'

'Oh, don't be. I never knew him and Mum and I were fine together. Better than fine. And Mum . . . well, I don't think she missed him that much to be honest. I'm sure she loved him, but I don't think she *loved* him, you know?'

'I do know.' He nodded, his eyes warm and intelligent. He was so far from the doddering, confused pensioner that his daughter had described that Nora wanted to laugh.

'And now? She married again?'

'No, never. It's always just been me and Mum.'

'I see.' His expression was an extraordinary mix of relief, disbelief, pain and hope. She wondered if she should be talking like this about her mother to a stranger, but she trusted him instinctively. 'And please,' he added, with an angular, endearing smile, 'don't call me Mr Jones. Call me Leo. Or, if you like, you can call me Llew.'

# Chloe

Three weeks after the accident, Chloe was curled up on the sofa in the living room at Kite Hill, wearing Uncle Harry's same jumper. Chloe had felt cold for three weeks now. She wouldn't leave Tenby. Mr Jones refused to let her see Llew at the hospital so she insisted on staying until they came home.

'In shock, poor dab,' said the neighbours. 'Thick as thieves, they were, and now no one knowing what's to become of the lad. And Mr Jones mad with grief! Fancy blaming a young girl when a natural disaster was all it was, and Leonard being reckless as usual. A tragedy, but no one's fault. But then, Mr Jones has always been queer. And his wife left him . . .'

But Chloe knew the truth: he was right to blame her. She was bad – Michael had said so and Mr Jones was saying so. She hadn't deserved Llew's love. She had been vain and so blind, going out with Iestyn when she knew it hurt Llew, thinking that Iestyn was somehow more right for her, not properly valuing the thing that was most precious to her in the whole world. She hadn't led *Michael* on, that much she knew, but she had been punished for her superficiality and selfishness – and so had Llew.

There had been gossip about Michael. That awful night, he had taken Annie Williams out. Annie had been floating for days beforehand, her mother told Auntie Susan, dizzy over his handsome face like all the girls, but now she didn't want to see him ever again. He'd come on very strong at the end of the night, Annie said. So strong she'd been frightened. She'd pushed him away and run home alone, leaving him wandering The Croft at night, all alone. And Annie was always such a good, polite girl. She must have been frightened to do that. What had come over that Michael then? Perhaps his popularity had gone to his head and he'd forgotten how to take no for an answer. Auntie Susan didn't say much.

Chloe overheard all this from the next room. So now she knew what he had been doing on the North Beach so late. He must have been angry and frustrated about Annie and then come across her, sitting alone . . . At night, in the attic, she kept waking from dreams of the moment when a pair of arms had stolen around her from behind and hot breath poured over her skin. They were all mixed in with dreams of falling earth, burying Llew, Chloe, Megan, Iestyn. The victim was different each night but it was always someone Chloe cared about, and always Chloe's fault. At least, up there in the roof, no one could hear her sobs.

She gnawed her fingernails. Llew was coming home from hospital today and she was going to see him whether Mr Jones wanted her to or not. What could he do? Keep them apart forever? She *had* to see him, she had to reassure him that it would be all right. And . . . she still had to tell him that she loved him. It had been in her heart all that night; when she was with Iestyn, during that ghastly time with Michael, and as she saw Llew running towards her through plumes of falling earth. She needed to let him know. Surely that would be something for him to hold on to in the midst of this terrible time. She still hadn't heard the doctor's conclusion. Perhaps it wasn't so bad after all, and they could be back to normal very soon now. Or . . .

All those fears she'd had about getting a job and leaving home – whether she'd be able to spend her holidays in Tenby – all so small and pointless now. Growing up was *good* because it meant they could be properly together. Chloe wanted that more than anything. But Llew didn't even know that she'd ever wanted it at all.

She jumped as the front door slammed; these days she was as nervous as a kitten. Then Megan burst into the room. 'He's home,' she said without preamble. 'Leonard, he's home.'

'How?' wondered Chloe, scrambling up and looking around as if she expected to see Mr Jones in any corner, pointing an accusing finger at her. 'Mr Jones told your dad he wasn't back until teatime.'

Megan shrugged. 'He may have done, but I've seen him, Chloe, I'm telling you. A taxi pulled up outside their house and Mr Jones carried him inside. I came straight back to tell you.'

'Thank you, Megan.'

She fled to the Jones's. It was the first time she had left the house alone since the accident. Her heart was hammering and not just from the exertion. Colours all seemed different – harsh, strident – and noises louder. She felt bruised all over, as if contact with anything at all would be painful. This was a world where the sky could fall in, where the people she loved could be crushed, where men might look at her and completely misread her intentions and feelings. Nothing was safe any more.

Llew's father answered the door looking harassed. 'What are you doing here?' he raged. 'You're not welcome. We've only got back this minute, I'm settling Leonard.'

'Please, Mr Jones. I'm sorry if it's not a good time. But I've been waiting and waiting, I have to see him, I *have* to.'

'Always about you, isn't it? That boy was always thinking of you. Trouble is, you are always thinking of you too. But maybe it's not what's best for *him*. Have you thought of that? Do you care?'

'Of course I care. It *is* best for him. Llew would want to see me. I have important things to tell him. And I need to know what the doctors have said. Please, Mr Jones, you can't keep it a secret forever! You know how much I . . . care about Llew.'

He looked at her with disgust. 'This is a private time, girl. Go home!' he said and slammed the door in her face.

Chloe stood on the doorstep. The panic that had periodically risen up inside her since that night threatened to engulf her again. She could feel her breathing change and her head spin; in a minute the sky would turn black . . . She couldn't let that happen here; she couldn't just collapse on the doorstep. Without thinking, she pushed the door open. The kitchen was empty, but she could hear voices in the sitting room. She went in.

'What the devil?' exploded Mr Jones. 'I told you to leave! You can't just waltz in as if you live here! Get on back with you now or I'll speak to your uncle and tell him to keep you away.'

'Please!' gasped Chloe, leaning on the wall for support. 'Please, Llew!'

'Let her stay, Dad,' said Llew's quiet voice from the sofa. 'It's all right.'

Mr Jones looked at his son with a wretched expression. 'You still want to see her, even now, after everything?'

'Of course. None of this is her fault, Dad. And we have to tell her. *I* have to tell her. Will you give us some time, please?'

Mr Jones stared at Llew for a long minute, then with an exclamation of disgust left the room.

Chloe walked on wobbly legs to the sofa. Just the sight of Llew helped her focus, as if some damaged compass were being restored.

'Pull up a chair,' he invited.

She perched at his side, wondering how to touch him now. There were blankets heaped over him, covering his limbs. She leaned forward to kiss his cheek and there was his familiar smell.

'Oh Llew!' she gasped. 'Oh Llew, at last!' She fell to her knees on the floor, chair forgotten, and started to cry. He didn't move to touch her and when at last she stopped she had the fearful thought that perhaps he couldn't. She looked up at him.

'Llew, are you . . . ?' She couldn't say, *are you all right*? That was preposterous. 'How are you?' she asked at last. 'I mean, what has the doctor said? How *are* you?'

There was a movement under the blanket and he slowly reached a hand to her, his fingers pale as they emerged. Chloe grabbed his hand and hung on to it fiercely. 'I've missed you so much,' she muttered. 'I've been so worried. Oh Llew, you have no idea. Please tell me everything. I never want us to be apart for so long again.'

He looked at her strangely. 'But we will be, Chloe. You'll go home and everything's different now. In fact, why *aren't* you home? You should be, by now.'

'How can you ask? I stayed because of you. I've been waiting and waiting. I wanted to come to Cardiff to see you but your dad—'

'He thought it was best. The doctor said I've had a terrible shock and it will take me a long time to adjust to everything.'

'I understand. I do. But I couldn't go home, Llew. And I won't, now. I'll stay at Auntie Susan's and we'll be together and we'll get through this.'

'Chloe,' he said gently. 'It won't be like that. The doctors have said . . .' Such a dark shadow crossed his pale, angular face that Chloe shivered. He was fighting back tears. 'The doctors have said that I'll never walk again. There, I've told you. I have a very different life ahead of me now.'

Chloe's body turned to pure ice. 'Llew,' she whispered. 'Truly? They said that?'

He nodded. 'Oh, they said many disabled people can live quite full and almost normal lives,' he said bitterly. 'But I never wanted to be normal, Chloe, I wanted to be extraordinary. *Quite full.* That's the best I can hope for. Oh, don't worry, I'll be all right. You know me, I'm always all right. But Doctor Meredith was right. It'll take a while to get used to, I expect.'

'I'm so sorry, Llew. I'm so, so sorry. But, are they sure? I mean, doctors can make mistakes, can't they? Can't you get a second opinion?'

'Had one. Dad called one in right away, of course. Said the same thing. Explained all about the spinal nerves, and the different sorts of injuries that arise when different vertebrae are damaged. I had two injuries: cervical – that's neck – and lower back. It's whether there's some sort of feeling in the first couple of days that bodes well for recovery. I had a little feeling in my arms and look. Look what I can do now!' He lifted his hand, just an inch, and gave a twisted smile. 'Dazzling, isn't it? But my legs are a different story. I'll be in a wheelchair, Chlo. Everything's finished.'

Tears came to her eyes again but she blinked them back because they were no help to Llew. 'It *can't* be all over. I know it must feel like that now but we won't let it be. I don't know how I'd feel if it was me . . .' She paused. 'But I know we can get through this and you'll be happy again, my love.'

If he noticed her endearment, which she'd never used before, he didn't comment. 'But it hasn't happened to you, Chloe. It's happened to me.'

'I know, I didn't mean—'

'I know you're upset. Thank you for caring. But I'm on my own with this, Chloe. At least, I'm on my own with Dad.'

'You're not, you'll always have me. We'll work things out together and gradually over time things will get better.'

'Chloe, this isn't chickenpox.'

She was stung. 'I know that! I'm not stupid.'

'I know you're not. I just don't think you know . . . I mean, I've had a week to let it sink in, and even then—'

'It will take more than a week, of course it will. But I do know what I'm saying, Llew. That's part of the reason I came here. I have to tell you something. That night . . . the night it happened—'

'Yes. Are you all right? When I saw . . . when I saw him on you and you were screaming . . . I couldn't see anything else, Chloe, I couldn't hear anything. Never mind the cliffs, the sky could've fallen in and I wouldn't have noticed. He didn't hurt you, did he? I wasn't too late?'

'Oh Llew, it was horrible, *horrible*. I'd never been so scared and I thought I never would be again. Then I thought I'd lost you and that was even worse. But no, he didn't hurt me, though he would have. You saved me, Llew, you saved me, and it's all my fault that this has happened to you.'

'It's not your fault. You didn't ask me to come looking for you. You didn't ask that bastard to attack you. Oh Chloe, I keep thinking that as soon as I'm up and about I'm going to beat him up and good. But I won't ever be up and about again, will I? I'll never be able to punish him for trying to—'

'And a very good thing too,' said Chloe, trying to keep her voice light. 'It was vile, Llew, but it's not your job to punish him. You did enough, you did the important thing, you stopped it happening. I owe you everything. Thank you.'

He pulled his hand from hers and lifted it again, reaching towards her face, but he couldn't quite get there, so she dipped her head so that his hand could touch her cheek. 'I'm so glad,' he whispered. 'So glad. I only want good things for you, Chloe.'

'And I for you. And we will have them, Llew, one way or another. It might not be the life we expected, but we'll find a way to make it good.'

'But this is *my* struggle, Chloe. I told you. You're so bright and beautiful . . . only good things for you. This, with me, it won't be a good thing. I don't want you to be part of it.'

She snorted. 'I'm already a part of it – and for always. That's what I was going to tell you. That night, before . . . everything happened . . .' She cleared her throat. It seemed like another lifetime, when nothing was clear and everything could be lost. 'Llew, I realised something I'd known for a very long time, but I didn't *know* I knew because . . . well, because I'm young, I suppose, and not too bright sometimes. I love you. Not just as a friend, Llew. All those dreams I had of romance and a home and a marvellous husband, it's *you*. I sat there and it dawned on me and then I wondered how I could ever have been confused. It's always been you and that won't change, not now or ever.

'I planned to come round and tell you that night. But then . . . anyway, I'm telling you *now*. I'm in love with you and I know you're young, but you won't be always, so you keep telling me, so I'm going to wait for you, Llew Jones. So there.'

She kneeled up and kissed him on the mouth, softly but firmly, then sat back to see his face. There were tears in his eyes and his skin was dotted with faint, brown freckles. His chest was rising and falling quickly and he looked at her with such a complicated expression in his golden eyes. He didn't say anything.

'Llew? Do you understand?'

He nodded.

'Well? Say something!'

'Oh Chloe,' he said. 'I'm so sorry. It was very brave of you to tell me this but . . . I'm sorry. I don't feel the same. I don't love you. Well, I do, of course, but not like that. I thought I did, I admit that. But it's confusing, at this age. We were together all the time, and you are very beautiful . . .' His eyes lingered on her face as though he were an artist making a sketch. 'But we're friends, that's all. It's something I realised while I was in hospital. But you'll be all right, Chlo, won't you? You'll meet someone else, you'll see.'

'But I don't *want* someone else! Llew! I've felt what there is between us. We care for each other more than for *anyone* else. We know everything about each other. We're so happy when we're together! It's *not* just me!'

'It is. I'm sorry.'

'You're just saying it because of your accident. Either you're upset and you don't know what you're saying, or you're trying to protect me because you think I won't have a good enough life with you. Well, I will, Llew. All the stupid things that mattered to me before like dancing and clothes and cities, they don't matter a bit. So don't you make my decisions for me! You don't know what will make me happy.'

He closed his eyes. 'I'm really tired, Chloe, I need to rest. This is all a bit much on top of learning that I'll never walk again. I don't want to be unkind but I really can't handle this as well.'

Instantly Chloe felt guilty. Of course. She had been so full to bursting with her feelings and hopes that she hadn't considered the timing. His mind must be reeling. No wonder he was confused. She was devastated . . . but she had to stop pushing now. Llew had enough to contend with.

She got up and bent to kiss him again. He turned so that she got his cheek. 'You rest now, Llew Jones. I'll come and see you tomorrow. I'll be with you all the way. I promise.' She hesitated, longing for him to say he'd changed his mind, that he wanted her with him. But he didn't and she left, legs still shaking, mind whirling. Mr Jones sat at the kitchen table and she wondered how much he'd heard.

'Goodbye, Mr Jones,' she said. 'I'll be back to see Llew again tomorrow.'

But he just watched with hooded eyes as she let herself out.

# Nora

It seemed to Nora that she talked for a very long time before Llew could get a word in. She told him about the unhappy change in her relationship with her mother, the mysterious vision that had brought her here and the life she had built since she came. She found herself drawn to confide in him. Also, she was afraid that whatever he said about her mother would lead them down a conversational rabbit hole. When she finally reached an end, it was Llew's turn.

He closed his eyes for a moment, as if thinking himself back in time, and when he opened them they held an expression of such tenderness that Nora's throat constricted.

'I first met your mother,' he began, 'in 1950. She was ten years old and I was eight, a fact she never let me forget. She kept telling me I was a boy, a child. I was, of course, but I never felt like one. My mother left when I was very small and back then it wasn't a commonplace thing. I was the only child of divorced parents in town.

'Until your mother came along, I had no one else. We were poor, I was ridiculed in school and had no friends. But I had

Dad, I had books, and I had photography, my first love, but not my greatest.

'I was sprawled in the dunes with my camera one evening when I heard running footsteps. Before I could move, someone tripped over my ankles and went flying. I turned around to see the most beautiful girl in the world sitting up, looking furious, covered in sand, long white-blonde hair down to here.' He flattened his hand and held it somewhere just below his heart. 'She might have been a mermaid thrown up by the sea.'

'Mum,' breathed Nora, in wonder.

'Your mother, yes. We were fast friends from that moment on. Oh, we had the best times, Nora. I can see that Tenby's woven its spell on you, but I wish you could've seen it then. It was a kind time, an innocent time.'

He continued reminiscing about the halcyon days of child-hood; little Chloe from Nant-Aur and Leonard Jones, the local misfit. Nora sat motionless, her coffee growing cold, drinking in his words instead. He was painting pictures for her, without even lifting a brush. At first it was hard to connect this blonde, carefree child with her mother, but as he talked, Nora realised that she wasn't so different from Jasmine after all. She had loved beautiful clothes and books and the luxury that she sorely lacked. She dreamed of London and Hollywood. She was warm and caring, loyal and funny. She took not just pleasure but pure delight in all the wonders of their bright world. It was as if two separate shadows in Nora's mind were drawing closer together, about to overlap.

Eventually he looked about him as if surprised to find himself in 2015. 'I'm getting pins and needles in my legs,' he said. 'Happens if I sit too long. Would you care to walk while I tell you the rest?'

They stepped out into the summer morning and turned towards the South Beach. Instinctively Nora wound her arm through his, the way she might have done with her own father if things had been different.

'I was in love with her, of course,' admitted Jones. Llew. 'I don't know when it started. No, that's not true. I know *exactly* when it started – that first moment I saw her. But an eight-year-old in love isn't the same thing as a young man in love, as a mature man in love, as an old codger in love . . . in my case, I've experienced all these different loves. They just happen to have been for the same woman. Even if I haven't set eyes on her for fifty-six years.'

'Fifty-six years. Oh Llew. But . . . your wife? Mrs Watkins' mother? God, I don't even know her first name. Why did Mum *leave*? Did she love you too?'

'Glenda, my daughter's name. Her mother was Sandra. I did love my wife. She was the first girl I ever kissed, as a matter of fact!' he smiled. 'She wasn't a Tenby girl but had some family connection here. We met once, as kids, and she took a shine to me. I didn't see her then for many years until she came back to the area. We got on well again. I worried at first that it wasn't fair of me to marry, knowing that the largest part of my heart was sealed off for someone else.

Then again, I was a good husband if fidelity and kindness and financial security count for anything. Anyway, I believe she was happy. She never told me otherwise and she wasn't one to hold her tongue. She died when she was only fifty-seven – cancer. We had thirty years together.' Their footsteps were soft on the damp sand, stepping between indigo mussel shells and frilly grey and peach oysters.

'I'm sorry, and for Mrs Watkins too. It must have been hard for you both.'

'Yes. I never married again – not that my marriage didn't give me pleasure. But there was an emptiness at the heart of it that I minded, even if Sandra didn't. I didn't want that again, knowing that however good something was, it would never be the way it was with Chloe.'

Nora grabbed his hand. 'I'm so sorry. It's heart-breaking. I'm not married. I . . . well, there's someone now but it's probably doomed. I don't know, it won't be easy anyway. But Mum never married again either and she was always so ambivalent about love and relationships.'

Abruptly she stopped. It was clear that her mother had been badly hurt by Llew. It was fine to warm to him; everyone made mistakes and it was all a very long time ago. Still, her mother commanded her first loyalty. She wondered suddenly if she had done the wrong thing in contacting him. Would her mother mind? She had just been so impatient to learn the mystery, and so determined not to have this important conversation with Jasmine while they were in different countries.

She looked out to the restless blue-purple expanse of ocean and the cornflower sky.

*You can't trust love, Nora. Anyone can let you down. Even the best of intentions won't stop disaster striking.* Disaster. It was a strong word. What on earth could have ruptured the idyllic friendship that Llew had described? Well, he was here with her now. She may as well plough on.

'So . . . what happened, Llew?' she asked, looking at him steadily. 'What went wrong?'

# Chloe

Chloe lay awake all night, appalled to find that she was worried for herself as much as for Llew — because he'd said he didn't love her. It had never occurred to her that he might not feel the same — was she so conceited? But no. It was her and Llew, that was all; magic. It didn't make her vain to see it for what it was.

He might be saying it to set her free. But he was quite wrong. The life they *might* have had together was gone, she saw that clearly, despite what he thought. But *a* life together was still within their reach and that was all that really mattered. It would need consideration, of course. Probably she would have to be the breadwinner, which would make them a very unusual couple indeed. But Llew was used to unconventional family arrangements and while Chloe was more sheltered, she could and would adapt. Her mam would advise and help her.

He might think she was doing it out of charity. Her father used to talk about men injured in the mines. Afterwards, he said, they felt like 'less of a man'. That was the phrase he always used when they turned to drink, turned on their caring wives, became morose and unreachable. He said it as though, were he in their shoes, he too would feel 'less of a man'. Chloe had never been able to understand that. But now that it was Llew, and not some distant adult, she could understand a bit. She knew that Llew, with his pride and ambition, would feel . . . less *Llew*, anyway. It was hard to imagine him without his camera, his mercurial passage around the town that was so dear to them, his quicksilver leaping off rocks, over cliffs, into waves . . .

But he had to see beyond that, he *had* to. Chloe knew the boy – the young man – he was underneath those habits. His courage and humour, his resourcefulness, his great wisdom, far beyond his years, would see him through. His bright spirit, too. These things would mean that he was Llew, with or without walking. But it might not be so easy for him to see that, not at first.

The next morning she was up at first light, parcelling up some food in the kitchen. Mr Jones wouldn't have thought of food, and he wouldn't be able to leave Llew yet. She didn't eat breakfast herself – her stomach was in knots – and slipped from the house down to Llew's place.

She didn't knock; she didn't want to give Mr Jones the chance to lock her out. She walked in and found him sitting at the kitchen table in his pyjamas, head in hands. He looked up wearily when she came in.

'Morning, Mr Jones,' she said in her mother's no-nonsense voice, the one she only ever used with the doctor or the school-teachers. 'I've brought some food for you and Llew. Would you like me to make you a cup of tea, before I go to him?'

She braced herself for a battle but he just shook his head. 'Go through. He's awake.'

The sitting room was dark with the curtains drawn and the air was stale. Chloe didn't think Llew had been washed either. But then how would Mr Jones manage? There were all sorts of practical things to be sorted out. She would talk to Auntie Susan, and Chloe would learn.

'Morning, Llew Jones,' she said, pulling back the curtains, kissing him softly and handing him a buttered bread roll. 'I know your appetite, so I've brought you food.'

'I'm not hungry.'

'Well, never mind, save it for later. Not too long, mind, they're lovely and fresh. I've been thinking all night Llew and—'

'Chloe, can you go, please?'

'But Llew, this is important. Are you tired? Is it too early?'

He sighed and turned his head with difficulty. He was in exactly the same position as yesterday, she saw; he must be so uncomfortable. Should she try to move him? But she didn't know if there was a right way to do it. Another thing to learn. 'No, it's not too early. I've been thinking all night too.'

'Tell me, then,' she said, making to sit at his side again.

'Don't!' he snapped. 'Don't get comfortable. You have to go, Chloe, and . . . I don't want to see you again. Not ever.'

She felt the blood drain from her. 'Llew, I know what you're doing, you're trying to protect me, but you don't understand. You really don't. *Please* just accept that I love you and I want

432

to be with you. I'll leave you for now if you want but I am coming back.'

'No.' His voice was strong and hard. 'I mean it, I'm not saying it for you. Having you here isn't good for me. In fact, it's the worst possible thing for me. You remind me too much of that night. You remind me too much of *before*. You were threaded through it all, Chloe, everything I loved, everything I've lost. I can't − *I can't* − do what I need to do − face up to this, adjust − with you around. You're the very last person who can help me.'

Fear darted through her. 'Llew! No! I don't want to hurt you. Please, tell me it will change. You'll start to adjust and then you'll be able to see me again. Won't you?'

'No.' His composure broke and his voice rose, breaking. 'Seeing you is too painful,' he wailed. 'Chloe, don't you get it? You make it *worse*! You make everything *worse*! So please just go, and good luck with your life, and don't come back. Ever!'

# Nora

'Nora Banquist!'

Nora was wandering around Tenby in a daze after Llew's story. It was lunchtime but she wasn't hungry; she could hardly take in her mother's story. Had Gran known about this? She *must* have known. Why had she never mentioned it?

'Nora! I want a word!' The shrill voice reached her like a breeze ruffling the surface of a pool. The breeze was getting stronger. She roused herself and saw Glenda Watkins barring her way.

'Oh, Mrs Watkins, I'm sorry, I was miles away. How are you?'

Something told her the answer wouldn't be good. Mrs Watkins was quivering, the black hair that sprouted from the mole on her chin trembled – her whole face was a vision of indignation.

'Very upset, as a matter of fact. I suppose you know my father is back?'

'Yes, I've just had breakfast with him actually. You've only just missed him. He's lovely, Mrs Watkins, it's such a pleasure to know him.'

Mrs Watkins snorted. 'Soft, is what he is. Breakfast, is it? I suppose you've been charming him into letting you stay in his house at that preposterous rate! And he's all for it, of course. Always was one for a pretty face.'

'Quite the contrary. I assumed he *would* want to return home and I offered to move out. But he won't let us. I assure you, Mrs Watkins, Kaitlin and I would never dream of staying if he wanted to move back.'

'You do know, I suppose, that my father's staying in a room over a pub? A man of his age, living as though he's twenty-three! A man with a reputation – in the *art* world at least – behaving like some young Bohemian. I think he does it just to plague me! Oh, I know I'm not the daughter he'd hoped for, we've never had the first thing in common, my father and I, but even so, to torment me like this . . . I'm a married woman! What will people *think*?'

Nora struggled to follow the train of thought. 'I don't understand, Mrs Watkins. What reflection is it on you where your father chooses to stay? And from what he's said to me today I'd say he's very proud of you indeed. I do mean it, you know – we'll move if he wants us to. But he was very clear that he didn't. Why don't you go and talk to him?'

'Oh! If I could find him, I would! But he's like a bloody seagull, flapping around the place, never in one spot for more than a minute. People will *wonder*, won't they, why he's not staying with me. But he *won't*, will he? "Best for us both to be independent, Glenda," he says to me.' Her imitation of her father's accent was quite good. 'As if I don't keep a clean, comfortable household. As if I don't put meals on the table. As if there's some sort of scandal going on underneath my very roof! That's what people will think, you know. Oh, he's a handful my father, and no mistake.'

Nora fought back a smile. 'I'm sure they won't think that. I'm sure he just wants to give you some space with your relatives staying, and perhaps he wants some peace and quiet to think.'

'What does he need to think about? What's happened?' Her eyes were trained on Nora like rifle sights.

'Nothing, I'm sure. I just meant in general, you know, after being away. Look, Mrs Watkins, I have to go, but please don't worry about anything. I'm sure you'll catch up with your dad soon. And if you want to call in for a cup of tea sometime, you're very welcome,' she added – an impetuous and inexplicable impulse for which Kaitlin would not thank her.

'A cup of *tea*?' echoed her landlord's daughter, staring after her in disgust, as if Nora had said 'a joint of marijuana'. She shook her head like a bull and stumped off in search of her errant father.

Nora hurried beneath the old stone arches of the West Gate and set off to Molly's house. All she wanted in the world was to find Logan and tell him everything she had learned today. But as she passed the pasty shop, she heard her name again and sighed.

It was Greg, Kaitlin's father. Impatient as she was to find Logan, she loved Greg so she stopped.

'Hi, Greg. How was your evening with Kaitlin?'

'Very nice, thank you,' he said in that belligerent voice, with that unsmiling face that belied his soft heart. 'Orright, Nor?'

'Yes, fine, thanks. Off to work?'

'Aye. I'm glad I've seen you, Nor. I wanted to say . . . and Anna too . . . we're glad the little one has you now. You're a good friend to her, Nor. You mean the world to her, like. So . . . thank you.'

Nora hesitated. 'Well, thank you!' It wasn't like Greg to initiate an emotional conversation. In fact, his face was red with the discomfort of it. 'You know, Greg, Kaitlin's just as good a friend to me. It goes both ways.'

'Aye, but with everything going on, like, with her mother. Some things are important to be said, that's all.'

*I knew there was something she wasn't telling me*, thought Nora, spotting her chance.

'Ah, of course,' she said, 'you mean with . . . ?'

'Aye, her mother,' he repeated, frustratingly.

It wasn't that Nora didn't respect privacy, but she had learned a thing or two from Kaitlin since they had met.

'And how *is* all that?' she asked sympathetically.

'Oh, as it is, you know. As it is. When the cancer went away, last summer, we were all so happy, like. To hear it's back again . . . well, Anna's strong but . . .' He shook his head. 'It's hard on all of us. The doctors say there's a good chance she'll fight this again, and Anna says I have to keep strong. But sometimes, when I'm chopping carrots, like, I'll suddenly think, but what if she doesn't?'

Nora let out a tiny gasp. Anna was *ill*. Of course. That was why they'd never met. That was why Kaitlin kept postponing dinners and coffees.

'I'm so sorry, Greg,' she said, laying a hand on his burly arm. 'I really am. Please give my love to Anna even though she's never met me. And if there's anything I can do for any of you, I mean it . . .'

'Thank you, love. Very kind. Well, best be off now. Keep an eye on that girl for me.'

'I will,' she promised. 'You don't know where she is now, do you?'

'Back at the house, I think she said. She's not working till tonight, I know that.'

'Right. Have a good shift, Greg.'

'Bye, love.'

Change of plan. Nora texted Logan, standing in one of the rare patches of signal in the town. She might have to change to a different network if she stayed, she thought inconsequentially.

Then she snapped her phone shut and headed back to the house to look for her ever cheerful, always philosophical flatmate. Who had a lot of explaining to do.

# Chloe

---

*I don't want to see you again, not ever . . . You make it worse . . . Don't come back.* Llew's words had haunted her for decades, chased her down the years.

Of course, she hadn't given up that easily, Jasmine reflected as she swirled a small amount of white wine around the bottom of her glass. The sun was sinking over the Tuscan hills. The fields were a patchwork of orange and lavender, muted and soft as smoke. God, it was glorious here. Italy truly was Jasmine's second favourite landscape in the whole world. And her months here had been perfect, really. She had shopped, lunched, wined, dined, talked, laughed and seen all the sights she could possibly long for. And Faith was easy company. If Jasmine had scripted the days and weeks herself, they couldn't have suited her better. But of course, she hadn't found the peace she was looking for.

Nora, by all accounts, was happy again. That knowledge eased an ache in her heart. But Jasmine had been plagued with thoughts of the past, and not just since Nora told her she was in Tenby – now *that* wasn't something she'd have scripted! But really, it hardly came as a surprise. Nora was her mother's daughter, after all. Why *wouldn't* she be drawn inexorably to that pretty town by the sea?

She wanted to be there too. She wanted to be with Nora, of course – she had held her at arm's length for too long now – and she wanted to see the place again. She had loved it so much, once.

Losing Llew and Tenby in one fell swoop, the trauma of the assault by Michael had . . . well, it was only now, in her refuge in Italy, that she was starting to realise exactly what it had done to her. She had thought that story had ended in London, in those crazy, runaway years. After that decade of slashing grief, covered over by parties and glamour and endless nights, she had moved again, found peace in another new life. Then she'd had Nora, and there was happiness and love again. But she had underestimated how it had continued to affect her, through all the years that followed. There came a time when pain and loss could stack up and reach a tipping point, from inevitable, to quite simply unbearable. Then it changed who you were, from free and spontaneous and loving, to brittle and bitter and bright – in the way an electric bulb was bright, capable of fusing at any moment. Somewhere along the years, exile from the people and places she loved had moulded her, had solidified into an identity. Sophisticate instead of country girl. Independent instead of inseparable. Jasmine instead of Chloe.

What she'd said to Nora was true: she didn't hold with obsessing about the past. She'd always thought that if she just kept moving, she would be all right. She always remembered

Blossom's words to her, that summer of '54. *Never regret anything, Chloe, just keep moving forward.* Life had offered her plenty of chances to do just that: modelling, single motherhood, career-building . . . surviving. Bringing up Nora to the best of her ability, trying to protect her from pain, as any mother would do.

Blossom. She wondered what had become of the vibrant, wonderful woman who'd made such an impression on her young self. Looking back now that she was older, worldly, she could see that Llew had been right – as usual. Blossom *had* been a restless spirit, was never going to stay in a small town for long. And she had become a lot like her, Jasmine realised suddenly. Dainty and dark-haired, with her flower name. Breaking ties, living life large, always moving on, always pushing forward.

In retirement, it was harder to keep moving forward. So she just *moved* – Egypt, Morocco, Thailand, Antigua . . . she had seen them all. But now that Nora was in Wales, with Mam, and she was here in Italy with Faith, she had understood that her true passion wasn't for seeing the world – splendid though that was. Travelling kept her busy but there was no landscape, no language, no lifestyle on earth that could smudge over the memory of that first glimpse of the Tenby sea, blue between the hills, and of stepping down from a wheezing bus, swinging a second-hand suitcase.

Jasmine gasped, sharp and desperate. Oh God. Everything she had fought to keep at bay so long was marching on her. Just for a second she could *see* it as if she were there! Llew's tawny eyes, lively and curious, and his hair, standing up in excitement; Auntie Susan's hourglass figure and matching suits and hats; the crumbling walls with their arches and oillets – she *still* remembered that word, even though she'd heard no one but Llew ever use it – and the long, clean sweep of the South Beach, bright as champagne beneath a cloudless sky.

For a moment the pain in her heart was so spearing, so visceral, that she thought she was going to die right there in Italy, on the terrace, with a half-finished glass of Sauvignon Blanc. A heart attack. Faith would have a right mess on her hands. She, Jasmine, would never see her mother or her daughter again; she'd never have the chance to explain.

As soon as she thought of Faith, Nora, Gwennan and all the reasons she wanted to live, the past – and the pain – cleared. Not a heart attack then. Just plain, old-fashioned heartbreak of the kind she had always hoped Nora would be spared, and from which she had been running all her life.

Iestyn went back to London, promising to write. She couldn't look him in the eye to say goodbye, and no letter ever came. For the first week she stayed away from Llew but wrote him letters. The second week she called every day, 'just in case he's changed his mind,' she said, while her uncle and aunt exchanged glances. He didn't.

Chloe's work placement was due to start. Her parents came to Tenby to talk to her.

'I don't want to push you when you've had such a terrible

shock, *bach*,' Mam explained. 'If I thought it was better for you, I wouldn't think twice about letting Mr Adams down. But you can't stay in Tenby forever, not like this anyway. Llew won't see you, *bach*. I hope he'll see sense in time, poor dab. But it could be weeks, lovely girl, it could be months. You can't help him by ruining your own life. The job is only for a few weeks and if he sends for you, you're not far away. I think it'll do you good, *cariad*, I honestly do – help you feel normal again.'

Normal. Chloe didn't think she'd ever feel that way again, but she could see the sense in her mother's suggestion. Guiltily she realised it even held some appeal. Tenby, her promised land, felt oppressive now. Without Llew it was sucked dry of all its magic. She *wanted* to stand in a shop, she realised, talking to strangers who didn't know Llew, didn't know that Chloe Samuels went to Tenby in the summers, didn't know that she was half a stone thinner than she had been two weeks ago. She *wanted* to talk about buttons on gloves and the different lengths of shoelaces.

So she wrote Llew another letter, explaining, telling him that she would return the minute he asked for her, job or no job. That no matter how much time went by, she would always return the minute he asked for her. He never did.

She went back anyway when her work placement finished. She stayed with Auntie Susan, went to see Llew every day, only to be denied entry by Mr Jones. He no longer seemed to hate her, he was just doing his son's bidding. He didn't even seem entirely happy about it.

No one knew how Llew was getting on. Mr Jones kept himself to himself, popping out early to shop for essentials, only exchanging the barest of greetings with others. Uncle Harry and Auntie Susan called regularly but only once got through the front door. They offered to help in any way they could; Mr Jones said they were managing fine. But he gave no specifics.

A full-time position opened up at Adams's. Chloe was offered the job, so she went home again, reiterating her promise to Llew, by letter and via the exhausted messenger of Mr Jones, that she would drop everything the minute he was ready to see her. She took up her new life as a shop girl in Carmarthen, hoping against hope, every day, that she would hear from Llew.

Then Richard was fired from the Sea Breezes. Embezzlement. It transpired that he had stolen thousands of pounds – a little here and a little there over the years, enough to add up to a significant outrage. And the town turned on the Schultzes. Richard's disgrace brought up all manner of censure – and renewed speculation about Megan's mysterious summer in France, from which she came back so changed and chastened. Rumour whispered that she'd had a baby out there, she'd always been fast.

The rumour was half true. Megan had had a baby. But she wasn't fast, that had always been bravado. Michael Everley had forced her, of course. It wasn't until many years later when Megan looked Chloe up in London one day and they treated themselves to tea at the Ritz that they could talk about it. Chloe's heart had broken all over again to think of her cousin going through the same thing that she had, but worse. Much worse.

Not content with tarring Megan with Richard's brush, Tenby tongues reached back still further and wagged some more. That Susan had remarried with indecent haste after losing her husband. And to a *German*! Right after the war, no less! Rubbing all their noses in it, she had been. Terrible. No grace to that. That Heinrich could call himself Harry all he liked, he could, but he was Heinrich the Hun and they all knew it.

The Schultzes moved to London. It was easier there, Auntie Susan explained when she came to Nant-Aur to say goodbye. And it was a fresh start; no one there knew what Richard had done, or looked at Megan and wondered. It was another nail in the coffin of Chloe's love affair with Tenby. That the town could turn on her aunt and uncle like that showed a dark underbelly that made Chloe feel sick.

Nant-Aur wasn't far enough to ease the nausea, nor Carmarthen. When a glamorous auburn-haired woman in a dark green trench coat came into Adams's in February 1959 and told Chloe she was a model's agent, Chloe couldn't believe her ears. She had long since decided that nothing would ever happen to her again, bar getting on the bus each day and going to work, then getting on the bus again and going home. The woman asked if Chloe would come to London for some test photos. She would cover all expenses, naturally.

Jasmine smiled, remembering Adele Brenneman, her first agent. Adele offered her a new career, a new way of life and a new place to live. It had been Adele's idea to dye her hair.

'There are so many girls plying the waif look at the moment,' she said after Chloe's first photo shoot, 'and they're all one shade of blonde or another. I believe you're prettier than all of them but mine is only one opinion. You need something to make you stand out, to edge you ahead of the field. I don't suppose you'd—'

'What?'

'No, never mind. Hmm.' Adele tilted her head and reviewed Chloe's contact sheets. 'These are very good. You're a natural in front of a camera. You wouldn't believe the girls who want to be models but stiffen up at the first sign of a lens. You've done this before, have you?'

Chloe thought of all those years posing for Llew, messing around mostly, the way he would catch her unawares. She would get so cross, only to see for herself, when the film was developed, that this unlikely angle or that unlikely outfit had something surprising to catch the eye, actually making a better picture than the pretty poses she would have preferred. 'No,' she said, 'nothing like this.'

'I don't suppose you'd . . . ? No.'

'What?' asked Chloe again.

'Consider dyeing your hair?' said Adele in a big breath, as though she were suggesting posing nude. 'Black.'

'Yes,' said Chloe at once. She could see it at once. Black was edgy, black was London. Black wasn't the hair of the girl who had been molested by a boy she hated and sent away by a boy she loved. White-blonde was the colour of sand, of sunlit surf, of moonlight, of innocence. Black was the colour of penitence, of the dark night of the soul and of winter, with its stark beauty and promise of re-emergence.

Adele looked startled. 'Heavens! If you're always this amenable, they're going to love working with you! Between your looks, your ease with the camera and your openness to suggestions, I'd say you have a very long career ahead of you indeed, if you want it.'

And Chloe did. What else was there for her? Back to Carmarthen to work in a shop for the rest of her life? As much as she missed her parents and even her brothers, it was, as Auntie Susan had said, easier here. No matter how much it hurt, London seemed determined to raise the stakes and fling one more new experience at her after another until her head was whirling and she hardly knew where she was, let alone who she was.

It had been disorienting when Megan finally looked her up, to meet and see her face after all these years and learn her story. Megan told her parents that it had been rape but begged them not to take any action. She couldn't bear anyone to know what had happened to her, she just wanted to forget. And it was a different time then; there was no guarantee Megan would have been pitied – or believed. She left the baby with her friend Charlotte's cousins in France, hoping to leave the whole experience behind. But reminders echoed through the years: every

Tenby Teens dance, every anniversary of the night he wouldn't take no for an answer, every anniversary of the baby's birth.

Chloe and Megan kept in touch for some time after that, meeting twice a year. But the longed-for friendship was tinged with pain and determined not-remembering. They drifted apart again.

Somewhere along the way, the part of the story where Michael had attacked Chloe just faded away. Time passed and Chloe realised that she'd never told anyone and then it seemed too momentous and strange suddenly to pipe up with it. 'So! Guess what happened to me?'

But now Jasmine found there was someone she wanted to tell very much indeed. Her daughter. She had filled Nora's head with so much nonsense over the years, about love and betrayal and disappointment and the perfidy of Wales. She wanted to explain. She wanted to put it right. Especially now Nora had met a man. She didn't want any of her distorted beliefs to live on in Nora and sabotage her. It was time to get it into the light of day at last.

Nora had always been like her – together on the outside. But the first time she crumbled, Jasmine had turned away. What kind of a mother did that? She'd always thought she was a good mother – a *great* mother. No one was perfect, but really, she wasn't proud of the last eighteen months.

Part of it was the timing. When things started going wrong for Nora, Jasmine had just found out that Llew had regained the use of his legs after all . . . Still he had never contacted her.

Tracy Rees

She would never forget that ordinary night alone in the cottage in Petersham, drinking a glass of Merlot and watching some thriller on television. Her thoughts had turned to Llew, as they did so often, and before she knew what she was doing her iPad was booting up and she was typing *Leonard Jones Tenby*, into the search engine. She found out that he was famous. That he was an artist. That he had married. Oh, and that he could *walk*.

He could walk! There was a photo of him standing on a stage at the Slade, presenting a prize. She ordered one of his painting DVDs from his website to be sure – and when she watched it, there he was, strolling over the cliffs of Pembrokeshire. She was glad for *him*, of course. But it had been the final, bitter epilogue to their story. All her life she'd blamed herself that he couldn't walk – only to learn, at the age of seventy-three, that he could. He must really hate her, still, not even to tell her the one piece of news that could have lifted her burden of guilt. She had bawled into her sofa cushions that night. She'd come close to telling Nora everything then, but chose to keep hiding it instead. She threw the DVD away.

She loved Nora, so very much. It had just grown so difficult to be close to her. Her own secrets and regrets kept getting in the way. When Nora told her that she was seeing a counsellor, leaving Simon, finishing work, Jasmine had been frantic – her darling girl's life was falling apart. Jasmine lived in fear of falling apart.

All through her glamour-girl days, all through her hippy phase, all through the career-driven eighties, she had been afraid

449

underneath it all. Everyone said Jasmine was a force to be reckoned with. But only Jasmine knew that on the inside she was Chloe, dizzy and frightened as Michael Everley pushed her legs apart and growled filth into her ear, dizzy and frightened as she crouched next to Llew wondering if he'd live or die, dizzy and frightened when he ordered her to leave him for good. She had felt that way the whole time she gift-wrapped gloves at Adams's, and all through the tumbling, glittering nights of London in the sixties. And when Steve left her, even though she had loved him only a little bit. *And* when she held her newborn daughter in her arms and felt such a flood of fierce love that she vowed to do everything in her power to make Nora's life happy, and safe, and pain-free . . .

'And the rest, as they say, is history,' she murmured, finishing her wine and debating whether she wanted another. She didn't. She wanted to see her daughter. And dammit, she wanted to see that town after all, the town that had captivated her heart and then broken it.

'Talking to yourself?' asked Faith, coming to join her in the muslin dusk.

'Sadly yes. Lost in remembering. What a cliché of old age.'

'You're hardly old, darling,' said Faith. It was what they said to each other all the time, Jasmine and Faith and their contemporaries, to reassure each other and themselves. They were a fine-looking set still, Jasmine thought, and certainly they weren't curling into their advanced years like an old blanket. But still.

'But really, darling, I am a little,' she said, smiling at her friend. 'And that's not a bad thing. Better than the alternative, you know! But you're right, there's still plenty of time left and I've been sitting here wondering what on earth I'm going to do with it! Faith sweetie, do you mind awfully if I go home earlier than planned? I really need to see Nora.'

'Of course not! I said come for as long as you like, not until I decide to release you. When will you go? I'll run you to the airport, of course.'

'Thank you, Faith. Tomorrow?'

# Nora

━━━━◈━━━━

While Logan drove Andy's car to Heathrow to collect Brendan and Sylvie, Nora spent the day with Gwennan, biting her nails and being far less help with the baking of Welsh cakes than she liked to think. Gwennan threw her granddaughter sympathetic glances as liberally as she threw sultanas and sugar into the mix. She baked by memory – and many years of practice. Nora kept dipping a teaspoon for a taste of batter, then getting another teaspoon for another taste until she found herself staring at an empty spoon section in the cutlery drawer.

'Never mind the spoons, we'll be running out of batter, *bach*,' commented Gwennan, observing her enormous bowl of creamy, sultana-dotted mix. For the Welsh, there was never any point making a few Welsh cakes; you might as well make enough to feed a village.

'Right,' said Nora, shutting the drawer and staring out of the window.

'Your mind's on Logan, I can see that. Or Kaitlin, perhaps. There's lemon shortbread in the cupboard if it will help, *bach*.'

'Thanks, Gran.' Nora opened the cupboard. It was a relief to be with someone who understood that baked goods really did help, or at least soothe, every problem. 'I've been thinking all day, *He's halfway there, He's nearly there, He's waiting at Arrivals*. It's huge! He's been missing them so much. And Kaitlin! Well, I can't bear to think of what she's going through with her mother. And I *still* don't understand why she didn't tell me.'

Kaitlin had told Nora everything after Greg had given the game away. How two years ago they had battled Anna's breast cancer and won, only to find, earlier this year, that it had come back. How it had made Kaitlin want to move closer to her parents and contributed to her break-up with Milo. He'd seen her through the weeping and the worry once and wasn't keen to face it again.

'I don't blame him, I guess,' Kaitlin had sighed. 'Some people aren't good at the deep stuff. But I want someone who's going to be there for me no matter what – it's not like I chose for this to happen.'

'But why did you leave that out when you told me about him?' wondered Nora. 'Why haven't you told me, all this time?'

Kaitlin shrugged, her animation dulled for once. 'I don't know. Meeting you was so great, so exciting. I guess I just wanted a part of my life that was free from all that, a part where I could be positive, cheery Kait again, and pretend it wasn't real. I don't want it to be real.'

Nora squeezed her hand. 'It doesn't have to change anything, Kait. We can still have fun. We can still obsess about *my* mother. But if you want to talk, I'm here, that's all.'

'A terrible thing,' tutted Gran. 'Poor Kaitlin. So much sadness and struggle in the world. And so much wonder too. Life is not for the faint-hearted, *bach*.'

'You're telling me! I'm so happy Logan's going to see his kids. And I'm looking forward to meeting them. But—'

'But you don't know how it'll be for the two of you now.'

'Exactly. And their coming marks the beginning of the end. Three weeks until he leaves. I don't know what will happen then.'

'If you really love him,' said Gwennan a little reluctantly, 'why don't you move out there, *bach*? People do it all the time nowadays.'

'I know. It's not that part of me isn't tempted. But I never really saw myself living halfway across the world. Have I known him long enough to warrant leaving everyone and everything and following him to New Zealand? But it's more than that . . . I've only just started to feel settled and happy in my skin. I've started thinking seriously about settling in Tenby if I can find work. And it feels really good. Whereas out there . . .'

'Well then, perhaps you could go for a holiday, *bach*, and see if it's somewhere you could be happy.'

'Yes. I'll go out there when I can – that's the first step really – then he'll come back here when he can . . . and if we still feel the same about each other, *then* we'll make decisions. But what if the kids don't like me? What if I don't like *them*? What if it's just too difficult for him and it all comes to an end before it's supposed to?'

Gwennan dropped her wooden spoon and gave Nora a floury hug. 'Everything happens when it's supposed to, *cariad*, you'll see. And of course they will like you. You'll meet them tonight, I suppose?'

'Tomorrow. We thought that after a long flight, and not having seen their dad for two months, meeting the new girl-friend might not be the first thing they'd want to do!'

'Very sensible,' approved Gran. 'It speaks well for him that he thinks of their needs like that, and for you too, Nora. You are both doing things the right way. You have to trust, now. Things will work out, you'll see.'

'But they didn't for Mum and Llew.' She had told Gwennan about Llew's return to Tenby, and what he had told her of his youth with Chloe. Gwennan had listened with tears in her eyes.

'A terrible accident, it was, I remember now. Well, it wasn't that I'd *forgotten*, of course, but I had children enough to worry about. Then Susan and the family moved away and our link with Tenby was gone. It was as if those summers had never been! But I did think about that poor boy from time to time. I asked Chloe if she heard from him and she said no, and it never felt right. Once or twice I even wondered about going to Tenby myself and looking him up, telling him Chloe needed him, but do you know why I didn't? I didn't really know how far things had gone between them, whether she was in love with him. I knew how good and loyal she was and I worried she might give up all her chances to look after him. I didn't like her being gone, but I didn't want that life for her either, tied and struggling, you know? I didn't know *what* was best, and I couldn't get her to talk to me about it, so I never did anything.'

Nora got back from Nant-Aur in a reflective frame of mind. Really, Llew's revelations had only raised more questions. Yes, he'd sent her mother away, told her that he never wanted to see her again. Her mother would have been traumatised by his accident and what must have felt like his cruelty. But surely somewhere over the years she must have realised he'd said those things in the heat of the moment? Had she never tried to get in touch with him again? Whatever the rights and wrongs of it, Nora felt she loved her mother more than ever. If Nora were in Kaitlin's shoes, if she were faced with losing her mother before she was ready – well, could you ever be ready? – she couldn't bear it. She got out of the car and took a large Tupperware container of Welsh cakes from the boot. She tucked it under her arm, slammed the boot and closed the garage.

There on her doorstep sat Logan and a young girl with riotous black curls. 'Wow! Hi!' Nora said. 'I didn't expect to see you until tomorrow.'

'Surprise!' said Logan, looking slightly anxious. He sprang up to kiss her and Nora's heart turned over. Things still felt normal between them! 'I hope it's OK that we're here but Sylvie was crazy to meet you. She *would not* wait! Anyway, it's late so we won't stay, but just quickly, Nora, this is my daughter, Sylvie, the apple of my eye, the peach of my heart, the fruit of my loins—'

'Urgh, Dad, don't say loins! Hi, Nora, it's so nice to meet you. Wow, you're really pretty. Dad said you were but you never know with men, do you? What's that? That smells good . . .'

Sylvie was tall for her age and seriously pretty herself behind large, round glasses. Nora had already seen photos but she was even lovelier in person. Naomi was Maori, and Sylvie had her dad's blue eyes with her mother's dark skin, smooth as a peach. She had incredible hair that reached her shoulders and was as wide as it was long. She had an expressive mouth, a beautiful smile and she wore a short skirt with a T-shirt and knee socks, one of which was pulled up starchily, the other crumpled around her ankle. Nora suspected this arrangement was not accidental.

'Oh my God, you're adorable.' It just came out. She had no idea if you were supposed to greet almost-teenagers that way but Nora was caught off guard. 'Sorry, I mean, hi, Sylvie, it's great to meet you! Thank you for coming to welcome me home.'

'Dad says you've been visiting your gran and she's ninety-three. That's so cool. Well, he's giving me that look like we need to get going. He said we could only come if I promised to be quick because you might be tired. But I hope I'll see you tomorrow?'

'Don't be silly! You both have to come in for hot chocolate and freshly baked Welsh cakes! Won't you, Logan? Can you?'

He grinned. 'Are you sure? We didn't want to ambush you, we just wanted to say hi.'

'*You* just wanted to say hi,' Sylvie corrected him. '*I* want to spend some proper time with Nora. Come on, Dad. What are Welsh cakes?'

Nora opened the lid for Sylvie to smell. She rolled her eyes and pretended to swoon, clutching her father's arm for support. 'Ohmigod, *so* delicious! Did you make them, Nora?'

'I'd like to say yes but sadly today I was even less help to Gran than usual. She made them. It's an old family recipe.'

'Cool. Let's go in then!'

Kaitlin was at work; the house was quiet. Nora switched on lights, poured milk into a pan and found plates and mugs. Sylvie wandered all around the hall and kitchen, wide-eyed. 'This is amazing! Dad told me about your landlord and your house and your housemate.'

'I hope he didn't bore you senseless, Sylvie.' Nora shot a look at Logan. What had happened to their plan to ease the kids into the idea of their being together?

'Oh no, I asked. Once I guessed he had a girlfriend I wanted to know everything. Oh, and don't think Brendan doesn't want to meet you. He does, it's just that he's asleep. You know boys, right, Nora? They're always sleeping, aren't they? They're so boring. But he's really fine about the whole situation. Can I use your toilet?'

'Oh, good! About Brendan, I mean. And yes, it's up the stairs, second door on the right.'

When Sylvie had thundered upstairs, Logan took advantage of the brief hiatus to kiss her deeply, but for once there was something Nora wanted more than his kisses: answers. '*How?*' she asked. 'How did this happen?'

'Couldn't have wished for anything easier,' he whispered. 'I didn't have to say a word. I tell you, some women are scarily psychic and even though she's only twelve she is one of them. We were just driving along and she took a good look at me and said, "Are you in love, Dad?" What was she seeing? I have no idea. But I just seized the day and said yes and then it was a million questions a minute. I eventually got the chance to ask how they felt about it and Sylvie was ecstatic and Brendan clapped me on the shoulder from the back seat and told me very manfully that he's happy for me. I said I hoped we could all spend some time together, but that if they weren't comfortable, I'd understand and we'd work something out.'

'And what did they say?'

'Well, you can see what Sylvie thought. She's just so *open*. It kills me. And Brendan told me very seriously that of course we must all spend time together because it wouldn't be cool of me to neglect my girlfriend. Seriously. I'm getting dating advice from my teenage son! I don't know how I feel about that.'

# Chloe

Jasmine landed in Heathrow at midday and headed straight for the hire cars. She knew herself a little better since Italy, she thought. She knew that if she went home for a shower and a good night's sleep, if she hesitated for even a moment, she wouldn't go at all.

*Are you chicken, Chloe Samuels?*

Too right she was. So although she would have given pretty much anything just then for a pot of Earl Grey, she collected a hire car and set off.

For the first hours of the drive she could fool herself that she was on any old journey. The M4 was long, straight motorway, impersonal and unremarkable. It was only when she reached the Severn Bridge and threw a handful of coins into the bin that fear or excitement or something combining the two kicked in. Wales! When had she last come home? Years ago, for some grandniece's wedding. When she reached Pont Abraham, her stomach lurched. She'd come so far west there was no more motorway – and she still had further to go.

Beyond Carmarthen she freaked out completely: all those

familiar names, like places from a dream. When she neared the turning for Nant-Aur she slowed down automatically, provoking a blare of the horn from an impatient driver behind.

'Screw you,' she muttered, narrowing her eyes at the road sign. She was so tempted to take that turning. She longed for her mother. But she must go on to Tenby while her resolve was intact. It wasn't Mam she was afraid to see. It never had been. She felt suddenly dizzy, and knew it had nothing to do with airport fatigue or the long journey. She pulled into a lay-by to gather herself; her neck was sore from hours of fixed, determined staring ahead.

Zoom. Zoom. She heard the traffic whoosh past and felt it too, her car tugging and shifting a little with every passing car and lorry. The sound of travel; she could be anywhere. But she wasn't. She was almost home. She wound down the window and beyond the traffic fumes she could smell fresh evening skies, the fields, the tang of manure. She looked up into a blue sky with polka-dot clouds that reminded her of a dress she'd once worn for a photo shoot with Jean Shrimpton . . . Two large birds circled above her car. Buzzards? Once she'd known things like that at a glance. She squinted and when they were at the right angle she saw their forked tails. Red kites. She'd heard that after years of being endangered they'd been brought back and were thriving. She'd felt glad, but had never come back to see. Now here they were to greet her.

*Welcome home, Chloe Samuels.*

What the hell had she been thinking all these years, keeping in touch with her mother by phone, meeting only a couple of times a year? She felt sick with guilt and regret. Her mother was old. She *hated* seeing so little of her and there would come a time when she wouldn't have a choice. You'd think she would have learned her lesson when her father died, seven years ago. She went home then, stayed with Mam for two months. Jasmine could still see him so clearly: cycling off to work at the crack of dawn each day to work on the railways in Llandeilo, Llandovery, Carmarthen; building her a doll's house out of orange boxes because she'd envied Megan's shop-bought doll's house; stroking her head when he found her shelling peas at the kitchen table; polishing her shoes late at night.

Jasmine heaved with sobs. It was unbearable. She had loved him so much and wasted so much time because she hadn't faced up to what had happened with Llew. It had poisoned everything; she had let it. She had to make the most of every minute that was left with her mother. But she *must* see Nora first.

Onwards. She started the engine and pulled out carefully. She was weary now, and wanted to arrive in one piece. At Kilgetty, she looked for the patch of scrubland where the gypsies had always been . . . it was still there! No gypsies now, though – only a couple of horses cropping the grass, as though time itself held echoes . . .

When she rounded the bend that afforded that first glimpse of the sea, the glimpse she had hungered for as a child, she nearly swerved off the road. It was so vivid and aquamarine as to seem almost confrontational. *See*, it seemed to say, *I'm still here. What will you do now?*

She steadied the car with a racing heart. 'Concentrate,' she muttered to herself, slowing right down as she took the bend into Tenby itself. It would help no one if she were to turn up dead. Oh God, it was just the same. Well, perhaps not *completely*, yet it was the same *enough* to make her feel as though she had just time-travelled somewhere along the A48. The railway bridge. The road winding uphill. The town walls and crumbling arches.

'Auntie Susan?' she whispered, looking to her right, fully expecting to see a glamorous woman in a tight suit and matching hat waiting on the side of the road. There was only a noisy hen party of four skinny girls and three fat ones wearing veils, L-plates and sashes hung with condoms. Susan had died fourteen years ago.

Jasmine had called ahead from a service station to book a B&B. She'd chosen somewhere tucked away and anonymous, not one of the hotels in the obvious places, like the Esplanade, or The Croft. Even so, the street name was as familiar to her as old wood. She could see it, smell it, even before she got there. There was, as her new hostess had assured her, a small parking space out front and there she drew to a halt.

She sat for another long minute. Outside was a pavement she had trodden a thousand, thousand times. She pulled out her phone to give Nora a little warning that her errant mother was about ten minutes away. No signal. The last time she'd been in Tenby there'd been no mobile phones, so she didn't know if this was typical or if she was just unlucky. She couldn't procrastinate any more.

After checking into the B&B, Jasmine headed out into the warm Tenby afternoon. It was too surreal, retracing the steps of a million summer days spent with Llew. She might have been going to meet him at the harbour, but she wasn't. She was going to find her daughter. Her *daughter*! The last time she'd walked these streets she was eighteen years old.

She decided to walk up Nora's street from the harbour because she didn't want to go the other way, overlooking the North Beach. Would she ever be able to walk that way again without seeing that night – Llew running, rocks falling, and life as they knew it ending forever? She walked among crowds of meandering families, excited children waving plastic spades.

At Nora's, she rang the bell. No answer. She lifted the bronze knocker – a tricksy mermaid – and gave three determined bashes. Silence. There was no sign of life in the windows and when she lifted the letter box no sounds drifted out. She turned to look at the sea. From here she could see Castle Hill. Easy to imagine Llew running through the archway from Castle Beach. *Chlo! Oh, there you are, let's go!* She could hear his voice in the wind.

She sighed. Turned back to the door, as if it could tell her something of what Nora's life had become.

'Are you looking for those girls?' demanded a voice behind her. Jasmine felt instantly and inexplicably guilty. That accent, that *tone*, reminded her of her childhood.

*You think you're big, you do, Chloe Samuels.*
*That Megan's a fast piece, mind you.*
*Married a German! How could she?*

Jasmine turned, reminding herself that she was seventy-five. She saw a woman of around fifty, whiskery-faced and with a thatch of unfashionable brown hair. She was stout and suspicious, dressed in an anorak of an indeterminate blue, sensible shoes and black trousers in some sort of polyester blend. This sort of woman and Jasmine could never understand each other.

'Hello. I'm Nora's mother. Do you know her?' she asked.

'Oh! The mother, are you? Well, well. Back from Italy, is it? I don't suppose she knows you're coming, does she? What's brought you here now then?'

Jasmine had forgotten – almost – the breathtaking intrusiveness of some people. But she was polite little Chloe Samuels no longer. 'Well, that's my business, isn't it?' she said. 'I don't suppose you happen to know where my daughter is?'

'Well!' The woman breathed in sharply, then puffed the air out again, like a bull. 'I've better things to do than keep tabs on those two. No doubt she's out with that flighty redhead, or that Kiwi chap of hers. Escaping tax or something I suppose he is – I know those overseas sorts. Or out with my father she could be. He prefers to spend his time with strangers rather than his own daughter, it seems! When you meet him, tell him I said hello! If he can even remember who I am. There we are, there's no telling what's what with the elderly, especially when they're as loose in the screws as my father.'

Jasmine could make little sense of this but she couldn't be bothered to argue. She knew this woman, or at least she knew her type.

'I'll try to find her, thanks for your help,' she said and hastened off. She wondered when Nora had befriended a senile old man – perhaps he was someone Kaitlin knew.

She walked through the town, noticing all the restaurants and shops that hadn't been there in her day. Well, of course they hadn't. Her day was long gone now. But the Paragon was the same, with its black Edwardian railings. The name had always made her smile. The Esplanade was also the same: bright pastel buildings and palm trees. And the South Beach was too: that long sweep of beach, silver-blond sand and the sea beyond. Swooping gulls on wings like blades. She paused for breath, gripping the railings. She really didn't know if she could go down there. It was *their* place more than anywhere, the scene of reunions, picnics, long sun-baked conversations, icy dips in the sea and such *laughter*. She didn't think she'd laughed quite like that ever since.

She headed back into town. She couldn't face the South Beach yet.

# Nora

<hr/>

Nora was wandering along Warren Street, looking for coins in the cracks in the pavement. She'd been keeping an eye out ever since Llew told her that he and her mother used to. She hadn't found any yet, but the thought that there could be lost change – hidden treasure! – under her feet was so compelling, so *Tenby*, that she lived in hope.

Other than money hunting, she was completely aimless for once. She had no classes today. Gran was having friends round for high tea and a monthly catch-up. Kaitlin was working. And Logan was out sailing with Brendan and Sylvie.

They'd invited her along but the children had only been here a few days and she felt they needed some time without her. It was hard to say no because she already loved being with the three of them. Even so, she wanted to respect the family unit; she didn't want to be 'all over it', as Brendan would say. She would see them tomorrow.

She needn't have worried that the kids' arrival would end the summer idyll; in fact, it was like being given a trailer of what life would be like if she and Logan were ever properly together. Nora had never really felt part of a family before – the double act of her and Jasmine was special, but different. Now the intense conversations and passionate nights Logan and Nora had enjoyed had morphed into swimming and visits to animal sanctuaries as a foursome, into barbeques with Molly and Andy and both sets of kids. Candlelit dinners in expensive restaurants had been replaced by ice cream parlours or chips scoffed sitting on the harbour wall and Nora found that she liked them just as much in a different way. Who knew?

She felt as close to Logan as she had before – less naked, obviously, but just as close – and now there were Sylvie and Brendan as well. Sylvie was offbeat, opinionated and quirky. She wasn't into pink, or make-up, or mainstream music. She liked indie bands and *Doctor Who* and graffiti art. She said whatever came into her head and it was usually hilarious, occasionally disastrous. Brendan was quiet and considered. He was academic, a bit of a preppie, and conversations with him were usually earnest and thought provoking. Nora could be flippant with Sylvie and serious with Brendan. She could be herself – this new, relaxed self – with both of them. She wondered what they would have made of the old Nora, attached to her smartphone, juggling demands from the office, never having time to eat or read or savour life.

If Logan was laid-back, his offspring were horizontal. They welcomed Nora enthusiastically and if she didn't deliberately make room for the three of them to be alone together, it would probably never occur to them. Now, when they went back to New Zealand, she would have three people to miss.

That was a depressing thought. Hastily she switched tracks.

She had met Anna at last that morning. Anna was having a good day and came into Tenby for coffee before Kaitlin's shift. She was a beautiful woman, willowy and curly-haired like Kaitlin, but with golden hair and dark sloe eyes. She was pale, though, and occasionally unsteady on her feet; Nora could see the strain of the last few months. Anna was currently undergoing radiotherapy and apparently the doctors had said there was every reason to hope for a full recovery again. Even so, Nora felt devastated for them all. Kait had been so good to her; Greg too – free paninis counted for much. She hoped that Anna's chances for recovery really were that good; she didn't trust Kaitlin not to downplay matters. If only she could have a sign . . .

And there it was, glinting silver in the join between sections of pavement – a shimmery, shiny fifty-pence piece! 'Oh!' she breathed. The street was empty. Good. She kneeled down and reached two fingers into the gap but she couldn't quite grasp it. Her efforts only shifted the coin further into the weeds growing through the crack. 'Bugger,' she muttered, wondering what to do. If only she had a ruler, but it wasn't the sort of thing she generally carried.

*It's only fifty pence*, said one part of her brain. *It's not exactly going to pay the rent.*

*It's a lucky coin*, the other part retorted. *I have to get it for Anna.* Nora rummaged in her bag and fished out her tweezers. She angled them carefully through the gap, making sure she had tight hold of them – all she wanted was to drop them. She was engrossed, oblivious to her surroundings, when a voice came out of nowhere.

'Nora darling? Are you all right? What *are* you doing?'

Nora looked up in astonishment. Auditory hallucinations! It sounded just like her . . .

'Mum! Oh my God! Mum! It *is* you! What are you *doing* here?' She sprang to her feet and threw her arms around the woman she had loved all her life. She pulled back to look at her incredulously. There she was. Small, indomitable, chic as could be in black palazzo pants and a black sleeveless shirt. Not in Italy, but *here*! Standing in front of Nora looking . . . nervous. Hopeful. They laughed and hugged again. Nora squeezed her eyes closed and thought, as hard as she could, *thank you*. Time was, she had only ever been happy to see her mother. That had changed for a while. But it had changed again. It had tilted back. Just at that moment there was no one on the planet she would rather see.

They hugged and jigged about in circles, laughing and crying. 'How are you here?' asked Nora again. 'Are you all right?' A thought hit her like electricity. What if her mother was ill? Was that why she had come back early? Anna's situation had rattled her. She held her mother still to examine her. She looked different, but well. For the first time in Nora's life, Jasmine had cut her hair. It was now a sharp bob, swinging just below her jawline. She was letting the colour grow out too so the top three inches were silver. On anyone else it would have looked as if the battle with old age was waning. On Jasmine it looked like a fashion statement. She was deeply tanned.

'Yes, yes, completely fine,' Jasmine assured her. 'I just wanted to see you, *very* much. I've been away too long. I'm so sorry I've been so lousy lately but that's all over now. How are *you*? Why were you on your hands and knees? You're not ill, are you?'

'No, I'm fine, I was just trying to fish out a coin from the crack.'

Jasmine looked amazed. 'You were? I used to do that when I was a kid.'

'I know,' said Nora, then remembered that her mother didn't know about Llew yet. 'I mean, I can imagine. There's fifty pence in there that I need to get for Anna as a lucky charm.'

'Who's Anna?'

'Kaitlin's mum. She's got cancer. Look, I've got my tweezers out—'

'No, no, you won't do it with those. You just need really little hands. Help me down.'

Jasmine manoeuvred painfully to her knees, Nora wincing on her behalf and pointing out the coin. Two men passed by and looked at them oddly, but didn't say anything.

'I see it! Wait a second . . .' Jasmine pulled off three huge rings, heavy with semi-precious stones, and handed them to Nora. Then she reached a practised hand into the narrow gap and withdrew the silver coin, triumphant. 'Voila!'

'Mum, you're a star. Let me help you up.'

She hauled her mother to her feet again. 'You look

wonderful,' she said softly. It wasn't just that she looked stunning – that was par for the course. But she looked more like the Jasmine Nora had missed. Up for a laugh, not so defended. Her blue eyes were clear and the corners of her mouth weren't primped in disapproval.

She gave Jasmine her rings and stuck the coin in her pocket. 'Kait will love this. You came along at just the right moment!'

'It's kind of you to say so but I'm afraid I'm about eighteen months too late. I wanted to be there for you, Nora, when you were struggling, and I couldn't be, but I'd like to explain, if that's OK.'

'Come back to the house and we'll talk about *everything*. Oh, and Mum? Welcome home.'

# Chloe and Nora

Home. Jasmine found herself in a sort of wonderment to be walking through Tenby with her daughter. Nora looked so well. Her hair was a little longer, whipped all ways by the breeze. It suited her to be less perfect, less formal. Her skin was golden from long walks and contentment and her tense, anxious manner was gone; she walked with a swinging stride as if expecting delightful things around every corner. Like a long-lost mother materialising from nowhere in front of her. And she was so *happy* to see Jasmine, despite everything – that made it all worthwhile, the long journey, facing her fears, kneeling on the pavement.

Jasmine tried not to look around too much. She didn't want the old memories overwhelming her before she'd made a coherent explanation to Nora. She looked at her daughter instead. When Nora was little, Jasmine had been her anchor. Now she looked at Nora to feel reassured.

Nora's house was exquisitely decorated and had an atmosphere of ease and comfort. 'It's perfectly beautiful,' she said as Nora put the kettle on. 'Did you ever get to the bottom of why the rent's so cheap?'

Nora put the kettle down and looked at her. 'Actually, yes. But Mum, we need to be sitting down. I don't think there's much we can talk about that isn't going to overlap with everything else.'

Jasmine wondered what Nora had learned about those long-ago summers since coming here. She wondered how much her own mother had told her.

'Are you hungry?' asked Nora. 'Tired? Do you want a rest before we talk?'

'I'm exhausted, but I want to talk to you first. It's so overdue and it's *so* good to see you. I would quite literally kill for some Earl Grey, though, if you have it.'

'Mum, I live with a foodie. We have everything. Seriously, whatever you fancy, name it, chances are it's here.'

'Well, Earl Grey, as I said, and . . . I am a bit hungry. Something savoury? Light?'

'Homemade mackerel pâté on sourdough? Oh, don't worry, not homemade by me. And some three bean salad?'

'Perfect.'

'And a couple of Gran's Welsh cakes?'

'Goodness. Yes.' To think that life went on here just as always, that her mother still baked Welsh cakes, tea was still poured for comfort, the tides came and went and people fell in love in Tenby . . . it was overwhelming. She had shut it all out for decades. Now she was agreeing to take comfort from these same old things again. She remembered learning to swim as a child, learning to trust the insubstantial, shifting water. This felt similar.

Upstairs, in a luxurious, spacious lounge, Nora headed to the window with an air of habit. Jasmine hesitated.

'What's wrong, Mum?' Nora looked over her shoulder.

'Nothing. Would you mind very much if we sat here? I . . . that is, the sofa looks so comfortable and I'm a bit achy after the drive.' She needed to stay away from the window. She couldn't look out on that view of Castle Hill, the path towards the rocks where Red Sam used to sit.

*Come on, Chlo! I'll get a good shot of him today, I can feel it!*

She blinked back tears.

Nora set the tray down on the coffee table then gave her mother another hug. She could only imagine what it had taken for her to come here, after so long. She could feel her small frame shaking a little and she held her hand, looking at her tenderly.

'Mum, please don't worry. I already know quite a bit of what you're going to tell me. I'm sure there's more as well, but I promise you things aren't as bad as you think they are. Everyone loves you, everyone's missing you. I want to hear everything you want to tell me, but nothing *matters*. All that matters is having you back.'

Jasmine sagged like a little leaf, and sank into the sofa. Nora poured two cups of tea then sat beside her mother, legs crossed. 'Who's going to start?'

'I'll start,' said Jasmine in a determined voice. 'I've been sitting in Italy missing you. Missing Mam. And even missing Tenby, since you wrote and told me you were here. Yesterday

I couldn't bear it any more, so I flew home this morning . . .'

'*This morning?* You haven't come straight from the airport?'
Jasmine nodded, her chic two-tone bob swinging.

What a pair her mother and Llew were, thought Nora,
both leaping on planes or trains and taking off to Tenby at a
moment's notice.

'No *wonder* you're tired! Anyway, I'm glad you're here. Carry
on.'

Just then Jasmine looked up at the mantelpiece. 'Is that my
old hourglass? The one you took from the cottage?'

Nora looked. 'Oh! Yes. I always loved that thing. I nearly
left it in the flat but I grabbed it at the last minute.'

'When I left Nant-Aur for London, I grabbed it at the last
minute too. It reminded me of Mam.'

Nora smiled. 'It reminded me of you.'

Jasmine nodded. 'I know all the symbolism, about the sands
of time and mortality, and being able to turn it over and make
a new start and all that, but do you know what it's always
meant to me?'

'What?'

'The bond between a mother and a daughter. I always used to
feel that one bulb was Mam and one was me. And we were connected, you know, by that thin but essential link in between.
And the sand was love, or life force, pouring from her to me,
but turn it over and it poured from me to her – I realised when
I had *you* how a daughter sustains a mother just as much as the
other way around.'

'That's lovely, Mum. That's just how it is.'

'On which note . . .' said Jasmine, looking at Nora, 'I want to apologise, properly, for being such a hag the last couple of years. You've always been so together, so *fine*, and that's all I ever wanted for you – at least, I thought it was. I suppose I knew *really* that you weren't happy, not properly, but you always *said* you were and it was what I wanted to hear. But life is more than work and financial security and routine. If *anyone* knows that, it's me. But love . . . I mean, the light-up-your-life sort . . . well, it can be dangerous, and I didn't ever want you to be hurt. But I've let you down so badly.'

'You haven't, Mum, please don't worry. When I went through all that stuff last year, I was terrified. Nothing felt the way it used to, the way I thought it should. I thought my world was coming to an end. And I was right, it did, it came crashing down. But that was *good*, because it meant I could build a new and better one. It's all good, I came through it OK.'

'I can see that. More than OK, you look wonderful, darling, so happy and beautiful . . . and it's what you deserve. You *really* deserve it. I just want you to know, I'm in awe of your courage. All that fear, all that confusion, you just stared it in the face, talked to Jennifer and really went through it. I'm sorry I didn't go through it with you. I'm sorry I turned away. But I couldn't bear to deal with your fear, because I never dealt with mine.'

Nora nodded and sat very still. She'd never thought of it like that. She'd never thought she had a choice about what she did when things started to unravel for her. It certainly hadn't *felt* like courage – she just wanted to make those crazy-making feelings go away. It was a long time since she had seen her mother so sincere, so serious. And she could see her pain, almost visible around her slender frame like an aura. How had she never seen it before? Presumably because Jasmine had kept it locked away in her innermost vaults. Her poor mother.

She sat quietly and listened while Jasmine told her of a family rift healed when ten-year-old Chloe Samuels started taking summer holidays in Tenby. She heard how, barred from the Tenby Teens dance, Chloe had run into the dunes, only to trip over – literally – the boy who was to become her best friend in all the world.

'I never told you about Llew,' said Jasmine quietly.

Nora shifted her position. She didn't want to interrupt her mother but she didn't want to listen as though she had never heard of Llew. It would feel like gaining a confidence under false pretences.

'Gran mentioned you had a friend called Llew,' she said. 'And – well – you're not going to believe this but . . . it turns out that Jones, my landlord . . . *is* Llew. I had no idea until last week.'

Nora watched her mother digest this remarkable fact. She grew a little pale. 'But he's not here, is he?' she asked at last. 'This is his house. You said he'd gone away.'

Nora swallowed. 'He did, yes. But he's back now, Mum. As soon as he found out I was your daughter, he came haring back. Don't worry, he's not *here*. He's staying in town. I've met him, Mum, he's lovely. But . . . he hurt you. And I'm so sorry.'

'He hurt me? Oh, yes, I suppose he did. But I wasn't sure you'd see it like that. I hurt *him*, you see, that's the thing. He doesn't mind you being here then, now that he knows who you are?'

'Of course not!'

'No. He wouldn't. Llew was never petty. He won't want to see *me*, though, Nora.'

'Well, actually, Mum, he does. He *really* does. He keeps asking me when you're coming back. It's completely obvious that he . . . well, that's jumping ahead. Won't you carry on with your story, Mum? I just thought you should know that I . . . know him. A bit.'

'I can't believe it,' Jasmine whispered. 'That you should end up in *his house* of all possible places! Is he related to Kaitlin? Is that how this happened?'

'No. Kaitlin is a completely separate Jones. It really is that random.' Best not to mention that Kaitlin was Alma's granddaughter at this point, thought Nora. That might derail the conversation completely.

Jasmine took a deep breath and tore off a fortifying bite of pâté and toast. 'This is spectacular! Kaitlin's a great cook.'

'Yes. I won't ever be able to let her marry and move away. I'd starve.'

Jasmine wolfed down her last piece and wrapped her hands around her china cup like a little girl. 'Mam always said that timing is a Godly thing. All this was obviously meant to come to light now. So let me tell you . . .'

Nora listened as her mother told her the same tales as Llew: coin-hunting and long days on the beaches; trailing around the town with Llew in search of the perfect picture; dancing and Horlicks; always trying to keep up with her moody cousin and her catty friends. She laughed when she heard about her mother's young crush on Iestyn and the embarrassing scrapes she had got herself into.

Jasmine was very careful to tell Nora everything about those last few summers, exhuming memories she'd ignored for a long time. She told her about Chickenpox Summer; how Llew had been her rock, then she had been his. She told her about the time when she and Llew teetered on the cusp of something more than friendship. How the threads wove together, she realised now, as she told her story. The timing of it all: the chickenpox interrupting the habitual flow of their childhood activities, forcing her to see him in a new light. Her father taking her aside, talking to her about the future. The hourglass tilting, about to swing around to a new phase, before she was ready.

'I always loved him, even before that last summer,' she said. 'Every time I tried to think about the future, Llew was there. As much as I told myself I should marry some suave city boy who could give me the life I'd always thought I wanted, there was Llew getting in the way. He was my soulmate, Nora. In a way we found each other too young. We weren't experienced enough to recognise what we had for what it was. I'd *almost* figured it out when Iestyn came back to Kite Hill. He'd travelled to California, he was living in London. He was all my girlhood dreams come true. I was dazzled, at first. And *validated*, because he finally saw me as the beautiful siren I'd always longed to be.'

Nora could understand. It was extraordinary to think there had ever been a time when her mother hadn't felt beautiful, hadn't been sure of her own power. To think that Chloe had gone through the doubts and embarrassments of adolescence just like everyone else. To Nora it had always seemed that Jasmine had just tumbled into the world, fully formed and glorious, at the age of twenty. An icon of feminine loveliness that Nora could never live up to. But it wasn't like that at all.

Llew hadn't told Nora about Iestyn, only that he had been on his way to meet Chloe when the terrible accident happened. Now Nora learned about the date and Chloe's realisation. Her eyes filled with tears. What had happened to Chloe and Llew was too cruel. She wasn't sure that timing had been Godly that night, whatever Gran might think. Some cruel fate had snatched the couple's future from them. She kissed her mother's soft cheek. 'I'm so sorry,' she whispered. No wonder Jasmine had run from love, steered Nora out of its crushing path, kept away from the place that held so many memories.

But the look of fear was back in Jasmine's eyes. She wiped Nora's tears away and the silence grew heavy with waiting. 'There's something else,' she said at last.

And then in a quiet voice, looking at her lap the whole while,

Jasmine told her about Michael Everley. About the things he'd said and the things he'd done and the terrible thing he'd tried to do, but failed, because of Llew, and the landslide.

Nora sat rigid, heart hammering, hating and dreading to hear what came next, hating that her mother had gone through such a thing. And when she learned that the worst had not, after all, happened, she breathed a sigh of relief. Timing *was* a Godly thing.

Jasmine started plaiting the fringes on a cushion with anxious fingers. 'I've never told anyone else,' she said. 'At the time, everyone was so caught up in the accident, in how Llew had been injured, and what those injuries meant, that the rest just got buried. He was injured because he was saving me, Nora, and the worst of it is . . . part of me has always been glad that he came when he did, relieved that Michael didn't get to . . . do what he did to Megan. Yes, he raped her,' she nodded when Nora gasped. 'That summer that she went to France, she did have a baby. She was broken afterwards, for the longest time, and we only talked about it years later. But the point is, I was glad it didn't happen.'

'Well, *of course* you are, Mum! *I'm* glad it didn't happen!'

'But at such a cost, Nora, such a cost to Llew.'

'But you didn't *choose* that, Mum, you didn't *make* it happen.'

'But he was looking out for me. I wouldn't have been there if I hadn't had my head turned by Iestyn. Llew wouldn't have been there if he hadn't been looking for me. If I could only have sorted out my feelings a day earlier. Even three *hours* earlier. If I had never gone on that picnic . . .'

'Mum . . . I understand, but you're being incredibly hard on yourself. You were nearly *raped*.' Nora shuddered. She hated to use that word about her own mother. About anyone. 'But you never talked about it. It just got lost beneath all the layers of what happened to Llew. You had two huge traumas in one night. Your head must have been *destroyed*! It was just a shit situation. The worst. But think of this, if Llew *hadn't* come along and saved you, he would have been safe, but you wouldn't. Think what would have happened to you. Llew would *never* have wanted that for you.'

Jasmine smiled and squeezed her hand. 'When did my little girl get so wise? You're right of course, he wouldn't. But no one ever knew *why* Llew was running hell for leather through the dirt and stones that night, and no one ever knew those terrible things Michael said to me. *Was* it my fault? Did I do something to make him think I would want to . . . ?'

'Oh Mum. *Mum!*' Nora scooted along the sofa and wrapped her arms around her mother. '*None* of it was your fault! It was just a terrible, terrible night. A whole series of horrible events that no one could have foreseen.' She shook her head in wonder.

*Don't trust love, Nora, anyone can let you down.* Now Nora understood. All those years it hadn't been her father that Jasmine had been talking about. It hadn't even been Llew. She still blamed herself; she'd been talking about herself.

The tears fell as Jasmine relaxed into her embrace. Oh, how good it felt to cry on the shoulder of someone who loved her.

Nora still loved her, despite knowing everything. The relief was immeasurable.

'Is Megan still alive?' Nora asked at last, when Jasmine was quiet again.

Jasmine shook her head. 'Susan's gone too, and Heinrich. They're all gone, Nora, except maybe Richard. Last I heard he was still living in Shropshire somewhere. I wish you could have met Susan, Nora. And she would have *loved* meeting you. She was very dear to me, you know. That poor family. They had so much to contend with, one way or another.'

'What happened to Megan's baby? Poor Megan.'

'Poor Megan,' Jasmine agreed and explained how Megan had looked her up in later years. 'Turns out the family in France were a godsend. Not only did they provide a place for her to have the baby, but they adopted him too. Megan came home thinking she could just leave it all on the other side of the Channel. But of course, it wasn't that easy for her.'

'Of course not. Was she happy in the end?'

'I think so. She married and they had two children. She opened her own hair salon. She wrote to me once, in the seventies, to say that her son in France had looked her up – Auguste, his name was. Megan wrote to me care of Mam, who forwarded it to me. She sent me his address, in case I ever wanted to get in touch with him.'

'And did you?'

'Never. But I kept the letter.'

'So we could . . .'

'We could . . . Anyway . . .' Jasmine roused herself. 'Now you know why I've been the sort of mother I've been, Nora. Exile is a painful thing and I was compensating, I suppose your Jennifer would say. I wanted to show you a strong, self-sufficient mother. I wanted to show you that it was possible to have a good life, a wonderful life, without romantic love, without roots, without *guilt*. Maybe I did you a disservice.'

'Oh Mum.' Nora smiled. 'I'm *grateful* you showed me how to be a strong woman. I'm *glad* I never settled for an OK relationship – not permanently anyway. If I had, I wouldn't be free now to be with Logan. And you have always been a legend, that's for sure. But it must have been . . .'

Jasmine nodded. 'I'm *exhausted*. And then I found out that Llew could walk after all . . . That was the last straw for me, I'm afraid. I'd been carrying around that guilt all those years and he'd never even let me know. I'm afraid I lost it, rather, realising he must still hate me *that* much. That's why I was no use to you when you were struggling. I'd only just found out. Bloody Internet!'

'Mum, he doesn't hate you, I can promise you that. Quite the opposite.'

'Well, then why did he never—'

'I don't know. You'll have to ask him that. You two need to talk and get everything out in the open.'

'I don't think I can, Nora. How can I face him again, after all these *years*?'

Nora gave her the look that Kaitlin had given her so often

when she first arrived in Tenby. 'Because avoiding it all has worked so well for you?' she demanded. 'Come on, Mum, how can you *not*? You've come this far.'

'Yes, to put things right with *you*! And Mam. I didn't know Llew was going to be here, did I?'

'But he is, and there must be a reason for that. You need to go forward happy. You can't do that if you're avoiding the gigantic fact that you and Llew are both in Tenby again.'

'I know. You're right. But I need to see Mam first. God, Nora, it's been too long. And she's ninety-three. What was I *thinking*? She won't be there forever. I need to see her before I do anything else.'

'OK, I agree with that. But then you come back here, you talk to Llew, you meet Kaitlin and Logan and life goes on, OK? No more running.'

Jasmine nodded, wiping her face with the back of her hand. 'No more running,' she agreed. She couldn't imagine how she would cope with seeing Llew again. But she would go home first, and Mam would help her. You had to laugh. Seventy-five years old, and all she wanted was her mother.

# Nora

&#10087;

The next day, Logan appeared on the doorstep begging Nora to come to London for a couple of days with him and the children. They were wild to see the city, apparently, and equally wild for Nora to come with them and show them around.

'I know what you're going to say,' he said, 'but they *really* want you to come. I promise.'

'Yes, why not?' said Nora, melting a little at the delight on his face. 'Mum went off to Nant-Aur this morning. It'll be nice for her to have a couple of days on her own with Gran.'

Logan's jaw dropped. 'Who's gone where now?'

Nora laughed. 'I'll explain on the drive.'

So they went. The time in London flew. Sylvie oohed and aahed at Madame Tussauds, the Tower of London, Camden Market . . . but Brendan looked honestly shell-shocked as they rumbled about on buses or took the Tube to the South Bank to emerge by the river and book a flight on the London Eye.

'He looks like he's in love!' Logan whispered to Nora as Brendan chatted to a waitress in the Tate Modern café. 'Not with the girl, with the city!' It was a happy time, if made bittersweet by the fact that Logan was leaving so soon.

On Friday morning Nora phoned her mother to say they were heading home. Logan had disappeared to help Sylvie with her bag, now swollen to twice its size thanks to the spoils of Camden market. Nora was leaning against the car with Brendan, who was staring about him like a boy hypnotised. While they waited, an email came through on her phone.

It was from Lou at the recruitment agency she had joined after leaving the university. That felt like another life now. When she saw the company name she felt as if they'd got the wrong person. She read it and couldn't quite believe her eyes. Lou had a vacancy that was just perfect for Nora, she wrote. And permanent.

I explained that you're not available yet, but they wanted to see your CV anyway. They were very impressed, and feel you'd be perfect for the job. Is there any way you could come for an interview next week? If they like you, and if you wanted the job, they would be happy to wait until you're ready to start. Late September if you like, to give you time to move back and sort things out.

'Oh God,' said Nora.

She opened the attachment giving details of the role. Very good salary, an interesting company by the looks of things, an events company. What she excelled at. She scrolled through the job description: organising events, co-ordinating with a wide variety of industries, managing the budget, managing the admin team, client liaison . . .

Her eyes blurred and she switched her phone off. It was a peach of a job, according to her old criteria. An impressive role, well within her capabilities, good benefits, a perfect fit. Why then did she feel . . . hunted?

'What's up?' asked Logan, appearing at her side. 'You OK, doll?'

'I'm fine. Is Sylvie OK? Oh! You're all here. Great, let's go.'

Flustered, she ducked into the car and bumped her head. Logan looked at her quizzically. But Nora finally understood why Kaitlin hadn't told her about Anna's cancer. She didn't want to tell him about the job offer yet, as though it might tarnish the time they had left. She didn't want to make the ending real.

That evening, Nora was getting ready for dinner, trying not to cry. She mustn't cry, because then she'd ruin her careful eye make-up. Shit. She was crying.

To celebrate their return from London, they were all going out for dinner: Logan, Nora, Sylvie and Brendan. Molly, Andy, Angie and Carter. And Kaitlin and Llew. Her mother was nearby, and life was perfect. Nora didn't want anything to change, but it would.

'God,' Nora muttered to herself, wiping underneath her eyes gingerly with the heel of her hand. 'Get a grip.' She grimaced in the mirror – funny how 'carefully smudged' and 'smeared by tears' could look so different.

They were going, of course, to the South Beach for dinner on the sand with cocktails for the adults and a view of the agate ocean for all. Nora was wearing a new dress made for her by Lilian – a soft turquoise that looked like the sea in certain lights, with a tulip skirt, a scooped neck and a V at the back. Sexy, but not so sexy you couldn't wear it in front of your boyfriend's kids. *Boyfriend.* What a word.

She felt reluctant to step outside, to count off another evening, bring another day to an end.

'Nora, you ready?' Kaitlin's voice flew up the stairs. 'Time to go!'

# Chloe

After three days with her mother in Nant-Aur, Jasmine felt like Chloe again. It had been a bittersweet, emotional time. Gwennan's face, when she answered the door to see her daughter, was a picture that Jasmine would never forget as long as she lived. They had fallen on each other weeping and didn't stir from the house for forty-eight hours as they talked and talked, only pausing to eat and sleep and brew countless pots of tea.

That morning they had taken a walk up the hill and through the woods. The old paths were unchanged, the smells and sounds were those of childhood. Gwennan and Jasmine – or Chloe as she always had been and forever would be to her mother – had changed, however. The gentle slope challenged Jasmine, with her stiff legs and aching back. Yet she was a creature of speed compared with Gwennan who could only creep, snail-like and determined. Her mother was very old, Jasmine admitted. Seeing her once every few months and talking on the phone didn't cut it. For some mothers and daughters it might be fine, but that wasn't how it was for them, just as it wasn't how it was for her and Nora. This family was close. This family was special. She was moving home, she decided, smelling the wild honeysuckle at the edge of the wood.

After their foray into nature, they both curled up on sofas in the sitting room and slept. When they woke, Gwennan looked at her carefully. 'You need to go and talk to Llew now, *bach*,' she said. 'I'll come and see you and Nora in a day or two. But you can't go any longer without talking to him. It's not good for you.'

Her mother and her daughter both! Jasmine was frightened. She would quite happily have stayed in Nant-Aur with Mam forever, but she knew that look in her mother's eye. And that tone of voice. The tone she used with doctors and teachers.

She was halfway back to Tenby when she remembered the text she'd received from Nora earlier. She'd be out tonight, with Logan and her friends. And Llew. Jasmine pulled over and thought about driving back to Nant-Aur, putting off Tenby til the next day. But she knew what Gwennan would have to say about that. So she carried on and checked into the same B&B. Nora would want her to stay at the house but she wanted to retain at least an illusion of control. Then she headed out, pausing in the same spot where she had stood overlooking the South Beach just a few days ago.

It was a glorious evening. Holidaymakers strolled to and fro. Gulls wheeled up and down on ice cream patrol. The sun splashed golden tracks over the water and sheer bridal veils of foam spread over the sand. She walked to the top of the path that led to the beach. It was hard not to feel fifteen again. Going to the South Beach and going to see Llew.

'God!' she exclaimed, stopping and gripping the metal railings. Was she really going to do this? Just turn up? Lay eyes on him for the first time in nearly sixty years in front of a roomful of strangers? But Nora would be there. It didn't have to be a big deal. If they could just be civil to one another, break the ice, make her realise she had no reason to avoid Tenby any more . . . that would be peachy. Now that she'd come this far she found she couldn't walk away. What else would she do? Spend the evening reading? Walk around the town? No. She was jangling with adrenaline. Nothing to do but go forward, now.

She started her way down the path. There was a large wood-and-glass structure on the beach, just exactly where the old Fountains Café used to be. How extraordinary that they'd picked the self-same spot for the restaurant. Well, it was a very *good* spot after all. The views must wash a meal down a treat. It was just so strange to see a place she had known so well, long gone, given a new incarnation. A boardwalk led to it over the sand and the dunes, she saw, were thick with dark green bushes, rather than the gently waving grasses of sixty years ago.

'Get your head out of the past,' she muttered grimly. 'Come on, go and see them and then get to bed. You'll need a sleep after this. A short coma would be nice.'

It took her a minute to work out which of all the glass facets of this new restaurant was the door and as she looked, a man came bursting through it, glaring at a mobile phone in exasperation. Her heart gave a lurch for he looked so very like Llew. She couldn't take her eyes off him for the sweetness of the illusion that she was looking at him again. He had a shock of white hair that sprang up at all angles, just as Llew's had. He had that same loping walk and air of confidence, quite flamboyant, she thought suddenly, though that wouldn't have been the right word for her scruffy friend back in the day.

'Eric? Eric, can you hear me?' he demanded in a loud voice and Jasmine froze. It was Llew's voice. Hell, it *was* Llew, of course!

'Llew?' she said, but no sound came out.

'Eric, hang on, the signal here is bloody terrible. Look, I'm at a special dinner so if I lose you now it'll have to wait til tomorrow,' said Llew with a scowl. 'What? What? Eric?' Then he gave up and snapped the phone shut, shoving it back into his pocket. 'Bloody things,' he said and turned to go back inside.

'Llew,' she said again, and then, louder, 'Llew Jones!'

He froze. Turned. Saw her. And his eyes, those familiar greeny-browny-yellowy lion's eyes, widened.

'Chloe?' he said, incredulous. 'Chloe, are you really here?'

She hung on to a railing. 'Yes.'

'But you're in Italy. I'm going senile. Oh, Glenda's finally right and I'm losing my marbles, aren't I?'

'No. It's me, Llew. I'm here.'

'Chloe? Oh dear God but it's good to see you. Chloe, I've never . . . I mean, I've always . . .'

'I love you, Llew.'

He laughed, stumbled a little, looked at her as if she might disappear at any second.

'I love you too. Well, we always did dive straight back in, didn't we? No small talk or polite stuff, even when I hadn't seen you for a year.'

'Or fifty-odd.'

'Or fifty-odd,' he agreed. 'God, Chlo, what a bloody waste of time. I'm so sorry. So very, very sorry.'

She watched his expression turn from stunned to horrified as she started to cry. 'I'm sorry too, Llew,' she sobbed. 'I'm so, so, so, so sorry and I love you so much.'

'Come here, girl, you daft woman. You don't say sorry to me. You did nothing wrong. It was *me*! A fool! Come here now.' His long legs reached her in easy strides and he took her in his arms to hold her tight as could be while she bawled her heart out, decades of longing washing over her like a wave.

Eventually they pulled apart. Llew looked at her wonderingly, tracing the outline of her face with his fingers. 'You're beautiful, Chlo,' he said simply, and happily. 'Although I hear you're Jasmine now. Should I call you that?'

'No.' She shook her head and her black and white hair swung. 'I'm Chloe, still Chloe.'

Llew pulled her close again. '*Duw*, I'm glad to hear that,' he said.

# Nora

'Where's Llew?' wondered Kaitlin, squeezing a lime wedge into her margarita. 'Is he all right? Shall I order him another beer?'

'He said he'd only be a minute,' mused Nora. 'Should I go and find him?'

'Oh my God!' exclaimed Sylvie. 'Look! He's snogging!'

'What? Don't be silly, Sylvie,' said Logan.

'*Daaaad*, old people have sexual feelings too, you know,' she reprimanded him.

'Oh God, don't say sexual. You're twelve. Wait until you're ninety.'

'Well, except you've only just gone and proved my *point*!'

'What do you mean, Llew's snogging?' demanded Nora in horror. Deep down, she realised, she had harboured a secret wish that he and her mother would get together after all. It would be belated, true, but they could be so happy . . . She got up and went to Sylvie's end of the table.

It was true. Llew was wrapped around a small woman in an elegant red sundress, her face invisible beneath his passionate

496

kisses. Wait a minute. Small. Elegant. It could only be one person.

Mesmerised, Nora supposed she should look away. It wasn't really the done thing to watch a couple in the throes of passion. But they didn't seem to care that it was broad daylight and children were all around. Now *that* was a first kiss that had taken a long time coming.

'Well,' she said eventually, 'they'll be in when they're ready. We'd better set an extra place for my mother.'

'Your *mother*?' gasped Kaitlin. 'Oh Nora, how *wonderful*! Now if you can just ask her to get Llew to let us stay in his house forever . . .'

# Chloe

———⌘———

Jasmine woke from a dream of Wales, so vivid and sweet that for a moment she thought she was home, that at any moment her mother might appear, smiling, telling her it was time to get up for school. Then she felt sunlight on her face, and heard a single cry slice through the morning silence, full of yearning, full of *hiraeth*. A gull. Tenby! She was in Tenby! The familiar butterflies in the pit of her stomach, the start of something wonderful . . . She sat up – and bumped her head. And then she gasped. It wasn't 1950-something and this wasn't a summer holiday. It was 2015 and she had spent the night with Llew!

There he lay, fast asleep beside her, hanging half over the edge of the bed. It was one of those one-and-a-half-size singles. She was squashed against the wall and Llew was clinging to the bed at some weird angle like a stick insect; how he hadn't fallen out in the night she would never know. She smiled and bit her lip.

*Duw, there's behaviour, Chloe Samuels!* whispered a chorus of voices in her head.

*I know!* she whispered back. *It's brilliant!*

*What would your mother say, look you?*
*I think she'd say it was high time.*

She snuggled back down gingerly so as not to wake Llew – and because her bones weren't what they were and a night in a too-small bed had done them no favours. She lay wide-eyed and staring about her. It was so like the first morning of her childhood holidays – awake and bursting with excitement but afraid to wake Megan. She giggled. It was so like it . . . but *not*.

Last night after the meal Nora had offered to walk her back to the B&B but Llew insisted that he would do it.

'I can walk myself!' Jasmine had protested. 'It's not as if I don't know the way.'

'It's a different time now,' said Llew. 'You can't just wander round in the dark the way we used to. I'll walk you.'

So he had taken her hand, bid the others goodnight and led her off into the night, the very picture of the respectable older gent chivalrously seeing his lady friend safely to her door . . .

'Bugger that,' he said when they were out of sight. 'You're coming home with me, Chloe Samuels. I've waited long enough and frankly, we aren't getting any younger.'

'But Llew! The B&B! They'll worry!'

'Ring 'em.' He had kissed her again then, his fingers playing in her hair at the back of her neck, and Jasmine went weak.

'Yes,' she mumbled dreamily. 'I'll ring them.'

But of course there was no signal so she had to ring from the pub. Much to her embarrassment the landline was behind the bar. The last few straggling drinkers had listened with interest as she explained to the B&B that she was staying the night with her daughter. When she hung up they sniggered. Llew watched her in amusement.

'Your daughter? I can't believe you're embarrassed at our age.'

'Well, what was I going to say? I don't usually stay with someone on a first date you know, Llew Jones!'

'First date!' He laughed. 'Yes, I suppose it is! Come on then, woman. Of course, ideally I'd take you home to my beautiful Tenby townhouse and impress you with my wealth and taste. But your daughter's living there so it's a room over a pub.'

And now here they were, waking up together for the very first time. The roller blind over the window wasn't sufficient to keep out the morning light. She looked around. A clothing rail in the corner with a few shirts, trousers and jackets on it. A door leading to a tiny bathroom. A chair. That was it. Bless him for staying here so that Nora and Kaitlin could continue to live out their dream summer in his wonderful home. There were cobwebs in the rafters and a faded rug on the floor. She wriggled her toes in excitement. She was in Tenby! She was in bed with Llew! She turned her face to his chest and breathed him in.

He opened an eye and stared at her. Broke into a wide smile. Tried to shift closer to her and realised his back had gone. After a bit of groaning and a bit of laughing they fitted together again, his long legs wrapped tightly around her, his lips kissing her neck.

'High time, Chloe Samuels,' he said. 'High time.'

★

They didn't leave the room over the pub until midday.

'And this from a boy who couldn't be indoors for five minutes when the sun was shining,' she teased him, running her fingers over his chest, toying with the grey hairs. When she had last seen Llew, he hadn't had any chest hair at all!

'Well, you see,' he explained, brushing her hair off her face and kissing her again and again. 'I'm not a boy any more, and I've discovered that some things are even better than swimming and milkshakes.'

She gasped. 'No! Really? What are they? Tell me. *Show* me.'

'*Duw*, there's wicked you are, Chloe Samuels. I'll show you all right . . .'

When they did finally emerge, Chloe still in her red dress of the day before, Dave the landlord and Mary the cleaner looked up from filling fridges and hoovering to wolf whistle and catcall.

'Good man, Leonard Jones!' approved Dave. 'About bloody time, if you don't mind me saying so!'

They went to The Cabin for breakfast. All she had done in the way of grooming was tug Llew's comb through her bed-hair and splash some water on her face. Moisturiser, make-up, fresh clothes, all hostage in the B&B. They could wait! That was the thing with Llew, she never had to pretend.

'We're old now,' she murmured, holding hands with him across the table.

'Do you feel old? I don't feel old. Apart from my damn hip.'

'No, but I was just thinking, I'm not wearing any make-up,

you're just seeing me as I am. And you always did. But now I'm not all peachy and young any more and—'

'Well, it's true you *are* two years older than me,' he mused. 'I don't know, Chlo, it's a bit grab-a-granny, isn't it? Ow!'

He laughed wickedly as she slapped his arm.

'After the hard time you always gave me about being younger,' he went on, grabbing her hands and holding them fast for his own safety. 'What do *you* know, Llew Jones,' he mimicked. 'You're only a *boy*!'

'You'll never let me live it down, will you? Perhaps you're not that mature after all!' But she grinned, and kissed him. 'Still, I suppose I can bear to have a toy boy now. If you don't mind being with an older woman.'

'Chloe, you're every bit as beautiful now as you ever were. We don't have time to waste being coy or self-conscious. Yes, we're a bit wrinkly. Yes, sex is going to be a little bit different from how it would have been fifty years ago. Yes, we've jumped straight from teenagers to the stage where we're wincing and groaning every half hour because of some weird ache or pain. Do you care? I don't care. We're together. That's all that matters. Let's not waste any more time doing anything but enjoying and celebrating every last minute we have together, every last inch of our bodies. They might be creaky but they can still give us pleasure.'

'You always did have a sensible head, Llew Jones. You always did have a perspective that was different from anyone else's. Better.'

'Except once.' His face grew serious. 'After the accident.'

'Oh Llew. It was only natural. What you went through! What the doctors said! I still can't bear to think of how afraid you must have been.'

'I know. But look what happened. We lost each other. I'm sorry, Chloe. I threw you away. I just . . . couldn't see how it was going to get any better. I didn't want you tied to me like that – for your sake and mine. I didn't want the woman I loved to be a carer, to see me compromised. How could we have kept any romance alive while every single thing – physical, emotional, practical – would have been a struggle? They told me things at the hospital and *nothing* would have been straight-forward for the rest of my life. Bowel control, Chloe, pressure sores, repositioning my legs regularly to stop the soft tissues shortening . . . these things were my whole life while I was recovering, my Dad's life. I didn't want them to be yours.

'You know it's funny, all those years without you I really regretted that choice. But now that I have you back after all, I find I'm rather glad we were spared that. Now, we have our time together and we are old enough to appreciate it. We've had lives. We can bring them together.'

Jasmine wiped her eyes. 'But bloody hell, Llew. I still wish we hadn't wasted fifty-five years! Oh, I'm going to make the most of every moment with you now, you can be sure, but it would have been worth every second of struggle to be with you. It would, you can't tell me otherwise.'

'Then I won't try, *cariad*.'

'So what happened, Llew? The last time I saw you, you were never going to walk again. The doctors said so, everyone seemed so sure, *you* were sure! Then I saw you on the Internet – not that long ago – and I sent for one of your DVDs. There you were walking around on the cliffs!'

'Which DVD? Not the painting birds one?'

'No, the seascape one.'

'Oh good. The bird one was crap.'

'Never mind the quality of the merchandising of your artistic empire! *Tell* me things! How long until you could walk?'

'Two years, as I was. Completely without feeling in my legs. Another year, then, until I could walk with a stick and hobble around. Maybe another two until I regained full use.'

Jasmine's eyes filled again. She had cried maybe ten times in all the intervening decades and now every five minutes! 'Oh Llew! I mean, it's better than a lifetime, of course, but still, you lost that time and it's all my fault.'

'Chloe, I'm shocked! You never thought that, surely? In what possible way was it your fault?'

'Of course I thought that. If I hadn't been on a date with Iestyn, you wouldn't have come looking for me. If Michael hadn't attacked me, you wouldn't have needed to rescue me, you wouldn't have put yourself in such danger. Oh Llew, *why* did you never contact me? I wrote and wrote that first year. I thought you'd never forgiven me for what happened to you!'

But Llew was frowning, and holding her hands more tightly than ever. '*Cariad*, that night was just as bad for you as it

504

was for me. The sound of you screaming . . . over the years that memory has caused me more pain than my accident ever did. But did you say *Michael* was attacking you? Not Michael *Everley*?'

'Well, *yes*, Llew, who did you think it was?'

'I assumed Iestyn.'

Of course. A dark night, a romantic spot for a date . . . she had been where Llew expected her to be, Jasmine realised, just not with the man he expected her to be with. Hurriedly she explained what had happened.

'Good God.' Llew looked shaken. 'That bloody Michael lived in Tenby for years! If I'd known it was him, I'd have killed him. I mean it. I've spent decades hating Iestyn. But in fact, he was a bit of a hero.'

'He was good to me,' Jasmine agreed. 'Did you ever hear what happened to Michael, Llew? He's not still here, is he?'

'Died a long time ago,' said Llew with some satisfaction. 'Massive heart attack, I remember hearing. But he was long gone from Tenby by then. He'd grown really fat before he left.' He frowned. 'You know, I seem to remember some gossip about him and one of the local girls, now I come to think of it. Something unsavoury.'

'Annie Williams? Megan?'

A bolt of shock crossed his face. 'You mean . . . ?'

Jasmine nodded and told him about Megan.

'Well, what a disgusting son of a bitch he was. I had no idea. And, my love, were you all right? You told me he never . . .

that I got there in time. Was that true? Or were you just saying it because you didn't want to worry me even more?'

'It was true. You saved me, Llew, and I'm forever thankful. I'm just sorry it cost you what it did.'

'I'd have done it no matter what the cost, you know I would.' He stroked her face. 'The thought of him trying to hurt you, I couldn't bear it. And Chlo, I'm sorry. You tried so hard to be there for me. But I wasn't there for you. You must have really needed me then.'

'I did. But what's done is done. Stop thinking of it now,' she said softly. 'We must let the past go and look to the future.'

'I know, you're right. And you must do the same about my accident. You know, indirectly it gave me an incredible gift. OK the first year was hell but then, when my father couldn't stand me brooding any more, he bought me paints and an easel and that was it! I painted the view from the window, I painted flowers he brought in, I painted *him* . . . and that was when I realised, it wasn't photography, per se, that was magic for me, it was just capturing life, the world, *people*. Now I had a new way to do it. I dug out all my old photos. I separated out the ones of you – I couldn't bear to see those – but it still left me with plenty to paint. Red Sam and Mrs Isaacs and Megan and the girls . . .

'Then Dad took me to visit people who were willing to sit for me. My urge to paint overcame my self-consciousness. And as I went out into the world again, my mood lifted and my head cleared. Remember that story Blossom told you about

Cyd Charisse? How she only took dance lessons to build up her strength after polio? It was like that. Life pushed me in a new direction, one I might never have found if I'd been able to carry on with the photography. One day I felt pins and needles in my legs, and then the shooting pains started. In all my life I'd never been so happy to feel pain, because I knew at once what it meant. I found out later that during those two years, while I was trying to come to terms with permanent paraplegia, my body had its own ideas. The nerves had started to regenerate.'

'A miracle, Llew! A sleeping miracle, like plants underground in winter. No sign of change, but when the time is right . . .'

'Exactly. A sleeping miracle. By the time I was twenty-two, I was completely able-bodied again. And there wasn't a day in all that time that I hadn't thought of you. In fact, always at the back of my mind was the idea that if I could ever walk again I might be able to be with you after all. I promised myself that then, and only then, I would look you up. It was my greatest incentive. But when the time came, I hesitated. You know the saying "He who hesitates is lost"? Never a truer word.

'I started to wonder how you could ever forgive me for how I treated you, and for staying silent so long. I considered going to Nant-Aur to ask your mother for your address but then I saw Evie in town one day. She'd heard from Megan and she told me you were a model, living in London, dating a film producer. Chlo, it was everything you'd ever wanted as a girl. Although I could walk again I'd lost a lot of time, I still had *nothing* to offer.

'I thought about it and thought about it. I never *stopped* thinking about it. But I was afraid that if I wrote to you you'd come back, because you'd promised you would, and you always were a girl to keep your promises. Then you'd turn your back on all your dreams. *And*, if I'm honest, I was equally afraid that you *wouldn't* choose me. I didn't know if I could bear that. Fear and indecision are just as paralysing as a spinal injury, Chloe. It wasn't that I made up my mind never to contact you again. It was that I didn't do it one day, or the next . . . and then another five years had gone by.

'I was living in London by then, working in a bank, trying to catch up financially. I went over to the receptionist one day to borrow a stapler and she had a copy of *Vogue* open on her desk. There you were, full page, full colour, advertising a diamond bracelet. Hair as black as night but unmistakeably you. Oh Chlo! You were stunning. It brought home to me in a way that news on the grapevine never could that you'd made it, belonged in a different world. You just weren't my Chloe any more. Oh, I know now that wasn't true, but that's how it felt at the time. I wish I'd held my nerve, Chlo. I wish I'd looked you up then.'

'Oh my love. I'm glad you *didn't* look me up then. Imagine, just the year before I met Steve! And if I hadn't met Steve, I wouldn't have Nora.'

He smiled. 'So it was good that I chickened out?'

'*Very* good. What did you do then, chicken boy?'

'That picture of you was my catalyst to run away, back to

Tenby, back to painting, to try again. Only this time I had money in the bank. I had something to offer . . . someone.

'And then I . . . met Sandra again. Sandra Sharples as was; you probably don't remember me mentioning her.'

Chloe smiled. 'Sandra Sharples from Llandeilo or Llandovery. Pretty girl. Your first kiss. I remember, Llew Jones.'

'Yes. She was still pretty, we still got on well. And I was *lonely*. Oh, she wasn't you, Chloe, but we were a decent match, all told, and we did care for each other very much.'

'I'm glad you had someone, I'm glad you had a family. I had Steve, well, for a little while. He wasn't you, either, but he made me laugh and he gave me Nora.'

'Nora's a special woman. I'm loving getting to know her. Now Chlo, about Glenda . . .'

Chloe grinned. 'We've met.'

'Yes, well. Glenda doesn't always create the best first impression, I know. She's not . . . that is, Sandra didn't think she was . . . very pretty. Looks and clothes and all that meant a lot to Sandra and she was always on at Glenda to be more graceful, more feminine. It was something we used to row about. I thought Glenda was lovely just as she was. Well, she was my little girl! But she's grown up quite bitter, I'd say, at not being the daughter her mother might have wanted. She's like her in other ways, though: sensible, practical. I drive her nuts with my . . . ways, as she calls them. And she'd hate me telling you this, by the way. But I just wanted you to know . . . she hasn't always had it easy. She expects people to see the worst in her. But she has a good heart and I love her and—'

'Llew, *cariad*, I will love her if it takes her four years to say a civil word to me. If anyone knows that appearances aren't the whole story, it's me.'

'I know. I just wanted you to understand her a bit.' He shook his head. 'All those years . . . haven't we wasted a lot of time?'

'Far too much.' Chloe looked out of the window at the busy street, then leaned over the table to lay her hands on his face. 'Let's put it all behind us now and move on. Let's be properly happy at last.'

# Nora

Nora sat in her usual seat in the window, looking over the harbour, listening to the phone ring in London. She felt a little nervous – was this the right thing to do? It was such a part of her old life . . .

She'd printed off the job description Lou had sent her; it was spread out on the table in front of her. Summer was ending, Logan was leaving, it was a great salary. And she was forty . . . Wasn't a good job the sensible next step? Five, six rings.

She hadn't talked to Logan or her mother about it. Her mother was so happy that Nora just wanted to leave her to it for a while. And with Logan, their conversations were like feeling around a bruise; they couldn't talk about anything that might happen after he went away.

Nine, ten rings. Nora could picture the busy city, busy London lives . . . Then the phone was answered.

'Nora? Sorry to keep you, there was someone at the door. How are you?'

'Hi Jennifer, I'm really well, thanks, and you?'

'Very good. Thanks for asking.'

'It's nice to talk to you again.' It really was, Nora realised with relief.

'You too! I've been wondering how you're getting on. Well, you know how it works. We've got fifty minutes, Nora, how can I help you?'

Nora laughed. 'I need a sounding board. I'm nearly at the end of my time in Tenby and it's been . . . incredible. In more ways than I could ever have imagined. But now I need to make some decisions and I've started going round and round in circles . . .'

'Ah, the eternal washing machine of the mind, perpetually stuck on spin cycle. Why don't you just start wherever feels right and we'll see what we can do.'

So Nora gave Jennifer a potted history of her summer in Tenby from start to finish.

'I could leave,' she concluded at last. 'I could go to New Zealand and be with Logan. But then I'd lose everything else I've gained this year. I have wonderful friends here. Mum's going to settle here now. Gran's nearby and she's very old – this isn't the time I want to be on the other side of the world. But . . . he's the man I love! Shouldn't I be willing to follow him to the ends of the earth? It's not as if I have a career here now. I'm in between jobs, lodgings, I feel as if I don't have a substantial reason to stay . . . That brings me on to the next thing. I have a possibility of a job. I need to ring the agency today and let them know . . .'

Then she told Jennifer about the job, being careful to focus on its benefits and positives and all the reasons why it was a good idea. Then she told her about the call she'd had only that morning from the estate agent in Kingston. Apparently her tenants had asked if they might extend their lease by another six months, or preferably a year.

'So I *could* stay a little longer . . .' mused Nora wistfully, 'but that's just buying time, isn't it? I can't keep renting out the flat and treading water forever. *Can I?*' Then she continued to list the pros and cons of various courses of action that had kept her awake the last few nights. 'I'm driving myself nuts,' she concluded.

There was a pause. Nora knew Jennifer was waiting to see if she had more to say. But she took a deep breath, and waited.

'Well, I'm hearing a few different things here, Nora. But first I want to ask you a question. Two questions, really. When you got the message about the job, how did you feel? I know, I know.'

Nora grinned. 'How did I feel? Um, bad. My first thought was, *Oh no*. Like a kid at playtime hearing the bell to go in to lessons. *Maths!*'

'That's a great comparison! And how about when you heard that the tenants want to stay in your flat? How did you feel then?'

Nora remembered talking to Sarah with the phone wedged under one ear while she took a jar of peanut butter out of the cupboard. 'Oh, happy!' she said at once. 'Festive, really. Like I had a reprieve and I didn't have to do this thing that I really don't want to do . . . Oh!'

'See, it can be a useful question sometimes, can't it?' Nora could hear Jennifer's smile.

'OK, you're vindicated. You know, I've spent all summer just assuming that I'd return to that kind of work. I thought I'd go back refreshed and grateful for the lovely time I've had and then go on with real life.'

'So what has this summer been for you, Nora – a pit-stop, a chance to refuel?'

'No,' said Nora decidedly. 'I thought it was, when I came. But now . . . I want it to have been more than that.'

'What then?'

'A . . . foundation.'

'A foundation, OK. Tell me more.'

'Well, I think what I've found here is more than just a reprieve. It's a whole new way of being. It's the start of . . . of a life. A *soulful* life, I guess. Oh, I know there has to be more. This summer's been all about personal relationships: my mother, and Kaitlin, and Molly and Gran. Logan of course . . . I need to get a job.'

'So you keep saying. And of course it's important to be financially stable. But Nora, I keep hearing you talk as though certain things have more value than others, even though they don't seem to be the things that are important to you personally. I hear you overriding your own judgement, just as you did when we first starting seeing each other.'

Nora was quiet for a minute. It was true that she didn't want to go back. She had grown used to walking with the roar of the grey-green sea at her side. 'I just feel as though I need more time,' she whispered.

'It makes perfect sense. I think perhaps you're underestimating how much you've achieved, Nora. I last saw you only six months ago and you were still having terrible anxiety, your relationship with your mother was in bad shape and you felt isolated and adrift in your world. Now you've found a place and people you love, you're relaxed and confident and learning a lot about what works for you and what doesn't. You've identified work as the next area you want to address – and you need time for that. You have this strong feeling that you "need more time". Can you give yourself that?'

Nora smiled. She felt a tingle inside her that unspooled from her stomach, up through her chest and into her face. Everything fizzed. A new career. There was still that pesky voice in her head saying it was too late for her to have a new career. But that same voice had once told her it was too late to find love. 'Can it really be that simple?' she wondered.

'I think you know the answer to that, Nora.'

She nodded. *It can be as simple as you let it be*, she realised suddenly. Humans have a million ingenious ways to complicate things, but it didn't mean it was a good idea to do it. She walked over to the mantelpiece, where her mother's old hourglass stood. She turned it over and the sand started pouring once again. Another new phase could begin, she realised. It already had.

'Thank you, Jennifer, everything seems much clearer now.'

'I'm glad, Nora. Any time you want to talk, please just get in touch. And good luck!'

# Chloe

'So when *did* you start to paint me?' asked Jasmine, adjusting her sunglasses and flicking through the programme for Llew's exhibition. Kaitlin had given it to her last night. It was astonishing to see her young self looking out from the pages.

'Hmm?' Llew reached down for the thermos of coffee they'd brought to the beach. They sat side by side on the South Beach as they had so many times before, although this time they had folding chairs borrowed from Glenda. Creaking down onto the sand and up from it was a hassle they could do without these days.

'You said you couldn't bear to look at the photos of me when you first started painting. But you did eventually, clearly.'

'Oh, it was after Sandra died and I didn't have to feel guilty for thinking about you. The pain had faded by then; there was just this bittersweet sadness. I dug the photos out and painted and painted. I knew I was doing my best work but I couldn't exhibit them. They were too precious and private. In a funny sort of way, that was the happiest I had been since the old days – hours and hours alone with you! Not the real you, but the next best thing.'

'God, Llew, I had no idea. I thought you couldn't bear the thought of me.'

'*Hardly*. And I did try looking you up online too by the way but of course the only mentions of Chloe Samuels were about the 1960s model. I didn't know you were Jasmine Banquist by then, did I? Anyway, earlier this year I was stuck for inspiration so I started painting you all over again. I was preparing to settle in and become a bit of a recluse – a regular thing with me, you know – when it struck me that starting a picture I'd already painted was about as low as it can get, for an artist. An utter impatience came over me. I thought, why am I painting her *again*? I should be *finding* her! I'm seventy-three. What am I waiting for *now*?'

'You crazy person, you wonderful fool,' said Chloe, taking his hand. 'Did you never think just to go to my mother and ask her where I was?'

'Yes, of course, but I didn't know if she was still alive. And even if she was, I knew she'd be very old. I didn't want to upset her. I didn't know how much you'd told her. I didn't feel I could just turn up . . . "Hello, I'm someone from your daughter's past. I may have broken her heart and I *did* tell her I never wanted to see her again but fifty years on I've changed my mind so can I have her number, please?" I didn't want to give her a heart attack or something.'

'I appreciate that.'

'Then I remembered that Eric, my agent, had written to me, oh, six months or so previously, about doing a retrospective. I'd said a resounding no at the time – I have to be in the mood for that sort of hoopla and the mood comes upon me less and less these days. I can be a little eccentric.'

'You don't say.'

'Well, I rang him and said I had all this previously unshown work and that I was willing to do an exhibition but only if he could guarantee maximum publicity. He jumped at it! Said he'd try the gallery who'd wanted the retrospective and get back to me when he had some news. Two hours later the phone rang, it was all sorted, but they wanted me to go to London immediately because they had a summer slot and wanted to see the paintings asap. So I upped and went. Just like that.'

'Why maximum publicity? I thought you were in a recluse phase?'

'Yes, but I had this idea that you would see the paintings, and get in touch with me. I was convinced! I couldn't bear just to sit around and hope, so I stayed in London until the exhibition opened, did a bit of channel hopping, gave some interviews and demonstrations, kept myself busy, you know. That's why I rented out the house so cheaply, that's why I left Glenda holding the fort . . . Then the exhibition opened and I received Nora's email, saying she was your daughter. You didn't see the paintings, but she did.'

Jasmine shook her head in wonder.

'And I missed it all because I was in Italy! See what you can miss when you run away. I didn't have a clue about any of it until I showed up and found Nora looking for coins in the cracks in the pavement, because *you'd* told her that's what *we* used to do!'

Llew smiled, tilting his face up to the sun and closing his eyes. 'I knew you'd find me.'

# Nora

It was a perfect autumn day. Red leaves drifted through a sparkling morning as Nora drove to Nant-Aur to collect her grandmother. Dark shapes of horses moved through the pale lilac mist wreathing the dells. Sunlight bloomed in hazy veils which parted to send occasional sharp glimmers through the trees.

Gwennan was waiting inside the front door, as though for a taxi, her small overnight bag packed and ready. Without stopping for so much as a Welsh cake they drove back to Tenby, arriving at the house before ten. Gwennan was going to stay in Nora's room that night and Nora would stay with Logan. He and the children had postponed their flights to be here for the wedding. *Leaving tomorrow*, thought Nora with a sinking heart before rousing herself. Today wasn't about that. And their goodbye would not be forever.

They got ready in Nora's room, Kaitlin occasionally invading to borrow tights or hairgrips or a bracelet.

'You and Mrs Watkins are going to be sisters,' she chuckled on one such occasion. 'Oh, who would ever have thought?'

'Mind you,' she continued on another. 'Hasn't she come good since Llew filled her in on everything? Hasn't she been a complete star with the wedding arrangements?'

In between interruptions, Nora told her grandmother her latest plans. She had let the flat in Kingston for a further twelve months. Not that she ever expected to go back there, but getting to grips with selling wasn't something she had the energy for just now. As before, the income from the flat would pay her rent, not on Llew's house, because it really was beyond time that he actually lived in it again, but on a new place that she was going to share with Kaitlin about half a mile away.

Llew and Jasmine were comical in their dismay that the girls would no longer have acres of space to rattle around in, expensive décor to luxuriate in or sea views. Nora and Kaitlin laughed at them. They would be a ten-minute walk from the sea. They would be happy and cosy in their new terraced house. They had a small garden that neither of them had a clue how to tend but Gran would advise them. They'd be living in one of the prettiest towns imaginable, surrounded by miles of beautiful countryside and coast.

'It's not too shabby!' Kaitlin told them. 'We really won't suffer much.'

'Besides,' added Nora, 'my stepfather's an artist. We've got luxury art on tap.'

'And on the job front, *bach*?' asked Gwennan, struggling and failing to fasten a star-shaped diamond pendant around her neck. She held out the chain in surrender to Nora.

'I've signed up with two temp agencies. I'm not committed to anything long-term, I can take some time and think about what I really want to do,' said Nora, fastening the necklace and looking at her grandmother. 'That looks so pretty against your blouse, Gran. I love your outfit.' Gwennan was wearing periwinkle blue, which brought out the colour of her eyes and looked bright and pretty against her long white hair, which was coiled in a loose chignon.

'Got to look my best, see, *bach*. Not every day you have a daughter getting married, is it? I can't deny, I'm much happier this time round. Nothing against your father, mind you, he was a nice enough lad, Steve. But Llew is the real thing, isn't he, Nora?'

'Hundred per cent. Are you ready, Gran?'

'I think so, *cariad*. *Duw*, you look beautiful. That's the loveliest maid of honour dress I've ever seen. But your mother always did have wonderful taste.'

'Yes, she does. Come on then, let's see if Kaitlin's ready. Oh, and I mustn't forget the present!' She picked up a soft package decorated with a champagne bow: the blanket she had made in Molly's class and raced to finish in time for today. Pieces of the past and the present stitched together: sky blue, peach, green and yellow – soft, pretty Tenby colours.

'Nora, I want you to know that I'm very proud of you. Do you know something? A few months ago I was feeling very sorry for myself – not something that happens often – and I said a prayer. Quite a demanding one it was. I was feeling so lonely, so sad that I never saw you and your mother.'

'Oh Gran, I'm so sorry.'

'Hush, *bach*, listen. So I said my prayer and told God that he had to bring you back to me, both of you, that there had to be a way for things to be better than they were. And not long after, there you are in Tenby. And a few months after that, your mother's back, and marrying Llew after all. I've often remembered that night lately. God works in mysterious ways, doesn't He?'

'I'll say,' said Nora, remembering, as vividly as if it were yesterday, that day at the office when she found herself dreaming of the South Beach, only knowing that she needed a different landscape, a different air to breathe. 'When was that night, Gran, can you remember? When did you say your prayer?'

'I remember. It was before Christmas. I remember looking out of the window at the frost on the fields and the moonlight shining down on them. I remember thinking that the power that can create that much beauty even in winter, even at our hardest times, can certainly do a little thing like bring my two girls home. And it has.'

Before Christmas. Just when Nora had seen that beach. When she had walked down the corridor to Olivia's office, as if in a dream, and resigned.

Jasmine was to be married in a simple oyster-coloured dress, mid-calf, with a gently flaring skirt, a plain bodice and a touch of lace. It was a little like a Ginger Rogers dress but simple, without feathers or flounces. Still, it made her want to dance.

Nora and Kaitlin were her bridesmaids and wore peach. Nora's dress was a gorgeous column of peach-coloured chiffon with a split all the way up one leg and Kaitlin wore strapless satin with a full skirt ending several inches above the knee. Glenda was getting ready in her own house but Jasmine had helped her choose a smart rose-pink suit. She was her father's best woman.

Smiling into the mirror in the hall, Jasmine tucked a small white rose into her silver hair, to match the luscious white lily in Nora's and the white gypsophila wound through Kaitlin's abundant curls. Her hair had been trimmed into a shorter, sharper bob now, so that the line of dyed hair ran around the bottom centimetre like a band of black piping. Her blue eyes were huge and bright and on the whole, she thought, she looked pretty damn good. Funny that she'd spent all that time in her teens worrying about whether or not she was pretty, then all of her twenties worrying about what would happen if she ever stopped being pretty . . . and now, now in her seventies, she felt really, properly pretty. A knock at the door announced Logan, who was escorting them to the church. His face when he saw Nora was a picture.

'Jeez, woman, can your mother spare you for the next hour or so?' he whispered into her hair.

'I don't think so,' Nora whispered back, 'but you know it's lucky to kiss the maid of honour after the ceremony, right?'

She looked at her mother, radiant with a love that had never died, even though she had given up on it. She looked at Logan, and marvelled that she had ever thought she'd left it too late for love to fit into her life, that she had been perplexed as to what it might look like, how it might feel. As if there was some great complication to it when really it was simple. Love is just love. At any age.

'Before we go,' said Logan, 'there's a tradition that must be upheld. I've received strict instructions from the groom.' He drew forth his phone with a flourish. 'Into the sitting room, ladies, please.'

'You mean I have to go back up those stairs again?' demanded Gwennan.

'I'm afraid so, darlin'. In front of the mantelpiece, Llew said. I can't disappoint a man on his wedding day.'

'Of course,' cried Jasmine, clapping her hands and leading the way. 'He's absolutely right!'

So Logan took the first photos of the day. Bride, maid of honour, bridesmaid and mother-of-the-bride, all clustered before the mantelpiece, beaming and be-flowered, before going out into the little town on the edge of the sea.

# Epilogue

Gwennan left the wedding party at eleven. *Pretty good going, for someone my age*, she thought. Nora, bless her, took her in the taxi to Llew's lovely house and saw her settled in bed in her own room. She brought her a hot chocolate to sip before she went to sleep and fussed over her until Gwennan ordered her back to the party. Then Nora went, back to Logan and his children, back to her mother and Llew, back to Kaitlin and her other friends. A good life she had here. And a good granddaughter she was, the very best. A shame Logan lived on the other side of the world.

She'd had to smile, though, when Brendan – lovely young lad he was, so serious – came over and sat down opposite his father and Nora halfway through the evening. He'd had half a glass of champagne and was feeling bold.

'Dad,' he'd said earnestly. 'Can we talk? I've come to a big decision these last couple of weeks and I'd like your blessing.'

*Good lad*, Gwennan had thought. *Sometimes you have to ask for what you want.*

Logan had looked all nervous; he'd reminded her of Dafydd

in that moment. Men were always so flustered by their children growing up; more so than women. Brendan had gone on to explain that next year, when the time came for him to apply to university, he wanted to come to London to study. It all came out in a rush and then he looked so anxious; did he really think his father wouldn't approve? The look Logan and Nora had exchanged was priceless.

Gwennan finished her hot chocolate and reached for the bedside lamp, then hesitated. She turned back the covers and walked across Nora's pretty room. It had been a big day. At long last she had seen her daughter remarried. She was coming home to live, and Nora was staying too, and Gwennan was the happiest woman alive.

She reached the window and drew back the curtain. A view very different from her own at home. Instead of fields, the waves of the harbour undulated in the moonlight. Instead of galaxies strewing the dark sky, she saw a few stars, and a mass of harbour lights. Out at sea was the dim shape of a big ship. In the morning, there would be sunrise over the ocean. At last Chloe would be in her place, just as Gwennan was in hers.

She struggled to kneel, then halfway to the floor thought better of it and pulled a chair nearer to the window. She folded her hands and kept her eyes fixed on the inky horizon, the shifting sea.

'Dear God,' she began. 'I apologise for not kneeling, but I'm ninety-three after all so I'm sure you will understand. First of all, I want to say thank you, again, for bringing my girls back. Thank you for this wonderful day, Lord, and all its many blessings. I know that after this miracle, I shouldn't ever ask for anything again. But this one's not for me, and perhaps you like granting prayers, giving people things. The ways you do it are so unexpected and ingenious that I think you must do. Anyway, this one's for Nora. Please give her a happy ending with Logan, dear God. Please let Logan come to settle here with his lovely family so we can all be together. If you can bring Chloe and Nora to me, I know you can do this, dear God, so without further ado, amen.'

She replaced the chair neatly and took a last look out to sea before drawing the curtain and going back to bed. She closed her eyes and smiled. She felt that she had been very clear.

# Acknowledgements

*The Hourglass* has been an absolute joy to research and write. Thanks as always to all the lovely people who support me in work and life. Particular thanks this time go to:

Mum, for her gorgeous, nostalgic, evocative tales of Tenby summers, which provided the seed of inspiration for this book. Dad, for his role as Research Assistant! And for ideas about Daf's backstory and employment. Both of them for so many magical escapes to Tenby. And, as always, for their unswerving love and support, and delight in my writing career.

Julia Joshua, for giving me ideas about Box Brownies and chickenpox, and Margaret Jones, for hands-on research for the sections about making – and eating! – Welsh cakes.

Huge thanks as always to the dream teams at Quercus and at Furniss Lawton – I know myself to be truly blessed in my agents and publishers and if I were to name everyone who is helpful and talented and indispensable for me and my books, I'd end up just reproducing your staff lists! Especial thanks of course to Kathryn Taussig and Eugenie Furniss, without whom my books would not be what they are and my writing life would not be half as fantastic as it is.

My early readers – invaluable as ever for their comments, encouragement and insights at the tender first draft stage. Jane Rees, Ellen Pruyne, Stephanie Basford-Morris.

All the staff at the Atlantic Hotel, Tenby, for warm welcomes, wonderful hospitality and for providing a much-appreciated home from home!

Rosie Jones and Angela Jones for help and advice regarding spinal injury.

Jules Rees for dance fitness – helping me keep body and soul vaguely connected.

Jacks Lyndon for lovely tea and patchwork instruction (even though apparently I spent more time scribbling down patchwork terminology than actually patchworking!)

Bruce Newman of Brains for giving me permission to use the name of the South Beach Bar Grill in the book.

# Tracy's Snapshots of Tenby!

A view of Castle Hill

My Mum and Aunt in the 1950s

My Aunts on North Beach

North Beach

My Aunt

*Here's a recipe for Welsh cakes, exactly like those Nora makes with her grandmother in The Hourglass ... except this is my gran's recipe!*
*Love, Tracy x*

# Gran's Welsh cakes
*Quantity: enough to feed a small village*

## Ingredients

2 lbs flour (self-raising)
16 oz butter or margarine (or half and half: the more butter, the richer the flavour)
16 oz sugar
8 oz sultanas
2 small teaspoons salt
4 large or 6 small eggs

## Method

1.  Mix flour, margarine or butter, and salt. Work through with fingertips until mixture resembles fine breadcrumbs. (Gran's tip: don't tickle it! Get stuck in!)
2.  Add sugar and sultanas and mix well.
3.  Lightly mix egg whites and yolk then pour into a well in centre of mixture. Mix well.

4. Heat a Welsh cake plank/cast iron griddle for quarter of an hour so that griddle is hot, then turn heat right down. Once griddle is hot, cook Welsh cakes on a low heat.

5. Gran's tip: The griddle must be the right temperature first so they cook evenly and don't get too dry. Try cooking one or two first and if they're browning too fast or not cooking through, adjust heat accordingly.

6. Spread flour over work surface. Take the dough, one large ball at a time, and roll out to a quarter of an inch thickness.

7. Gran's tip: Use flour sparingly on surface and rolling pin so the mixture doesn't get too dry, otherwise the Welsh cakes will be too biscuity.

8. Using a round cutter of approximately 2.5 inches across, cut Welsh cakes close together. Set aside the leftover bits of dough in a separate bowl of second rollings, until the first batch of dough has all been rolled and cut. Then repeat process with second rollings and so on until all dough is used.

9. Heat slowly, turning them often. Don't let them get too brown but they must be cooked through.

   Gran's tip: It's nice to have company to make them so one person can be rolling and cutting and the other can be heating. You can have a nice chat then, too.

*Eat and enjoy!*

# My Top Five Fictional Heroines

Being asked to pick just five favourite fictional heroines is hard! It's a bit like being asked, 'What's your favourite book?' Literature is a treasure trove of memorable, wonderful characters . . . how do you choose?

It's also a particularly salient question for me just now. With my second novel, *Florence Grace*, I was delighted by readers' responses so far to my heroine, Florence. Amy, in *Amy Snow*, inspired so much love, which was wonderful, only Florence is very different . . . I wondered if readers would take to her in the same way. But I think that to imagine that only one kind of heroine will find love and approval is just like saying only one kind of person will be well liked. Literature, like humanity, has room for all sorts and brims over with glorious variety. Where would we be as readers, otherwise?

Which is all preamble to the evil moment when I must choose just five . . . OK, here they are in no particular order:

1. One, of course, is Jane Eyre. I love her fierce integrity, her determination to do what's right according to her own principles – the flashes of temper, spirit and passion that get her into so much trouble at various points in her troubled life – she won't take the easy road and that is something I admire.

2. Another great favourite from my childhood is Jo March in *Little Women*. I loved how she would shut herself away in her attic, bristling with indignation about all the injustices in life, then forget it all by plunging into a fictional world. As long as she's scribbling stories, or doing something creative, she feels alive. No parallels there! Louisa May Alcott also makes her gloriously human – her scowls, her envy, her indignation . . . she's no paragon of unattainable feminine perfection – she's a person, with feelings and faults and brilliance. I love that.

3. Talking about faults . . . I really love Emma Woodhouse in Jane Austen's *Emma*. I think it's rare for a heroine to be quite so imperfect, yet you can't help but love her, even though she's absolutely infuriating most of the time: short-sighted, vain and meddling. In fact, the fact that Jane Austen could make her likeable at all is quite a feat!

4. I'm completely enchanted by Yvaine, in Neil Gaiman's *Stardust*. A heroine who's not, in fact, a woman, but a star! What a beautiful, tantalising idea. Although, she too acts so very humanly! Throwing mud at Tristan when they first meet, calling him names, fuming at his short-sighted romantic devotion (to someone else). She's a great combination of relatable and yet magical. I think that's a wonderful recipe for a heroine.

5. My fifth choice is another childhood favourite, Emily Byrd Starr, from LM Montgomery's *Emily of New Moon*. She's a dreamy, soulful girl, at one with nature and deeply bonded

with the landscape around her. She's also another creative type, like Jo March. Why do writers love reading about writers so much I wonder? I used to love reading about Emily curling up under an apple tree and losing herself in a story as she scribbled in one of her precious notebooks and searched for just the right word . . .

So there you have them! My top five. I think what they all have in common is heart. They are essentially warm, courageous people who don't give up when difficulty strikes, but find a way to grow beyond it. Like Amy, Florence, Chloe and Nora, they are also all a little different from those around them! This gives them the advantage of having a unique perspective on their world, but it can also create trouble on their path. I like heroines who don't get it right all the time, and keep bumping up against the established world and asking questions!

If you enjoyed *The Hourglass*, don't hesitate
to try Tracy Rees' first novel . . .

# Amy Snow

## THE RICHARD AND JUDY BESTSELLER

**'My favourite novel of the year'**
**Lucinda Riley**

Abandoned on a bank of snow as a baby, Amy is taken in
at nearby Hatville Court. But the masters and servants
of the grand estate prove cold and unwelcoming. Amy's
only friend and ally is the sparkling young heiress Aurelia
Vennaway. So when Aurelia tragically dies young, Amy is
devastated. But Aurelia leaves Amy one last gift. A bundle
of letters with a coded key. A treasure hunt that only Amy
can follow. A life-changing discovery awaits . . . if only
she can unlock the secret.